THE WORD
STUDIES IN THE GOSPEL OF JOHN

J. Otis Yoder

First Printing: 1979
Second Printing: 2006
Revised and Printed: 2022

The Word: Studies in the Gospel of John
Copyright © by Heralds of Hope, Inc.

HERALDS OF HOPE, INC.
Box 3, Breezewood, PA 15533-0003
www.heraldsofhope.org

ISBN-13: 978-1-7361524-8-5
ISBN-10: 1-7361524-8-3
Cover Design: Illustra Graphics, Bedford, Pennsylvania

Printed in the United States of America

HERALDS OF HOPE

TABLE OF CONTENTS

John 1

1. The Logos God — 1
2. God's Children — 5
3. Make Jesus Personal — 9
4. Answers To Questions — 13
5. Who Is He? — 17
6. Meet The Messiah — 21
7. Clear Proofs — 25

John 2

8. Do You Need A Sign? — 31
9. Do What Is Right — 35

John 3

10. Born A Second Time — 41
11. God Did All He Can — 47
12. What Is Really Important? — 51
13. The Essence Of Truth — 55

John 4

14. Jesus At Jacob's Well — 61
15. How To Have Inner Peace — 65
16. What Is Worship? — 69
17. How To Test What Is Important — 73
18. How To Know Christ Truly — 77
19. How To Find Help — 81

John 5

20. Faith That Acts — 87
21. God The Son—His Nature — 91
22. God The Son—His Purpose — 97
23. God The Son—His Call — 101

TABLE OF CONTENTS

John 6

24. Five Loaves For 5,000 People	107
25. How To Conquer Fear	113
26. The First Thing In Life	117
27. The True Bread	121
28. Believing For Life	125
29. More Than Existence	129
30. Beyond The Material	133
31. The Final Choice	137

John 7

32. Live In The Open	143
33. Obedience Opens Understanding	147
34. Is This The Very Christ?	151
35. End The Search	155
36. He Is Different	159

John 8

37. Be Careful How You Judge	165
38. We Need Help	169
39. Understanding Yourself	173
40. How To Be Free	177
41. Some Important Comparisons	181
42. Why Is Jesus Supreme?	185

John 9

43. Establishing Reasons	191
44. Measuring Values	195
45. Weighing Evidences	199
46. Reaching Conclusions	203

John 10

47. The Abundant Life	209
48. Self-Giving Love	213

TABLE OF CONTENTS

John 10 *cont.*
49. True Security — 217
50. Correct Your Misunderstandings — 221

John 11
51. Overcoming Trouble — 227
52. Testing The Heart — 231
53. Thinking Right — 235
54. Meeting The Impossible — 239
55. Facing The Facts — 243

John 12
56. Jesus And True Love — 249
57. Jesus Is King — 253
58. Jesus—The One For All — 257
59. Jesus—The Son Of Man — 261
60. Jesus—The Sent One — 265

John 13
61. Love Symbolized — 271
62. Love Exemplified — 275
63. Love Petrified — 279
64. Love Clarified — 283

John 14
65. Faith—The Cure for Fear — 289
66. How To Experience God — 293
67. Personal Possibilities In Prayer — 297
68. Deliverance From Doubt — 301
69. True Peace — 307

John 15
70. How To Live Right — 313
71. More Than Servants — 317
72. Why Christians Suffer — 321

TABLE OF CONTENTS

John 16

73. Think Right	327
74. The Comforter	331
75. The Spirit Of Truth	335
76. How To Cure Worry	339
77. Plain Speech	343

John 17

78. The Difference In Jesus	349
79. Jesus's Goals For Disciples	353
80. The High Calling	357

John 18

81. Judas—The Betrayer	363
82. Peter—His Failure	367
83. The High Priest	371
84. Pilate—The Roman Governor	375

John 19

85. Who Is Guilty?	383
86. The Final Choice	387
87. The Crucifixion	391
88. The Completed Act	395
89. The Wonder Of It All	399
90. Where Did They Lay Him?	403

John 20

91. Haunting Fear	409
92. Crushing Sorrow	413
93. Comforting Joy	417
94. Rewarding Faith	421

John 21

95. How Jesus Showed Himself	427
96. The Final Test	431

Preface - Original

John, the Beloved Disciple, wrote the story of his Master's life, death, and resurrection so people could respond in faith and be saved. With Holy Spirit power and illumination, John began in the beginning with the WORD.

When Bro. Yoder began the radio messages, he followed John's pattern. In 1968, *The Voice of Hope* radio programs were begun in the beginning with Genesis, followed by the Gospel of John. About six years later, in response to Trans World Radio's challenge to go international, the *Hope For Today* program was begun. Again the pattern was followed, and Genesis sermons prepared the way for the Gospel of John.

In response to listeners, these HOPE messages were printed in booklets. So there were eighteen booklets of beautiful, simple, expository sermons published for the Gospel of John, each with a cover designed with a simple line drawing, appropriately illustrating that particular chapter of John. Those little booklets were mailed to listeners in countries overseas. Even today, a pastor in Nepal is translating, printing and distributing them in Nepal and neighboring countries.

This volume has gathered all the John sermons together in one. We thank God who blessed Ray Peters in designing the first covers and Brian Tucker in producing this paperback cover. We give thanks for God's supply of strength to secretary Audrey Van Pelt and printer Mark Atkinson. And it has been my pleasure and Holy Spirit enablement to edit, or shall I say, re-edit, this volume. May God's Spirit and Grace use this presentation of truth in the hearts and lives of all who receive it.

Isabelle K Yoder (Mrs J.O.Y.) April 2006

Preface - 2022 Update

John, the Beloved Disciple, wrote the story of his Master's life, death, and resurrection so people could respond in faith and be saved. With Holy Spirit power and illumination, John began his gospel "in the beginning was the WORD."

When Dr. Yoder began the radio messages, he followed John's pattern. In 1968 *The Voice of Hope* radio programs began with Genesis and were followed by the Gospel of John. About six years later, in response to Trans World Radio's challenge to broadcast internationally, the *Hope for Today* program began. Again, Genesis sermons prepared the way for the Gospel of John.

In response to listeners, these HOPE messages were printed in eighteen booklets produced in our in-house print shop. The booklets were beautiful, simple, expository sermons published for the Gospel of John. Each had a cover designed with a simple line drawing, appropriately illustrating their theme. Those little booklets were mailed to listeners in many countries, and the expository messages have been translated into other languages by our international ministry partners.

In 2006, we gathered these sermons into one volume. Fifteen years later, it is time for a thorough update. We thank God for the work of Illustra Graphics in redesigning the cover and Luronda Hege in updating the layout. We give thanks to each member of our Staff Team who helped in a variety of ways. May God's Spirit and grace use this presentation of truth in the hearts and lives of all who receive it.

J. Mark Horst, Radio Bible Teacher

Things to remember as you are reading this book:

These are verbal sermons that were compiled into book form. We have taken the liberty to change them slightly for easier reading, but some places still are hard to read.

Scripture portions are from the King James Version translation.

STUDIES FROM
JOHN 1

Chapter One

The Logos—God

The idea of God has puzzled many people, especially the fact that God became man in the person of Jesus of Nazareth. I was speaking to a friend of mine once, a Jewish friend, and he raised a real question about this. I can understand well why he raised the question. He said, "I cannot understand how another Jew can be God." Well, I can't either, really, but that is not the problem or the question. It is not how a man can become God, but the question is can God become man? That is the question to which we must address ourselves.

We have the right to ask these questions. Who is the *Logos,* the Word? Where did the Word come from? What did the Word do?

I don't believe any other questions are any more puzzling than these. I would like to say, dear friend, that we must take our starting point from God if we are going to find our way in this world. You see, my friend, it's not so smart or intelligent not to believe the Bible. I believe the Bible is the way to get to God. In fact, the most intelligent response you can make in life is to take the Bible for what it is, God's Word. Faith in God's Word will open great doors in your understanding. Whole new fields of truth will open to you. So why deny yourself this great opportunity when you could, by simple faith in God's Word, have doors of understanding open before you?

When I turn to the book of John and begin to read, I notice an important word. It is the word, 'Word.' "In the beginning was the Word." Some writers tell us that this Greek word, *Logos*, is a special kind of word in this particular passage. It does open a tremendous door of understanding to us once we hear what the Bible has to say. A great depth of meaning is contained in this word, *Logos*. So my message is entitled **THE LOGOS-GOD.**

Let us read these five verses from John 1:1-5.

1 In the beginning was the Word, and the Word was with God, and the Word was God.

2 The same was in the beginning with God.

3 All things were made by him; and without him was not any thing made that was made.

4 In him was life; and the life was the light of men.

5 And the light shineth in darkness; and the darkness comprehended it not.

In these five verses, the writer lays down three basic **PROPOSITIONS** about the Word to lead us to a fuller understanding. Here are great doors of understanding immediately before us.

The first Proposition: **The Word Is God.**

That is a basic proposition. The writer proceeds to support this proposition by pointing out that the Word was there in the beginning. Saying it another way, never was there a time when the Word did not exist. This emphasizes that the Word is eternal. I readily recognize that in our human expression we find it difficult to think of the meaning of the word, eternal. The reason is we are bound constantly by time considerations; by minutes, hours, days, weeks, months, years, and centuries. But the Word is God because He was there in the beginning. This is proof of the proposition.

The writer further supports his proposition, the Word is God, by stating "the Word was with God." The *Logos* was there beside God; He was in His presence. He was there-face to face with God.

I must insist, dear friend, on this particular translation of the clause because in my study of the Greek language of the New Testament, I have found that the proper way to translate this passage is "The Word was God."

We find in other passages similar truth, clear and certain. The Word is God is a basic proposition you must accept to enter this door of understanding.

The second Proposition: **The Word Is Creator.**

Observe carefully verse 3: "All things were made by him." That immediately clears up our understanding of the beginning of matter. This one called the "Word" is the Creator of everything, all things visible and invisible. In fact, the verse goes a bit further to say, "All things were made by him; without him (apart from Him) was not anything made that was made." This verse then establishes the proposition; the Word is Creator.

If we were to turn to Genesis 1, we would see how God created the heavens and the earth. He made all things; He made everything. Whether it be the general or the details of the creation, the Word was active as Creator. Here the Scripture clearly asserts and affirms this proposition; the Word is Creator.

The third Proposition: **The Word Is Revealer.**

This fact is established by the statement, "the life was the light of men." Rationality, the power to think, in the human race is light. We often refer to it as the light of reason, and God has so made us that we have this light of reason. In Him, the Word, was life and no overpowering darkness could ever subdue that light. The darkness could not overcome it.

A great many attempts have been made to put out the light. But because He is the Revealer, the light still shines. The Word is the Revealer is our third proposition that opens a great door of understanding for us.

In these five verses, by these three basic propositions, we must clearly see who the *Logos* is: He is God; He is Creator; He is Revealer.

Chapter Two

God's Children

God, in His wisdom, created the first pair, male and female. Then He commanded them to be fruitful and multiply and replenish the earth. In other words, it was expected of Adam and Eve that they would bear children, that children would be born to them. But, you know, all that parents can do is reproduce themselves. No human parents have ever given birth to any other creature than human children. What you are is what you bring forth.

A man once said, "All you can do is bring forth little heathen!" In a sense, that is true because all of us are separated from God until we take a step of faith in His direction. There is a part in each of us that must be touched by the Spirit of God to be born in a spiritual way. And the *Logos*, the Word, has a part in making us **GOD'S CHILDREN**. John 1:6-13 is the Scripture basis for this meditation.

> *6 There was a man sent from God, whose name was John.*
>
> *7 The same came for a witness, to bear witness of the Light, that all men through him might believe.*
>
> *8 He was not that Light, but was sent to bear witness of that Light.*
>
> *9 That was the true Light, which lighteth every man that cometh into the world.*

10 He was in the world, and the world was made by him, and the world knew him not.

11 He came unto his own, and his own received him not.

12 But as many as received him, to them gave he power to become the sons of God, even to them that believe on his name:

13 Which were born, not of blood, nor of the will of the flesh, nor of the will of man, but of God.

In these few verses, several **ACTIONS** of God are set forth by which we can become God's children. Will you take note?

The first Action: **He Included All Men.**

He included all men by His messenger. God sent a messenger. His name was John. He came to bear witness of the Light: to bear witness, to point out the Light, to help people see the Light, to instruct them who the Light is. The reason was "that all men might believe." Note, He included all men.

John was not that Light. That was made very clear. He was sent to point out who the Light is. Please notice carefully that no one can take the place of the Light. This one who came was to say Who the Light is and where the Light can be found.

In doing so, God was working out His purpose to include all men, the Scripture says, "that all men through Him might believe." The actions of God are seen in another way.

The second Action: **He Influenced Every One.**

He influenced everyone by His mission. He, the Light, was sent to lighten every man. That was the true Light to which John bore witness and it is the Light that lights every man who comes into the world. There is something of a response to the Light in your soul, in your being. God has given you a bit of Light.

Jesus, the true Light, was in the world. It is His creation. He came here as the Light, and yet His own creatures whom He made did not receive Him. His own did not receive Him.

Yet, His coming as the Light influenced everyone. I'm so glad for this because it means no one is excluded. Everyone is included, but even more, so is everyone influenced by the Light. We have a capability of responding to that Light.

In fact, you have been influenced by Him. You may not really know it, but you have been, because the light of God has been placed within you so that light can be responsive to this light, the true Light. The Bible here clearly tells us that Light has lightened every man. In the action of God, He influenced everyone.

The third Action: **He Enables Certain Ones.**

He enables certain ones by His ministry. I want you to follow carefully how this is written. All men are included, everyone has been influenced, but only certain ones come to the light. He enables certain ones by His ministry. Who are those certain ones? The ones who receive Him. "But to those who received him, to them he gave the authority to become the children of God." God's children.

The basic turning point is right there. As many as receive Him, He enables to become children of God. He changes you. After that change, you become God's child, born of God, not in the normal process of blood or flesh or the will of man, but born of God.

I said earlier when God made the first pair, He ordered them to be fruitful and replenish the earth. They could only bring forth and reproduce themselves. It is therefore important that you have another birth, that you be born of God.

But this is only possible to those certain ones who receive Him. Only believers in the Logos are then made children of God. You can become a child of God if you will receive Him.

Let me go over that again. You must receive Him, Jesus Christ. You must believe in Him, and then He will give you power to become a child of God because you believe in Him.

So the actions of God as expressed in the Logos to bring us into God's family are: He included all men in the potential belief; He influences everyone because He has made man with the capability to come to God; He enables certain ones, those who truly believe in Him. That is why I keep insisting, my friend, that faith will open great doors of understanding and experience to you. But you must take that step of faith in Him.

Chapter Three

Make Jesus Personal

Faith is important if you expect to find hope and peace, but not faith in just any object. Faith in the right object. I have studied some of the religions of the world, and I am convinced, the help we need the most is found in God's revealed Word.

For many people, their religion is only an obligation. It is a duty which they have imposed upon themselves. Either they do it to satisfy some god or to keep away the evil spirits. There is nothing very personal about it. Their religion puts God far off, and they come to think of Him as a mean tyrant.

Religion should be meaningful, should be personal. That is, it should come to you as a part of your total being. I am glad to tell you that true Christian faith is personal. You can know God in a personal way. You can learn to **MAKE JESUS PERSONAL.**

It is my interest to show you from John 1:14-18 how faith in Jesus Christ can afford you a personal experience.

> *14 And the Word was made flesh, and dwelt among us, (and we beheld his glory, the glory as of the only begotten of the Father,) full of grace and truth.*
>
> *15 John bare witness of him, and cried, saying, This was he of whom I spake, He that cometh after me is preferred before me: for he was before me.*

16 And of his fulness have all we received, and grace for grace.

17 For the law was given by Moses, but grace and truth came by Jesus Christ.

18 No man hath seen God at any time; the only begotten Son, which is in the bosom of the Father, he hath declared him.

In this paragraph, we have the several **RESPONSES** to the Lord which you must make to bring Him out of the unreal into a personal experience.

The first Response: **You Must Recognize His Glory.**

The Word was made flesh, I read. Think of the humility of God, the Logos, to become flesh. God, we read in other Scripture passages, is a spirit. Yet the Spirit God became flesh, that is, He took on human flesh and dwelled among us. A human being, He lived here on earth as a man. The Word became flesh!

Here we learn something of His true relationship with the Father. He had glory, "the glory as of the only begotten of the Father, full of grace and truth." There are three attributes here: glory, grace, and truth. Attributes are characteristics. We are urged in these verses to recognize His glory which puts Him in a unique position, in a particular position, in a position all by Himself. He is spoken of here as "the only begotten of the Father." That puts Him in a particular place all His own. That gives Him glory. You must recognize His glory if you are to make Jesus personal.

The second Response: **You Must Realize His Grace.**

John bore witness about Him and said, "He is the One of whom I spoke. He is preferred before me even though He comes after me." This would very clearly indicate that John understood that Jesus is eternal. He is before all things. He was before John. According to human age, John was six months older than Jesus in his natural birth, but John said, "He was before me."

Please note carefully verse 16, "And of his fullness have all we received, and grace for grace." Only by grace can you find Jesus personal. It is a fullness; it is a reality.

It is difficult for me to explain this to you unless you have opened your heart in faith to receive this grace. Once you have opened your heart in simple faith to receive His grace, then I will not need to explain it to you because faith opens that door of understanding by which you can make Jesus personal. You must realize His grace.

The third Response: **You Must Emphasize His Message.**

Verse 17 tells us the Law was given by Moses. We can go back to the book of Exodus and find that fact. There can be no question about that because the historical record is there.

In order for grace and truth to come by Jesus Christ, it was necessary that the law be given to Moses. I would like you to understand that the thought in this verse is not to contrast grace and truth with law. Rather, it says that, to make it possible for grace and truth to come, the law needed to be given. The law is the foundation of grace. In fact, the law is a very part of that grace. This is the message we must emphasize.

God cannot be gracious, show His grace to us, unless we know what He requires, and the requirements are set forth in the Bible, God's law. Observe further that no man has seen God at any time, but this One who has come, Jesus, the *Logos*, can declare Him unto us because He has been in the bosom of the Father.

You must therefore emphasize His message to find Jesus personal. You must accept His grace and truth based on the law. You must accept what He says about God the Father because He was in the bosom of the Father.

These are the responses which will make Jesus personal.

You must recognize His glory; He is uniquely, in His own right, the only begotten of the Father.

You must realize that we have all received this grace to believe when we received Him.

You must emphasize His message; because He is the One who has been in the bosom of the Father, He can tell us about the Father ,and His message will be truth.

You can make Jesus personal right now.

Chapter Four

Answers To Questions

Does anyone actually have all the answers? The answer to that question is yes and no. God has all the answers to be sure. No human being has all the answers. However, if he has faith in God, he will have more answers to the deep questions of life. That is, he will have more answers to questions; more of his questions will have answers.

All of us have questions for which answers are hard to find. In some cases, it is because we are not able to see everything as God sees. We must live with some unanswered questions. But that is not without solution because we can rest those questions with God if we truly know Him as a personal God.

However, for some people, those hard questions become traps from which they never escape. They are snared by those questions. For others, those questions create a search which leads them to true answers, the answers that can be found in God's Holy Word and by a relationship to Him.

In order to get answers to those questions, and the right answers, we must go to the right source. I am not surprised that some people are still struggling with questions, not finding satisfying answers, because it is impossible to find satisfying answers to the questions of life until you go to the right source; and the right source is the Bible.

Faith makes the difference. Faith makes the difference, but faith in the right object. This is what I want to lead you to in this discussion from John 1:19-28, **ANSWERS TO QUESTIONS.**

> *19 And this is the record of John, when the Jews sent priests and Levites from Jerusalem to ask him, Who art thou?*
>
> *20 And he confessed, and denied not; but confessed, I am not the Christ.*
>
> *21 And they asked him, What then? Art thou Elias? And he saith, I am not. Art thou that prophet? And he answered, No.*
>
> *22 Then said they unto him, Who art thou? That we may give an answer to them that sent us. What sayest thou of thyself?*
>
> *23 He said, I am the voice of one crying in the wilderness, Make straight the way of the Lord, as said the prophet Esaias.*
>
> *24 And they which were sent were of the Pharisees.*
>
> *25 And they asked him, and said unto him, Why baptizest thou then, if thou be not that Christ, nor Elias, neither that prophet?*
>
> *26 John answered them, saying, I baptize with water: but there standeth one among you, whom ye know not;*
>
> *27 He it is, who coming after me is preferred before me, whose shoe's latchet I am not worthy to unloose.*
>
> *28 These things were done in Bethabara beyond Jordan, where John was baptizing.*

In this recorded conversation, we find the answers to two of the most basic **QUESTIONS** facing all of us.

The first Question: **Question Of Identification.**

They came to John the Baptist with the question, "Who are you?" He was very quick to identify himself and to make clear to them that he was not the Messiah. "Christ" in English is the Greek word which means "the Anointed One" and is parallel to the Hebrew word for

"MESSIAH." "I am not the Messiah," John the Baptist said.

Then they asked him, "Are you Elijah?" Malachi predicted that Elijah would come before the great and notable day of the Lord will come, so they were asking him if he were Elijah. He said, "No."

They said, "Are you that prophet?" What prophet? Well, the prophet Moses spoke about in Deuteronomy 18:15. Moses said the Lord was going to raise up unto them a prophet like unto him, and they ought to listen to that prophet. So they asked the question, "Are you that prophet?" John the Baptist identified himself and said, "No, I am not that prophet."

They then asked, "Well, who are you then?" And he quoted from Isaiah, "I am the voice of one crying in the wilderness, make straight the way of the Lord."

From this conversation, we readily learn that John the Baptist had a special place. He was the voice which was to prepare the way for the Messiah. But I must ask you, "Who are you, and what place do you have?" I am convinced you do have a place. Have you found it? Are you doing what God wants you to do?

If I were to ask you, "Who are you?" What would be your answer? John made it clear in his answer. He said, "I am the voice of one crying in the wilderness, make straight the way of the Lord." That is a most noble task.

So it was first the question of identification, and that was answered clearly.

The second Question: **Question Of Explanation.**

They then asked Him, "Why do you baptize then if you are not the Messiah or Elijah or that prophet?" Then John gave them the explanation. He said, "I baptize with water." That was true. When we turn to other texts in the New Testament where John's baptism is explained, we learn further that he said, "I baptize you with water unto repentance." So the water baptism of John was a baptism as a sign of repentance.

But he said, "Somebody else is coming greater than I am. He is, in fact, standing among you now, but you do not know Him. And when He comes, I will not be able even to loose His shoe latchet. I will not be worthy to do that. He is so much greater than I, that I would feel unworthy to loosen His shoe latchet."

Now let me ask you, why you are doing what you are doing? Can you answer that question? John the Baptist answered it quite well because he had a particular relationship with the Messiah, and he was fulfilling his calling. What kind of relationship do you have with the Messiah? Why are you doing what you are doing? How do you answer me?

The answers to these questions show us the relation we ought to have to Jesus Christ. As you answer the question of identification, do you know Him as the One who has come? As the coming One? Are you interested in making a straight way for Him? How do you answer the question of explanation? Why are you doing what you are doing? Does it relate directly to the Anointed One?

The Messiah is coming! John saw it that way in His day. How do you see it? Have you a personal relationship with Him, the Messiah, Jesus Christ? You can have that relationship right now.

Chapter Five

Who Is He?

Men still puzzle over who Jesus is. They puzzled over Him when He lived here, and they still puzzle over Him. Many are not sure how to answer the question, **WHO IS HE?** Some say He is a very good man. He is a very good man. He is kind, compassionate and tenderhearted. He loves people. Yes, that is true, He does.

Others say He is a prophet because He taught as one having authority. He predicted events that came to pass. In that sense, He was also a prophet. But does that really answer the question, Who is He? It is a crucial question, a very important question, one that everybody will answer someday.

When He lived here, the people were immediately faced with the question, Who is He? We will look for the answer, In John 1:29-34.

> *29 The next day John seeth Jesus coming unto him, and saith, Behold the Lamb of God, which taketh away the sin of the world.*
>
> *30 This is he of whom I said, After me cometh a man which is preferred before me: for he was before me.*
>
> *31 And I knew him not: but that he should be made manifest to Israel, therefore am I come baptizing with water.*
>
> *32 And John bare record, saying, I saw the Spirit de-*

scending from heaven like a dove, and it abode upon him.

33 And I knew him not: but he that sent me to baptize with water, the same said unto me, Upon whom thou shalt see the Spirit descending, and remaining on him, the same is he which baptizeth with the Holy Ghost.

34 And I saw, and bare record that this is the Son of God.

In this significant text, John the Baptist gave us two **ANSWERS** to our question so that we might know who He is. They are quite simple answers, and yet they carry a great deal of heavy thoughts. Who is He? In the first answer, John the Baptist said,

He Is The Lamb Of God.

You see that in verse 29. "The next day John seeth Jesus coming unto him and saith, Behold the Lamb of God." One answer to our question is, He is the Lamb of God. It may seem strange that a man would be said to be a lamb. Let's examine the meaning of the word *lamb* in the way John the Baptist used it because he spoke of Him as "the Lamb of God who takes away the sin of the world."

To get the meaning of lamb, we need to go back to the early days of Israel's history. When the Children of Israel were ready to leave the land of Egypt under the guidance of Moses, God instituted what is called the Passover. You will find this recorded in Exodus 12. The Passover was a ritual that Israel was to keep in order to protect themselves from the death angel that was to go through the land. They were to select a spotless lamb. They were to keep it for a number of days to make sure that it was absolutely perfect, and then they were to kill it, catch the blood in a basin, and sprinkle the blood on the lintel and side posts of the doors of their houses. In this way, God said He would protect them. The death angel would pass over and not kill the firstborn sons in the homes where the blood was on the door.

Now we can understand better what John meant when he said, "Behold the Lamb of God who takes away the sin of the world." You see, the purpose of the lamb was to protect the people who lived in the house where the blood had been applied. We could say that the lamb was the substitute for the firstborn. In that way, the lamb died for one who would have died if the lamb had not died.

In a very literal sense, that was a physical death. The Lamb of God, as John the Baptist answered our question, also died so that we need not die. He died a physical death and shed His blood on Calvary so that you and I may be delivered from the sure and certain sentence of death as the result of sin. So He is the Lamb of God.

Let's go further and see what else John says of Him. In the second answer, John said,

He Is The Son Of God.

The Son of God you will find in verse 34, "And I saw and bore witness that this is the Son of God." That may also seem strange. Some people don't seem to be able to understand how God would have a Son, but here in this Scripture, Jesus is called the Son of God. Notice that John the Baptist said, "He was before me." In the actual historical record, Jesus was six months younger than John the Baptist. But John said, "He was before me." He is clearly implying that Jesus was eternal with God the Father.

He further said that He was to be made manifest to Israel; that is, He was especially chosen, a particular person by whom God would bring His program to pass. That is very important to keep in mind. God has a plan, and He is carrying out that plan. In that plan, the Son of God was to be made known to the people of Israel. John the Baptist was an Israelite. He was baptizing in the river Jordan, and those who came to him to be baptized were Jewish people. God was making manifest His will to the people of Israel. The Son of God was coming to them. This is a particular part of the divine revelation God brought to us.

I notice that He was anointed by the Holy Spirit. John the Baptist said that when he saw the Spirit descending and remaining on a certain person, he would know that this was the Son of God.

The Gospel of Matthew tells us that is exactly what happened. The Holy Spirit came down and rested on Jesus at the time of His baptism. The answer to our question then, from the lips of John the Baptist who saw Him is, He is the Son of God. That may be a mystery for us, but it is a reality. God became man. It is not that man became God but that God became man.

There are, then, two answers to our question, Who is He? John the Baptist said He is the Lamb of God, and that solves the sin problem; He is the Son of God, which solves the communications problem. He came as man to make God manifest to us.

Chapter Six

Meet The Messiah

We like to meet new people, don't we? Especially important people. We are glad to learn to know them.

In the time of Andrew and Peter, many were expecting the Messiah to come. They were looking for Him.

They had reasons to look for Him because the prophets had foretold His coming. Yet long years passed, and He had not come. Some lost hope, but many kept looking for Him. They were expecting Him. Let us read John 1:35-42 and look in on several who met Him.

> *35 Again the next day after John stood, and two of his disciples;*
>
> *36 And looking upon Jesus as he walked, he saith, Behold the Lamb of God!*
>
> *37 And the two disciples heard him speak, and they followed Jesus.*
>
> *38 Then Jesus turned, and saw them following, and saith unto them, What seek ye? They said unto him, Rabbi, (which is to say, being interpreted, Master,) where dwellest thou?*
>
> *39 He saith unto them, Come and see. They came and saw where he dwelt, and abode with him that day: for it*

was about the tenth hour.

40 One of the two which heard John speak, and followed him, was Andrew, Simon Peter's brother.

41 He first findeth his own brother Simon, and saith unto him, We have found the Messias, which is, being interpreted, the Christ.

42 And he brought him to Jesus. And when Jesus beheld him, he said, Thou art Simon the son of Jona: thou shalt be called Cephas, which is by interpretation, A stone.

At last, He had come, and He was being introduced to different people. Do you hear them saying one to another, **"MEET THE MESSIAH?"** John the Baptist saw Him and first understood Him. Andrew saw Him and brought Peter to Him.

In this account are several **INSIGHTS** into the nature of the Messiah as we meet Him. I want you to meet Him too.

The first Insight: **His Identification.**

His identification is the Lamb of God, for so John the Baptist identifies Him. This is a very descriptive term and full of meaning: The Lamb of God.

In verse 29, John the Baptist went farther and said that He takes away the sin of the world. That is why this identification, the Lamb of God, is full of meaning. All of us have sinned. All of us have come short of the glory of God.

What are we going to do about this? We cannot do much at all until God has done something, and He has done something. He sent the Lamb of God, the One who takes away the sin of the world.

I want to show you something else, however. John the Baptist identified Jesus to two of his disciples. John the Baptist had disciples, men who followed him and listened to his teaching. When those two men understood that Jesus was the Lamb of God, they followed Jesus. Jesus, the Lamb of God, is being followed by two disciples. I want to point Him out that way to you: He is the Lamb of God, and He is worthy to be followed. They followed Him, and as they followed Him, He turned and asked, "What do you want?" They said, "We want to know where you live."

The second Insight: **His Invitation.**

Come, "Come and see." It was their curiosity. They wanted to know more about Him. They wanted to become more intimately acquainted with Him, so as they followed and He asked them what they wanted, they said, "Where do you live?"

There is something interesting about this question. They felt if they could know where He lived, they would know more about Him. That was true. That is true today. If you can find a man's house, you'll find out more about him. Their question was a natural question.

Notice His response, "Come and see." That is His invitation, come and see. Wasn't that kind? There are some who throw great fences about their buildings, their houses. They have guards, dogs, men, and machine guns. That is not Jesus.

His invitation is still good. He would like to say to you, "Come and see." I'd like to echo that invitation to you "Come and see!"

The third Insight: **His Introduction.**

Andrew was one of those two disciples who followed Jesus when John had identified Him. He heard John, and He followed Jesus. He was convinced completely that He had found the real Messiah. So He went to find his brother, Simon Peter. When he found him, he said to him, "We have found the Messiah." They were looking for Him. They were expecting Him. They were trusting God that He would come. Andrew was overjoyed that they had found the Messiah, so he brought Simon, his brother, to Jesus, and Jesus knew him. Yes, Jesus knew him and said, "Thou art Simon the son of Jona: Thou shalt be called Cephas (which is by interpretation, a stone)."

Here is a wonderful introduction. Andrew brought Simon Peter, his brother, to meet the Messiah. You know, you are just like Simon. You need to meet Him too. I'd like to be like Andrew. I'd like to bring you to meet Jesus and say, "Meet the Messiah: the only One, the true Messiah, the Anointed One of God."

I want you to meet Him. I want you to meet Him because He is the One we are looking for. I can say, too, He will receive you. He knows you, and He wants you to follow Him.

Chapter Seven

Clear Proofs

Some people are too quick to accept anything that comes along. They don't ask for proof. They are like a bird flitting everywhere. Everything is attractive, and they accept things too quickly. Some are too slow to accept. They refuse to recognize proofs when they see them. It is a state of mind, a blocked, closed state of mind.

We ought to be careful. That certainly is true, but we ought also to be convincible. In other words, when the proofs are presented to us, we should then accept them clearly, wholeheartedly, and convincingly. In John 1:43-51, there are evidences that Jesus was the One they looked for.

> *43 The day following Jesus would go forth into Galilee, and findeth Philip, and saith unto him, Follow me.*
>
> *44 Now Philip was of Bethsaida, the city of Andrew and Peter.*
>
> *45 Philip findeth Nathanael, and saith unto him, We have found him, of whom Moses in the law, and the prophets, did write, Jesus of Nazareth, the son of Joseph.*
>
> *46 And Nathanael said unto him, Can there any good thing come out of Nazareth? Philip saith unto him, Come and see.*
>
> *47 Jesus saw Nathanael coming to him, and saith of him,*

Behold an Israelite indeed, in whom is no guile!

48 Nathanael saith unto him, Whence knowest thou me? Jesus answered and said unto him, Before that Philip called thee, when thou wast under the fig tree, I saw thee.

49 Nathanael answered and saith unto him, Rabbi, thou art the Son of God; thou art the King of Israel.

50 Jesus answered and said unto him, Because I said unto thee, I saw thee under the fig tree, believest thou? Thou shalt see greater things than these.

51 And he saith unto him, Verily verily, I say unto you, Hereafter ye shall see heaven open, and the angels of God ascending and descending upon the Son of man.

In this Scripture, we can find **CLEAR PROOFS** that Jesus of Nazareth is the one we look for, and I would like to point them out.

First there is the Proof: **By Jesus' Word.**

He said to Philip, "Follow Me." You will notice that Jesus was in Galilee when He said that. He found Philip there along the shore of the Sea of Galilee because his hometown, Bethsaida, was on the west shore of the Galilee.

First, I'd like to focus our attention on these two words that Jesus spoke to Philip, "Follow Me." There must be something compelling about these words or about the tone of the voice Jesus used because Philip, without any hesitation, followed Jesus.

Yes, I would say there is something compelling about those words when they come from Jesus. "Follow Me." And Philip followed. He was, as I say, from this town Bethsaida, the town of Andrew and Peter, on the shore of the Sea of Galilee. But today, there is nothing much there. The town is completely covered over with the sands of time, but the word of Jesus to Philip comes through clear today. It's the same word, "Follow Me."

We find the second Proof: **By Philip's Witness.**

Philip was convinced. The word of Jesus convinced him, and Philip set out to find a friend. He found him, Nathanael, and he witnessed to him. "It's real," he said. "We have found Him of whom Moses in the law and the prophets did write, Jesus of Nazareth, the son of Joseph." We have found Him.

I want you to notice how broadly Philip related Jesus to the Bible. He said Moses wrote about Him, and the prophets wrote about Him. Indeed they did! Philip's witness was exactly correct. He said then to Nathanael, "Come and see." Nathanael doubted. He could not understand how any good thing could come out of Nazareth. Nazareth was not a famous town in those days. It was the crossroads of the nations, alright, because the trade routes passed close by. It was the crossroads of the Gentiles. And a man's town seems to be important, too, for Nathanael could not understand how anyone could come out of Nazareth who could be worth very much.

Philip's witness, "Come and see," put the responsibility on Nathanael. He went on the basis of Philip's witness.

The third Proof is found: **By Jesus' Wisdom.**

When Jesus saw Nathanael coming, He commended him, "Behold an Israelite indeed, in whom is no guile." Now that is an attainment. There is hardly any question about that. To have this kind of commendation, an Israelite, indeed, in whom there is no guile, this is outstanding.

Nathanael was puzzled until Jesus explained to him that He saw him under the fig tree. It so moved Nathanael that he cried out, "Rabbi, thou art the Son of God, thou art the King of Israel." He was right. The wisdom of Jesus convinced him, and he made a confession that was absolutely correct.

But Jesus had more instruction for him. Jesus told him he hadn't seen much yet nor heard very much. "There is much more ahead, Nathanael. You will see greater things than these. You will see heaven open and the angels of God ascending and descending on the Son of man."

This is a very serious consideration. Nathanael was convinced by the wisdom of Jesus. He knew him, and He knows you. Yes, He understands more about you than you understand about yourself.

Here are proofs enough for you! Jesus' words to Philip come

down to you, "Follow me."

    I'd like to take His place and say to you, "Come and see." I hope you will come so that Jesus will be able to speak to your heart like He spoke to Nathaniel's heart.

STUDIES FROM JOHN 2

Chapter Eight

Do You Need A Sign?

The Bible records times of revelation. Each period of revelation was accompanied by signs or miracles. Let me suggest two for you.

In the days when Moses brought the Children of Israel out of the land of Egypt, God performed miracles by the hand of Moses. We can read about them in the books of Exodus and Numbers. God sent flies, hail, darkness, etc. To convince Pharaoh to let Israel go. When the people of Israel had departed from the Lord and were worshiping idols, God raised up the prophet Elijah. Elijah performed miracles by the hand of God. You can read about them in the book of I Kings: for example, no rain for three and one-half years.

When Jesus came and lived among men, God performed miracles by His hand. I'm telling you the Bible records times of revelation, and signs and miracles accompanied each of them. When Jesus lived, He performed such signs.

The Gospels, all four of them, record 38 such miracles that Jesus performed. Of course, the Bible says in those accounts that many other signs also did Jesus. We have one of them, the first one, right here before us in John 2:1-11. **DO YOU NEED A SIGN?** I want to show you what this sign of Jesus may mean to you.

1 And the third day there was a marriage in Cana of Galilee; and the mother of Jesus was there:

2 And both Jesus was called, and his disciples, to the marriage.

3 And when they wanted wine, the mother of Jesus saith unto him, They have no wine.

4 Jesus saith unto her, Woman, what have I to do with thee? Mine hour is not yet come.

5 His mother saith unto the servants, Whatsoever he saith unto you, do it.

6 And there were set there six waterpots of stone, after the manner of the purifying of the Jews, containing two or three firkins apiece.

7 Jesus saith unto them, Fill the waterpots with water. And they filled them up to the brim.

8 And he saith unto them, Draw out now, and bear unto the governor of the feast. And they bare it.

9 When the ruler of the feast had tasted the water that was made wine, and knew not whence it was: (but the servants which drew the water knew;) the governor of the feast called the bridegroom,

10 And saith unto him, Every man at the beginning doth set forth good wine; and when men have well drunk, then that which is worse: but thou hast kept the good wine until now.

11 This beginning of miracles did Jesus in Cana of Galilee, and manifested forth his glory; and his disciples believed on him.

In connection with this sign, we note several **COMMANDS** to the servants that are important to us as well.

The first Command: **Do It!**

Jesus, the disciples, and the mother of Jesus were invited to a wedding. A wedding is a time of joy. In all cultures weddings are times of rejoicing. There was great joy here, but they ran out of wine, so Jesus' mother came to Him and said, "They have no wine."

That is not the important statement in this passage. The important statement is not so much what she said to Jesus but what she said to the servants, "Whatever he says unto you, do it." She left no choice to them.

Here is a great lesson. A great lesson! My friend, do you need a sign? There is no hope unless you do what He says, exactly what He says. There is no choice left to you.

The second Command: **Carry it!**

Then Jesus spoke to the servants, "Fill the waterpots with water." They filled them, six of them. Then He said, "Draw out now, and carry it unto the governor of the feast."

You could say that these commands were simple, yet they must be followed carefully. There can be no departure from the clear instructions of the Lord. Many people today want a sign, but they do not want to do what the Lord has asked them to do.

How do we find out what God is asking of us? We find out when we read the Bible. I am not suggesting that you should find yourself six waterpots of stone, fill them with water, draw out, and expect that the water should be turned to wine. That is not the point. The point is to learn this great abiding principle: if you want to understand the Lord, you must be ready to follow His instructions carefully, totally.

The third Command: **Taste it!**

They took this water turned to wine to the governor of the feast. He tasted it and said, "This is better than we had before."

I am in no position to make a judgment on the wine because I do not drink wine. I do not know exactly on what basis the governor made his judgment, but he said, "You have kept the best until last."

There is something beautiful about that, isn't there? Whatever Jesus does is best. And here is a case to be considered. The governor, who knew nothing about the activities or how the wine was made, said it was the best. Yes, there is a principle here—whatever Jesus does is best.

This sign showed forth the glory of Jesus, and His disciples believed on Him. Do you need a sign? Signs cannot be ignored.

Signs must be acknowledged, not ignored.

The commandments Jesus gave to the servants ring true today. The commandment that the mother of Jesus gave to the servants rings true today. You cannot really know Him until you obey Him.

Let me remind you of what Mary said to the servants, "Whatever He says to you, do it." Now, if you will take this attitude of complete yielding to what Jesus says, then you will see the glory of God, too, and the signs will add confirmation to what you know to be correct.

Chapter Nine

Do What Is Right

It seems, that for many people, right and wrong are simply preferences. Such persons have little on which to base their conclusions. The decision of right and wrong is often made on the basis of whatever pleases them, so they do as they want to.

But the definition of right and wrong is far more clear. The Bible sets forth the standards of right and wrong. That's the reason this message is **DO WHAT IS RIGHT**.

Sadly, for many people, right and wrong are only convenient terms. The reason is they have never actually sought out the basic standards on which we can make proper judgments. Then, because men are depraved, they seek out and do wrong. By the word 'depraved,' we mean they do not think straight; they have no basis from which they can think straight. I'm glad the Bible sets forth the standards of right. The Scripture in John 2:13-25 helps us to understand how to do what is right.

> *13 And the Jews' passover was at hand, and Jesus went up to Jerusalem,*
>
> *14 And found in the temple those that sold oxen and sheep and doves, and the changers of money sitting:*
>
> *15 And when he had made a scourge of small cords, he drove them all out of the temple, and the sheep, and the*

oxen; and poured out the changers' money, and overthrew the tables;

16 And said unto them that sold doves, Take these things hence; make not my Father's house an house of merchandise.

17 And his disciples remembered that it was written, The zeal of thine house hath eaten me up.

18 Then answered the Jews and said unto him, What sign shewest thou unto us, seeing that thou doest these things?

19 Jesus answered and said unto them, Destroy this temple, and in three days I will raise it up.

20 Then said the Jews, Forty and six years was this temple in building, and wilt thou rear it up in three days?

21 But he spake of the temple of his body.

22 When therefore he was risen from the dead, his disciples remembered that he had said this unto them; and they believed the scripture, and the word which Jesus had said.

23 Now when he was in Jerusalem at the passover, in the feast day, many believed in his name, when they saw the miracles which he did.

24 But Jesus did not commit himself unto them, because he knew all men,

25 And needed not that any should testify of man: for he knew what was in man.

From this experience in the life of Jesus, I bring forth several **COMMANDS** that should point us to the right way.

The first Command: **Clean Up.**

When Jesus came to the temple of God, that holy place where God had said He would put His name, He found it polluted. He found there men selling oxen, sheep, and doves and changing money: there in the holy place, the place which had been set aside for the worship of God. It was the place where God's presence had been evident, for in the days of Solomon's temple, the glory of God had come down and filled the temple.

At this time, Jesus found these people selling oxen, sheep, and doves, and changing money. He commanded them, "Take these things from here." Jesus wanted His Father's House to be kept clean and fit for worship.

There is a consideration that we must look at in a clean-up program. Not only should we keep the houses of worship fit and clean, but since the Holy Spirit of God dwells in us who are born again, we must keep our lives and bodies clean and pure. That means to do right.

The second Command: **Speak Up.**

After this experience of cleaning up the temple the people who were affected by the program came and asked Jesus a proper question. They said, "What sign shewest thou unto us, seeing that thou doest these things?" How is it that you act so? You must have some kind of authority that you have done these things. For them, a sign or a miracle would be the proper proof.

Miracles had accompanied the prophets of old, such as Moses and Elijah. Their question was therefore a proper question. He gave them a puzzling answer. Here is the sign: He said, "Destroy this temple, and in three days I will raise it up." They immediately thought of the temple in which they stood. They said, "This temple has been in construction for forty-six years, yet you propose to raise it up in three days?"

This was a misunderstanding of His intention because we are informed here that, instead of referring to the physical temple which Herod had built, Jesus was referring to His body. He was making a prediction as to how He was going to be crucified, and how He would rise from the dead after three days. This became very clear to the disciples after His death and resurrection. They then saw that His comment had to do with His body, not with the temple of stone where they stood.

I'd like to point out to you that the way Jesus spoke up would help you do right, because implied in His statement is the importance of belief. You must believe in Him even if you can't see sign or miracle.

The third Command: **Open Up.**

Jesus was present at the Passover feast for the Jewish people. It is a time of commemorating their deliverance from the land of Egypt under the hand of Moses many years before. Jesus was there in the city of Jerusalem observing this memorial feast of deliverance. Many who saw Him and saw the miracles that He performed believed in Him. The miracles opened up their faith in Him.

Then we note that Jesus knew all men. In other words, even those who tried to hide from Him couldn't really because Jesus knows all men. It was not necessary that anybody should testify to Him of man, for He knew what was in man. There was nothing to hide.

Some still try to hide from Jesus, but that is impossible. When He was here, He knew all men. Surely now, after His resurrection, He would have knowledge of everybody. He has knowledge of you. You may try to hide, but you can't, really. It is important to understand that He knows who you are and where you are. Doesn't that help you do right?

Do what is right. But you ask me, "How shall I do that?" Well, first clean up; He will do it like He cleaned up the temple. He will clean you up. Then speak up; let Him tell you what He wants you to know. And open up; He knows you anyway. Now that's simple: clean up, speak up, and open up. Then you'll be able to do what is right.

Studies from John 3

Chapter Ten

Born A Second Time

World population is increasing daily. Thousands are born every hour; thousands of others are dying every hour. But many of these only experience one birth, the physical birth.

Do you know that you can be **BORN A SECOND TIME?** That's right. The Scripture I'm using for this meditation tells us this very clearly. A Jewish leader came to Jesus one night, and they had a conversation. There was a thought in this Jewish leader's mind that he wanted to get cleared up. He wanted to get more information. So he came to Jesus for a talk. The account is in John 3:1-13.

1 There was a man of the Pharisees, named Nicodemus, a ruler of the Jews:

2 The same came to Jesus by night, and said unto him, Rabbi, we know that thou art a teacher come from God: for no man can do these miracles that thou doest, except God be with him.

3 Jesus answered and said unto him, Verily, verily, I say unto thee, Except a man be born again, he cannot see the kingdom of God.

4 Nicodemus saith unto him, How can a man be born when he is old? Can he enter the second time into his mother's womb, and be born?

5 Jesus answered, Verily, verily, I say unto thee, Except a man be born of water and of the Spirit, he cannot enter into the kingdom of God.

6 That which is born of the flesh is flesh; and that which is born of the Spirit is spirit.

7 Marvel not that I said unto thee, Ye must be born again.

8 The wind bloweth where it listeth, and thou hearest the sound thereof, but canst not tell whence it cometh, and whither it goeth: so is every one that is born of the Spirit.

9 Nicodemus answered and said unto him, How can these things be?

10 Jesus answered and said unto him, Art thou a master of Israel, and knowest not these things?

11 Verily, verily, I say unto thee, We speak that we do know, and testify that we have seen; and ye receive not our witness.

12 If I have told you earthly things, and ye believe not, how shall ye believe, if I tell you of heavenly things?

13 And no man hath ascended up to heaven, but he that came down from heaven, even the Son of man which is in heaven.

Did you notice Jesus tell this man, Nicodemus, "you must be born again?" In this talk with Nicodemus, I point out the necessary **STAGES** so you, too, can experience being born a second time. It's possible. Would you like to know how? Then read on.

The first Stage: **The Assertion.**

Here is a learned man, a ruler among the Jews who came to Jesus. When he came to Jesus, he made a very positive assertion. He said, "We know that thou art a teacher come from God." That was a very worthy acknowledgment Nicodemus made. Jesus was a teacher come from God. There can be no question about that. When you read the Gospel records about Him, He was a teacher come from God. Then Nicodemus went a little farther. He said, "No man can do these miracles that thou doest except God be with him." So Nicodemus acknowledged not only that Jesus was a teacher come from God but also that He was a worker of miracles.

That is very, very important. That is stage number one. Jesus is not an ordinary person. No, Jesus is an extraordinary person. He's a teacher come from God and a worker of miracles. That isn't all that Jesus is, but that much Nicodemus already knew. My friend, it is a tremendous assertion.

The second Stage: **The Direction.**

Jesus gave a direction to Nicodemus. He started out with a very solid statement. He said, "Truly, truly, I say unto you, unless a man be born again, he cannot see the kingdom of God." I want you to notice that Jesus isn't particularly addressing Nicodemus, although He is talking to him. By the very fact that He said, "Except a man be born again," means any man, and that includes you and me. It means every man, every person. No matter in what station of life you may find yourself, it means you.

Here was a learned Jew, a ruler of the Jews, who was told by Jesus, "You must be born again." Now if it was necessary for him, I confess that it is necessary for me. And I must tell you, it is necessary for you. That is a very solemn statement. It was to Nicodemus a very puzzling statement because he immediately raised the question, "How is it possible?" Is it possible for old men to be born a second time? How is the process accomplished? In what way is it done? Do old men enter the second time into their mothers' wombs and be born? That is a rather puzzling statement Jesus made. At least it was puzzling to Nicodemus. Maybe it is puzzling to you.

Let's notice the revealing answer that Jesus gave. He said to Nicodemus, "Except (or unless) a man is born of water and of the Spirit, he cannot enter the kingdom of God." The reason being that whatever is born of the flesh is flesh, and whatever is born of the Spirit is spirit. That very clearly states that there must be a spiritual birth. Now we have all been born of the flesh, for we have our physical bodies. The evidence is clear that the flesh produces the flesh. The evidence is also clear that the Spirit produces the spirit. A very deep and profound truth is here expressed by Jesus. It is this: you and I are creatures of flesh and spirit, not just flesh, but flesh and spirit.

We have plenty of proof by our human bodies that we are of the flesh. We also have plenty of proof that we are of the spirit in those around us. If you are born again or born the second time, you know what I am talking about. That which is born of the Spirit is spirit. Jesus said, "Marvel not that I said unto you, you must be born again." You can be born a second time.

The third Stage: **The Conclusion.**

Jesus used a very interesting illustration. He said the wind blows where ever it wills. You can hear, it but you can't see it. You don't even know what creates the wind. Oh, I suppose our weathermen have some theory about the wind, but they don't know for sure what causes the wind, where it comes from or where it goes. All we can do is feel it passing by or see what happens as it passes by, by the way in which it affects the dust, or the trees. But we do not know very much about the wind, not much.

Jesus said, "So is every one who is born of the Spirit." There is some mystery about this, perhaps some unsolved mystery. We only know that the Spirit is at work. For Nicodemus, his mind stood in his way because he raised the question, "How can these things be?" Oh, there are many people like our friend Nicodemus who allow their minds to rob them of the deeper experiences of life. Yes, to them, the most important answer is that it must convince the mind.

But we also have a will with which to believe! Jesus went on to talk to Nicodemus about the earthly things and the heavenly things. He said, "We know what we're talking about, but you don't receive our witness." Jesus gave Nicodemus enough for his mind, but the reason Nicodemus did not receive the witness of Jesus is that he had yet to exercise his will for faith.

Earthly things tell us of heavenly things. Yes, they do. Jesus made that comment and made it very clear. Earthly things and heavenly things have a relationship. The earthly tell us of the heavenly. Therefore, because we are flesh and we are born of the flesh, which is earthly, we can also be born the second time of the spirit and be in relation to the heavenly.

To be born a second time, you must agree that Jesus is more than any other man; One come from God. You must will to believe and receive His direction to be born of the Spirit. You must give your will to Him. You can't afford to argue with Him, He knows what is in your heart. Why don't you believe on Him now?

Chapter Eleven

God Did All He Can

When we get into trouble, we are often inclined to blame God; at least, some of us are. Sometimes I hear people say, "If there is a God, why all this trouble?" Such men do not know the real nature of God. They do not know even their own nature. Why does a man make such a statement, "If there is a God?" The reason is they do not know themselves, and they do not know the real nature of God.

I want to explain something about you and me. We can make our own choices. But many times, the basis of our choices is not right. That is why I always come to you with the Bible. Here in the Bible, we have the basis for all right choices. So we cannot really blame God for our troubles. He has given us the right to make the right choices.

Our Scripture is a continuation of the conversation that Jesus had with Nicodemus that night long ago in Jerusalem. It is found in John 3:14-21.

> *14 And as Moses lifted up the serpent in the wilderness, even so must the Son of man be lifted up:*
>
> *15 That whosoever believeth in him should not perish, but have eternal life.*
>
> *16 For God so loved the world, that he gave his only begotten Son, that whosoever believeth in him should not*

perish, but have everlasting life.

17 For God sent not his Son into the world to condemn the world; but that the world through him might be saved.

18 He that believeth on him is not condemned: but he that believeth not is condemned already, because he hath not believed in the name of the only begotten Son of God.

19 And this is the condemnation, that light is come into the world, and men loved darkness rather than light, because their deeds were evil.

20 For every one that doeth evil hateth the light, neither cometh to the light, lest his deeds should be reproved.

21 But he that doeth truth cometh to the light, that his deeds may be made manifest, that they are wrought in God.

From these verses in the Bible, I want to show you the **REASONS** why I can say emphatically, **GOD DID ALL HE CAN!**

The first Reason: **The Comparison.**

Jesus said, "As Moses lifted up the serpent in the wilderness, even so must the Son of man be lifted up." So Jesus is taking an experience out of the life of Israel when they were coming from Egypt to Canaan many, many years ago.

They began to complain against God, and He sent poisonous snakes among them. Many of them were bitten. There was no cure. Many of them died. If God had not instructed Moses what to do, there would have been no cure at all. But God told Moses to fashion a snake out of bronze and put it up on a pole, and everyone who would look at this image of the snake would live. It was desperate with these people. There was no other hope for them.

Now notice what Jesus said to Nicodemus. "As Moses lifted up the serpent in the wilderness, even so must the Son of man be lifted up." In other words, we also have an incurable situation. Unless God does something, we are without hope.

But God has done something. See? God did all He can do. So

when we look unto Jesus, we also will live. The direct instruction from the Lord is in this comparison. He said whoever believes in Him, the Son of man, should not perish but have eternal life. That is a quality of life, my friend; you cannot get in any other way.

I can say emphatically that God has done all He can.

The second Reason: **The Compassion.**

John 3:16 has often been referred to as the golden text of the Bible. "For God so loved the world, that he gave his only begotten Son, that whosoever believeth in him should not perish, but have everlasting life."

Now, wait a moment. Look at the compassion of God: His love, how broad was it? What was its magnitude? God so loved the world, that he gave his only Son, that whoever believes in Him should not perish, but have everlasting life.

Then it was God's act: so merciful that He gave His only begotten Son. You couldn't ask for more, could you? Didn't God do all He could when in this act of love, He sent His only Son, gave His only Son? That compassion was merciful.

Then there was God's offer: How gracious, for it includes you and me. This Scripture says, whoever believes in Him.

There was God's purpose: it is redemption. How redemptive is God in His compassion! Whoever believes in Him should not perish but have everlasting life. The implication is clear. Whoever does not believe in Him will perish. That's what Jesus said later on, but it's implied here, too. God's compassion is for the salvation of everybody, for the next verse tells us, "God sent not his Son into the world to condemn the world; but that the world through him might be saved."

I must insist that God's compassion includes me, and it means you. How marvelous! How wonderful! You and I can be included. Praise the Lord. Yes! God did all He can.

The third Reason: **The Condemnation.**

I want you to notice very carefully, Jesus makes it absolutely clear, the sentence has been passed. The condemnation is on us, unless we believe. He said that the one who believes on Him is not condemned. Belief is the escape from the condemnation, from the sentence of death. Unbelief brings it on you. "But he that believeth not is condemned already, because He hath not believed in the name of the only begotten Son of God."

It is very serious when God has done all He can, and you do nothing. Just to remain as you are without believing in Jesus Christ means you are under the condemnation of God. The sentence has already been passed; the execution is on the way. That's certain. "And this is the condemnation, that light is come into the world, and men loved darkness rather than light." Isn't that a pity? Men choose darkness because of their evil deeds. So the condemnation is absolutely certain.

But there is security. Praise God! I want you to notice verse 21. Truth leads to light, and light reveals. When we understand by the light of God who we are and what condition we are in, then we have taken a great step forward. For he who believes in Jesus Christ is not under condemnation.

God did all He can! The proof is Jesus lifted up like Moses lifted up the serpent. The proof is God's compassion gave His only begotten Son. The proof is deliverance from condemnation can be yours.

Chapter Twelve

What Is Really Important?

I look around, and I see that some people must surely believe that clothes are the most important thing in life. I'm reminded of what Jesus said to the disciples one time. They had that same problem. He asked them why they were thinking so much about clothing. "Consider the lilies of the field, how they grow; they toil not, neither do they spin; and yet I say unto you, that even Solomon in all his glory was not clothed like one of these."

Then I look around, and I think I can see that some people believe that money is the most important: if I just had more money! Again I'm reminded of what Jesus said to the disciples. He said some people lay up treasure on earth, but treasures on earth can spoil, thieves can steal them. So money can't be the most important thing in life.

Well, **WHAT IS REALLY IMPORTANT?** I believe some people think that friends are really important, and they are. But friends die, and sometimes they prove untrue.

We still have the question of what is really important? If we can get to the really important things, we will find the answer to our question. We'll get the answer to our question in John 3:22-30.

> *22 After these things came Jesus and his disciples into the land of Judea; and there he tarried with them, and baptized.*

23 And John also was baptizing in Aenon near to Salim, because there was much water there: and they came, and were baptized.

24 For John was not yet cast into prison.

25 Then there arose a question between some of John's disciples and the Jews about purifying.

26 And they came unto John, and said unto him, Rabbi, he that was with thee beyond Jordan, to whom thou barest witness, behold, the same baptizeth, and all men come to him.

27 John answered and said, A man can receive nothing, except it be given him from heaven.

28 Ye yourselves bear me witness, that I said, I am not the Christ, but that I am sent before him.

29 He that hath the bride is the bridegroom: but the friend of the bridegroom, which standeth and heareth him, rejoiceth greatly because of the bridegroom's voice: this my joy therefore is fulfilled.

30 He must increase, but I must decrease.

Ah, what is really important? On the basis of this Scripture, I'm going to raise three **QUESTIONS** which will help you find out what is really important. We focus our attention upon this portion of God's Word.

The first question from John the Baptist's ministry: **Is It Baptism?**

What is really important? Is it baptism? I read that John was baptizing in Aenon near Salim, and people came to him and were baptized. I also read that Jesus and his disciples came into the land of Judea, and there they were baptizing.

Perhaps you would think then that baptism is really important. Many arguments have been brought together as to how the baptism should be done. In some cases, the reason for baptism has been almost lost. Because people have insisted so much on how the baptism should be done, many never experience the reality which it is to convey.

So I'm raising the question, what is really important? Is it baptism? Is that really the most important thing? No.

Well then, I'm raising a second question which comes from those who observed John the Baptist: **Is It Purification?**

I read that some of John's disciples had a dispute with the Jews about purifying. Among the Jewish people in those days, it was commonly practiced that one should wash his hands coming from the market before saying prayers. Yes! The Lord had instructed Moses in the years gone by that they were to appear before the Lord with their bodies washed in pure water. There is a principle set forth here: God wants us at our best, not our worst.

But the question remains, is purification really that important? Yes, Jesus said, "Blessed are the pure in heart: for they shall see God." There are some who go through very careful outward forms, everything is precisely done, but they never reach God. How sad!

Then those who came to John tried to plant the seed of jealousy in his heart. Watch them inform him. Listen to what they said. "He that was with thee beyond Jordan, to whom thou barest witness, behold, the same baptizeth, and all men come to him." They were trying to plant impure thoughts in the heart of John the Baptist. Now inner purity is better than outer purity.

How do you attain purification? It starts inside as John's answer clearly told them. My question holds, what is really important? Is it baptism? Is it purification? NO!

Another question comes from John the Baptist's words.

The third Question: **Is It Position?**

John the Baptist made it clear that one only receives: "A man can receive nothing, except it be given him from heaven." That is quite humbling because some people think they are self-made, that they made themselves. But John the Baptist came through clearly and said 'whatever you have, you received.' Now, don't forget that.

Then John the Baptist said, "I am not the Christ. I'm only sent before Him." Were we to return to the first chapter of John's Gospel, we would learn there exactly how this all came about. He was just reviewing for these people what he had said earlier, "I am not the

Christ, but I am sent before him." John was the announcer of the Christ.

He said, "I'm not the bridegroom; I'm just a friend of the bridegroom. The bridegroom is the one who has the bride. My joy is fulfilled because I am his friend."

Now I want you to see what is the real answer to this question: Is it position? Well, yes, if you take verse 30 for what it says, "He must increase, but I must decrease." When we see it correctly, when we understand it exactly like John the Baptist put it, then we can say to put Jesus Christ in His rightful place is the most important thing in life! He must increase, but I must decrease! Let Jesus increase in your life. Only by this way can you know what is really important.

I am not saying that baptism is not important, that purification is not important. I'm only pointing out to you that the most important thing, that which is really important, is to put Jesus Christ in His rightful place in your heart.

Chapter Thirteen

The Essence Of Truth

So much today has the label "truth," but contains error. We must be able to tell the difference between truth and error.

How can we be sure that we have found the truth? Everybody wants to find the truth. I think only the depraved will rejoice in error. We all want the truth. **THE ESSENCE OF TRUTH** can be tested from John 3:31-36.

> *31 He that cometh from above is above all: he that is of the earth is earthly, and speaketh of the earth: he that cometh from heaven is above all.*
>
> *32 And what he hath seen and heard, that he testifieth; and no man receiveth his testimony.*
>
> *33 He that hath received his testimony hath set to his seal that God is true.*
>
> *34 For he whom God hath sent speaketh the words of God: for God giveth not the Spirit by measure unto him.*
>
> *35 The Father loveth the Son, and hath given all things into his hand.*
>
> *36 He that believeth on the Son hath everlasting life: and he that believeth not the Son shall not see life; but the wrath of God abideth on him.*

John the Baptist sets forth the **TESTS** which we ought to apply so we will not be deceived. We want to know the essence of truth.

The first Test comes by: **The Source.**

John suggests to us that there are two possibilities from which information may come. It may come from the earth; that is from, beneath. If it does, it is only humanistic; that is, it makes man the measure of all things. When it comes from the earth, it speaks of the earth, John the Baptist said.

Then there is the other possibility that information may come from heaven; that is, from above. Then it would be divine truth, and we can be fully confident that it is, in fact, true truth. It would not be mixed with error at all.

Now, these two sources may in some way be related. That which is expressed from heaven is related to earth because God had us in mind. We are creatures of earth. When God spoke, He spoke with us in mind. Even though these two sources are somewhat related, they are not the same. We must therefore test very carefully the source of what is proposed to be the truth. If it comes from heaven, we can be confident, we can be sure: we have true truth.

Then John the Baptist said there are two responses to the source of truth. First, he who has heard and seen tells what he has seen and heard; he bears testimony to the truth. Those are two valid ways of learning: seeing and hearing. One who has seen and heard the divine truth bears witness to that truth. Those who receive this testimony are sure that God is true.

Then there is the other response which John the Baptist mentions, where no man receives his testimony. In other words, they turn away from the evidence.

The response to truth is locked in the breast. It is tied very firmly to the will of man. You can decide to receive heaven's truth, or you can decide to reject heaven's truth. According to John the Baptist, there are two sources from which information may come: One source is from earth; the other from heaven. All information must be tested as to its source. If it comes from earth, then beware.

There's a second Test that comes by: **The Spirit.**

Again, there are two ideas. The one is related to God. We're told that God is true. This is a very important consideration because it deals with the very nature and character of God. In His inmost person, way inside there where nobody can measure or understand, God is true. The Spirit witnesses that to us. Here you have the idea of God's person; He is true, absolutely true, with no mixture of error or falsehood.

The other area is the Word of God, used here in the plural, "Words of God." Now there is a direct relationship between the true God and His Words. We find His words revealed in the Bible. These two ideas are very, very important: the nature of God and the WORDS of God.

Then there are two affirmations. First, I believe that John the Baptist was telling us that there is a certain standard by which we make our measurements. That standard is the seal of God. It is as though you were to go to a bureau of standards and find there the absolute genuine character of truth. Yes, God has such a standard, the seal of God.

The second affirmation speaks of boundless measure of the Spirit. You see, to get down to the essence of truth, every idea and affirmation must be tested by the Spirit.

Then there is a third Test that comes by: **The Son.**

This Scripture knows two ways. They are very sharply contrasted. The one is the way of belief; he who believes on the Son has everlasting life. That, my friend, is very basic and I'm glad to tell you it is possible. God has made us in such a way that we can believe, and He has made us in such a way that belief is very basic. So John the Baptist tells us that one who believes, one who takes that way, will have everlasting life. That's one way.

The other way is the way of unbelief. He states that one does not believe the Son. There are two ways: one is the way of belief; the other is the way of unbelief. Both are possible. Also, there are two results. The result that comes from belief is everlasting life. The result of unbelief is the wrath of God.

These are very closely connected with the Son because John the

Baptist tells us that he who believes in the Son has everlasting life. And he who does not believe in the Son does not have everlasting life. In fact, the wrath of God abides on him. So everyone must test his belief by the Son.

We all look to John the Baptist as the forerunner or the announcer of the Messiah. He said there are three tests that must be made if we are to be sure we have the truth. We must test the source, whether it comes from heaven or from earth. We must test it by the Spirit as it is directly related to the person and Words of God. We must test it by the Son so that the result will be belief and everlasting life.

Notice how he puts it so well: He who believes the Son has everlasting life, and he who does not believe that Son shall not see life. The wrath of God abides on him. Where are you?

Studies from John 4

Chapter Fourteen

Jesus At Jacob's Well

In my experience, I have learned that certain professional people put a sign on their office door something like this: by appointment only. Anyone who wants to see that person must call for an appointment. I have had many such experiences. I suppose you have, too. In that way, they can control each day's work and how many people they will see.

Jesus was not that kind of person. He didn't say by appointment only. No, Jesus made Himself available. Sometimes He seemed to arrange a meeting before the other person knew about it.

In a beautiful way, Jesus arranged such an appointment with a woman of Samaria. He was traveling from Jerusalem to Galilee and sat down by a well to rest at noontime when a woman came to the well to draw water. He made that arrangement before the woman knew that He was anywhere around.

The Bible record which tells the experience of **JESUS AT JACOB'S WELL** is from the fourth Gospel, John 4:1-10.

> *1 When therefore the Lord knew how the Pharisees had heard that Jesus made and baptized more disciples than John,*
>
> *2 (Though Jesus himself baptized not, but his disciples,)*
>
> *3 He left Judea, and departed again into Galilee.*

4 And he must needs go through Samaria.

5 Then cometh he to a city of Samaria, which is called Sychar, near to the parcel of ground that Jacob gave to his son Joseph.

6 Now Jacob's well was there. Jesus therefore, being wearied with his journey, sat thus on the well: and it was about the sixth hour.

7 There cometh a woman of Samaria to draw water: Jesus saith unto her, Give me to drink.

8 (For his disciples were gone away unto the city to buy meat.)

9 Then saith the woman of Samaria unto him, How is it that thou, being a Jew, askest drink of me, which am a woman of Samaria? For the Jews have no dealings with the Samaritans.

10 Jesus answered and said unto her, If thou knewest the gift of God, and who it is that saith to thee, Give me to drink; thou wouldest have asked of him, and he would have given thee living water.

It is helpful for us to see what **PROCESSES** Jesus used in His meeting. It was an informal meeting as far as the woman was concerned, but carefully planned by Jesus.

I want you to notice first in the life of Jesus that: **He Lived Under A Requirement.**

He seemed to know exactly where He was going, what each day would hold, and where He ought to be at what time. You'll notice in the beginning of this chapter that He was in Judea and was going to go to Galilee. It was necessary for Him to go through Samaria. We could say that the roads led Him through Samaria. The traditional road would have led Him around this country, so there was another reason why it was necessary for Him to go through Samaria. It was not that there was no other way to go. It was that He had planned a meeting with this woman at Jacob's well.

That was the plan. See? So He made his way through Samaria

in spite of the fact that Samaria, for many Jews, was off bounds. They normally did not travel through there. Oh, the reason is very clear if we go back into Biblical history. We learn that when Nebuchadnezzar came into the country and carried many of the Jews captive to Babylon, that he brought some other people and settled them there. They intermarried and became a mixed race. The Jews had a problem with people of mixed races. God had spoken to them about it. So they thought it best just to avoid them.

But Jesus lived under a certain requirement which meant that He must be in a certain place at a certain time. Every day He felt this requirement, so it was necessary for Him to go through Samaria even though there was a road that would have taken Him around.

That was process number one. Process number two: **He Made A Request.**

When He got to Jacob's well, it was noon. I am sure it took Him more than a half-day to go from Jerusalem to Samaria. I have traveled that area by bus, and He was walking most likely, so it took Him perhaps two days to get to Jacob's well. But here was a convenient place to stop. A nice place to stop because here was a good well of refreshing water, and here was a resting place not too far from the nearby village where the disciples might go and get food for them all.

It was also a likely place to meet someone, and, as I say, it was noon. I don't think Jesus was at all surprised when this woman came. Because, as I had intimated to you, I believe that He was planning this meeting. I believe He had it in His mind all along. So when she came, because He was thirsty, He said, "Give me a drink." Such a request from a Jew to this Samaritan woman really surprised her. "How is it that you, being a Jew, would ask a drink of me, a woman of Samaria?" She knew the Jews had no dealings with the Samaritans.

But do you know that didn't make any difference to Jesus? No, that didn't make any difference to Jesus. He did not see the artificial social barriers that were erected. He went on across them. He overcame the barriers and told her what He wanted. He wanted a drink. Well, as I study this text, I cannot find anywhere in it that she actually gave Him a drink. I suppose she did. At any rate He asked her for a drink, and she was surprised.

The third Process was: **He Led Her To A Response.**

After she had expressed her surprise, He said, "If you knew who it is who is talking with you, why, you would ask of Him; you would ask a drink of Him." And she couldn't understand that at all. But anyway, He understood her deeper thirst way down in her spirit, in that part of her makeup that you can't see. Her thirst was different from His. He had a physical thirst that could be quenched with water from Jacob's well. But she had a kind of thirst that needed another supply of water.

He said, "If you knew the gift of God, and who it is that says to you, give me to drink; you would have asked of Him, and He would have given you living water." That kind of water can't be drawn from Jacob's well. It is impossible to get that kind of water from a well like Jacob's well. He knew what she needed, and He had it. He knew what He needed, and she had it. So He asked her for a drink and offered her living water.

I'm sure before Jesus ever left Judea, He knew He was going to meet that woman at that well. Jesus showed the woman what everyone really needs to satisfy the thirst of spirit. She was important to Him. He went from Judea to Galilee, passing through Samaria to meet her. He stopped at the well, and He told her what she needed. He'll do that for you. He'll meet you right where you are, and He'll give you a spring of living water. You'll have to meet Him, though.

Chapter Fifteen

How To Have Inner Peace

It was Bishop Augustine of Africa many years ago who said, "My soul is restless until it finds its rest in Thee." He was talking to God when he said that. He was expressing that inner longing that everybody has, that inner longing that you have. You long to have peace way down deep in your spirit. But you wonder, "How can I have that peace?"

That's exactly what this message is about: **HOW TO HAVE INNER PEACE.** I want to help you find that peace because everybody has such a longing, and everybody tries to satisfy it, but many only create a worse condition. That was the way it was with this woman; she thought by having all those men around her, she could have inner peace, but she didn't.

Our Scripture is from John's Gospel, the fourth book in the New Testament; John 4:11-19.

> *11 The woman saith unto him, Sir, thou hast nothing to draw with, and the well is deep: from whence then hast thou that living water?*
>
> *12 Art thou greater than our father Jacob, which gave us the well, and drank thereof himself, and his children, and his cattle?*
>
> *13 Jesus answered and said unto her, Whosoever drinketh*

of this water shall thirst again:

14 But whosoever drinketh of the water that I shall give him shall never thirst; but the water that I shall give him shall be in him a well of water springing up into everlasting life.

15 The woman saith unto him, Sir, give me this water, that I thirst not, neither come hither to draw.

16 Jesus saith unto her, Go, call thy husband, and come hither.

17 The woman answered and said, I have no husband. Jesus said unto her, Thou hast well said, I have no husband:

18 For thou hast had five husbands; and he whom thou now hast is not thy husband: in that saidst thou truly.

19 The woman saith unto him, Sir, I perceive that thou art a prophet.

Now she had an eye-opening experience, didn't she? But all she needed was that inner peace which Jesus is able to give. I want to talk with you about having inner peace, how to get it, how to receive it. In the talk Jesus had with this woman, there are beautiful **DIRECTIVES** which will lead you to inner peace.

Directive number one: **Assess The Situation.**

Take account of how things are. When Jesus offered her living water, she looked at Him and said, "Where are you going to get that living water? You have nothing to draw with. This well is deep. How are you going to get living water? You must be greater than our father Jacob, who gave us the well and drank from it himself, as did his children and his flocks and herds."

She was doing some good, straight, and careful thinking; she assessed the situation. She thought from every human standpoint the water He wanted to give her was impossible. Impossible! Where is He going to get water? How can He provide living water?

That's a good directive, my friend, to assess the situation and see how utterly helpless and hopeless it is strictly from a human viewpoint. There's not much hope if you look at it like this woman looked at it. She understood how deep the well was. She also understood that before He could get any water from Jacob's well, He would need something to draw with. She did right by assessing the situation.

The second Directive is also there: **Express Your Need.**

Jesus said, "You come here often, every time you are thirsty. Whoever drinks of this water shall thirst again." Of course, the very fact that she came with her water pot indicated that she was thirsty. Her household needed water, so she came every day with her water pot. It was a drudgery. Most likely, it was a kind of thing that kept her going every day. It was what she must do.

She came here often, but she was always thirsty. Whoever drank of that water would thirst again. But Jesus said, "Whoever drinks of the water that I shall give him shall never thirst because it will be inside of him a well of water." It will be meeting that longing deep in the soul and spirit. It will not be like the physical thirst that brings you here to the well. It will be something altogether different.

When she heard that, she said, "Give me to drink." Most likely, the woman wasn't understanding everything that Jesus was pointing out to her at this moment. But when she expressed her need, give me to drink, it opened the door, the way for Jesus to bring peace to her inner spirit. That inner peace I'm talking about comes when you are willing to express your need. It will lead to peace.

These two directives are very important: assess the situation and express your need.

But the third one is just as important: **Confess Your Condition.**

In order for her to get this drink, she asked for, Jesus said to her, "Go, call your husband." That was right at the place where she was most distressed. That was where peace was absent. Jesus understood her, and He said, "Go, call your husband and come here." She immediately responded by saying, "I have no husband." That was a confession of her condition. Her whole life was exposed, for He said to her, "You are right. You have no husband. You have had five husbands, and the one you now have is not your husband." Her whole life was completely laid bare by the Lord.

She had confessed her condition, and Jesus understood it completely. Her response was, "I understand you are a prophet." Well, when Jesus offered her that inner peace, that peace of inner spirit, He had to go where the restlessness really was. Once the real condition was clear, He could offer her real peace.

Jesus can bring inner peace to you. These are the directives: assess the situation, see how hopeless it is unless He does something other than what you can do; express your need, ask Him to give you that living water; then confess your condition, open the place of your restlessness. Yes, that way, inner peace is possible. Jesus can give you peace.

Chapter Sixteen

What Is Worship?

King David once wrote these words: "Oh, worship the Lord in the beauty of holiness." But another king, long before David asked this question: "Who is the Lord that I should obey Him?" Who the Lord is and what David meant when he said, "Oh, worship the Lord in the beauty of holiness" will help us to understand **WHAT IS WORSHIP?**

I would say worship is acknowledging who God is. One man explained worship as looking or gazing at God. But then, how are you going to get that visual image of God? How are you going to see God?

Together we are going to have a blessing. We will go to a part of the Bible, the Gospel of John, the fourth book in the New Testament, and read John 4:20-26.

> *20 Our fathers worshipped in this mountain; and ye say, that in Jerusalem is the place where men ought to worship.*
>
> *21 Jesus saith unto her, Woman, believe me, the hour cometh, when ye shall neither in this mountain, nor yet at Jerusalem, worship the Father.*
>
> *22 Ye worship ye know not what: we know what we worship: for salvation is of the Jews.*

23 But the hour cometh, and now is, when the true worshippers shall worship the Father in spirit and in truth: for the Father seeketh such to worship him.

24 God is a Spirit: and they that worship him must worship him in spirit and in truth.

25 The woman saith unto him, I know that Messias cometh, which is called Christ: when he is come, he will tell us all things.

26 Jesus saith unto her, I that speak unto thee am he.

In this text, Jesus talked about worship. The story opens with a woman talking with Jesus regarding worship. I want to talk to you about the idea of how to worship God.

There are no people in the world who have no desire to worship. Oh, there are certain countries and lands where they've tried to outlaw it, but still, the desire to worship is there. There are different methods and different objects, but people all over the world have a desire to worship.

We may wonder what is the right way to worship. I am sure that everybody who has heard about Jesus is convinced that He was a great teacher. You can't read the Gospel records without being impressed with the way Jesus was able to teach the truth. He taught as no one else taught. In fact, the people of His day said, "No man ever spoke like this man." Even people who did not agree with Him had to admit that here was somebody who stood tall as a teacher. He had a way of teaching that got the truth across.

Therefore, I want you to pay close attention to this Scripture in which Jesus comments about worship. From His words, we find the **ANSWERS** to the deep question, "What is Worship?"

There is: **The Answer Of Place.**

The woman asked a very important question, "Our fathers worshiped in this mountain, but you Jews say that in Jerusalem is the place where men ought to worship." You might wonder why these Samaritan people insisted on worshiping in that mountain. Even today, there are still a few Samaritans living in the same place where this woman lived. Today they worship on Mt. Gerizim. God had told Moses they were to read the law to the people of Israel from that mountain when they got into the land of promise. So the Samaritans chose that as the place to worship.

Later the Jewish people set their temple in Jerusalem. David took Jerusalem from the Jebusites a thousand years before Christ. Solomon set the temple there on Mount Moriah where Abram offered Isaac. It was the place God had chosen.

So the woman said, "We'll worship here; you worship there." There are many people who think it is important in which city you worship; for example, Rome, Bombay, or Mecca. Places are really important to some people.

Jesus said they had mistaken the whole purpose of worship. He said, "The time is coming when neither in this mountain nor in Jerusalem are you going to be worshiping the Father." By that, He did not say you can worship God nowhere, but He said you can worship God anywhere. It's not so much this mountain or that mountain or any other place; it is that you are worshiping the Father. So Jesus gave an answer to the question of place.

Then He gave: **The Answer Of What.**

He asked, "Do you know what you are worshiping?" When He said that, He answered clearly for many people because many worship in ignorance; they do not know what they are worshiping. In my study of religions of the world, I have found that many people are like that. They worship in ignorance. That is not criticism, but simply to point out that just as Jesus remarked about this woman, there are many others in the world today who worship but have no idea what they worship.

Then Jesus said, "We know what we worship: for salvation is of the Jews." Now, my friend, you can't rewrite Bible history. The history of revelation has it this way. God chose the sons of Jacob and their descendants. He gathered them at Mount Sinai many years ago and came down in revelation to them. They had the prophets. They were the ones to whom God spoke. He spoke to the world through them. God chose one people to receive the revelation of Himself. They are the Jews. Jesus said, "Salvation is of the Jews."

Now, my friend, these words cannot be changed. Maybe some people would like to change them, but they cannot be changed. The God of revelation is the true God. Jesus said that God came to the people of Israel in salvation. Salvation is of the Jews. So in that, He answered the question of what.

He gave a third answer to the question of worship when He gave: **The Answer Of Whom.**

All religions are not the same. Jesus defined the Father in this Scripture. He said you are going to worship the Father and the Father seeks worshipers. He is a spirit, therefore we must worship Him in spirit and in truth.

The physical is important but not all-important. That's why Jesus said it's not this mountain or this city or that city or that mountain; we must worship God in spirit and in truth.

The woman responded with a tremendous statement, "We know that the Messiah is coming, and when the Messiah has come, He will tell us all things." Now listen carefully. Jesus said, "I that speak unto you am He."

I would think that what Jesus said about worship, since He is the Messiah, would be foundational to our thought of how to worship God. We must listen to Him because He understands who God is. How shall we worship God? Jesus answers, we can worship God anywhere, not in this mountain or that city, but wherever we are we can worship God. He said we know what we worship for we have the revelation; salvation is of the Jews. He gave the answer of whom we worship; He said the Father, God. So it's all put together for us. Praise the Lord! Are you worshiping the true God?

Chapter Seventeen

How To Test What Is Important

Every one of us has a set of values by which we judge events and experiences. We also use this set of values to judge the quality of an object: a garment, a purchase of food. We use this set of values in a number of ways. All of us have also learned that quality is not always determined by the price one has to pay. Some items are overpriced. Some items may be under-priced. So we use our set of values to judge the quality of whatever item or object we may wish to buy at a reasonable price.

Then some values are priceless. Some ideas cannot be bought. For example, Jesus said once, "What will it profit a man if he should gain the whole world and lose his own soul?" Do you see what I mean, that some values are priceless? All the wealth of the world is not worth as much as the soul.

The experience of Jesus in John 4:27-38 teaches us **HOW TO TEST WHAT IS IMPORTANT.**

> *27 And upon this came his disciples, and marvelled that he talked with the woman: yet no man said, What seekest thou? Or, Why talkest thou with her?*
>
> *28 The woman then left her waterpot and went her way into the city, and saith to the men,*
>
> *29 Come, see a man, which told me all things that ever I*

did: is not this the Christ?

30 Then they went out of the city, and came unto him.

31 In the mean while his disciples prayed him, saying, Master, eat.

32 But he said unto them, I have meat to eat that ye know not of.

33 Therefore said the disciples one to another, Hath any man brought him aught to eat?

34 Jesus saith unto them, My meat is to do the will of him that sent me, and to finish his work.

35 Say not ye, There are yet four months, and then cometh harvest? Behold, I say unto you, Lift up your eyes, and look on the fields; for they are white already to harvest.

36 And he that reapeth receiveth wages, and gathereth fruit unto life eternal: that both he that soweth and he that reapeth may rejoice together.

37 And herein is that saying true, One soweth, and another reapeth.

38 I sent you to reap that whereon ye bestowed no labour: other men laboured, and ye are entered into their labours.

This is a very interesting experience in the life of Jesus, and from this scene, we can discover the **CLUES** which should help us to test what is important.

First there is: **The Woman's Invitation.**

This woman, who went into the city and invited the men to come and see the man who told her everything, was the woman that Jesus was talking with there at Jacob's well. The conversation between Him and the woman was a surprise to the disciples. They could not understand why Jesus would be talking with this Samaritan woman, but they would not ask Him.

The woman's invitation was to the men of the city. She said, "Come, see a man who told me all things that ever I did. Is not this the Christ?" She was convinced. She had made a commitment unto this One who spoke with her. She understood that He knew all about her. In her statement to the men, she made a confession of Christ. "Is not this the Christ?" she asked. "Is this not the Messiah?" Then they went out of the city to meet Him.

In our set of values, we must do like this woman did; we must put Jesus Christ in His rightful place. In her invitation to these people of the city, she did exactly that. She said, "I have met Him; He has told me all things ever I did; surely this must be the Christ." Yes, in your set of values, you will need to place Jesus in His proper position.

There is a second Clue which comes out of: **The Disciples' Supplication.**

When the disciples returned from the city where they had gone to buy food, they found Jesus talking with the woman. You know, hunger is a part of our existence. To stay alive, we must eat. Our physical bodies must have food. So naturally, when the disciples came back with the food they had purchased in the village, they were expecting the Master to share it with them.

But He was unconcerned about food at that moment. They could not understand it. It was their second surprise. Even more was it a surprise to them when He said, "I have food to eat that you know not of." By this, He meant that there are considerations more important than the physical. Jesus saw and accepted that truth.

There are some considerations more important than food and the physical. The disciples had no answer for Him. They only wondered if somebody had given Him something to eat. Then Jesus made it clear. He said, "My food is to do the will of Him that sent me and to finish His work." For Jesus, to do the will of God was more important than having lunch.

Now in our sets of values, we must see the relationship of the physical to the spiritual. Or, we must see the relationship of the spiritual to the physical. Jesus understood that. His set of values put the spiritual above the physical. That is where you will need to put it in your set of values.

There is the third Clue: **The Master's Evaluation.**

Jesus went on to say, "Say not ye, There are yet four months, and then cometh harvest?" He corrected the timetable of harvest. They thought there would be four months to harvest time. But He said, "Lift up your eyes, and look on the fields; for they are white already to harvest." Now quite surely He was referring to a kind of harvest other than the wheat or barley harvest. As Jesus looked upon the conditions around Him, He saw that the harvest was now, not four months from now.

Jesus also understood the relation of sowing and reaping. "One sows, and another reaps," He said. They must go together. They are dependent one upon the other. Each is very important. You can't have a harvest without somebody sowing the seed, and you can't have seed unless there is a harvest. So Jesus helped them to understand the relation of sowing and reaping.

Jesus directed the disciples into their labor. He sent them to reap that on which they had not labored. Other men had labored, and they were to reap the harvest. Jesus put value on the harvest.

We must put the Master's order of priorities in our sets of values; the spiritual must be over the physical. We must see that the time is now; we should not put off what needs to be done now. Here in this scene, we note the necessity of putting Christ in His rightful place, like the woman inviting others to Him. We must value the necessity of putting God's will above personal comfort. That's what Jesus did. He put the Father's work above physical food. We must also see the necessity of laboring in the spiritual harvest NOW.

Above all, put Christ in His rightful place. Have you done that?

Chapter Eighteen

How To Know Christ Truly

In the experiences of my life, I have found there are levels of learning. We come to know truth in a number of different ways. We may read it in the Bible or we may read it in a magazine. That's one level of learning. Another level is that we may hear someone speak the truth. Then we may experience the truth. That is a third level of learning. We often think about this experience level. After some experiences, we say we need to write that up to the school of experience. We can say experience is a most valid way of learning. Sometimes it's very costly. We can avoid unhappy and wasteful experiences if we will listen or read, but experience is foundational. It is right there at rock bottom.

Then there are many kinds of learning: the skills we need to know to earn a living which we might call a trade; the ways of doing a job easily; how to do it smoothly and with a minimum of effort.

There are persons we need to learn to know: those who will guide, train, and teach. Someone once said to me, "It's not so much what you know as who you know." That may be true in Christian experience, but it is also important to know the facts of life. From John 4:39-45 I bring to you **HOW TO KNOW CHRIST TRULY.** him that he would tarry with them: and he abode there two days.

39 And many of the Samaritans of that city believed on

him for the saying of the woman, which testified, He told me all that ever I did.

40 So when the Samaritans were come unto him, they besought him that he would tarry with them: and he abode there two days.

41 And many more believed because of his own word;

42 And said unto the woman, Now we believe, not because of thy saying: for we have heard him ourselves, and know that this is indeed the Christ, the Saviour of the world.

43 Now after two days he departed thence, and went into Galilee.

44 For Jesus himself testified, that a prophet hath no honour in his own country.

45 Then when he was come into Galilee, the Galileans received him, having seen all the things that he did at Jerusalem at the feast: for they also went unto the feast.

In the introduction, we noted different levels of learning and different subjects to be learned. From this text, I mean to show you the several **CHARACTERISTICS** of Jesus Christ so you can know Him truly. You can read about Him, listen to Him and you can experience Him.

The first Characteristic: **He Is The Revealer Of All Things.**

That woman with whom Jesus had spoken by Jacob's well suddenly realized that her life was like an open book before the Lord. He seemed to read every part of her life. She told Him all the truth and added, "I perceive that you are a prophet." She concluded this because her life was completely open before Him.

Many of the Samaritans believed because she said, "He told me all that ever I did." Her front was taken away. She could no longer hide behind the things she had hidden behind in the presence of other people. Now in the presence of Jesus, she couldn't hide anything because He is the Revealer of all things. So she simply confessed and said, "He told me all things that ever I did!"

Well, that's Jesus for you. Yes, He understands everything about you. In fact, I would like to say, you cannot know yourself until you let Him tell you what you are. That is what happened to this woman. That is what can happen to you, because He is the Revealer of all things! That's one characteristic about Him.

The second Characteristic: **He Is The Redeemer Of All men.**

Jesus stayed with these Samaritans two days, and during that time, many more believed because of His own word. You see, it was necessary for them to hear Him. The woman could tell them, and she did, and many believed because of what she told them. But when they heard Him themselves, they said, "Now we believe, not because of thy saying: for we have heard Him ourselves." Yes, one can hear the testimony of what Jesus did for another, but it is also good to hear Him. They said, "Now we believe... and know that this is indeed the Christ, the Saviour of the world." That's what I say: He is the Redeemer of all men. These Samaritan people saw Him that way. They said, "We understand; we believe; we have heard Him, and we are convinced that here is the Messiah, the Saviour of the world!

I'm glad I know Him that way. I know He is the Redeemer of all men. He is my Redeemer; He is my Saviour. I have confessed and acknowledged Him as the Messiah, the Saviour of the world. Do you know Him that way? You must know Him like this. He is the Redeemer of all men who believe. Of course, now you can be one of those and believe this very moment.

The third Characteristic: **He Is The Restorer Of All Good.**

There are some serious tragedies in life. One of those Jesus mentioned here. He said that the prophet has no honor at home in his own country. That really is a tragedy. It is what I call the tragedy of neighborhood. Isn't it a pity that some of the people who live closest to us, we are unable to appreciate as we should? But Jesus is the Restorer of all good things.

The Galileans believed. They received Him because they had seen all the things which He had done in Jerusalem. Jesus was a worker of miracles. The Gospels record thirty-eight miracles which Jesus did. So I believe, too. All of them but one were miracles of mercy! His deeds told the people who He was, and who He is. The

Galileans knew Him. They received Him because they had seen the things which He did: His acts of mercy; His words of compassion and love. Yes, He is the Restorer of all good.

By this text, we see Him as He is: the Revealer of all things; the Redeemer of all men; the Restorer of all good. How do you know Him? How can you come to know Him? Believe on Him. Receive Him. Then you can know Him truly just like these people did, and just like I do.

Chapter Nineteen

How To Find Help

We are all dependent creatures. We cannot make it on our own. Nobody is completely independent. All of us need the help of those around us. Some of us seem to be more helpless than others. All of us are dependent upon those around us, but sometimes even they cannot really help us.

One of my African friends told me this experience. At one time during our radio broadcast, as I was bringing the program to a close, his sister who had been sick with tuberculosis picked up the radio and held it to her bosom, and, as I was praying at the close of the program, God healed her. Praise the Lord!

Sometimes people around you can't help you; then God can! When there seems to be no one to help you, where do you turn? Do you have a place where you can go? Do you have a person you can go to? In John 4:46-54 notice carefully what this nobleman did when he had a problem.

> *46 So Jesus came again into Cana of Galilee, where he made the water wine. And there was a certain nobleman, whose son was sick at Capernaum.*
>
> *47 When he heard that Jesus was come out of Judea into Galilee, he went unto him, and besought him that he would come down, and heal his son: for he was at the*

point of death.

48 Then said Jesus unto him, Except ye see signs and wonders, ye will not believe.

49 The nobleman saith unto him, Sir, come down ere my child die.

50 Jesus saith unto him, Go thy way; thy son liveth. And the man believed the word that Jesus had spoken unto him, and he went his way.

51 And as he was now going down, his servants met him, and told him, saying, Thy son liveth.

52 Then inquired he of them the hour when he began to amend. And they said unto him, Yesterday at the seventh hour the fever left him.

53 So the father knew that it was at the same hour, in the which Jesus said unto him, Thy son liveth: and himself believed, and his whole house.

54 This is again the second miracle that Jesus did, when he was come out of Judea into Galilee.

Here was a man who had a very deep problem. By looking at the experience of this nobleman, we have **EXAMPLES** which will show us **HOW TO FIND HELP** for our needs too. Because this nobleman had his problem and found a solution for it, we are able to find the examples which will show us how to get help, too.

Example number one: **The Nobleman's Purpose.**

His son was very sick. The father had done all he could possibly do. He told Jesus his son was at the point of death. So when he heard that Jesus had come out of Judea into Galilee, he set out for Cana on foot. I measured the distance on the map, and it would be thirty kilometers. That's a day's journey, especially in that particular part of the country. Capernaum is down by the seaside and Cana is up in the mountains. He would have walked uphill thirty kilometers to get to Cana.

But he had heard that Jesus was in Cana, and he would not be turned aside. He set out to find Jesus, and he found Him. He would not change his course. He would not be diverted; he kept on going until he came to Jesus.

I call this a consuming purpose. The nobleman's need developed a consuming purpose. He would not give up until he had found Jesus, the source of help. How will you find help? Let that kind of consuming purpose possess you, and you will find help.

Here is a second Example: **The Nobleman's Prayer.**

When he came and asked Jesus to heal his son, Jesus said to Him, "Except ye see signs and wonders, ye will not believe." I call that a test because Jesus put it to him quite straight, didn't He? He wanted to be sure this nobleman had examined his heart. Jesus wanted to be sure the man was not there just for some great sign or wonder. So the Lord put it that way to him; He said, "Except ye see signs and wonders, ye will not believe."

The man by his reply expressed his honest motive. "Sir, come down before my child dies." Please dispense with all this extra and let us get down to the urgent need that I have in the life of my son. Jesus said very simply, "Go thy way; thy son liveth."

Watch that man! Watch that nobleman! If you want help, watch him. "And the man believed the word that Jesus had spoken unto him, and he went his way." Do you get it? The man prayed to Jesus, "Come down before my son dies," and when Jesus responded and said, "Go, your son lives," he believed it, and he went! There were no doubts in his mind, not one.

If you want help when you really need it, take this nobleman's example and pray like he did. That's what I call a pleading prayer: "Come down before my son dies." This nobleman prayed that kind of a pleading prayer, and he got help. When Jesus spoke to him, he believed. He is a good example. Pray a pleading prayer and believe the answer to your prayer. That is the way to get help when you need it just like this man did.

A third Example: **The Nobleman's Persuasion.**

It is already reflected in the fact that he just believed Jesus. That is why he was persuaded. For all practical purposes, he had no evidence; just the word of Jesus. But he was persuaded and went.

Whom should he meet on the way but his servants coming to find him. They said to him, "Your son lives!" What a joy that must have been for him. He heard it right from home. You might say he believed it before he had left Cana, but now he has the assurance of it by the word of his servants. So he began to ask, "When did he get better? When did he start improving?" And they said, "Yesterday at the seventh hour the fever left him." He figured a little bit and realized it was exactly the time when Jesus spoke the word.

Wasn't that a tremendous confirmation? He was thoroughly persuaded. That proof was convincing for him, and he and all his house believed on Jesus.

That's what I call forcible persuasion. That kind of forcible persuasion will find help. It found help for this nobleman. Surely, it did! He believed and all his house. Take this man's example, and you can find help. Be persuaded that what Jesus says is absolutely true, and you'll have the evidence to go with it just like he did. Such forcible persuasion will find help.

When you need help, let me commend to you this nobleman's example: set out with a consuming purpose to find Jesus; pray a pleading prayer to Jesus; adopt a forcible persuasion about Jesus and you'll find help.

Seek Him out with consuming purpose; let nothing hinder you. Present your need to Him with pleading prayer; let no doubt confuse you. Accept the answer with forcible persuasion; let no barrier stop you! Help is available!

Studies from John 5

Chapter Twenty

Faith That Acts

In my experience and study, I have learned that everybody believes in something. The widespread practice of religion proves it. Even though a man may be practicing a very strange and odd religion the very fact that he does practice religion proves that he believes in something. In fact, I would say that even the attempt to stifle religion proves that everybody believes in something. Those who deny God would not work at it so hard if they did not believe down deep in their hearts that He does exist.

We are made with the ability to believe. That is one distinguishing quality which separates us from the animals. They can't believe; they were not created that way. We are made so we can believe. There was King David who said once, "The fool has said in his heart, There is no God." I'm quoting the Bible, my friend, the words of King David who said only the senseless person, only the fool, will say, "There is no God."

That brings me back to my statement, everybody believes in something. It is of the utmost importance what we believe in, and then how our faith acts. In this Bible text, John 5:1-14, we have the experience of Jesus when He performed a miracle in Jerusalem.

> *1 After this there was a feast of the Jews; and Jesus went up to Jerusalem.*

2 Now there is at Jerusalem by the sheep market a pool, which is called in the Hebrew tongue Bethesda, having five porches.

3 In these lay a great multitude of impotent folk, of blind, halt, withered, waiting for the moving of the water.

4 For an angel went down at a certain season into the pool, and troubled the water: whosoever then first after the troubling of the water stepped in was made whole of whatsoever disease he had.

5 And a certain man was there, which had an infirmity thirty and eight years.

6 When Jesus saw him lie, and knew that he had been now a long time in that case, he saith unto him, Wilt thou be made whole?

7 The impotent man answered him, Sir, I have no man, when the water is troubled, to put me into the pool: but while I am coming, another steppeth down before me.

8 Jesus saith unto him, Rise, take up thy bed, and walk.

9 And immediately the man was made whole, and took up his bed, and walked: and on the same day was the sabbath.

10 The Jews therefore said unto him that was cured, It is the sabbath day: it is not lawful for thee to carry thy bed.

11 He answered them, He that made me whole, the same said unto me, Take up thy bed, and walk.

12 Then asked they him, What man is that which said unto thee, Take up thy bed, and walk?

13 And he that was healed wist not who it was: for Jesus had conveyed himself away, a multitude being in that place.

14 Afterward Jesus findeth him in the temple, and said unto him, Behold, thou art made whole: sin no more, lest a worse thing come unto thee.

This sick man's experience demonstrates for us the **PROCESSES** by which faith is brought to action. That's what I want to talk about, **FAITH THAT ACTS.**

Here is the first of these Processes: **The Man Was Waiting.**

The Bible tells us there was a multitude waiting. There was a great multitude of helpless sick people waiting expectantly because this pool was known as a place for healing. So they came, many of them; all of them sick: people with paralysis, people with blindness, people with fevers, people with all kinds of problems. This man came waiting, waiting, waiting for the moment of healing.

I would like to tell you, my friend, in order for faith to act, there must be a kind of waiting, of expectancy when the moment of experience will come. This man was in that process, waiting for the exact moment when that healing could take place in the pool.

But there was more to faith that acts than simply waiting. When Jesus came by and saw the man, that he had been sick like this thirty-eight years, He asked if him would he like to be well. The man told him how helpless he was.

The second Process: **The Man Was Weary.**

He had been sick thirty-eight years. Maybe he was born with this sickness; maybe he was only thirty-eight years old and had known nothing except to be sick. He said, "I come here and wait and wait. When the water is troubled I try to get to the pool but while I am coming, another steps down before me."

In other words, the man said, "I am totally helpless. I've come here many times, and I always go away the same as I came. I can't do anything for myself, and nobody helps me."

Ah, he did not know that his faith was going through a process of extreme importance. He admitted he could do nothing for himself. Then it was possible for the Lord to do something for him. That's true of you. Waiting is important; weariness is important. Then you come to the place where you realize that nothing you can do is going to help. Jesus said to that man, "Rise, take up your bed and walk!"

Here we have the third Process: **The Man Was Walking.**

When Jesus gave him that startling command, he arose. Immediately he was made well. He took up his bed and walked. There was no hesitance. There was no questioning. No, there was no waiting. When Jesus gave him that startling command, he immediately rose up. He did what Jesus told him to do. No delay, nobody else needed to come raise him up because the word of Jesus had made him well, and he arose and was walking.

He picked up his bed and started for the temple to worship and praise God that he was healed. Do you know why he was able to walk? He was able to walk because he did exactly what Jesus told him to do. He did not argue or go around another way. When Jesus gave him that startling command, he immediately responded. That's why he was walking. His faith took action right at that point.

This leads to the fourth Process: **He Was Well.**

You might call this the result of faith in action. The question was, "Would you like to be well?" And after he was made well, he responded to those who questioned him about his work of carrying his bed on the Sabbath day. He said, "He that made me well told me to carry my bed." And when Jesus found him later in the temple, He said, "Behold, thou art well." For thirty-eight years, he had been sick, but now he was well, cured of a thirty-eight-year-long sickness.

"Behold, thou art well." I don't know what your problem might be. Perhaps you have some physical sickness. If you do not know Jesus Christ, I know that you have a spiritual sickness, and it may be of long standing. But just like this man, you must act in faith and listen to what Jesus says to you. Would you like to be well? Act on His Word, and you can be well in your spirit.

To put faith into action, notice these four processes: the process of waiting, the process of weariness, the process of walking, and the process of being well. Now see how these may apply to you. Don't give up in your weariness; when He says walk, walk; and you will be well by His Word.

Chapter Twenty-One

God The Son—His Nature

Honestly, we all have problems that are difficult to understand. We have situations or conflicts in life that are not easy to solve. We are surrounded with mysteries even in everyday life. I'm sure that you must say with me, "There are some things I don't understand." But I'm also glad that there are some things that can be cleared up when we get to the right source of information.

In this message, we will go to the right source of information to learn about God's Son. The Bible speaks about God's Son in the second Psalm in these words: "I will declare the decree: the Lord hath said unto me, Thou art my Son; this day have I begotten thee." Maybe you didn't know that was in the Bible: "Thou art my Son; this day have I begotten thee." From the book of Proverbs, the 30th chapter, we have another very interesting portion in verses 1-4:

> *1 The words of Agur the son of Jakeh, even the prophecy: the man spake unto Ithiel, even unto Ithiel and Ucal,*
>
> *2 Surely I am more brutish than any man, and have not the understanding of a man.*
>
> *3 I neither learned wisdom, nor have the knowledge of the holy.*
>
> *4 Who hath ascended up into heaven, or descended? Who hath gathered the wind in his fists? Who hath bound*

the waters in a garment? Who hath established all the ends of the earth? What is his name, and what is his son's name, if thou canst tell?

These questions in the book of Proverbs surely describe God Almighty, "Who hath ascended up into heaven? Who hath established all the ends of the earth?" This can mean none other than God. Then the question follows, "What is his name, and what is his son's name, if thou canst tell?"

"When Jesus was conceived by the virgin Mary, the angel Gabriel told her that her Son would be called, "The Son of the Highest." You'll find that in Luke's Gospel, chapter 1. I believe the Bible is God's revelation to us which means we learn from the Bible what we otherwise could not know. So it's entirely appropriate and proper for us to talk about **GOD THE SON—HIS NATURE.** In this message from John 5:15-29, we learn which are the words of Jesus.

15 The man departed, and told the Jews that it was Jesus, which had made him whole.

16 And therefore did the Jews persecute Jesus, and sought to slay him, because he had done these things on the sabbath day.

17 But Jesus answered them, My Father worketh hitherto, and I work.

18 Therefore the Jews sought the more to kill him, because he not only had broken the sabbath, but said also that God was his Father, making himself equal with God.

19 Then answered Jesus and said unto them, Verily, verily, I say unto you, The Son can do nothing of himself, but what he seeth the Father do: for what things soever he doeth, these also doeth the Son likewise.

20 For the Father loveth the Son, and sheweth him all things that himself doeth: and he will shew him greater works than these, that ye may marvel.

21 For as the Father raiseth up the dead, and quickeneth them; even so the Son quickeneth whom he will.

22 For the Father judgeth no man, but hath committed all judgment unto the Son:

23 That all men should honour the Son, even as they honour the Father. He that honoureth not the Son honoureth not the Father, which hath sent him.

24 Verily, verily, I say unto you, He that heareth my word, and believeth on him that sent me, hath everlasting life, and shall not come into condemnation; but is passed from death unto life.

25 Verily, verily, I say unto you, The hour is coming, and now is, when the dead shall hear the voice of the Son of God: and they that hear shall live.

26 For as the Father hath life in himself; so hath he given to the Son to have life in himself;

27 And hath given him authority to execute judgment also, because he is the Son of man.

28 Marvel not at this: for the hour is coming, in the which all that are in the graves shall hear his voice,

29 And shall come forth; they that have done good, unto the resurrection of life; and they that have done evil, unto the resurrection of damnation.

In Jesus' teachings, we have several **DESCRIPTIONS** which should help us understand the nature of God the Son.

First Description: **There Is Equality.**

Jesus said They work together. "My father works hitherto, and I work." The people who heard Him say this knew exactly what He meant. They judged Him for making Himself equal with God because He referred to God as His Father. That Father/Son relationship spelled for them and for us equality. God the Son is equal with God the Father.

When John began to write his Gospel, he said,

1 In the beginning was the Word, and the Word was with God, and the Word was God.

2 The same was in the beginning with God,

3 All things were made by him; and without him was not any thing made that was made.

Here Jesus said, "My father works and I work." Because He referred to God as His Father those who were around Him understood that He meant He was equal with God. There was equality between Him and God the Father.

The second Description: **There Is Unity.**

There is unity between God the Son and God the Father. Jesus said that He can do nothing but what He sees the Father do. Whatever the Father does, the Son does in the same manner. He said, "The Son can do nothing of himself." They work in absolute harmony. The purpose of one is the same as the purpose of the other, so whatever the Father does, the Son does. "The Father loves the Son and shows him all the things that He himself does. And he will show him greater works than these," Jesus said.

He has the power to give life. As the Father has power, so the Son has power. The Father has committed all judgment unto the Son. There is absolute unity between the Father and the Son. Therefore, we can talk about God the Son. We are correct because here we see there is absolute unity between the Father and the Son.

Now for some people, that creates difficulty. I would like to point out to you two references we should note: one in Genesis and one in Deuteronomy.

When God brought Eve to Adam, Adam responded and said, "Because the woman is bone of my bone and flesh of my flesh she shall be called woman." And then he said, "They shall be one flesh," *basar echad* my Hebrew Bible reads. That means these two became one. There is a unity between man and woman, which is like the unity in God. Let us note Deuteronomy 6:4: "Hear, O Israel: the LORD our God is one LORD." A unity, *echad*. Jesus in this Scripture in John 5 was talking about that kind of unity when He said that the Father and the Son do exactly the same things.

The third Description: **There Is Authority.**

There is no conflict between the Father and the Son, because the

Father has given all authority unto the Son. Let us look at that 27th verse just as it is: "And hath given him authority to execute judgment also, because he is the Son of man." He also has authority to raise the dead because they shall hear the voice of the Son of God and those who hear shall live. So He has authority to give life, to raise the dead, to execute judgment, and to assign for eternity! Those who are called up from the grave, who hear his voice, shall come forth, some unto the resurrection of life and some unto the resurrection of damnation.

God the Son has that authority, for He is now risen from the dead. When Jesus spoke these words, He was here in His earthly body as the Son of man, but we know from the record He is now risen from the dead. He has, therefore, conquered all opposition and has absolute authority.

The nature of the Son of God is described in these words of Scripture. The people then living understood the implications of what He was saying, but many of them did not believe; some did. How is it with you?

He is not merely a man aspiring to be God. He is not only a prophet. He is God come in the flesh! As such, He possesses equality with the Father, He possesses unity with the Father, He possesses authority with the Father. It is therefore important, my friend, that you and I both pay attention to God the Son.

Chapter Twenty-Two

God The Son—His Purpose

Some of the names that are used for Jesus are in combination. Jesus Christ in Greek is *Christos*, which means Jesus, the Anointed One. In the Old Testament language, Hebrew, it is *Mashiach*, Jesus, the Messiah. This tells me that He is the Special One. There is no one like Him! He has a particular place in all of the human family. Nobody can take His place. He came to show us God.

One time Philip asked Him to show them the Father, and Jesus answered, "He who has seen me has seen the Father." So He came to show us the Father.

Jesus Christ came to fulfill God's purpose perfectly, and He did. We learn this from John 5:30-38.

> *30 I can of mine own self do nothing: as I hear, I judge: and my judgment is just; because I seek not mine own will, but the will of the Father which hath sent me.*
>
> *31 If I bear witness of myself, my witness is not true.*
>
> *32 There is another that beareth witness of me; and I know that the witness which he witnesseth of me is true.*
>
> *33 Ye sent unto John, and he bare witness unto the truth.*
>
> *34 But I receive not testimony from man: but these things I say, that ye might be saved.*

35 He was a burning and a shining light: and ye were willing for a season to rejoice in his light.

36 But I have greater witness than that of John: for the works which the Father hath given me to finish, the same works that I do, bear witness of me, that the Father hath sent me.

37 And the Father himself, which hath sent me, hath borne witness of me. Ye have neither heard his voice at any time, nor seen his shape.

38 And ye have not his word abiding in you: for whom he hath sent, him ye believe not.

These are straightforward words coming from the lips of Jesus. From Jesus' own personal testimony, we can see the several **AREAS** where He accomplished His purpose. This message is about **GOD THE SON—HIS PURPOSE.**

The first of these several Areas where Jesus accomplished His purpose: **In The Will Of The Father.**

He said He came not to do His own will but the will of the Father. There was complete submission on His part. He had no will of His own. He realized His highest joy by doing the will of the Father. There is something comforting about that because it becomes very clear that there is a kind of unity here which no other one has experienced.

He received His Father's witness because He did His Father's will. He said He did not bear witness of Himself, for if He did, His witness would not be true. But the Father bore witness of Him. Jesus received His Father's approval.

Now, my friend, without doubt, Jesus carried out the Father's will. On another occasion, He said, "I do always those things that please the Father." In this area, His purpose was clearly spelled out. Nothing mattered to Jesus except the will of the Father. It was His total purpose to carry out the Father's will.

I don't know whether that comes through to you in all its force or not. It really means that God the Son purposed to do nothing except the will of God the Father.

The second Area where Jesus accomplished His purpose: **In The Works Of The Father.**

There is a very close relationship between the will of the Father and the works of the Father. Jesus goes back and recalls that John the Baptist bore testimony to Him. We could find that in the first chapter of John's Gospel. What did John say about Jesus when he saw Him coming? He said, "Behold the Lamb of God, which taketh away the sin of the world." John had a message. He urged those who came to him to bear fruit as evidence of repentance, because they were in the presence of the Lamb of God.

Jesus remarked how the people came and rejoiced in the light John brought them. Jesus said the works of God are more important than the testimony of John. Jesus had a special work to do; a work outlined for Him even beyond the teachings that He taught, because there was a particular and distinct work that Jesus came to do: the work of the Father.

He doesn't say exactly what that work is in this Scripture, but if we go on to the end of John's Gospel, we can see what it is. Jesus came to make a satisfactory sacrifice for our sins. He went to the cross; He died on the cross and shed His blood that we might be forgiven of our sins. That is the work of the Father. Without doubt, Jesus accomplished the work of the Father. There can be no question about that.

The third Area where Jesus accomplished His purpose is: **In The Witness Of The Father.**

Several times in these verses, you notice that Jesus said, "The Father hath sent me." Jesus was sent by the Father. On other occasions, a voice came from heaven affirming Jesus. One of those times was at His baptism by John the Baptist in the River Jordan. A voice came from heaven saying, "This is my beloved Son in whom I am well pleased." God the Father bore witness to God the Son.

In addition, Jesus' teaching agreed with God's Word. He said the Father sent Him and has borne witness of Him. The words of Jesus are important because Jesus was teaching in harmony with God's Word. He said to those who were around Him that they did not have God's Word dwelling in them, because they did not believe in

Him whom God had sent. The invisible God became visible in Jesus.

God's Word is a picture of God and His dealings with mankind. If they refused to look at God's Word and to accept it, how could they expect to understand whom God the Son was? You see? The witness of the Father is that third area in which Jesus worked out His purpose. Without doubt, Jesus received a witness of the Father.

Now, my friend, we must see how Jesus, God the Son, carried out His purpose closely associated with the Father: He performed the will of the Father; He accomplished the work of the Father; He received the witness of the Father. Do you see that this Someone who is distinct and absolutely unique is God the Son? How do you respond to Him? Peter once said, "Thou art the Christ, the Son of the living God!" That must be your confession, too.

Chapter Twenty-Three

God The Son—His Call

There are many who know something about Jesus. Some know only His name. Others know little more about Him. They know He was born in Bethlehem. They know He grew up in Nazareth and Galilee. They know His teaching was carried on throughout the Holy Land and often in the city of Jerusalem. They even know that He was crucified on Calvary outside the old city of Jerusalem. They know the record says that He was raised from the dead. But all this knowledge is useless unless the person who knows these facts about Jesus accepts Him for who He is, **God the Son**.

There must be an acceptance. There must be a response. Jesus understood human nature and issued His call first to His own people, the Jews. And He did it in these words found in John 5:39-47. Here is a word from Jesus to the people of His day.

> *39 Search the scriptures; for in them ye think ye have eternal life: and they are they, which testify of me.*
>
> *40 And ye will not come to me, that ye might have life.*
>
> *41 I receive not honour from men.*
>
> *42 But I know you, that ye have not the love of God in you.*
>
> *43 I am come in my Father's name, and ye receive me not: if another shall come in his own name, him ye will*

receive.

44 How can ye believe, which receive honour one of another, and seek not the honour that cometh from God only?

45 Do not think that I will accuse you to the Father: there is one that accuseth you, even Moses, in whom ye trust.

46 For had ye believed Moses, ye would have believed me: for he wrote of me.

47 But if ye believe not his writings, how shall ye believe my words?

You see how He issued His call to His own people, the Jews? And now He issues it to us. In His teaching, Jesus included several **CALLS** He wanted us to heed.

The first: **The Call Of Eternal Life.**

He said, "Search the scriptures." Eternal life is found in the Bible. How precious! How wonderful that God has offered to us the opportunity of finding eternal life in that He has given us the Bible. We can open God's Word and find life. Jesus said so. "Search the scriptures; for they are they which testify of me." And He said, "In them you think you have eternal life."

Not only do they think so, but the Scriptures actually generate life. The goal of eternal life is found in the Scriptures.

Here is another great truth. Jesus said that eternal life is bound to the will. He said, "You will not come to me that you might have life." My friend, I want you to hear the word of Jesus. You wonder, "How can I get eternal life?" Here it is. Break down your will and come to Jesus. You are responsible. He said, "You will not come to me that you might have life." Your will stands in your way. Decide now to exercise your will in His direction and come to Jesus. Then you will have life.

In issuing His call, He wanted us to reach the call of eternal life. His call includes for you the great call of eternal life. Search for it.

The second: **The Call Of Divine Love.**

Divine love is necessary for real living, and it is only possible with the proper attitude toward God the Son. He said, "I know you do not have the love of God in you." He was talking to His opponents gathered around Him. He said, "I am come in my Father's name, and you do not receive me.

Do you see what I mean? Divine love is only possible through a proper attitude toward God the Son. Divine love can come into your heart when you receive Jesus. He came in His Father's Name. And He said to those about Him, "You do not receive me: if another shall come in his own name, him you will receive."

I warn you; deception is very possible. Jesus warned us about that. He goes on to say, "How can you believe, who receive honour one of another and seek not the honour that comes from God only?" They were deeply concerned about those people around them. They were not so much concerned about the One above them.

If we could get things straightened out and recognize that our most important relationship is to God through God's Son, we could then experience divine love. The love of God can be shed abroad in our hearts. This is the goal.

When He issued the call, He included the goal of divine love. Let the love of God fill your heart. How do you do that? Open your heart to Him. Acknowledge and recognize the Son who came in the Father's Name. That is how you get the love of God. That is how you attain the goal of divine love. You confess that the Son came in the Father's Name and that He is the Son of God.

There is a final goal: **The Call Of United Learning.**

Here is something of utmost importance, my friend. It is this: Moses and Jesus agree. Jesus said, "I am not going to accuse you. Already there is one who accuses you, and he is Moses in whom you trust."

Jesus took no position against Moses. Moses was God's man to receive the law on Mt. Sinai. Jesus said that Moses wrote about Him. There is no opposition between Moses and Jesus. There is no disagreement between them.

Now, what did Moses write about Jesus? You'll find that in

Deuteronomy 18:15-19.

"The LORD your God will raise up unto you a Prophet from the midst of you, of your brothers, one like me. Unto him you shall listen...I will raise them up a Prophet from among their brothers, like you, and will put my words in his mouth. And he shall speak unto them all that I shall command him. And whoever will not listen to my words which he shall speak in my name, I will require it of him."

Jesus said, "Moses wrote about me." Moses can teach us truth about Jesus. Now listen, Jesus also said, "If you believe not his writings, how shall you believe my words?"

My friend, Jesus insisted there is united learning. What you learn from Moses, you learn from Jesus. What you learn from Jesus, you learn from Moses. Jesus' call for you includes the goal of united learning, understanding how Moses and Jesus agree.

God the Son calls you and me. Have you heard His call? He calls you to eternal life. He calls you to divine love. He calls you to united learning. These goals can be yours when you respond to Him.

Studies from John 6

Chapter Twenty-Four

Five Loaves For 5,000 People

We all have faced great difficulties in life. Since you have come for some time along your life span you know what I mean. We have had great difficulties. Perhaps right now, you are having such a difficulty. You hardly know how to examine it, how to solve it. You look at it. As you look, it gets bigger, doesn't it? How do you plan to deal with that difficulty you are in now?

Let me offer a suggestion: to deal with difficulties, you must examine each one to find where its solution is and how you can work with it. When stone masons want to break a stone they examine that stone and decide where to strike it with the hammer so that it will break at the right place. They must know how to strike that stone so that it will break with the proper angles at the best places.

A difficulty is like that. Your difficulty has a solution if you look at it carefully. Examine it from all sides, and you will find your difficulty can be solved. Right here in John 6:1-14 there is a difficulty that had its solution as Jesus examined it and dealt with it.

> 1 After these things Jesus went over the sea of Galilee, which is the sea of Tiberias.
>
> 2 And a great multitude followed him, because they saw his miracles which he did on them that were diseased.
>
> 3 And Jesus went up into a mountain, and there he sat

with his disciples.

4 And the passover, a feast of the Jews, was nigh.

5 When Jesus then lifted up his eyes, and saw a great company come unto him, he saith unto Philip, Whence shall we buy bread, that these may eat?

6 And this he said to prove him: for he himself knew what he would do.

7 Philip answered him, Two hundred pennyworth of bread is not sufficient for them, that everyone of them may take a little.

8 One of his disciples, Andrew, Simon Peter's brother, saith unto him,

9 There is a lad here, which hath five barley loaves, and two small fishes: but what are they among so many?

10 And Jesus said, Make the men sit down. Now there was much grass in the place. So the men sat down, in number about five thousand.

11 And Jesus took the loaves; and when he had given thanks, he distributed to the disciples, and the disciples to them that were set down; and likewise of the fishes as much as they would.

12 When they were filled, he said unto his disciples, Gather up the fragments that remain, that nothing be lost.

13 Therefore they gathered them together, and filled twelve baskets with the fragments of the five barley loaves, which remained over and above unto them that had eaten.

14 Then those men, when they had seen the miracle that Jesus did, said, This is of a truth that prophet that should come into the world.

In this exciting text, the Bible records a difficulty and how Jesus solved it. Let us examine the **DETAILS** of this account of **FIVE LOAVES FOR FIVE THOUSAND PEOPLE.**

Here is one Detail we should examine: **The Multitude.**

We are told that a great multitude followed Him. Jesus and the disciples were gone over the Sea of Galilee or the Sea of Tiberias. This little sea is located in the northern part of the Holy Land. It is a nice little freshwater lake being fed by springs at the base of Mt. Hermon, which form the headwaters of the Jordan River. It is a very lovely little lake, and many villages were settled on its shores in Roman times. So it was that a great multitude followed Jesus.

They were following Him because they had seen the miracles which He had performed for those who were sick. So everyone wanted to be near Him. Well, we can understand that. Who would not want to be near someone who would be able to heal the hurts we all have or will have?

But Jesus and His disciples went up into a mountain, and there He sat to rest with them. There was also a very important religious holiday near, a feast of the Jews called the Passover. It comes in March or April of each year. Well, you see the multitude gathered there around Jesus. They were really very much interested in Jesus, so much so that they had not provided food. So you have the multitude as one detail in this experience.

A second Detail: **The Mystery.**

You read that Jesus asked Philip, one of His disciples, where to go to get bread for all this multitude. He said, "Where shall we buy bread that these may eat?" Certainly, they were not close to any baker. It would be impossible for them to make little fires and bake their own cakes over those fires. There was no way as far as Philip could see. He answered Jesus, "Well, even if we bought two hundred pennies worth of bread, it would not be enough." Now a penny in the days of Jesus was a day's wages. Think of the earnings of a full day's work and then multiply that by two hundred, and you can understand what Philip was saying. Of course, he was right. Certainly, it would take more than two hundred days of work to feed five thousand people.

Then Andrew, Simon Peter's brother, came to say, "There is a lad here who has five loaves and two small fishes: but what are they among so many?" We can understand that if two hundred days of work would not pay for the bread that these people would eat, certainly five loaves would come nowhere near feeding the five thousand people.

You read, though, that Jesus knew what He was going to do. He asked Philip that question in order to test him. So when Andrew brought this boy to Jesus with five barley loaves and two small fish, Jesus knew exactly what He was going to do. To Philip and Andrew, there was no solution, but to Jesus, there was. Do you see what I'm saying? Your difficulty has a solution.

In these two details: the multitude and the mystery, Jesus knew what He would do, even though Philip and Andrew did not know how to handle this particular difficulty.

There was the third Detail: **The Miracle.**

In the first step in this detail, Jesus said to these disciples, "Make the men sit down." You see, there needed to be some preparation. Get ready, we're going to solve this difficulty. So the men sat down. In the second part of the miracle, Jesus took the loaves and gave thanks to God for five loaves and two fish to feed five thousand people. He took what He had and gave thanks to God for it. Then He began to distribute it to the disciples, and the disciples began to give it to those who were seated.

The Bible says that they did the same with those two small fish. They gave the people as much as they would eat. In other words, everybody ate until he was satisfied. From five loaves of bread, five thousand people ate as much as they would! That is not the end because Jesus then said to the disciples, "Gather up the fragments (crumbs) that remain that nothing be lost." From five loaves of bread, they had twelve baskets of crumbs? I call that a miracle, don't you? "Little is much when God is in it."

Ah, yes, you see how this difficulty was solved. These details speak to us of conditions today. There are multitudes everywhere. How can their needs be met? There is a mystery, too. We do not always know and sometimes we don't know at all how we are going to meet the difficulty. Then comes the barley bread. Jesus performs miracles. In this story, He took five loaves of bread and two fish and fed five

"Little Is Much When God Is In It" Kittie L. Suffield (1924) Public Domain

thousand people. That tells me that Jesus cares about our difficulties.

While this exact situation may not be repeated, to have a multitude fed with five loaves of bread, the Lord does care for us. That much we can learn from this experience. He knows what He wants to do for you and to you, but you must trust Him!

Chapter Twenty-Five

How To Conquer Fear

Medical doctors tell us we were born with fear. It is a basic human emotion. We all come into the world with it. We need not develop fear; we already possess it at the moment of birth. Our emotion of fear takes various shapes as we are conditioned by where we live, by the fears of our parents, or others around us.

My mother was afraid of thunderstorms because as a girl she was in a house that had been struck by lightning. She implanted fear in all of us. I remember well as a boy how distressed she was whenever a thunderstorm came up.

Is there help for inborn fears or fears that we develop? If we take the right course, there is a way to conquer fear. We will find this help in our Scripture text: John 6:15-21.

> *15 When Jesus therefore perceived that they would come and take him by force, to make him a king, he departed again into a mountain himself alone.*
>
> *16 And when even was now come, his disciples went down unto the sea,*
>
> *17 And entered into a ship, and went over the sea toward Capernaum. And it was now dark, and Jesus was not come to them.*
>
> *18 And the sea arose by reason of a great wind that blew.*

19 So when they had rowed about five and twenty or thirty furlongs, they see Jesus walking on the sea, and drawing nigh unto the ship: and they were afraid.

20 But he saith unto them, It is I; be not afraid.

21 Then they willingly received him into the ship: and immediately the ship was at the land whither they went.

As we observe the disciples' experience, we can draw three CONCLUSIONS on **HOW TO CONQUER FEAR**.

The first Conclusion: **The Need For Meditation.**

Jesus was able to test the mood of the crowd around Him. He understood what their intentions were. The Bible tells us here that when He "perceived (that means knew or understood) that they would come and take him by force... He departed again into a mountain himself alone." He needed some time for meditation. This was not the time for His coronation, not the time to crown Him king. He understood that. The crowds did not understand. In order to avoid the crowd's actions, He withdrew for meditation. He went into a mountain by Himself for a time of reflection. I'm sure Jesus knew then, as He knows now, that someday He will be king, King of Kings and Lord of Lords. In fact, He is that now, but He has not yet exercised Himself fully in that way.

He understood that there is a necessity of withdrawing for meditation and fellowship with God. So one conclusion we draw from this experience is the need for meditation in our confrontation with fear.

The second Conclusion: **The Fact Of Frustration.**

I want you to see His disciples. The Sea of Galilee is a freshwater lake in the northern part of the Holy Land. It has been very famous through the years. It supplies the people of the countryside with some fine fish. During Jesus' ministry, He and His disciples crisscrossed the lake many times and in many ways.

In this experience, the disciples went down to the sea as the evening drew on and took a boat for Capernaum. They may have taken one of the disciple's boats. Andrew, Peter, James, and John were fishermen along the shores of the Sea of Galilee before Jesus called them. They understood the ways of the sea, but on this particular day, as it became dark, a storm arose. Most likely, this wasn't the first storm the disciples had experienced on the Sea of Galilee, but now it was dark and stormy.

They were trying to go to the village of Capernaum but made very little progress. They had rowed twenty-five or thirty furlongs, which in modern measurement would be about 1,700 meters or a kilometer and a half. They were trying to get to their destination but with very little progress.

Now get this picture together: it is dark; there is a storm at sea; they are making very little progress; and they see Jesus walking on the water and drawing near unto the boat.

Don't you understand what kind of frustration that must have been? What kind of fear that struck in their hearts? In a storm at sea, one has very little that he can do except try to stay afloat. Well, they wanted to go to Capernaum, but they weren't making much progress, and here came Jesus walking on the sea. So, to conquer fear, Jesus understood the necessity to withdraw for meditation, and the disciples faced the fact of frustration.

The third Conclusion we draw on how to conquer fear: **The Call For Identification.**

Not knowing who He was created fear in their hearts. The Bible records these words: "And they were afraid." They feared because they did not know Him. His voice calmed their fears, for He called out to them above the noise of the storm, "It is I; be not afraid." The voice of Jesus calmed the fears of the disciples.

It was still dark and stormy, but Jesus was there, and His voice made all the difference in the world. When they knew Him, they willingly received Him into their boat. Immediately they were at the land to which they went.

The presence of Jesus calmed their fears. Fear can be conquered for you even though you are alone, struggling against great difficulty. You may think you are alone, but be assured Jesus is near, ready to relieve your fear as He did for the disciples. The secret is this: Hear His voice and take Him into your boat.

What a beautiful lesson we can learn from the experience of the disciples. Jesus had withdrawn for meditation but He had not forgotten His disciples. When they were so seriously frustrated because of their difficulty, Jesus made Himself known to them, relieved all their fears, and they came quickly to the point of their destination. I want to point out to you, fear can be conquered if you respond to Jesus in the same way. His presence relieves fear.

Chapter Twenty-Six

The First Thing In Life

Everyone wants to do what is first in life. We struggle hard sometimes to find out what that is. It is not always easy to decide which should be first. The evidence of adulthood is to have the ability to do what is important. Children do the thing for the moment.

I think back on my own boyhood. My father died when I was thirteen years old. After his death, I had to make decisions beyond my ability. I tried but could not do it because I lacked experience. God was very gracious to me, but I often felt that I lacked something that my friends had. I lacked a great deal: my father's guidance through my young manhood days. I know what it is to try to sort out the first things in life and do them.

I want to talk to you about **THE FIRST THING IN LIFE.** We ought not waste our time with less than the important things in life. We ought to learn how to make decisions so that the most important things can be done in their proper order. As we learn from John 6:22-29, we will find the first thing in life.

> *22 The day following, when the people which stood on the other side of the sea saw that there was none other boat there, save that one whereinto his disciples were entered, and that Jesus went not with his disciples into the boat, but that his disciples were gone away alone;*

23 (Howbeit there came other boats from Tiberias nigh unto the place where they did eat bread, after that the Lord had given thanks:)

24 When the people therefore saw that Jesus was not there, neither his disciples, they also took shipping, and came to Capernaum, seeking for Jesus.

25 And when they had found him on the other side of the sea, they said unto him, Rabbi, when camest thou hither?

26 Jesus answered them and said, Verily, verily, I say unto you, Ye seek me, not because ye saw the miracles, but because ye did eat of the loaves, and were filled.

27 Labour not for the meat which perisheth, but for that meat which endureth unto everlasting life, which the Son of man shall give unto you: for him hath God the Father sealed.

28 Then said they unto him, What shall we do, that we might work the works of God?

29 Jesus answered and said unto them, This is the work of God, that ye believe on him whom he hath sent.

I submit to you, in this text, the Master defines the first thing in life. To attain the first thing in life, we must comply with these **DEMANDS** which Jesus taught in this text.

The first Demand: **We Must Seek Jesus.**

The people saw when they got to the seaside that the boat was gone, that Jesus and His disciples had gone away. When they understood that He was not there and His disciples were not there, they got into their boats and started out for Capernaum to find Jesus. They were seeking Jesus. The distance was not too great; the risk was not too great.

I want you to notice there was a restlessness among the people when Jesus was not there; a restlessness that took them down to the sea and into boats and across the sea to Capernaum to seek Jesus. Yes, to attain the first thing in life, we must comply with this demand: we must seek Jesus. Let nothing turn you aside from your search to find Jesus.

The Apostle Paul said, "He is not far from every one of us." But we must comply with this demand; we must seek Jesus like these people did when they saw He was not there.

There is a second Demand we must meet: **We Must Hear Jesus.**

Notice the conversation that went on between them and Jesus. When they found Him, they asked Him this question, "Rabbi, when camest thou here?" The question is "when?" But Jesus did not answer their question in the way they expected. I want you to hear what He said to them, "Truly, truly I say unto you, you seek me not because you saw the miracles, but because you ate the loaves and were filled."

Do you see what Jesus did when He answered them? His words touched the very heart from which motives arise. They were not so much interested in what He was doing or what He was teaching. They were interested in getting their stomachs full of loaves and fish. For that reason, Jesus warned them, "Labor not for the food that perishes, but for that food which endures unto everlasting life, which the Son of man shall give you."

You see, Jesus directed them toward the first thing in life. What is the first thing in life? Everlasting life and the food which brings it. Jesus directed their minds and their thoughts toward the spiritual side of life. They were tied up with the physical, but He directed their minds higher. He said, "the Son of man will give you that food, for God the Father has sealed him."

We must comply with this demand if we are to attain to the first thing in life. We must hear Jesus. Do you know what He will do? He will uncover our real motives, just like He did for those who came to Him. He did not answer their "when" question, but He answered their "why" question. Why are you seeking for them? You ought to seek for Him, because He has everlasting life to give.

We must comply with a third Demand: **We Must Believe Jesus.**

Here comes a question again from the people. They say unto him, "What shall we do that we might work the works of God?" What shall we do? That is a good and necessary question. Every one of us ought to ask this question, "What shall I do that I might work the works of God?"

Notice very carefully how Jesus answered their question. They expected Him to give them some kind of work to do, a job perhaps or some task, maybe a hard one. Instead, He said, "This is the work of God that you believe on him whom he (God) has sent." To them, and most likely to you that does not sound like much work. Jesus implies that believing is work. Here is what you can do.

Jesus corrected their view. Instead of doing some hard work, He said, "Believe on him whom he hath sent." Of course, He was referring to Himself. That is the work of God. To attain the first thing in life, we must comply with this demand: we must believe Jesus. Our approach will be opened wide when we believe in Jesus. Jesus answered their question very well. That answer will apply to you and me. The first thing in life is to believe on the One whom God has sent. Who is He? Jesus of Nazareth.

Now, how do we attain to the first thing in life? We comply with these demands: we must seek Jesus; we must hear Jesus; we must believe Jesus. My friend, this is a very effective order. When you come that way, you will also attain to the first thing in life. "This is the work of God that you believe on him whom he hath sent." Do you believe?

Chapter Twenty-Seven

The True Bread

Bread has been called the staff of life. It is usually made from grain: wheat, barley, rye, or rice. Grain was the first food given to man. When God made man He said, "You may eat of the herb of the field." Grain is usually field-grown.

However, during the trip from Egypt to Canaan, when God was first bringing the Children of Israel into His land, God provided a different kind of bread for them. It was called manna. He gave it to them daily. The Bible tells us it was white like coriander seed when it lay on the ground. It was sometimes called "bread from heaven."

Then when Jesus taught the disciples to pray, He included this idea in that model prayer: "Give us this day our daily bread." Of course, such bread satisfies only for the day. Whether it be the bread we now make or whether it is the bread we pray for in the model prayer, or even the bread from heaven that God gave to the Children of Israel, it only lasted a day.

Is there better bread? Oh, yes, there is **THE TRUE BREAD**. You may read about it in John 6:30-40.

> *30 They said therefore unto him, What sign shewest thou then, that we may see, and believe thee? What dost thou work?*
>
> *31 Our fathers did eat manna in the desert; as it is writ-*

ten, He gave them bread from heaven to eat.

32 Then Jesus said unto them, Verily, verily, I say unto you, Moses gave you not that bread from heaven; but my Father giveth you the true bread from heaven.

33 For the bread of God is he which cometh down from heaven, and giveth life unto the world.

34 Then said they unto him, Lord, evermore give us this bread.

35 And Jesus said unto them, I am the bread of life: he that cometh to me shall never hunger; and he that believeth on me shall never thirst.

36 But I said unto you, That ye also have seen me, and believe not.

37 All that the Father giveth me shall come to me; and him that cometh to me I will in no wise cast out.

38 For I came down from heaven, not to do mine own will, but the will of him that sent me.

39 And this is the Father's will which hath sent me, that of all which he hath given me I should lose nothing, but should raise it up again at the last day.

40 And this is the will of him that sent me, that every one which seeth the Son, and believeth on him, may have everlasting life: and I will raise him up at the last day.

In this Bible text, I find several **IDEAS** which will help us understand the true bread.

The first Idea: **A Compelling Demonstration.**

The people desired a sign. They said they wanted Jesus to demonstrate a sign, make it visible, make it tangible like Moses when he gave their fathers the bread in the desert. They were saying, We want to see a sign from you; make it a compelling demonstration so we know what kind of work you are doing. Then they drew that illustration from Moses. They said, Moses gave our fathers bread in the wilderness. They had manna, that bread from heaven. We want a compelling demonstration from you.

Well, many today insist on demonstration beyond necessary proof. They sought a compelling demonstration like the manna Moses gave to their fathers in the wilderness. Well, God did it once. Will He do it again?

There is a second Idea here: **An Impelling Supplication.**

Jesus made a correction to their idea immediately, because He informed them that Moses did not give them the bread from heaven. The manna which God gave them in the desert was hardly the bread from heaven. It only did for them what ordinary bread would do: sustain life for a time. Jesus said that God gives you the true bread from heaven and that true bread is He who came down from heaven. When you come to Jesus you will find Him to be the bread from heaven which gives eternal life.

Then there was their supplication. They said, "Lord, evermore give us this bread." Let it never cease; let it always be our portion, the bread from heaven. That's what we want: a continual supply; never let it stop. You see, they were still thinking in terms of that manna in the wilderness. They did not understand that their imploring supplication was much broader than they imagined. They just wanted it on a day-by-day basis, just like their fathers had when they were traveling in the wilderness.

It was an imploring supplication because they cried out like this: "Lord, evermore give us this bread."

There is the third Idea: **A Pressing Invitation.**

I want you to notice very carefully how Jesus answered them. He said, "I am the bread of life: he that cometh to me shall never hunger; and he that believeth on me shall never thirst." That definitely is a pressing invitation. He who comes and he who believes will never hunger and will never thirst. Do you see that this calls for a voluntary response to the invitation of Jesus? That means a willing response from him who comes and him who believes. I want you to notice further that Jesus said, "All that the Father giveth me shall come to me; and him that cometh to me I will in no wise cast out."

My friend, that is absolutely sure. You need not ask any question whatever about that. Jesus said, "I will in no way cast out him who comes to me." That is absolutely certain. Then He further said, "I will raise him up at the last day." That, too, is just as sure as God is sure because Jesus said so. See, this pressing invitation is voluntary on your part; it is absolute on His part because God will follow through with what He said. Jesus made this absolutely clear.

There is no alternative here, my friend, because Jesus confined His comments and His invitation to what He said. "All that come to me I will in no way cast out." But He also said you can come and never hunger; you can believe and never thirst. Think about these ideas: a compelling demonstration: bread from heaven; an impelling supplication: Lord, evermore give us this bread; a pressing invitation: come and never hunger, believe and never thirst.

Chapter Twenty-Eight

Believing For Life

As people, we are able to sort out what we accept. We can choose; we were made like that. That is both a personal right and a personal responsibility. It is our right to think for ourselves. It is our responsibility because we must live with the results of our choices.

Both the mind and will are involved in the choices we make. These must be properly balanced. When it comes to believing, the will is important, especially when Jesus is the subject. He once said to the people around Him, "You will not come to me that you might believe." That is why the will is very important, especially when Jesus is the subject of belief.

Think with me on this topic: **BELIEVING FOR LIFE**. I invite you to read from John 6:41-51 as follows.

> *41 The Jews then murmured at him, because he said, I am the bread which came down from heaven.*
>
> *42 And they said, Is not this Jesus, the son of Joseph, whose father and mother we know? How is it then that he saith, I came down from heaven?*
>
> *43 Jesus therefore answered and said unto them, Murmur not among yourselves.*
>
> *44 No man can come to me, except the Father which hath sent me draw him: and I will raise him up at the last*

day.

45 It is written in the prophets, And they shall be all taught of God. Every man therefore that hath heard, and hath learned of the Father, cometh unto me.

46 Not that any man hath seen the Father, save he which is of God, he hath seen the Father.

47 Verily, verily, I say unto you, He that believeth on me hath everlasting life.

48 I am that bread of life.

49 Your fathers did eat manna in the wilderness, and are dead.

50 This is the bread which cometh down from heaven, that a man may eat thereof, and not die.

51 I am the living bread which came down from heaven: if any man eat of this bread, he shall live for ever: and the bread that I will give is my flesh, which I will give for the life of the world.

These verses provide us with several direct **INSIGHTS** into what it means to believe for life.

The first Insight: **The Critical Examination.**

I want you to weigh this with care like they did. They weighed the whole situation very carefully. They made a critical examination of who Jesus was. They knew Him, you see. They knew He grew up in the city of Nazareth. They understood who His parents were, at least they thought they did. They were acquainted with His community. They said, "Is not this Jesus, the son of Joseph, whose father and mother we know?" They had the right to ask some very hard questions. They were making a critical examination of what it means to believe in this One who said, "I am the bread which came down from heaven."

Now I invite you to make a critical examination of who Jesus is. Don't take other people's words for it. Listen to what He is saying here in this text. See how those around Him were also asking some very hard questions. He was among them as one of them, which, indeed, He was. He was born of the virgin Mary, and Joseph was His father in a real sense, because Mary was Joseph's wife. He took her to him as his wife after she was with child.

So you see, they had the right to make a critical examination, and you do too. I invite you to make a critical examination of who Jesus is, but as I say, take His word for it, not those of someone else.

There is another Insight: **The Careful Exception.**

Jesus said this, "No man can come to me unless the Father who has sent me draw Him." That's a very careful exception: no other way. There is here a very definite unity between the Father and the Son. Jesus said His Father must draw whoever comes to Him. There is that activity of the Father in coming to Jesus. That unity is inseparable, and, I should say, you cannot refute it from the words of Jesus. It is absolutely clear that there is this careful exception: you cannot come to God any way you want to. You'll come as the Father has outlined it.

Jesus said, "He who has known me has known the Father. Every man, therefore, who has heard and has learned of the Father comes to me." Now that's something, isn't it? Some people claim to know God the Father, but they do not recognize Jesus the Son. Here Jesus makes that absolutely plain: to know God is to know Jesus.

I prefer to say that no one else has seen God at all except the One who has come from God. I must insist, my friend, that your own way cannot work. Jesus made a very careful exception. He set the bounds.

The third Insight: **The Certain Expectation.**

He said, "Whoever believes on me has everlasting life." That is a present reality. Do you know that when you believe on Jesus Christ, your everlasting life begins right at that moment? That's right. Jesus said he has it, "Whoever believes on me has everlasting life." But even more, there is a future to it because Jesus went on to say, "A man will not die if he eats the bread that comes down from heaven."

Jesus explained, "I am the living bread which came down from heaven: if any man eat of this bread, he shall live forever." Just praise the Lord! Everlasting life is a present reality and everlasting life is a future certainty! Then His sacrifice was totally necessary for you and me to have life. He said, "The bread that I will give is my flesh, which I will give for the life of the world." That is a kind of exchange. Do you understand? He gave His life so that we might have life and that is a certain expectation.

I offer you this same expectation in a present reality and a future certainty. You can be just as sure of it as Jesus' own word. No test is more demanding. If you want life, you must believe in Jesus Christ. It is not wrong for you to make a critical examination of His claims. But here is what He said, "No man can come to me, except the Father…raise him up." We know that belief in Him puts quality in your expectation.

Chapter Twenty-Nine

More Than Existence

Our earth is teeming with life: plant life and animal life. Scientists have made hundreds of classifications. There are land animals and sea animals, all shapes and sizes. Some are too small to see. They all are affected by the life-death cycle. Some live for many years and some only a few minutes.

We are a part of the earth's life. But we have another quality which puts us in a different level of existence. We have more than mere existence. Jesus spoke of that extra quality of which we are capable. Let's see what Jesus has to say about **MORE THAN EXISTENCE** from John 6:51-59.

> *51 I am the living bread which came down from heaven: if any man eat of this bread, he shall live for ever: and the bread that I will give is my flesh, which I will give for the life of the world.*
>
> *52 The Jews therefore strove among themselves, saying, How can this man give us his flesh to eat?*
>
> *53 Then Jesus said unto them, Verily, verily, I say unto you, Except ye eat the flesh of the Son of man, and drink his blood, ye have no life in you.*
>
> *54 Whoso eateth my flesh, and drinketh my blood, hath eternal life; and I will raise him up at the last day.*

55 For my flesh is meat indeed, and my blood is drink indeed.

56 He that eateth my flesh, and drinketh my blood dwelleth in me, and I in him.

57 As the living Father hath sent me, and I live by the Father: so he that eateth me, even he shall live by me.

58 This is that bread which came down from heaven: not as your fathers did eat manna, and are dead: he that eateth of this bread shall live forever.

59 These things said he in the synagogue, as he taught in Capernaum.

From these words of Jesus I draw several **STATEMENTS** to show you the possibility of our having **MORE THAN EXISTENCE**.

There is the first Statement: **An Unavoidable Decision.**

This must be individual: "If any one eats of this bread he shall live for ever." This is an unavoidable decision you must make. This decision nobody else can make for you. It is your individual decision, and it is conditional: if any man. It is not compulsory. There is no force in here. It is rather all your decision. The fact is, it is an unconditional and unavoidable decision and you must make it.

And then it is directional because Jesus is the focal point. He spoke like this: "I am the living bread...If any man eat of this bread... unless you eat the flesh of the Son of man you have no life." So this is an unavoidable decision, which you must make.

I want you to see that this means there is a possibility of more than existence. Those who heard Him sometimes tried to reason it out without success. But Jesus made it very clear that this is an unavoidable decision and it is individual.

There is also a second Statement: **An Unequaled Provision.**

Jesus said, "Unless you eat, you have no life in you." Recall verse 35. For all this is so beautiful. There Jesus said, "He who comes to me shall never hunger, and he who believes on me shall never thirst."

Without that experience, there can be no life. Jesus made that positive here. There is an unequaled provision: coming and believing.

So He said, "Whoever eats my flesh and drinks my blood has eternal life, and I will raise him up at the last day." Do you understand that Jesus says when you come, you are satisfied? When you believe your thirst is quenched? "Because my flesh is food indeed, and my blood is drink indeed." Keep in mind that verse 35 tells us exactly how that is experienced. It is an unequaled provision.

Experience assures us relationship because as the Father had sent Jesus and He lives by the Father, so those who believe in Him live by Him. That is really beautiful. There is complete union in Jesus. This is an unequaled provision. He gave all that we might receive life by believing. This gives us more than existence. We are not merely an animal though we have mortal life, but ours is much more than that. There is here an unequaled provision.

In the third Statement there is: **An Unquestioned Possession.**

Just as sure as God is sure, Jesus said, "As the living Father hath sent me, and I live by the Father: so he that eateth me, even he shall live by me." Just as sure as God the Father and God the Son were thus related so surely we are related to Him when we come as He has defined for us.

The realization can be yours. I'm glad to testify that I have had that relationship, because I believe in Jesus Christ. I've come to Him, and my thirst has been quenched; my hunger has been satisfied.

Manna was no protection against death. Their fathers ate manna in the wilderness and died. But Jesus said, "He who eats this bread shall live forever." I am pointing out to you that we have more than existence, and this bread provides the basis for that more than existence. Jesus included you when He said, "He shall live by me."

The Lord has made a wonderful provision, and your possession can be exactly what He said it would be if you live by Him. This is no sign of weakness; it results in great strength.

The Bible informs us about that. These statements should show you this truth: we have more than existence. There is an unavoidable decision which you must make. But there is also an unequaled provision which God has made, and there is an unquestioned possession which can be yours. We do have far more than existence.

Chapter Thirty

Beyond The Material

In this life, we are quite limited by location and the hard facts of life. I don't really know where you are, but wherever you are, you are limited by your location. Being physical, we deal with the material of life. We are up against the hard facts of living from day to day. But our minds can take us beyond the material.

The Lord has made it possible for me to travel in some twenty-nine countries of the world. Experiences of travel come before my mind right now. But in my mind, I am able to go **BEYOND THE MATERIAL** world. By our thoughts, we can transport ourselves far beyond our material surroundings.

Jesus taught us some great truth on this fact. I want to share it with you from John 6:60-65.

> 60 Many therefore of his disciples, when they had heard this, said, This is an hard saying; who can hear it?
>
> 61 When Jesus knew in himself that his disciples murmured at it, he said unto them, Doth this offend you?
>
> 62 What and if ye shall see the Son of man ascend up where he was before?
>
> 63 It is the spirit that quickeneth; the flesh profiteth nothing: the words that I speak unto you, they are spirit, and they are life.

64 But there are some of you that believe not. For Jesus knew from the beginning who they were that believed not, and who should betray him.

65 And he said, Therefore said I unto you, that no man can come unto me, except it were given unto him of my Father.

In this discourse, Jesus brings together certain **FACTS** that prove we can live. He had been instructing them of the necessity to eat and drink of Him if they would live. Let us consider those facts together.

The first Fact: **A Sensible Barrier.**

These people who murmured at Him and said, "This is a hard saying," were depending completely and entirely upon their five senses: touch, taste, sight, hearing, and smelling. They do form our material boundaries. We are aware of the things around us by our five senses. This is a sensible barrier. The people said, "We do not understand what He is saying." It was a hard saying; it was a hard statement; and it was hard for them to break out of their five senses. To do so required more than touch, taste, sight, hearing, and smelling.

What does it require? It requires faith; it requires belief which is an experience beyond the five senses, beyond the material. Many a person has come up against this barrier and stopped there. They have said, "I can't understand this," and turned away. You need not turn away because this is a sensible barrier, and it is not an impossible one because, by faith, you can overcome and pass that barrier.

A second Fact: **A Spiritual Body.**

Physical food is for the physical body; we all know that. Physical food for the physical body is necessary; we know that, too. And yet Jesus said, "The flesh profits nothing." In other words, there comes an end to the physical body; death comes. We are certain by the word of Jesus that He will raise that body again in the last day. At the same time, there is an end to physical existence, to our mortality. That is why Jesus said, "The flesh profits nothing."

There is also spiritual food for the spiritual body. Did you notice in the text that Jesus said, "It is the spirit that makes alive … The words that I speak to you are spirit and life." That means there is a spiritual body. Not only are we physical, my friend, but we are also spiritual. That is an important truth for you and me to catch hold of. It is a fact that Jesus sets forth here when He said, "The words that I speak to you are spirit and life." That means that there is another existence; there is something beyond the material.

We have spiritual bodies. Do you know you have a spiritual body? How are you going to feed that spiritual body? You know how to feed the physical body, but how about the spiritual body? It must be fed, too. But you can't feed that with physical food; it must be fed with spiritual food. For the material is not all that basic. We need food for the body to be sure, the physical body, but by the same fact, we need food for the spiritual body. Jesus said the words that He has spoken are that food. That means there is a spiritual body.

A third Fact: **A Supernatural Bridge.**

Now, this is very, very crucial. Right here we must pay very close attention because the crucial point is belief. Jesus said, "I know there are some of you who do not believe." Oh, what a world is shut out of life by unbelief! What a whole new world is opened by belief! Because they did not believe, they shut out for themselves a great world. They did not cross over that supernatural bridge that has been already built. When Jesus further explained that the crucial way is by the Father, there can be no doubt about that, He said, "Therefore I said to you that no one can come to me unless it was given to him by my Father." The very important bridge has been built. That's exactly what a friend said to me one time. He said, "The bridge has been built; it is Jesus Christ."

Don't try to find another bridge or another way, there is no other. A supernatural bridge has been built, and you cross over it by faith. It is beyond the material. You too must accept the supernatural bridge which has been built; then you can go beyond the material.

We are made for this, we fit into it, once we have accepted the facts that Jesus brings together here. The facts prove to us we are made for life beyond the material because our senses cannot overcome the barrier. It is there, believe me. But there is also a spiritual body and a supernatural bridge by which we can go beyond the material.

Chapter Thirty-One

The Final Choice

All of us are forced to choose. Every day there are some very simple choices; for example, how I answer a question. There are also choices of long-standing results, such as a job or a life partner. Perhaps there are many possibilities before us when we make such choices. They are, however, of long results.

Then there is a final choice where there are only two ways, just two possibilities. In John 6:66-71, from the words of Jesus, I want to show you what I mean by **THE FINAL CHOICE.**

> *66 From that time many of his disciples went back, and walked no more with him.*
>
> *67 Then said Jesus unto the twelve, Will ye also go away?*
>
> *68 Then Simon Peter answered him, Lord, to whom shall we go? Thou hast the words of eternal life.*
>
> *69 And we believe and are sure that thou art that Christ, the Son of the living God.*
>
> *70 Jesus answered them, Have not I chosen you twelve, and one of you is a devil?*
>
> *71 He spake of Judas Iscariot the son of Simon: for he it was that should betray him, being one of the twelve.*

In these verses, we can find the **FACTORS** which make the final choice so serious.

The first Factor: **The Particular Question.**

This text opens with the observation that many of those who had followed Jesus as disciples left Him. They went back and walked no more with Him. His requirements were too difficult. They somehow couldn't match their lives with what Jesus required.

But there is no hope of success apart from Him. He is the way, the only way. The only way to have real success in life is to follow Jesus. But many of them quit following Him, so Jesus turned to the twelve and said to them, "Will you also go away?" Will you be followers of the crowd, or will you follow me? Will you stand against the current? The rest are leaving me; are you going to leave me too?

You see, these disciples had only two possibilities: either to follow Jesus and go with Him or to go with the crowd. Can you see how important this question is? Will you also go away? It is a particular question and, I should add, a question you will need to answer. Will you also go away? Will you be a crowd follower, or will you follow Jesus? See, that is the final choice. That is the choice I'm placing before you from the words of Jesus on that particular question.

The second Factor: **A Positive Confession.**

Peter answered Jesus with a positive confession. He said, "To whom shall we go? Thou hast the words of eternal life." No one else is here to whom we can turn. We have made our choice. Peter was speaking for the other disciples, who most certainly agreed with him. Peter said, "Thou hast the words of eternal life, and we believe and are sure that thou art that Christ, the Son of the living God."

Those were not just mere words, my friend. That was a positive confession from Peter, who was speaking for most of the disciples. They were expressing in positive confession that no one else was like Him. "We believe, we are sure that you are that Christ, the Son of the living God."

Can you understand the importance of this confession? It is a most important confession. It is one that you are going to need to make in this final choice of whether you are going to follow Jesus or whether you are going to follow the crowd. The other people left, but Peter put it straight when he made this positive confession.

I want you to think about that confession when he said, "We believe that thou art the Christ." That means Peter regarded Jesus as the Messiah, the Anointed One, the One whom God had promised would come. He further said he believed that Jesus is the Son of the living God. Now I know some people have real problems with Peter's confession but there it is and I want to remind you that this same confession you will need to make. This is a most important confession, one that Peter made for the disciples and the one that you and I will need to make as well. We are sure that Jesus Christ is the Son of the living God.

The third Factor: **The Penetrating Assessment.**

After Peter's confession, Jesus made a prediction. He said, "Have I not chosen you twelve, and one of you is a devil?" I would surely think that Judas in Jesus' presence would have shrunk back. By this statement, Jesus clearly expressed that He knew exactly what was in the heart of man. He had absolute knowledge of people. He disclosed the bare truth, the awful truth that one whom He had chosen was possessed of a demon. He had absolute knowledge, absolute knowledge of life. He knew that Judas was soon going to betray Him. He was about to betray Him being one of the twelve.

That is a most penetrating assessment. It leaves nothing to chance because Jesus knew exactly what was in Judas' heart. He knew exactly what was in the disciples' hearts, too, the rest of them.

Can you understand the importance of His assessment? If by this statement it is clearly revealed that He understood Judas' heart, then we must conclude that Jesus understands your heart and mine as well. He knows you and me just as clearly and as thoroughly as He knew Judas.

The final choice lies with us, as well. I would like to make it even more direct because I have made my choice to follow Jesus. How is it with you? The final choice lies with you. I urge you to follow Jesus. He is the one to whom you can go, and you can learn of Him. Don't turn away. He is that Christ, the Son of the living God. May the Holy Spirit help you to make your final choice right now.

Studies from
John 7

Chapter Thirty-Two

Live In The Open

We like people who have nothing to hide. We don't like those people who are always living in the darkness. We like people whom we can trust. It seems every community and every family responds the same way. When someone unknown comes around, we wait to see what will happen. We are never quite sure until we have tested them out.

Jesus of Nazareth seemed to be a stranger even to his brothers. The reason was His calling was so utterly different from what they could conceive of Him. They could not think of Him being whom He said He was. They thought He should live out in the open. In their response in John 7:1-13, you will understand what I'm saying.

> *1 After these things Jesus walked in Galilee: for he would not walk in Jewry, because the Jews sought to kill him.*
>
> *2 Now the Jews' feast of tabernacles was at hand.*
>
> *3 His brethren therefore said unto him, Depart hence, and go into Judea, that thy disciples also may see the works that thou doest.*
>
> *4 For there is no man that doeth any thing in secret, and he himself seeketh to be known openly. If thou do these things, shew thyself to the world.*
>
> *5 For neither did his brethren believe in him.*

6 Then Jesus said unto them, My time is not yet come: But your time is alway ready.

7 The world cannot hate you; but me it hateth, because I testify of it, that the works thereof are evil.

8 Go ye up unto this feast: I go not up yet unto this feast; for my time is not yet full come.

9 When he had said these words unto them, he abode still in Galilee.

10 But when his brethren were gone up, then went he also up unto the feast, not openly, but as it were in secret.

11 Then the Jews sought him at the feast, and said, Where is he?

12 And there was much murmuring among the people concerning him: for some said, He is a good man: others said, Nay, but he deceiveth the people.

13 Howbeit no man spake openly of him for fear of the Jews.

In these conversations, I will lift out several **RESPONSES** to the challenge Jesus faced to **LIVE IN THE OPEN** which ought to lead us, I trust, to faith.

The first Response: **The Brothers Of Jesus Urged Him.**

His brothers said, "Show yourself to the world." Now let us get the setting of this conversation. The Jewish feast of tabernacles was at hand, and that particular feast would bring a great many people to Jerusalem. It was one of the feasts from the time of Moses which every man was to attend. They were to go to Jerusalem for the feast. This would be a wonderful opportunity to meet the crowds, and His brothers urged Him to go.

I think how readily men today would jump at such an opportunity. Such an occasion would be a wonderful opportunity to be in the limelight, to be in the forefront, to be where people could see you. But not Jesus. These brothers' unbelief left them without hope. Jesus said, "You go up to the feast, but I will not go up just now." But the Bible tells us that His brothers did not believe on Him.

Some people, it seems, ask for more and more evidence. No matter how much evidence they already have seen, they still keep asking for more and more. They said to Him, "Show yourself to the world so that your disciples might also believe on you." They said that not because they believed but because they wanted to make it difficult for Jesus.

The second Response: **Jesus Answered His Brothers.**

"You go up to the feast. My time is not yet," He said. I see in that statement a very clear indication that Jesus had His life very carefully ordered. He lived on a schedule. He sensed timing with care. He told them their time is always, but His time had not yet fully come.

I am not sure what all Jesus implied by that statement but I am quite sure that He understood that His life was lived according to the divine plan of God. He sensed this. He realized that His life was planned beforehand. He said, "Your time is always near." In many respects that meant they had nothing to lose and nothing to gain. It wasn't as important for them as it was for Him so they could go, and He urged His brothers to go to the feast. They went.

I think some people do not know the value of timing. The importance of the moment gets away from them. It was not so with Jesus. As He lived in the open, everything was very important with Him. So He told His brothers to go up to the feast, and they went up. Later, Jesus also went up. I have read that there was a great discussion among the people who had gathered at the feast when they could not find Him.

The third Response: **The People Argued About Him.**

Some said, "No, but he deceives the people." There were those who saw in Him a good man and they said, "Where is he. He's a good man." Others said, "No, he deceives the people." They saw Him as a deceiver, for they failed to understand Him. The final conclusion was that no one spoke of Him openly for fear of the Jews.

I have learned as I get around that people still wonder and argue about Jesus. During His lifetime they puzzled about Him, and they still do. Even some of the most brilliant minds in the world stumble and wonder about Him. Let me tell you, He is the Christ. He is not only a good man, He is the Messiah. Jesus had nothing to hide. He arranged the timing so that He would be there at exactly the right moment. He understood human nature; He understands you. As you think of Jesus, how do you respond to Him? What do you think of Him?

Chapter Thirty-Three

Obedience Opens Understanding

Obedience opens understanding. Many people have hesitated to believe because they were not able to understand. They have the mistaken notion that they must understand everything before they believe, when really it is the other way around. We believe, and then we understand. All of us have asked questions from our childhood. To us they were important questions. We probably have some questions that are still unanswered.

One secret to understanding spiritual truth is obedience. This is an important principle. Obedience is closely related to belief. Some people think they must understand everything before they can believe. Others think they must understand everything before they will obey. But I want to point out to you that **OBEDIENCE OPENS UNDERSTANDING.**

This truth is illustrated in John 7:14-24.

> *14 Now about the midst of the feast Jesus went up into the temple, and taught.*
>
> *15 And the Jews marvelled, saying, How knoweth this man letters, having never learned?*
>
> *16 Jesus answered them, and said, My doctrine is not mine, but his that sent me.*
>
> *17 If any man will do his will, he shall know of the doc-*

trine, whether it be of God, or whether I speak of myself.

18 He that speaketh of himself seeketh his own glory: but he that seeketh his glory that sent him, the same is true, and no unrighteousness is in him.

19 Did not Moses give you the law, and yet none of you keepeth the law? Why go ye about to kill me?

20 The people answered and said, Thou hast a devil: who goeth about to kill thee?

21 Jesus answered and said unto them, I have done one work, and ye all marvel.

22 Moses therefore gave unto you circumcision; (not because it is of Moses, but of the fathers;) and ye on the sabbath day circumcise a man.

23 If a man on the sabbath day receive circumcision, that the law of Moses should not be broken, are ye angry at me, because I have made a man every whit whole on the sabbath day?

24 Judge not according to the appearance, but judge righteous judgment.

In these verses, we can develop several **PROPOSITIONS** from which we must conclude that obedience opens understanding.

The first Proposition: **You Must Earn The Right To Speak.**

For the people, it meant you go to school; it meant you get an education. They looked at Jesus while He was teaching and said, "How can this man teach never having gone to school?" He doesn't know very much; he's never been to our schools. Well, I know what it means to work hard for an education, to spend long hours at a study table. I know what they meant, but Jesus went on to say it's not so much where you have spent your time, at this or that educator's table; it is whether or not you know Him. For Jesus, it meant a proper relationship to God because He explained that anyone who does the will of God shall know whether His teaching is of God or not. He said, "I speak what God gives me," and He challenged them to believe and do.

I want you to especially notice how Jesus said, "If any man will do his will, he shall know of the doctrine, whether it be of God, or whether I speak of myself." I point out to you that you must earn your right to speak, and when you obey, great areas of understanding are opened to you. In that way, proof is forthcoming. Before you turn off Jesus' words, make sure that you test them. Don't just walk away from this and say, "No, there is nothing to it." Do what He says and see whether I'm not right that obedience opens understanding.

A second Proposition: **The Law Of Moses Was Given To Keep.**

Jesus said, "Moses gave you the law, and nobody keeps it." We all acknowledge that Moses is the lawgiver. Maybe we should change that just a bit; Moses was the law revealer, for God gave him the law. We can read about this in the Old Testament book of Exodus. Moses went up on the mountain, and God gave him the law. But in that law was this statement: "this do and thou shalt live." Yet Jesus, looking upon the situation of His day, said nobody keeps the law. Well, I could add, were Jesus here today, He would say the same thing: nobody keeps the law. Yet in His day and ours, some of the people who are strongest in their condemnation of others are those who do not practice the law themselves. So it was in His day. He said, "You don't keep the law, but you condemn me."

Now how could that be? The law of Moses was given to be kept. Now before you take sides, my friend, make sure you do not condemn in others what you allow in your own life. I'm speaking to you right there, right now.

The third Proposition: **The Basic Truth Everyone Must Meet.**

Jesus used the illustration of circumcision. That rite was given to Abraham many years before Moses came on the scene. That's why Jesus said it wasn't of Moses; it was of the fathers. God instructed Abraham that the circumcision should be done on the eighth day. It could, at times, fall on the Sabbath day. In the time of Jesus, it was important enough for them to go ahead with the circumcision. So in order to keep this law of the circumcision, they set aside another law, the law of the Sabbath. This law took first place. Then Jesus raised a very important question with them because He had healed a man on the Sabbath day. He said, "Are you going about to kill me because

I made a man every bit whole on the Sabbath day?" He questioned their form of reasoning.

Well, I question their reasoning, don't you? If to circumcise a boy baby on the Sabbath day is right, then surely to heal a man, make him whole, would also be right. Such basic truth we all meet. Before we decide, we must make sure we have all the facts. Truth must be faced with honesty. We can't shirk it.

From Jesus' words, we must conclude simply that obedience brings depth of understanding. These propositions make that very clear: you must earn the right to speak; the law of Moses was given to keep; such basic truth everyone must meet.

Chapter Thirty-Four

Is This The Very Christ?

Various religions and sects take different views regarding Jesus of Nazareth. Some say He was an outstanding miracle worker, and indeed He was. Some say He was a prophet, maybe not quite equal to Moses but a very important prophet. We would say with them, "That's true."

Christians of every nation, however, believe Jesus to be the promised Messiah and the Saviour of all who accept Him, all who believe in Him. We call them believers. I have met them in many different places and from many different lands. For example, I have met believers from India. I have met Japanese believers. I have met a believer from Swaziland, from Ethiopia, from Egypt, from Greece, from Germany, from Lebanon, from Israel, from the United States, and many other countries. Yes, believers in every nation believe Jesus to be the Messiah, the One whom God had promised and the Saviour of all who accept Him, all who believe in Him.

In every generation, the question about Jesus must be answered, for to many people, Jesus is a puzzle. They ask the question, **IS THIS THE VERY CHRIST?** We can find the answer in John 7:25-31.

> *25 Then said some of them of Jerusalem, is not this he, whom they seek to kill?*
>
> *26 But, lo, he speaketh boldly, and they say nothing unto*

him. Do the rulers know indeed that this is the very Christ?

27 Howbeit we know this man whence he is: but when Christ cometh, no man knoweth whence he is.

28 Then cried Jesus in the temple as he taught, saying, Ye both know me, and ye know whence I am: and I am not come of myself, but he that sent me is true, whom ye know not.

29 But I know him: for I am from him, and he hath sent me.

30 Then they sought to take him: but no man laid hands on him, because his hour was not yet come.

31 And many of the people believed on him, and said, When Christ cometh, will he do more miracles than these which this man hath done?

Is this the very Christ? I propose to answer this question. Yes, yes, this is the very Christ. In this text are set forth several definite **EVIDENCES** which support my answer that this is the very Christ.

The first Evidence: **The Mystery Of His Coming.**

In identity He was the one they wanted to kill. There was something mysterious about Him because they said, "We know where he comes from." Yet they were very unsure about Him. They said, "Who is this man? Do the rulers really believe that he is the very Christ?" But they said they knew Him. You could go over there right now to the country where He lived. You could find the town in which He was born. You could find the place where He grew up. You could find the area where He ministered around the Sea of Galilee. They knew Him and yet there was something mysterious about Him because they were so unsure about Him.

The Bible predicted about the Messiah's coming. Genesis 3:15, that early, God said that the seed of the woman was going to crush the seed of the serpent. When Jacob bid his sons goodbye in Genesis 49, he said of Judah that the scepter should not depart from Judah until Shiloh come; unto him should the gathering of the people be. The prophet Isaiah in Isaiah 7:14 predicted the virgin birth. He said, "A virgin shall conceive, and bear a son, and shall call his name Immanuel, God with us."

Now I have only quoted three passages in the Old Testament predictions about the coming of Jesus. There's something of a mystery about His coming but that mystery clears up when you see the predictions in the Bible about Him.

There is a second Evidence: **The Manner Of His Coming.**

When Jesus replied to these people, He said, "You know both me, and you know where I come from and I have not come of myself, but He who sent me is true." He said He had been sent by the True One. Now, who might that be? Moses asked when God called him from the back side of the desert, "Whom shall I say sent me?' And God said to Moses, tell them, "I AM" hath sent you." The prophet Isaiah speaking about God, said there is no one like God. Who would they compare Him to? Jesus said, "He that sent me is true, whom ye know not. But I know him: for I AM from him, and he hath sent me."

It is possible for us to know God, too. Not in the same sense in which Jesus has known Him, but in a very real sense, we can understand God. The manner of Jesus' coming is very clearly set forth here. No one else has been able to make such claims. He was known by His neighbors and His family, to be sure, and yet He was unknown by them. The reason being He had been sent from God. That is the manner of His coming.

There is a third Evidence: **The Miracles Of His Coming.**

They were not able to take Him. They would have, but they were not able because His time had not yet come. They tried it, but it did not work. We can very confidently say Jesus' life was kept until the time came for them to take Him. He Himself was a miracle. We are told in this text that many believed on Him because of the miracles which He performed. His miracles testified to His truthfulness. Thirty-eight are recorded in the Gospels that Jesus performed during His three and a half years of ministry. No wonder they said, "When Christ comes will he do more miracles than these that this man has done?" Of course not, because He was the Christ.

Both His birth and His death were miracles. He was born of

the virgin. No one else had been, or ever has been. He gave His life on the cross for you and me. He dismissed His spirit and sent it back to God. He said on one occasion, "Nobody takes it from me. I lay it down of myself. Then I take it up again." His whole life was a miracle. The miracles of His coming are clear if you will study the record carefully.

The answer to the question then is this: He is the very Christ. Yes, on the ground of these evidences: the mystery of His coming, the manner of His coming, and the miracle of His coming. If you study the record carefully, you will find that the answer must be yes; this is the very Christ. Have you believed on Him?

Chapter Thirty-Five

End The Search

Are you still searching, seeking, looking, and longing for something? Do you know what you need? Deep in the heart of every man, woman, and child is a longing for rest. One great African Christian many years ago said, "Our souls are restless until they find their rest in Thee." But the question is, "Where can I find Him?" That is a most important question.

I want to help you **END THE SEARCH.** I take you to the Bible and the words of Jesus in John 7:32-39.

> *32 The Pharisees heard that the people murmured such things concerning him; and the Pharisees and the chief priests sent officers to take him.*
>
> *33 Then said Jesus unto them, Yet a little while am I with you, and then I go unto him that sent me.*
>
> *34 Ye shall seek me, and shall not find me: and where I am, thither ye cannot come.*
>
> *35 Then said the Jews among themselves, Whither will he go, that we shall not find him? Will he go unto the dispersed among the Gentiles, and teach the Gentiles?*
>
> *36 What manner of saying is this that he said, Ye shall seek me, and shall not find me: and where I am, thither ye cannot come?*

37 In the last day, that great day of the feast, Jesus stood and cried, saying, If any man thirst, let him come unto me, and drink.

38 He that believeth on me, as the scripture hath said, out of his belly shall flow rivers of living water.

39 (But this spake he of the Spirit, which they that believe on him should receive: for the Holy Ghost was not yet given; because that Jesus was not yet glorified.)

These words teach us what **STEPS** are necessary if we ever expect to end our search.

The first Step: **The Search Is Clarified.**

Time, according to Jesus, was very important. He said there is only a little while, "Yet a little while I am with you." He was showing that time is limited. You can't just waste time and expect to end your search. Jesus clarified the search. The time is now, not later.

The object is also important because there's nobody like Jesus. He said, "You are going to seek for me, and you will not be able to find me." My friend, it is very important that you make the right search and that you have the right object in view. Believe me, time is important. The opportune time is now, not tomorrow; this very moment, because Jesus said, "You are going to search for me (He said this to those Pharisees), and you are not going to be able to find me." Men have often tried in vain; they have searched and searched, but they have found no rest because they have not found Him.

My friend, today is your day to seek Jesus. I am glad to tell you that you can find Him. Ah, but you must search for Him while you can. You must be sure that the object of your search is Jesus Christ.

Well, Jesus clarified the search. But when He said what He did to clarify, they thought:

The Search Is Mystified.

They said, "Where is He going to go? How can He say we cannot come to Him?" You see, human reason blocked their understanding. Their minds got in the way. He had come from God, you see, and they failed to understand that.

Some still fail to understand that. They still believe that Jesus did not come from God. But He said, "I'm going back to God." On this occasion, they did not understand where He was going. But He said, "I am going, and you are not going to be able to come where I am."

Let me point out something to you. Human existence is unqualified to go where Jesus is. The flesh has its limitation. Your bodily physical existence now is going to need to undergo some changes if you are going to go where He has gone. That is what these people did not understand.

There is another existence beyond the flesh. It comes after death. So in one sense, we can say that Jesus mystified the search. He made it more difficult because they tried to reason out what He was saying. My friend, don't let your mind block your search. Be sure that you understand that Jesus came from God and went back to God. That will clarify your search, not mystify it.

There is a final step to end your search: **The Search Is Satisfied.**

It was on that last great day of the feast when Jesus stood and gave that great invitation, "If any man thirst, let him come unto me and drink." Well, everybody does thirst. I said in the beginning that in the heart of every man, woman, and child, there is a longing for rest. Jesus knew that. He said it this way, "If anyone thirst," because He wanted that decision to rest with the thirsty one, "let him come and drink." Let him submit himself and understand that he will find the end of his search right here by me.

There was a great invitation. There was also a great satisfaction because Jesus said that inner longing down deep in your heart will be satisfied when you come to Him. He said out of his innermost being shall flow rivers of water. His soul thirst will be satisfied. Praise the Lord!

Take Jesus' words seriously if you want to end your search. You can come to Him, Jesus Christ, and when you do, that deep soul thirst inside of you will be satisfied. The search will end when you find Him. He can and will satisfy your innermost being. So come to Him now. Surrender to His invitation and find rest for your soul.

Chapter Thirty-Six

He Is Different

We are all alike in many ways: we get hungry; we get tired; we get thirsty. We have many needs that are alike: food, clothing, shelter. Of course, these are physical needs. But in the spiritual area, we are also all alike. The Bible tells us in Romans 3:23, "For all have sinned and come short of the glory of God."

My friend, that Scripture makes no exception. We are all alike. In all of human history, only One lived who is different from us and yet like us. He lived here among men. They saw Him as a man, and yet He was different. He is Jesus the Messiah.

What evidence do we have that **HE IS DIFFERENT**? We find the evidence in this Scripture: John 7:40-53.

> *40 Many of the people therefore, when they heard this saying, said, Of a truth this is the Prophet.*
>
> *41 Others said, This is the Christ. But some said, Shall Christ come out of Galilee?*
>
> *42 Hath not the scripture said, That Christ cometh of the seed of David, and out of the town of Bethlehem, where David was?*
>
> *43 So there was a division among the people because of him.*

44 And some of them would have taken him; but no man laid hands on him.

45 Then came the officers to the chief priests and Pharisees; and they said unto them, Why have ye not brought him?

46 The officers answered, Never man spake like this man.

47 Then answered them the Pharisees, Are ye also deceived?

48 Have any of the rulers or of the Pharisees believed on him?

49 But this people who knoweth not the law are cursed.

50 Nicodemus saith unto them, (he that came to Jesus by night, being one of them,)

51 Doth our law judge any man, before it hear him, and know what he doeth?

52 They answered and said unto him, Art thou also of Galilee? Search, and look: for out of Galilee ariseth no prophet.

53 And every man went unto his own house.

From this text, we learn that the presence of Jesus started several **MOVEMENTS** in which we see the evidence that He is different.

The first Movement: **He Made A Division.**

They wondered who He was. Some said, "He is the prophet." By that, they were referring to the quotation from Exodus where Moses said God was going to send them a prophet. In fact, God said it to Moses, that He was going to raise up from among them a prophet like Moses. So they said, "He is the prophet."

Then others said, "He is the Christ." The word Christ means Messiah. They were expecting Him, so some said, "This is the Messiah." But they wondered where He came from. They knew He came from Nazareth in Galilee, and there was no record of any great prophet coming from Galilee. They had it right. They said the prophets said that the Messiah was to come from Bethlehem, David's town, and from David's seed.

Well, He was born in Bethlehem. In the genealogies in the Bible, His family line goes back to David. The Bible says that because of this, there was a division. He made a division. Oh, I find people today who are divided on who Jesus is. Is He the prophet? Is He the Messiah? Who is He? He made a division.

A second Movement: **He Created A Discussion.**

Some said, "Let's arrest him; let's take him." But they were unsure what to do. Now the officers who had been sent to take Him came back without Him. They had not arrested Him. When they were asked why they hadn't brought Him, they answered, "Nobody ever spoke like this man." So they had a discussion. They talked it over. The Pharisees said, "Are you also deceived?" It was only the common people who believed in Him. "The rulers and the Pharisees don't believe in Him, do they?" The common people, though unlearned, were trusting in Jesus. So they had a discussion; some wanted to arrest Him; others wanted to investigate.

I have found people today who can talk about Him without making any careful investigation as to who He really is. A good bit of discussion goes on around Him as to who He is, but I find that some never make up their minds. They are just there talking about Him. He can create a discussion. Yes, the subject of Jesus, who He is, can create a rather warm discussion.

The last Movement: **He Forced A Decision.**

Nicodemus, one of the Pharisees who had come to Jesus by night, made a very interesting statement. He said, "Does our law judge a man before it hears him?" Hold your sentence: a man is innocent until proved guilty; pass no judgment on Him until you have heard his case. But He was forcing a decision. He challenged them to give some consideration to all the facts, to weigh everything before they rendered a decision, to hear Him themselves. Don't just stand there; arrange for the Man to speak for Himself.

Oh, that is so important today, my friend. Many people read what others have said about Him, but they never listen to Him. I have found people who judge without the facts. But any fair-minded person will weigh all the facts; he will examine all the evidence before he makes a decision. But he will have to make a decision; he must make it.

Jesus is different because He will make a division, He will create a discussion, He will force a decision. It is today just like it was then. No one can take His place. You are brought face to face with Him. You must make your decision yourself. Are you ready to do that?

STUDIES FROM JOHN 8

Chapter Thirty-Seven

Be Careful How You Judge

We are all made with the ability to decide. God has placed within us reasoning powers. Those reasoning powers cover the whole of life, every area, and make us continually responsible. Some have developed this ability to a high degree. In the legal profession, they are appointed judges, to interpret the laws of our communities and to hand down decisions. Though not as highly developed, every one of us has this ability because we are human. Because of this, we must be sure we use our powers properly and impartially.

Most of us judge our neighbors much more harshly than we judge ourselves. It may be because we do not have all the evidences. So our judgment of them is unfair and most likely unfair of us when we judge ourselves.

During the life of Jesus, people came to Him with many of their problems. They wanted help. On a number of occasions, certain persons planned to create a situation which left Him no real choice, no way to decide without violating God's holy law. Such an occasion is reported in John 8:1-11.

1 Jesus went unto the mount of Olives.

2 And early in the morning he came again into the temple, and all the people came unto him; and he sat down, and taught them.

3 And the scribes and Pharisees brought unto him a woman taken in adultery; and when they had set her in the midst,

4 They say unto him, Master, this woman was taken in adultery, in the very act.

5 Now Moses in the law commanded us, that such should be stoned: but what sayest thou?

6 This they said, tempting him, that they might have to accuse him. But Jesus stooped down, and with his finger wrote on the ground, as though he heard them not.

7 So when they continued asking him, he lifted up himself, and said unto them, He that is without sin among you, let him first cast a stone at her.

8 And again he stooped down, and wrote on the ground.

9 And they which heard it, being convicted by their own conscience, went out one by one, beginning at the eldest, even unto the last: and Jesus was left alone, and the woman standing in the midst.

10 When Jesus had lifted up himself, and saw none but the woman, he said unto her, Woman, where are those thine accusers? Hath no man condemned thee?

11 She said, No man, Lord. And Jesus said unto her, Neither do I condemn thee: go, and sin no more.

In this experience, we should see the several **CONCLUSIONS** that are necessary to help us **BE CAREFUL HOW WE JUDGE**.

For example, the first Conclusion: **Guilty In Act.**

The evidence was proof. They brought her. They said she was taken in the very act. So they set her in the midst as a victim. They awaited the verdict. They went to the law of Moses, a very good and legitimate law. They said Moses said in the law to stone her, that such a one should be stoned.

What's your verdict? What do you say? Here is one guilty, taken in the very act; how shall we judge her? How do you judge her? They were very quick to condemn. Had they not delayed bringing her to

Jesus to tempt Him to find out what He would say, they would have stoned her on the very spot.

The second Conclusion: **Guilty In Heart.**

They put Jesus on trial. Instead of answering them immediately, He began to write on the ground. We do not know what He wrote, but they kept pressing Him. They kept asking for a verdict. They kept wondering how and what He was going to say. So He raised Himself up and said, "The one who is without sin, let him cast the first stone at her." Then He went on writing.

Did you notice in the text that they were convicted in their hearts and began to leave, from the oldest to the last? Surely they found her guilty in act, but they were guilty in heart. So they left. It is very important, in your process of judgment, that you search out your inner spirit before you begin to condemn. Yes, it is easy to be very harsh until the case is turned to you, yourself.

After they were all gone, except Jesus and the woman, He looked around at her and said, "Where are your accusers?"

This brings me to the third Conclusion: **Guilty But Pardoned.**

There was Jesus and the woman. She was still waiting for the verdict. When He asked her, "Has nobody condemned you?" she said, "No, no one." Jesus spoke to her like this: "Neither do I condemn thee. Go and sin no more." He acknowledged her guilt. But He said, "I'm not going to condemn you." The sinless One who could have by His verdict thrown the first stone said, "No, I don't condemn you." Evidently, this poor woman was repentant, so He said, "Go and sin no more." Imagine how she must have felt, deep in her soul, that she was not condemned to death, for Jesus had pardoned her.

When you judge, take into account these conclusions: the guilty in act, and "who has not sinned;" the guilty in heart, "and who must not confess that;" guilty but pardoned, who does not want to hear Jesus' words, "Neither do I condemn Thee. Go and sin no more."

If God were to deal with us as we deal with one another, there would be no hope at all. But once pardoned, the word of Jesus should restrain us to go and sin no more.

Chapter Thirty-Eight

We Need Help

The greatest curse of our time, my friend, is go it by yourself, do your own thing. It is not new. Men in other days tried that as well. Long before King David's time, the Bible reports every man did that which was right in his own eyes. That is what we see today on every hand. Independence then brought a harvest of anarchy, and society went to pieces. We are living in days uncomfortably like those days long ago. **WE NEED HELP** to find the way in life. Our most important step in life is to admit our need. Why are we so slow to understand what our problem is?

A conversation Jesus had with the people of His day will provide us with some very helpful suggestions. It is recorded in John 8:12-20.

> *12 Then spake Jesus again unto them, saying, I am the light of the world: he that followeth me shall not walk in darkness, but shall have the light of life.*
>
> *13 The Pharisees therefore said unto him, Thou bearest record of thyself; thy record is not true.*
>
> *14 Jesus answered and said unto them, Though I bear record of myself, yet my record is true; for I know whence I came, and whither I go; but ye cannot tell whence I come, and whither I go.*
>
> *15 Ye judge after the flesh; I judge no man.*

16 And yet if I judge, my judgment is true: for I am not alone, but I and the Father that sent me.

17 It is also written in your law, that the testimony of two men is true.

18 I am one that bear witness of myself, and the Father that sent me beareth witness of me.

19 Then said they unto him, Where is thy Father? Jesus answered, Ye neither know me, nor my Father: if ye had known me, ye should have known my Father also.

20 These words spake Jesus in the treasury, as he taught in the temple: and no man laid hands on him; for his hour was not yet come.

From these words of Jesus, I wish to point out to you the **REASONS** why **WE NEED HELP**.

The first Reason: **The Prevailing Darkness Of Self-will.**

Jesus plainly set us the contrast. He said, "I am the light of the world. He who follows me shall not walk in darkness." Immediately by implication, I understand that Jesus said anywhere else besides following Him is darkness. But there must be a yielding to follow Him. "If any man follow me, he shall not walk in the darkness."

Self-will is the path of darkness. You may think you have light when you don't, because Jesus said if you follow Him, you will walk in the light; you'll not be walking in the darkness. So if you are not following Him, then you are walking in the darkness.

King David once said, "Thy word is a lamp unto my feet and a light unto my path." The prevailing darkness of self-will is one reason why we need help.

The second Reason: **The Assailing Error Of Human Judgment.**

They came back to Jesus like this: "You bare record of yourself. Your record is not true." That had a very shallow basis; it had no footing. It was a response without depth. They had little time for reflection. It was a one-sided evidence for Jesus said, "You judge after the flesh." All matters were not taken into consideration. They had uncertainty because the flesh is shifting. It was unreal because it was partial. You can't make a partial judgment and come anywhere near reality.

We need help. Jesus said, "Your law says that in the mouth of two or three witnesses, every word shall be established." I affirm, my friend, that God's law will give us help. I affirm we need help because human judgment is not enough. There is error in human judgment. We need help because of the assailing error of human judgment.

The third reason we need help: **The Alienating Ignorance Of The Rational Mind.**

We were made to think. Oh yes, God made us that way. Our reasoning ability is part of God's gift to us. But the mind has sidetracks that separate us from God. These people got sidetracked. They said, "Where is your father?" Many let their minds throw up roadblocks.

This was a show of unbelief because they did not believe in Him. But Jesus said, "The Father and I are one." There was a union between Him and God. As the Son of God, Jesus could make such a statement: "If you had known me, you would have known my Father also."

Yes, my friend, we need help. We cannot take this step into knowledge without taking the step of faith. Our minds are too limited. Our rational mind is hemmed in with ignorance. Jesus will open a whole new field of knowledge for you. We need help for the alienating ignorance of the rational mind keeps us away from God.

Your greatest step forward will be when you agree with God that you need help. Your self-will has you in darkness; Jesus can give you light. Your human judgment has you in error; Jesus can give you truth. Your rational mind has you in ignorance; Jesus can give you knowledge. You need help, and He can give it to you.

Chapter Thirty-Nine

Understanding Yourself

I received a letter from a listener to our radio program. She told me of her deep struggle of soul, until she came to call out to the Lord for rest and peace! God heard her. When she needed help, she could call on the Lord, and the Lord heard her.

What she needed was an understanding of herself. In fact, she needed to understand her need. That is what all of us need. Yet sometimes, it seems we cannot reach it.

It was so in Jesus' day. As He met with the crowds, they struggled to understand Him. Their problem really was to understand themselves. Jesus was able to touch those areas of life which are essential even for us today. We come to better understanding from the Scripture text, John 8:21-30, and the words of Jesus.

> *21 Then said Jesus again unto them, I go my way, and ye shall seek me, and shall die in your sins: whither I go, ye cannot come.*
>
> *22 Then said the Jews, Will he kill himself? Because he saith, Whither I go, ye cannot come.*
>
> *23 And he said unto them, Ye are from beneath; I am from above: ye are of this world; I am not of this world.*
>
> *24 I said therefore unto you, that ye shall die in your sins: for if ye believe not that I am he, ye shall die in your sins.*

25 Then said they unto him, Who art thou? And Jesus saith unto them, Even the same that I said unto you from the beginning.

26 I have many things to say and to judge of you: but he that sent me is true; and I speak to the world those things which I have heard of him.

27 They understood not that he spake to them of the Father.

28 Then said Jesus unto them, When ye have lifted up the Son of man, then shall ye know that I am he, and that I do nothing of myself: but as my Father hath taught me, I speak these things.

29 And he that sent me is with me: the Father hath not left me alone; for I do always those things that please him.

30 As he spake these words, many believed on him.

Here are several **INSIGHTS** into human behavior which should help us understand ourselves.

The first Insight: **Unbelief Is The Roadblock.**

Jesus issued a warning. He said, "You shall seek me, but you shall not find me, and you shall die in your sins." He said, "Where I go, you cannot come." Now that was a very solemn warning Jesus issued to these people.

He then went on to say, "If you do not believe that I am he, you shall die in your sins." So Jesus stated a condition; a condition, my friend, beyond which there is no help. He said, "I am the Messiah, and if you do not believe that I am He, you shall die in your sins."

The conclusion is that unbelief is the roadblock.

There is no escape because Jesus made it very clear. There is only one way, believe that Jesus is He.

The second Insight: **Understanding Is The Doorway.**

Then Jesus answered a question for them. They said, "Who are you?" He said, "I am the same one that I told you before." I go back to verse twelve of this chapter, and I find that Jesus there said, "I am the light of the world. He that followeth me shall not walk in darkness but shall have the light of life." I believe that Jesus answered their question with reference to that particular statement when they said, "Who are you?"

He said, "I am the same one I told you before. I am the light of the world." And then Jesus made this statement: "I have much to say to you, and I get my message from the true One, the One who sent me. I speak what He tells me to say, but you do not understand. You do not understand."

You see, I am pointing out to you that one of the insights into human behavior is that understanding is the doorway. On the one hand, unbelief is the roadblock. But on the other hand, understanding is the doorway to let you through. There is no other route.

Jesus was helping these people and you and me to realize that understanding is the doorway.

The third Insight: **Unequal Is The Decisive Point.**

Jesus made a prediction. He said, "When you have lifted up the Son of man, then you will know what I have said. When you have lifted up the Son of man, then you shall know that I am He." There was a time to come, Jesus predicted, when they would lift Him up.

Lifting Him up certainly must have brought to their minds the experience of their forefathers in the wilderness while coming from Egypt to the Holy Land. When the serpents got among them, Moses cried out unto the Lord. The Lord instructed Moses to make a brazen serpent and put it upon a pole. Everyone who looked at that serpent was healed. Jesus said, "When you have lifted up the Son of man then you shall know that I am He." It was a very important prediction.

Then Jesus stated a very vital principle. He said, "The Father is with me, and I do always those things that please the Father." Not another human being has ever been able to make such a statement. Nobody but Jesus has been able to say, "I do always those things that please the Father."

That's why I say unequal is a decisive point because He is not like you and me. No one is equal to Him. He stands above all others.

These insights should lead you to faith in Him. Are they not significant insights to the needs of human behavior, just like you and just like me? You can overcome the roadblock of unbelief by faith. You can enter the doorway of understanding by faith. You can resolve the decisive point by faith. He is the Messiah. Do you know Him? Do you believe in Him?

Chapter Forty

How To Be Free

Liberation movements are everywhere. People want to be free; they want to be independent. I am not criticizing anybody, but I wonder sometimes how these very small nations are going to make it. Often the true meaning of freedom is overlooked. Sometimes the meaning of freedom is actually distorted, twisted, so people do not really understand what freedom means.

To want what is not good for us is to become misfits, and that surely leads to bondage, not freedom. I often think of the way children demonstrate this. They want what is not good for them and in that way create more problems for themselves than they solve.

But the most serious bondage is the bondage of the spirit. And the most joyous freedom is freedom of the spirit. Because we are so fleshly, we often fail to understand this fact: the most joyous freedom is freedom of the spirit.

The way to freedom is set forth in the Scriptures. I have chosen John 8:31-36 for the foundation of this instruction on **HOW TO BE FREE.**

> *31 Then said Jesus to those Jews which believed on him, If ye continue in my word, then are ye my disciples indeed;*
>
> *32 And ye shall know the truth, and the truth shall make*

you free.

33 They answered him, We be Abraham's seed, and were never in bondage to any man: how sayest thou, Ye shall be made free?

34 Jesus answered them, Verily, verily, I say unto you, Whosoever committeth sin is the servant of sin.

35 And the servant abideth not in the house for ever: but the Son abideth ever.

36 If the Son therefore shall make you free, ye shall be free indeed.

How can we be free? Jesus offers several expert **COUNSELS** as to how we can be free in the true sense.

The first Counsel: **Continue In My Word.**

I point out to you that Jesus by making this statement, "continue in my Word", suggested that this is not a momentary experience. This is an abiding or a dwelling place. "If you continue (if you live, as it were) in my Word, then you will be my disciple indeed."

There is a definite relationship: my disciple. This whole idea of disciple and Lord is exciting because it simply means that when you become a disciple of Jesus Christ, then He orders your life. You need no longer be so concerned about where you are going or what you are doing because Jesus as Lord of your life, will give you direction.

There is also a distinct discovery here because Jesus said, "You shall know the truth, and the truth shall make you free." Oh, people are searching for truth, but they don't find it because they don't search for it at the right place. Jesus said His word will bring you to truth. Some find it. Praise the Lord! I'm glad to point out to you that truth is found in Jesus' words.

To be free means to continue in the word of Jesus. Don't miss the full force of this counsel. He said if you want to be free, then you continue in His word.

The second Counsel: **Consider Wisdom.**

They really denied their condition. They said, "We are Abraham's children. We have never been in bondage to anybody." They fell into a serious state. They thought that family lines can override the spiritual problem. They overemphasized their family background. They ignored the daily situation because, at that time, they were under the bondage of Rome. The Roman rulers had the say over them, but in their desperation, they did not consider the wisdom of Jesus. So He needed to point out to them that true freedom is not in their family line, but true freedom comes in the spirit. So He showed them that sin enslaves. Sin makes slaves out of people.

Oh yes, I know that to be true. I have witnessed it. What's more, I have experienced it. He taught them that sin enslaves and yet there is hope in the Son. For He said, "The slave does not abide in the house forever, but the Son abides forever." In other words, you can break the bondage of sin if you respond to the wisdom of Jesus.

To be free means to consider the wisdom of Jesus. Sin enslaves. It creates bondage of the spirit, but Jesus can liberate you.

The third Counsel: **Confess My Work.**

That is the only way, for Jesus said when the Son makes you free, then you are free indeed. Oh, my friend, I want you to catch this in verse 36: "Therefore if the Son shall make you free, you shall be free indeed." It is His work to set you free. You can struggle all you want, but you will never be free until you are willing to confess His work.

Then you have true freedom! And without a doubt, for Jesus said, "You shall be free indeed." Indeed, without doubt. Yes. Praise the Lord! When we come His way, then we experience that freedom of the spirit, the most important area where freedom can be experienced.

To be free means to confess Jesus' work. He liberates the spirit. And that's the most important place for liberation to happen, in your spirit and mine.

How to be free then involves accepting the counsels of Jesus: continue in my word, consider my wisdom, confess my work. He said, "If you continue in my word, then you are my disciples indeed, and you shall know the truth and the truth shall make you free. If the Son therefore shall make you free, you shall be free indeed."

I invite you to find this freedom of which Jesus spoke, freedom of the spirit.

Chapter Forty-One

Some Important Comparisons

In everyday life, we learn by comparing one thing with another. Most likely, in your community, you have certain sayings like "hard as stone" or "dark as night." These are familiar comparisons.

To make comparisons is a good way to learn because what we do not know, we can compare with that which we do know. Sometimes we may see someone who reminds us of a friend or a member of our family. If we watch carefully, we can observe traits that identify that person or object, but we must know what we are looking for. We have a saying in English like this: "Birds of a feather flock together." No matter what kind of bird, stork, or whatever, they usually travel together, don't they?

So, it is true in other considerations of life. We learn by **COMPARISONS.** The same things go together. Let us see what we find in John 8:37-47.

> *37 I know that ye are Abraham's seed; but ye seek to kill me, because my word hath no place in you.*
>
> *38 I speak that which I have seen with my Father: and ye do that which ye have seen with your father.*
>
> *39 They answered and said unto him, Abraham is our father. Jesus saith unto them, If ye were Abraham's children, ye would do the works of Abraham.*

40 But now ye seek to kill me, a man that hath told you the truth, which I have heard of God: this did not Abraham.

41 Ye do the deeds of your father. Then said they to him, We be not born of fornication; we have one Father, even God.

42 Jesus said unto them, If God were your Father, ye would love me: for I proceeded forth and came from God; neither came I of myself, but he sent me.

43 Why do ye not understand my speech? Even because ye cannot hear my word.

44 Ye are of your father the devil, and the lusts of your father ye will do. He was a murderer from the beginning, and abode not in the truth, because there is no truth in him. When he speaketh a lie, he speaketh of his own: for he is a liar, and the father of it.

45 And because I tell you the truth, ye believe me not.

46 Which of you convinceth me of sin? And if I say the truth, why do ye not believe me?

47 He that is of God heareth God's words: ye therefore hear them not, because ye are not of God.

From our text, we examine **SOME IMPORTANT COMPARISONS** that help us understand Jesus' teaching.

The first Comparison: **Father Likeness.**

We may say this is family identity. Each of us have certain traits that make us clearly a part of our family. You have yours; I have mine. And Jesus drew a comparison on that very point. He said to the Jews who were questioning Him, "You do what your father says; I do what my Father says."

Jesus went beyond the physical likeness. He took it to the moral and spiritual dimensions, to that part of life which controls conduct. For the most part, conduct is controlled by the model we follow. Jesus said He does the Father's will, and they do their father's will.

They appealed to the fact that Abraham was their father. While they said Abraham was their father, they were thinking only of the physical. Jesus answered them that what they were seeking to do to Him, their father Abraham, if indeed he was their father, would not have done.

No claim will do in family lines until the deeds match the claim. So here is one comparison: father likeness.

There is a second Comparison: **God Likeness.**

Here they made a very futile proposal. They said God was their Father. They implied that Jesus was born of fornication because He was born of the virgin. They said, "We are not born of fornication; God is our Father." They tried to make a spiritual appeal. Jesus tested them with a proof. He said, "If God were your Father, you would love me, but you do not love me. I came from God, and I am going to God but you do not love me. I proceeded forth and came from God; neither did I come of myself, but he sent me."

Heart attitude is so very important. He said, "Why do you not understand my words? Because you cannot hear my word." Heart attitudes are so very, very important. Empty claims are useless unless backed by proper conduct. No one can claim to be God-like and not love Jesus.

Say, I think I'd better repeat that: no one can claim to be God-like and not love Jesus.

There is a third Comparison: **Truth Likeness.**

Here Jesus sets forth a very significant exclusion. He excludes the devil. He says there is no truth in him; there is no peace in him; he is a murderer and a liar from the beginning, and all who follow him are like him. He never knew what it was to walk in truth. He speaks a lie, and when he does, he speaks of his own because he is the father of lies. The conclusion is a very sober one, all who follow the devil are like him. So there is also the exclusion of unbelievers.

I discovered something here, my friend; truth divides. The truth of God divides. "Why do you not believe me? I tell you the truth, but you do not believe me," Jesus said. He went on to explain that truth has its source in God. God's words are truth.

I want you to be sure and understand this. "Which of you

convicts me of sin," Jesus asked. "If I say the truth, why do you not believe me? He who is of God hears God's word." I must insist, my friend, that truth divides. It separates error from truth. Only those who follow God can have any claim on truth.

These comparisons strike home to us, do they not? What does your conduct reveal about you? Your father-likeness is showing. I appeal to you, believe God, accept the truth, and your God-likeness will be showing.

Chapter Forty-Two

Why Is Jesus Supreme?

Christians over all the world believe that Jesus is different from all other people. He is supreme. There are others who look to Jesus as a great teacher, as an outstanding reformer, as a prophet ranking with Moses. But Christians go farther in their belief. They believe Jesus is much more. They believe He is the Son of God. They believe He is supreme. They do so on the basis of the records in the Bible.

In certain cases, His own words tell us this in the books of the New Testament called the Gospels. The arguments for His supreme position are established on the reliability of the record. Is the Gospel record true? Yes, my friend, it is true. I want you to read with me from John 8:48-59 and listen to the words of Jesus as He was talking with these people near Him.

> *48 Then answered the Jews, and said unto him, Say we not well that thou art a Samaritan, and hast a devil?*
>
> *49 Jesus answered, I have not a devil; but I honour my Father, and ye do dishonour me.*
>
> *50 And I seek not mine own glory: there is one that seeketh and judgeth.*
>
> *51 Verily, verily, I say unto you, If a man keep my saying, he shall never see death.*
>
> *52 Then said the Jews unto him, Now we know that*

thou hast a devil. Abraham is dead, and the prophets; and thou sayest, If a man keep my saying, he shall never taste of death.

53 Art thou greater than our father Abraham, which is dead? And the prophets are dead: whom makest thou thyself?

54 Jesus answered, If I honour myself, my honour is nothing: it is my Father that honoureth me; of whom ye say, that he is your God:

55 Yet ye have not known him; but I know him: and if I should say, I know him not, I shall be a liar like unto you: but I know him, and keep his saying.

56 Your father Abraham rejoiced to see my day: and he saw it, and was glad.

57 Then said the Jews unto him, Thou art not yet fifty years old, and hast thou seen Abraham?

58 Jesus said unto them, Verily, verily, I say unto you, Before Abraham was, I am.

59 Then took they up stones to cast at him: but Jesus hid himself, and went out of the temple, going through the midst of them, and so passed by.

In this text, we must acknowledge He made certain special **CLAIMS** that set Him apart from all others. **WHY IS JESUS SUPREME?** He is supreme upon the basis of several claims.

The first Claim: **To Have Power Over Death.**

His own people brought an accusation against Him. They said, "You are a Samaritan." That was a mean thing to say in those days. They said, "You have a demon." That also was a mean thing to say because that meant that He was deranged; He was mentally incompetent; He couldn't think straight anymore. That was the accusation they brought against Him.

But Jesus refuted what they said by saying, "I honour my Father, God; you dishonour me, but God honours me; I seek not mine own glory but the glory of Him who sent me."

And He made an affirmation. Did you notice as you read? He said, "If a man keeps my saying, he shall never see death." His sayings will liberate those who keep them from death, eternal death. In other words, Jesus is supreme because He claims to have power over death. Doesn't that strike you as something special? Something different? Nobody else could make that claim. Of course not.

The second Claim: **To Have Direct Contact With God.**

This claim sets Him apart as being Supreme. His accusers said, "Now we know that you have a demon." This was confirmation in their hearts. They said Abraham is dead; the prophets are dead; everybody dies. How can He say that if one keeps His saying, he shall not taste death? Is He greater than Abraham? They said, "Now we are sure that you must have a demon."

But then Jesus gave a different presentation. He said, "My Father honours me, and you claim that He is your God. You have never known Him, really. I know Him in ways that you do not know Him. I have direct contact with God."

The Bible says in another place about Jesus that He is the only one who has ever seen God face to face. He was in the bosom of the Father before He became flesh and dwelt among us. That sets Him off as being supreme because He has direct contact with God. That was His claim, and it was correct.

The third claim: **To Have Lived Before Abraham.**

They denounced Him. They said, "You are not yet fifty years old, and you have seen Abraham?" Well, if you begin to figure a little bit, you soon find that Abraham lived many years before Christ was here on earth. Yes, many years.

But Jesus clarified this for them. He said, "Abraham rejoiced to see my day, and he saw it." I wonder how Abraham saw Jesus' day. Well, I remember one time when God sent Abraham to Mount Moriah to offer his only son, Isaac, on the altar. God provided a ram to be slain in Isaac's place and Abraham said, "In the Mount of the Lord, it shall be seen." He saw the sacrifice of the ram for his son. In that way, I think, he saw the day of Jesus.

Then Jesus went on to say, "Before Abraham existed, I AM." Do you remember that when Moses was sent by the Lord to Egypt to bring the children of Israel out, Moses asked the Lord, "What shall I say? Whom shall I say sent me?" And He said, "tell them 'I AM' hath sent you." So Jesus could say, "Before Abraham existed, I AM." He claimed to have lived before Abraham, and indeed He did.

Why is Jesus supreme? Because He is God in the flesh. He is not a human being trying to be God. The eternal Word became flesh and dwelt among us. He has the right to claim power over death. He has the right to say He has direct contact with God. He has the right to say He lived before Abraham.

It is, therefore, important, my friend, for you to have the proper relationship with Him. Have you responded in faith?

Studies from John 9

Chapter Forty-Three

Establishing Reasons

"Why?" is an important question. It gets to the central issue. It is, we may say, the basic question. "Why?" leads us to the reasons for whatever exists. Many never bother to ask why. They keep doing the same things without even thinking, just going through the routine day after day without any bother to ask why.

Now, my friend, we are not a machine to do only one thing one way. God has given us minds with which we can think. We have the right, therefore, to establish the reasons for our actions. We can change if we want to, and there are reasons to change. Of course, just to change for the sake of change isn't really very smart. But we are not machines. We can make changes, and we can think over the reasons why we do what we do.

From a very interesting experience in the life of Jesus in John 9:1-12, we learn about **ESTABLISHING REASONS**.

> *1 And as Jesus passed by, he saw a man which was blind from his birth.*
>
> *2 And his disciples asked him, saying, Master, who did sin, this man, or his parents, that he was born blind?*
>
> *3 Jesus answered, Neither hath this man sinned, nor his parents: but that the works of God should be made manifest in him.*

4 I must work the works of him that sent me, while it is day: the night cometh, when no man can work.

5 As long as I am in the world, I am the light of the world.

6 When he had thus spoken, he spat on the ground, and made clay of the spittle, and he anointed the eyes of the blind man with the clay,

7 And said unto him, Go, wash in the pool of Siloam, (which is by interpretation, Sent.) He went his way therefore, and washed, and came seeing.

8 The neighbours therefore, and they which before had seen him that he was blind, said, Is not this he that sat and begged?

9 Some said, This is he: others said, He is like him: but he said, I am he.

10 Therefore said they unto him, How were thine eyes opened?

11 He answered and said, A man that is called Jesus made clay, and anointed mine eyes, and said unto me, Go to the pool of Siloam, and wash: and I went and washed, and I received sight.

12 Then said they unto him, Where is he? He said, I know not.

From this text, we learn to follow the **INSTRUCTIONS** which will help us to establish reasons for what we do.

The first Instruction: **Examine The Problem.**

This was indeed a very critical problem, for the man was born blind. The disciples asked a right question. They said, "Who sinned, this man or his parents?" That's what I meant by saying a "why?" question is a very basic one. It is hidden in their question. Why is this man like he is? Who sinned?

They reasoned that any problem like a disease or a handicap was indeed the result of somebody's sin. But Jesus corrected that. While they were examining the problem, He answered, "Neither hath this man sinned nor his parents."

He gave them a correction. This is a situation where the glory of God is going to be manifest. He answered them to help them understand exactly what the problem was. But they had a right to examine the problem, and that's the instruction I'm bringing to you. First of all, to establish the reasons, examine the problem.

Then Jesus went on with a directed acknowledgment. He said, "I must work the works of Him who sent me while it is day because the night comes when nobody can work." Do what is yours to do when you ought to do it.

So here we have instruction number one: examine the problem that is before you when you are ready to establish the reasons.

The second Instruction: **Accept The Prescription.**

Here was a man born blind. How was he to be made whole? How was he to receive his sight? We are told that Jesus spit on the ground, and of the spittle He made clay salve and put it on the eyes of the blind man.

We do not know if there was any medicine in that clay or in that saliva. However, Jesus went about it in a very simple way. After He had anointed, or put the salve on the man's eyes, He gave him a very simple command: "Go, wash in the pool of Siloam." He went and washed. Very simple obedience. He went his way and washed and came seeing.

We do not have any explanation as to how this man got to the pool of Siloam. Perhaps someone led him. But he did not doubt that the prescription Jesus gave him would indeed make him well. So he went, he washed, he came seeing. He had no hesitancy to do what he was told. He did exactly what Jesus told him to do.

The third Instruction: **Study The Puzzle.**

When he came back seeing, the people who knew him, the neighbors and friends, first doubted that this was indeed the man who had been blind. So they tried to get his identification. They talked among themselves. They said, "Is not this he who was sitting and begging?" And some of them said, "Yes, this is the same man." But others said, "No, no, this is not the blind man. This is another like him." But he said, "I am he." And then they asked him how he received his sight.

Again, you see, they were studying the puzzle. They did not know exactly what the situation was, but they were trying to arrive at the reasons for what had happened.

Listen to the explanation: he said, "A man who is called Jesus made clay, and anointed my eyes, and said to me, Go to the pool of Siloam, and wash: and I went and washed, and I received my sight." That should be simple enough for anybody. The answer was clear. It was no longer a puzzle because the man had answered the question.

Here then, we have the instructions we must follow if we would establish the reasons for our actions: examine the problem, accept the prescription, and study the puzzle. Be sure you come out at the right answer like this man did.

Chapter Forty-Four

Measuring Values

Sometimes we are puzzled to know what is the most important thing in life. At such times we need help. Where do you turn for help? I turn to God's Word. Here is a helpful verse for times like that: "I will lift mine eyes unto the hills, from whence cometh my help. My help cometh from the LORD, which made heaven and earth." Psalm 121:1-2.

To know how to choose the best in life is our problem. One time Mrs. Yoder and I were visiting a shop to buy a Persian rug. We had no idea of the value of Persian rugs. When the shopkeeper told us what the price was, we couldn't buy one. It was too costly. The price was more than we could afford. So we had to leave the Persian rugs. They were beautiful, but we could not afford to buy even one.

In life, we must take care to measure the values by which we live. Some are too costly. For some, the price is too high. For some, the price is much too cheap. Are there any ways of **MEASURING VALUES** in life properly? Yes, there are. We shall see what happens here in John 9:13-23.

> *13 They brought to the Pharisees him that aforetime was blind.*
>
> *14 And it was the sabbath day when Jesus made the clay, and opened his eyes.*

15 Then again the Pharisees also asked him how he had received his sight. He said unto them, He put clay upon mine eyes, and I washed, and do see.

16 Therefore said some of the Pharisees, This man is not of God, because he keepeth not the sabbath day. Others said, How can a man that is a sinner do such miracles? And there was a division among them.

17 They say unto the blind man again, What sayest thou of him, that he hath opened thine eyes? He said, He is a prophet.

18 But the Jews did not believe concerning him, that he had been blind, and received his sight, until they called the parents of him that had received his sight.

19 And they asked them, saying, Is this your son, who ye say was born blind? How then doth he now see?

20 His parents answered them and said, We know that this is our son, and that he was born blind:

21 But by what means he now seeth, we know not; or who hath opened his eyes, we know not: he is of age; ask him: he shall speak for himself.

22 These words spake his parents, because they feared the Jews: for the Jews had agreed already, that if any man did confess that he was Christ, he should be put out of the synagogue.

23 Therefore said his parents, He is of age; ask him.

In this conversation, I find several helpful **PROCESSES** by which values can be measured, for we must measure the values of life. Let's look at these processes.

Process number one: **Seek A Clarification.**

Don't be satisfied with just a report. Go right to the source and find out what happened. That's what these people did. They tried to find out clearly what had taken place. This blind man had been healed by a miracle that Jesus had performed. Jesus had put clay salve on his eyes and had sent him to the pool of Siloam to wash.

So, they came to find out, to get a clarification, and they asked the man. He told them exactly what happened. He said, "He put clay upon my eyes, and I washed, and I see." Just as simple as that. No great enlargement, no complex way. Just a very simple answer of exactly what happened.

But do you know that some of these people came to the wrong conclusion? They concluded that since the miracle was performed on the Sabbath day, that whoever performed it could not possibly be a man of God. He must be a sinner. But the man who was healed said that surely a sinner could not do miracles like this.

Well, let's see who came to the wrong conclusion. It was not really the man who was healed this time. It was others who were standing around who said a sinner cannot do miracles like this.

To measure the values of life, it is appropriate and important to seek clarification of the problem. Make sure you understand exactly.

Let's take Process number two: **Stress The Verification.**

Gather more facts. Talk to other people who know. So these people called the parents. Now they certainly should have known. If he was their son then they would know whether or not he had been born blind and surely they ought to know how he received his sight. So they called them in and asked, "Is this your son?" They said, "Yes, this is our son. He was born blind." But then they went on to say, "We do not know how he received his sight, and we do not know who healed him."

Well, they said part of the truth, but they would not tell all they knew. We are going to see why they wouldn't. But I have to admire these people for trying to get all the facts together. That is a very important process. Don't be satisfied until you have all the facts brought together.

To measure values, you must stress the verification, make sure that all the facts have been well verified.

The third Process: **Face The Excommunication.**

Let me warn you, don't be afraid. You read in this text that these parents would not tell everything they knew because they were afraid. They had been threatened with excommunication; that means to be put out of the synagogue. If anybody confessed that Jesus was the Messiah, they had already agreed among themselves that such a person could not have fellowship in the synagogue.

That was a very serious threat. But don't be afraid. If you are going to really come out on the side of truth, then you must measure values and not be scared. Don't close your mind to the truth. Don't draw conclusions before the evidence is in.

Be sure that you verify everything, but do not be afraid if someone threatens you. To measure values, you must face the threats of excommunication, the threats of others. I suppose these parents were afraid. Therefore they had their problem and could not really come to the measuring of values. They put the wrong weight or the wrong value on the wrong side.

Measuring values in life properly will require these processes: seek a clarification, ask to know; stress the verification, make certain of the facts; face the excommunication, stand on the side of the truth. Don't draw any conclusion before the evidence is in.

Chapter Forty-Five

Weighing Evidences

When I was in high school, our teacher in physics quoted a law of life: "For every action there is opposite and equal reaction." For that reason, I can walk because I have the strength to react against the pull of the earth's gravity. Such physical evidences are easily seen once we understand them and accept them.

In other areas of life, we are often very slow in admitting or accepting the evidences which are available to us. Often we are stubborn, reluctant, sometimes rebellious about **WEIGHING EVIDENCES** that may be right before us. So it was in Jesus' days in the text in John 9:24-34.

24 Then again called they the man that was blind, and said unto him, Give God the praise: we know that this man is a sinner.

25 He answered and said, Whether he be a sinner or no, I know not: one thing I know, that, whereas I was blind, now I see.

26 Then said they to him again, What did he to thee? How opened he thine eyes?

27 He answered them, I have told you already, and ye did not hear: wherefore would ye hear it again? Will ye also be his disciples?

28 Then they reviled him, and said, Thou art his disciple; but we are Moses' disciples.

29 We know that God spake unto Moses: as for this fellow, we know not from whence he is.

30 The man answered and said unto them, Why herein is a marvellous thing, that ye know not from whence he is, and yet he hath opened mine eyes.

31 Now we know that God heareth not sinners: but if any man be a worshiper of God, and doeth his will, him he heareth.

32 Since the world began was it not heard that any man opened the eyes of one that was born blind.

33 If this man were not of God, he could do nothing.

34 They answered and said unto him, Thou wast altogether born in sins, and dost thou teach us? And they cast him out.

That's what they did. This formerly blind man's experience furnishes us with certain **REALITIES** with which we must deal to be able to weigh the evidences.

The first Reality: **Assurance Comes By Experience.**

Empty arguments can never satisfy. What has happened is far more basic. So this man said, "I know one thing; I was blind, but now I see." Do you understand that an improper affirmation can only lead to a false conclusion? You can't start wrong and come out right. You must start right if you expect to come out right.

And this man said, "I know one thing; I was blind, and now I see." He could have said, "When you ask me to enter into the theological discussion of the background, I am not equipped for that. But I can tell you that I was once a blind man, and now I can see."

I am telling you, my friend, that assurance comes by experience. What you have experienced cannot be denied.

The second Reality: **Ignorance May Come By Evasion.**

We may plead ignorance by avoiding what has been told. They

asked the healed man to please report and please repeat. Perhaps there was a flaw in the first report. But then the man came through and said exactly what had happened; in fact, he would not even tell them. He said he had told them once before, and they did not hear. Why did they want him to repeat it?

You see, he had told the truth. He had said exactly what had happened. Jesus took clay and anointed his eyes, and sent him to the pool of Siloam to wash. He went and washed and came seeing. But they were trying to cross-examine him and put him into a position where he would say something other than what he had said before.

I was really interested in how he responded. He said, "Why do you want to hear it again? Do you also desire to be his disciple?" So he gave himself away, and they caught him immediately and began to revile him, to humiliate him.

Now ignorance sometimes does that: humiliates the opponent, reviles the opposition, and asserts a superiority. But they were not open to the truth. They would not open their minds to what the man said. They closed their minds. You see? Willful ignorance is never the mark of intelligence. I must run that past again: Willful ignorance is never the mark of intelligence.

The third Reality: **Certainty Comes By Admitting The Effects.**

What is done bears its own testimony. The opening of blind eyes is not a sinner's work. Everyone ought to be able to acknowledge that. This was a bona fide miracle performed by Jesus of Nazareth. These men who were accusing the man of being a disciple of Jesus would not admit what had happened. They kept insisting that whoever performed that miracle, because it was done on the Sabbath day, must of necessity be a sinner.

But the man began to lecture these who were supposed to know. He said, "This is a marvelous thing that you do not know where he is from, and yet he has opened my eyes. We know that God does not hear sinners. But this man has opened my eyes."

The effect must be convincing. Certainty comes by admitting the effects, what can be seen. The effects must be accepted if truth is to be obtained. Don't close your mind to what is clearly evident.

I urge you to be sure to weigh the evidence. Here are the realities that will help you to do this: assurance comes by experience; ignorance may come by evasion, not being willing to face up to it; certainty comes by admitting effects. Do not close your mind. Keep your mind open to the truth.

Chapter Forty-Six

Reaching Conclusions

Some people who claim to be the wisest and the smartest never make up their minds about religion. They think it is a mark of intelligence to suspend judgment on such a vital subject. It is wise to think carefully about the subject of religion because of the way it affects our lives here and for eternity. But to simply refuse to decide is to decide by default. We reach a conclusion by inaction.

As human beings, we are made to reach conclusions. We cannot live with our judgments in suspense indefinitely. To be undecided is a very difficult position to hold. While our thought processes should be active, they should lead us to a position, to a conclusion, and not just all the time say, "I don't know."

One of the marks of an intelligent person is his ability to state his conclusions on a subject, even though those conclusions may need to be modified when more truth is available. We ought to become concerned about **REACHING CONCLUSIONS**. Let us think about that with John 9:35-41 as a basis.

> *35 Jesus heard that they had cast him out; and when he had found him, he said unto him, Dost thou believe on the Son of God?*
>
> *36 He answered and said, Who is he, Lord, that I might believe on him?*

37 And Jesus said unto him, Thou hast both seen him, and it is he that talketh with thee.

38 And he said, Lord, I believe. And he worshipped him.

39 And Jesus said, For judgment I am come into this world, that they which see not might see; and that they which see might be made blind.

40 And some of the Pharisees which were with him heard these words, and said unto him, Are we blind also?

41 Jesus said unto them, If ye were blind, ye should have no sin: but now ye say, We see; therefore your sin remaineth.

We had better put together our thought patterns so that we can reach proper conclusions. From this text, I purpose to show two **MANDATES** which you will need to follow in order to reach satisfying conclusions.

The first Mandate: **Answer The Most Important Question.**

What is it? What is the most important question? Is it, "Who am I?" Well, that is an important question, but is that the most important question? Or is it, "Why am I here?" That, too, is an important question, but is it the most important question? Or is it "Where am I going?" Now that also is a very important question. But none of these is the most important question.

The most important question is the one that Jesus asked this blind man. It is this, "Do you believe on the Son of God?" This is the most important question you can ask, and I am asking that question now. Now don't turn me off. Hear me through. This is the most important question anybody can ask you.

This question you must answer, just as the man in our story in the Bible needed to answer. He could not come to a satisfying conclusion until he said, "Lord, I believe." He first asked, "Who is he?" And when he learned who He was, he said, "Lord, I believe." Now, do you believe on the Son of God? You cannot indefinitely hold your judgment in suspense. I ask you that question now, and you must answer it sometime.

The second Mandate: **Trust The Most Certain Cure.**

What is it? Well, men say today you must put yourself out front. You must say, "I am number one." No, but that is not a cure. In fact, that may be a disease. They tell me you must say to yourself, "I am self-sufficient; I will make it." No, no, my friend, that sounds like the devil. The prophet Isaiah in chapter 14 of his book, tells us that Lucifer, son of the morning, said just exactly that, "I will be like the most High." No, that is not the most certain cure.

What is the most certain cure? Accept healing for your blindness. Notice how Jesus replied to these Pharisees when they said to Him, "Are we blind also?" He said, "If you were blind, you would have no sin, but now you say, we see; therefore your sin remains."

I get a tremendous truth out of that statement from Jesus. I get this: you had better admit, my friend, that you cannot see. Then Jesus can give you sight. He can help you see. There is a blindness much worse than physical blindness, much worse than this man who was born blind. That blindness is spiritual. When people are deliberately blind, they will not see the truth. That, my friend, is awful. That is a blindness that will curse you. But Jesus said if they were blind, then it would be possible for them to see. But since they say they are not blind, they are hopeless and blind.

Now it's very simple, very simple. Come to Jesus for healing. That is the most certain cure. There is no other cure as effective as this one. I am especially talking about the kind of blindness that Jesus addressed Himself to when He was talking to these Pharisees, a blindness of the mind. Not a blindness of the eye, but a blindness of the mind.

To reach the really satisfying conclusion, these two mandates or requirements must be met. Answer the most important question. What is it? Do you believe on the Son of God? Trust in the most certain cure, that He can give you sight.

Studies from
John 10

Chapter Forty-Seven

The Abundant Life

Are you satisfied with your life? Do you long for something better, something new, something different? Our materialistic world philosophy ties everything to money. But there are values more worthy than money. Those values have to do with peace in the heart and soul. An abundant life is possible whether there is little or much.

From the words of Jesus in John 10:1-10, let us bring our thoughts to **THE ABUNDANT LIFE.**

> *1 Verily, verily, I say unto you, He that entereth not by the door into the sheepfold, but climbeth up some other way, the same is a thief and a robber.*
>
> *2 But he that entereth in by the door is the shepherd of the sheep.*
>
> *3 To him the porter openeth; and the sheep hear his voice; and he calleth his own sheep by name, and leadeth them out.*
>
> *4 And when he putteth forth his own sheep, he goeth before them, and the sheep follow him: for they know his voice.*
>
> *5 And a stranger will they not follow, but will flee from him: for they know not the voice of strangers.*

6 This parable spake Jesus unto them: but they understood not what things they were which he spake unto them.

7 Then said Jesus unto them again, Verily, verily, I say unto you, I am the door of the sheep.

8 All that ever came before me are thieves and robbers: but the sheep did not hear them.

9 I am the door: by me if any man enter in, he shall be saved, and shall go in and out, and find pasture.

10 The thief cometh not, but for to steal, and to kill, and to destroy: I am come that they might have life, and that they might have it more abundantly.

In this text Jesus clears up several **IDEAS** about the abundant life. Let's think about their relationships.

The first Idea: **A Close Intimacy.**

This close intimacy is experienced between the shepherd and the sheep. Jesus said that the gatekeeper knows Him, the Good Shepherd. He opens the gate to Him. All that came before Him and all that climbed up some other way were thieves and robbers. The gatekeeper knows the Shepherd. There is a kind of warm acquaintance there between the gatekeeper and the Shepherd.

There is more to this intimacy. The Shepherd is also known by the sheep. They know his voice. "When he puts forth his own sheep, he goes before them, and the sheep follow him, for they know his voice." Yes, sheep are very personable animals. They learn to know the shepherd very well. They can tell his voice. They can tell by his appearance whether or not he is, in fact, the true Shepherd.

You'll notice that Jesus said this intimacy means good following. He goes before his sheep, and they follow him. I have seen shepherds in the Holy Land (Israel) leading their sheep. They always go before them. They never drive the sheep, they lead them. Jesus said He goes before His sheep and they follow Him. They will not follow strangers because they do not know the voice of the stranger.

This is the kind of intimacy that the abundant life can bring to you. Jesus is the leader of that abundant life. In His close acquaintance with you, His intimacy, He can walk before you, and you can know His voice.

A second Idea: **A Careful Instruction.**

Jesus told them this parable, but they did not understand what He was telling them. So Jesus explained further to lead them to a real understanding. He said in clear tones, "I am the door of the sheep." If you are going to enter into the abundant life, you must accept what Jesus is saying, "I am the door." Then He said, "All who ever came before me are thieves and robbers: but the sheep did not hear them."

"I am the door." That is a very careful instruction which simply means that there are no other entrances beside the one that Jesus has prepared, in fact, the one that Jesus is. If you are going to enter into the abundant life that Jesus is talking about in these verses, then you must come by that door which He said He is. So to lead you to understanding, Jesus gave a very careful instruction here.

Then He also warned against others. He said, "All that came before me are thieves and robbers." Very important it is, then, to get our directions clear. We have only one that we dare or care to follow and that one is Jesus. The true sheep do not hear the voice of strangers and will not follow thieves and robbers.

Jesus was very careful to give them clear instruction. It was necessary to come to a clear understanding from this careful instruction. Jesus said, "I am the door of the sheep. All that ever came before me are thieves and robbers."

There's a third Idea in which Jesus clears for us the relationships of the abundant life: **A Considered Intention.**

He said, "I am the door: by me if any man enter in, he shall be saved, and shall go in and out, and find pasture." It is possible for you, just as for me, to enter in by this door, Jesus, and find a safe place. He said, "he shall be saved, and shall go in and out, and find pasture." All others are excluded. Only He is the way. Once you have entered in through Him you are safe and satisfied.

I wonder, really, do you know what it is to be satisfied? Satisfied in Jesus with this abundant life? Here is a very considered intention for you, that you might find out with me what it really means to go in and out and find pasture, to have a perfectly satisfied life.

But Jesus goes a bit farther than that. He said, "I am come that they might have life, and that they might have it more abundantly." That's why I called my message The Abundant Life. Life for us can be much more than just existing physically. Much more. In fact, God expected us to have more in life than just to live from birth till death. He expected us to have the abundant life, the overflowing life, the kind of life that comes when you enter in by the door, Jesus, and find in Him your satisfying portion. It's more than existence; it is satisfying relationship.

I trust you to consider this intention very seriously because Jesus wants to impart unto you that abundant life of which He spoke to the disciples. He said, "I am come that they might have life," yes, but that they might have more abundant life, life more abundantly, overflowing life, the kind of life that gives you real joy and peace.

All provisions have been made for you and me. I have chosen that way for the abundant life. Have you? If you choose it, you'll have a very close intimacy with Jesus, the kind of fellowship that provides true leadership. You'll have a careful instruction so you'll be able to discern who is right and who is wrong and not follow the thieves and robbers. You can have a considered intention to receive that more abundant life which provides satisfying joy and peace.

Chapter Forty-Eight

Self-Giving Love

Many years ago, King David had an experience in the time when the Philistines came in and harassed the people of Israel. He said to three of his brave men, "Oh, how I long for a drink of water from the well at Bethlehem's gate." And do you know, those three men broke through the Philistine ranks and brought water to David from the well at Bethlehem's gate? And do you know what David did? He said he couldn't drink it. He wouldn't drink it because this represented blood. They had taken their lives in their hands to get the water from the well at Bethlehem's gate.

Some people will die for a friend. These three brave men risked their lives for their king. But, who will die for an enemy? Who would even dare to die for one he does not love?

We are told self-preservation, to keep alive, is the first law of human existence. There is a higher law though, **SELF-GIVING LOVE.** That's what I want you to think about as we come to the words of Jesus. Three times in John 10:11-18 Jesus tells how He will give His life for the sheep.

11 I am the good shepherd: the good shepherd giveth his life for the sheep.

12 But he that is an hireling, and not the shepherd, whose own the sheep are not, seeth the wolf coming, and leaveth the sheep, and fleeth: and the wolf catcheth them, and scattereth the sheep.

13 The hireling fleeth, because he is an hireling, and careth not for the sheep.

14 I am the good shepherd, and know my sheep, and am known of mine.

15 As the Father knoweth me, even so know I the Father: and I lay down my life for the sheep.

16 And other sheep I have, which are not of this fold: them also I must bring, and they shall hear my voice; and there shall be one fold, and one shepherd.

17 Therefore doth my Father love me, because I lay down my life, that I might take it again.

18 No man taketh it from me, but I lay it down of myself. I have power to lay it down, and I have power to take it again. This commandment have I received of my Father.

In this Bible text, we find **EXPLANATIONS** why Jesus died for us or why He would give His life for the sheep in self-giving love.

Explanation number one: **There Is One Shepherd.**

He is the good Shepherd. He is the trusted Shepherd. He is the faithful Shepherd. The One who is faithful even until death. He said, "I give my life for the sheep." The others are hirelings, hired to do the job, but they don't care for the sheep. They only care for themselves. So their central thought is "my life." I want to be sure that I am protected. So when the wolf comes, they run away and leave the sheep to their fate. Jesus said so. That's the way the hireling operates.

But Jesus said He gives His life for the sheep. There's only one shepherd who would do that, and that is the good Shepherd. What a wonderful fact this is, one shepherd. Not many shepherds, my friend, one shepherd. And Jesus said, "I am the good Shepherd."

There is a second Explanation: **There Is One Fold.**

Notice how He said there is not separation between the shepherd and the sheep? They won't follow strangers. We learned that before.

But there's no separation between the shepherd, the true Shepherd, and the sheep. There is one fold.

There is also a relationship between the Shepherd and the Father. He spoke of the reason why the Father knows Him and He knows the Father. He said, "As the Father knoweth me, even so know I the Father: and I lay down my life for the sheep." There is unity of thought between the Father and the Shepherd. And Jesus is that Shepherd, you understand.

Then there is the Shepherd and the fold. All true sheep are in the true Shepherd's fold. Jesus said, "And other sheep I have, which are not of this fold: them also I must bring, and they shall hear my voice; and there shall be one fold, and one shepherd."

Oh, how I rejoice in that, my friend. It doesn't make any difference where you are reading this. Whether you are in the Far East, or whether you are in South Africa, West Africa, or the Middle East. It doesn't make any difference where you are. Jesus said there is going to be one fold and one Shepherd. From many countries, they come into one fold.

Praise the Lord! Isn't that wonderful! Jesus said He was going to give His life for the sheep so that there will be one flock, one Shepherd, one fold.

Then there is one central truth: the Father's love. He said, "For this reason the Father loves me, because I am going to give my life for the sheep." This was the Father's intention from the beginning. This was the Father's plan from the very start, that the Shepherd would give His life for the sheep.

Then Jesus made a very striking prediction. You'll find that in verse 18: "No man taketh it from me, but I lay it down of myself. I have power to lay it down, and I have power to take it again. This commandment have I received of my Father."

No matter how you examine the record, it becomes absolutely clear that this prediction that Jesus made came to pass. He gave His life. Oh, it's true the Roman soldiers crucified Him. But in reality, He gave His life because the Bible says, from the cross, He cried with a loud voice, "It is finished." Then He gave up His Spirit and said to God the Father, "Into thy hands I commend my Spirit."

Yes, my friend, Jesus gave His life so that He might take it again. He arose from the dead just like He said He would. He is alive today. Right now, He is alive. He is now seated at the right hand of God in heaven, so the Bible informs us. There is one truth that He did lay His life down and that He did take it again. What a wonderful fact! The death and the resurrection of Jesus was truly self-giving love.

He said, "I'm going to lay down my life for the sheep." No one else has ever done what Jesus did. He is the one Shepherd. He is the good Shepherd. And He is the one who is going to bring all His sheep into one fold. It makes no difference where we're from; if we are true sheep of the true Shepherd, we're all in one fold. This is done on the basis of one truth: He gave His life for the sheep.

Chapter Forty-Nine

True Security

How can you be sure of what you really believe? Where does your security lie? Some trust in horses and chariots, the Bible says. Some trust in uncertain riches. Some trust in princes and kings. Some may trust in their intelligence. You see, I was a Bible teacher on a college campus and seminary for twenty-one years, and so I know some of the routes that students take. Some trust in their intelligence.

All of these pass with time. But how can we be sure what we trust in will really endure, endure for the times beyond this life? Jesus' conversation with the people in John 10:22-30 reveals where **TRUE SECURITY** lies.

22 And it was at Jerusalem the feast of the dedication, and it was winter.

23 And Jesus walked in the temple in Solomon's porch.

24 Then came the Jews round about him, and said unto him, How long dost thou make us to doubt? If thou be the Christ, tell us plainly.

25 Jesus answered them, I told you, and ye believed not: the works that I do in my Father's name, they bear witness of me.

26 But ye believe not, because ye are not of my sheep, as I said unto you.

27 My sheep hear my voice, and I know them, and they follow me:

28 And I give unto them eternal life; and they shall never perish, neither shall any man pluck them out of my hand.

29 My Father, which gave them me, is greater than all; and no man is able to pluck them out of my Father's hand.

30 I and my Father are one.

Here in these Bible verses, my friend, are set forth the **DIRECTIVES** to attain true security. I'm asking you, "Where have you placed your trust?"

The first Directive: **Make A Direct Investigation.**

Here is a time and place. We are told that it was the feast of dedication. The Jews still observe that feast, the dedication of the temple 165 years before Christ, or before the common era. It was that time, and the place was in the temple, Solomon's porch. They came to that particular time and place and raised a question with Jesus. They asked, "Who are you? Why don't you tell us who you are? How long do you make us doubt? If you are the Christ, tell us plainly."

That word, Christ, is a very important word. It is the English word for the Greek word *Christos*, which is a translation of the Hebrew word *Meshiach*, the Messiah. Tell us if you are, in fact, the Messiah. Why do you keep us wondering?

I invite you to make a direct investigation of the record. Jesus said He had told them who He was, and He told them He was the Messiah. But still, they wanted some additional confirmation. So I am suggesting that you do what they did. You make a direct investigation.

The second Directive: **Be Prepared For A Decisive Evaluation.**

Then Jesus said, "I told you, and you did not believe. The works that I am doing in my Father's Name, they bear witness of me." Now, what did He do? The Bible records thirty-seven miracles of mercy that Jesus performed. Thirty-seven miracles of mercy are recorded in the Gospel records, like healing the sick, raising the dead, casting out the demons, etc. Now, they should bear some testimony as to whom Jesus is, shouldn't they? Of course.

Besides that, He was teaching the truth. One time the people sent the temple guards to take Jesus, and they came back without Him. The people asked, "Why didn't you bring Him?" And they said, "Well, nobody talks like this man talks."

You see, He taught the truth. So you must be prepared for a decisive evaluation. And Jesus made it very clear that belief is a certain step. It's a step of certainty. He said, "You did not believe because you are not of my sheep."

I tell you. Jesus made a decisive evaluation of these people that were listening to Him. But I'm asking you, "Where do you stand now? What would Jesus say about you? Would He also say about you that you are not a true sheep?"

When you ask, when you make a direct investigation, you must be prepared for the decisive evaluation. Are you a believer?

There is a third Directive: **Receive The Definite Declaration.**

Again Jesus refers to the sheep and the Shepherd. He said, "My sheep hear my voice, and I know them, and they follow me." There is that intimacy and satisfying relationship. Jesus went on to say, "I give to them eternal life; and they shall never perish, neither shall any man pluck them out of my hand."

Think of the security there can be in faith in Jesus. That is where it is, belief in Jesus. That is where security actually comes from. He goes on to say that they are also secure in the Father's hand because, "My Father, which gave them me, is greater than all; and no man is able to pluck them out of my Father's hand."

You see the oneness between these two: the Father and the Son? He said, "Nobody is able to pluck them out of my hand...nobody is able to pluck them out of my Father's hand."

Once you believe in Jesus Christ as the true Shepherd and the Son of God, then you experience true security. That is the result. So long as your faith remains secure, He will hold you fast. You can be sure of that. You must receive this, however, as a very significant and definite declaration.

You see how true security deals not with the material, but with the heart and its peace. That is only possible in Jesus. So make your investigation. I implore you; I invite you to make a decisive and direct investigation. Study the case and see who Jesus is. But be prepared for His evaluation because He said if you do not believe in Him, then you are not a true sheep. And receive His declaration. Once you really believe in Him and know Him as the true Shepherd, and become a true sheep, He holds you fast.

Chapter Fifty

Correct Your Misunderstandings

What causes misunderstandings? One cause may be the lack of information, not having all the facts together, or the inability to communicate, that is, not able to tell it like it really is.

There may be another cause for misunderstanding, that of not hearing correctly. I may say a word that you do not quite understand. If you do not understand what I am saying, then you may misunderstand what I mean.

How can misunderstanding be corrected? It is quite simple. Gather all the information that you can, sift the facts from the falsehoods, and listen carefully so as to understand.

I believe among the subjects most frequently misunderstood is the nature and mission of Jesus of Nazareth. On that subject, though, hangs the most serious of life's outcomes.

My dear friend, it is very important that you understand as well as possible who Jesus of Nazareth is and what His mission is. From John 10:31-42, I want to show you how Jesus helps you to **CORRECT YOUR MISUNDERSTANDINGS.**

31 Then the Jews took up stones again to stone him.

32 Jesus answered them, Many good works have I showed you from my Father; for which of those works do ye stone me?

33 The Jews answered him, saying, For a good work we stone thee not; but for blasphemy; and because that thou, being a man, makest thyself God.

34 Jesus answered them, Is it not written in your law, I said, Ye are gods?

35 If he called them gods, unto whom the word of God came, and the scripture cannot be broken;

36 Say ye of him, whom the Father hath sanctified, and sent into the world, Thou blasphemest; because I said, I am the Son of God?

37 If I do not the works of my Father, believe me not.

38 But if I do, though ye believe not me, believe the works: that ye may know, and believe, that the Father is in me, and I in him.

39 Therefore they sought again to take him: but he escaped out of their hand,

40 And went away again beyond Jordan into the place where John at first baptized; and there he abode.

41 And many resorted unto him, and said, John did no miracle: but all things that John spake of this man were true.

42 And many believed on him there.

Here then, in these verses we have the **DETAILS** which clear up most misunderstandings about the person and work of Jesus.

The first Detail: **The Condemnation.**

They were about to render an execution without trial. Moses' law required the execution of a heretic, but not without a hearing. He was to be brought before the elders, and people were to testify of his unsound faith, and after careful examination, then, they were to stone or execute the person.

So, Jesus protested. He said, "Many good works have I shewed you from my Father; for which of those works do ye stone me?" Their reply is very significant because they said, "For a good work we stone thee not; but for blasphemy; and because that thou, being a man, makest thyself God."

You see, there is one of the misunderstandings that they had because it was not really that at all. They lacked information. One cause for misunderstanding is lack of information. And they lacked information. They thought that Jesus, being a man, was trying to be God. But it's the other way around. Here was God being man, and they were not understanding this at all. So they sought to condemn Him and stone Him without a trial.

Here is the second Detail: **The Vindication.**

Jesus made an appeal to the Word of God. He said there was a Scripture where people were called gods. Here is the exact quote: "I have said, Ye are gods; and all of you are children of the most High." I found it located in Psalm 82:6. The people were called gods. They were mortal, yet they were called the children of God.

Now Jesus raised a very important question on that and vindicated Himself because He said, "Say ye of him, whom the Father hath sanctified, and sent into the world, Thou blasphemest; because I said, I am the Son of God?"

A part of the problem was that they did not understand the nature of this miracle of God becoming man. I am trying to point out to you that Jesus vindicated His position and His statement, "I and the Father are one." Because this was the miracle of God becoming man. And they misunderstood that.

Do you understand it? They needed to accept His statement, and so must you. He is the sanctified sent One and is the Son of God.

The third Detail: **The Verification.**

The record continues that Jesus left that part of the country and went over beyond the Jordan where John had been baptizing, and many of the people came unto Him, and many believed on Him. He found a place where He would not be harassed and where they would not be threatening to stone Him, in the place where John the Baptist had been ministering and most likely where John the Baptist had baptized Jesus. There He found a kind of resort or retreat.

Many of the people came unto Him, and from them, the

response was that everything that John the Baptist said about this man is coming true. John the Baptist performed no miracles, but his prophecies regarding this man are coming true. And many believed on Him there.

When you take it all together, the evidence is convincing. The verification is absolutely established. How can you still hesitate when many today are believing? Letters come from radio listeners in many countries telling us, "I am a believer."

Why don't you take that step, too, and become a believer? If you have any misunderstandings about Jesus, consider with care these details: the condemnation without a trial; the vindication and the appeal to God's Word; the verification that many believed on Him. Surely these can be helpful to you. These details give us certainty of the truth.

Correct your misunderstanding, and learn to know who Jesus is by accepting Him, the Son of God, as your personal Saviour.

Studies from John 11

Chapter Fifty-One

Overcoming Trouble

Because we have limitations, we often face troubles. Our humanity is the source of much of our trouble. We are bound in this body, and because we have the limitations of our human nature, many of our troubles arise.

There is another reason why we have trouble. We have a common enemy, the devil. For that reason, we all face trouble. Yes, my friend, I sincerely believe the Bible teaches us that we do have a common enemy, the devil, and for that reason, we face trouble.

I rejoice to tell you there is a way to overcome trouble. Even though you may be going through very hard trouble right now, there is hope for your help. I'm glad to tell you that there is hope for help.

In John 11:1-16, let us see where two sisters went for help in **OVERCOMING TROUBLE.**

> *1 Now a certain man was sick, named Lazarus, of Bethany, the town of Mary and her sister Martha.*
>
> *2 (It was that Mary which anointed the Lord with ointment, and wiped his feet with her hair, whose brother Lazarus was sick.)*
>
> *3 Therefore his sisters sent unto him, saying, Lord, behold, he whom thou lovest is sick.*

4 When Jesus heard that, he said, This sickness is not unto death, but for the glory of God, that the Son of God might be glorified thereby.

5 Now Jesus loved Martha, and her sister, and Lazarus.

6 When he had heard therefore that he was sick, he abode two days still in the same place where he was.

7 Then after that saith he to his disciples, Let us go into Judaea again.

8 His disciples say unto him, Master, the Jews of late sought to stone thee; and goest thou thither again?

9 Jesus answered, Are there not twelve hours in the day? If any man walk in the day, he stumbleth not, because he seeth the light of this world.

10 But if a man walk in the night, he stumbleth, because there is no light in him.

11 These things said he: and after that he saith unto them, Our friend Lazarus sleepeth; but I go, that I may awake him out of sleep.

12 Then said his disciples, Lord, if he sleep, he shall do well.

13 Howbeit Jesus spake of his death: but they thought that he had spoken of taking of rest in sleep.

14 Then said Jesus unto them plainly, Lazarus is dead.

15 And I am glad for your sakes that I was not there, to the intent ye may believe; nevertheless let us go unto him.

16 Then said Thomas, which is called Didymus, unto his fellow disciples, Let us also go, that we may die with him.

From our text, I gather several **COUNSELS** which should help you and me in overcoming our troubles.

The first Counsel: **Send For Help.**

Here in this home of Mary and Martha, a very serious problem arose. Trouble overshadowed that home because their brother was sick, very sick. It came right close to them. And Lazarus was close to our Lord because they said, "He whom thou lovest is sick."

Here was a need, a very deep need. They were passing through great trouble. How would they overcome that trouble? Well, one counsel is, send for help when the need arises. So they sent for help. They sent a call to Jesus. They said, "He whom thou lovest is sick."

Jesus was a loving friend. In fact, the Bible tells us that Jesus loved Mary and Martha and Lazarus. So they sent for help. They sent to the right place for help. They sent to One who really cares.

Do you bear your trouble alone? Like these sisters, you, too, can send for help. Believe me, Jesus will respond to your need as well. You can say, "Lord, he whom thou lovest is in trouble," and Jesus will pay attention to your need.

A second Counsel: **Consider The Opposition.**

So Jesus, after He had waited several days, said, "Let us go into Judea again." But the disciples immediately warned Him about the opposition, "Master, the Jews of late sought to stone thee; and goest thou thither again?" Your life is at stake, Master. And Jesus said, just watch how you walk. If you walk in the daytime, you will not stumble. If you walk in the nighttime, you cannot see, and you will stumble because you have no light in you.

What I want you to see is that Jesus considered the opposition, yet His response was, "Let us go." Later, He said to them, "Our friend Lazarus sleepeth; but I go, that I may awake him out of sleep." The disciples thought He was talking about rest and sleep. But He said, "Lazarus is dead. I am going to help these sisters." Jesus considered the opposition and, with determination, said, "I am going to help them."

My friend, take this counsel in overcoming trouble: look at the opposition and then go forward. That's the way Jesus did. He went forward in spite of the opposition and what it might mean.

A third Counsel: **Face The Danger.**

When the disciples thought that Jesus referred to Lazarus' rest and sleep, He said plainly to them, "Lazarus is dead." But He said, "Your faith is going to grow; I am glad for your sakes that I was not there, to the intent ye may believe." Here Jesus stated the stark reality: Lazarus is dead, but I am going so that your faith may grow.

Then I hear Thomas say to his fellow disciples, "Let us also go, that we may die with him." This is a kind of resignation. A resignation that meant that they were going to go along with Jesus no matter what the danger might be. My friend, take this counsel in overcoming your trouble: face the danger with resignation and go on through with it.

These counsels will help you overcome troubles: first, send for help; second, consider the opposition; third, face the danger. These counsels are most helpful when you know Jesus Christ as your personal helper. He is the One to send for, and He is the One who will help you.

Chapter Fifty-Two

Testing The Heart

Whenever you go to the doctor for an examination, he most likely will check your heart. He will test your heart. He will listen, and he will check your pulse. I want to talk to you about **TESTING THE HEART** in another way.

We all have certain standards by which we measure or test the propositions we hear or the articles we buy. We make certain tests, and we want to be sure that what we buy is of good quality.

We must also make certain tests to determine the realities we have to deal with. The inner part of our being must also undergo some of these testings. That's why I'm talking about testing the heart. The conditions in life sometimes form those testings.

From John 11:17-27, we read of an experience of two sisters' hearts that were tested.

> *17 Then when Jesus came, he found that he had lain in the grave four days already.*
>
> *18 Now Bethany was nigh unto Jerusalem, about fifteen furlongs off:*
>
> *19 And many of the Jews came to Martha and Mary, to comfort them concerning their brother.*
>
> *20 Then Martha, as soon as she heard that Jesus was*

coming, went and met him: but Mary sat still in the house.

21 Then said Martha unto Jesus, Lord, if thou hadst been here, my brother had not died.

22 But I know, that even now, whatsoever thou wilt ask of God, God will give it thee.

23 Jesus saith unto her, Thy brother shall rise again.

24 Martha saith unto him, I know that he shall rise again in the resurrection at the last day.

25 Jesus said unto her, I am the resurrection, and the life: he that believeth in me, though he were dead, yet shall he live:

26 And whosoever liveth and believeth in me shall never die. Believest thou this?

27 She saith unto him, Yea, Lord: I believe that thou art the Christ, the Son of God, which should come into the world.

From Martha's experience, I discover certain **APPROACHES** to the testing of the heart.

The first Approach: **The Limitation Of Friends.**

The neighbors came. This text told us the neighbors came to comfort Mary and Martha. It was what you might call a community of comfort. What could these people do? The brother was dead. So all they could do was try to sympathize. I'm sure the sisters appreciated this, but it didn't restore the brother or help a great deal in lifting their sorrow. Here was a real test of heart, to be able to endure this trial. At the same time, these friends tried their best to comfort.

Then Martha heard that Jesus was coming, and she quickly went out to meet Him. But Mary sat still in the house. Mary mourned alone. But Martha quickly went to meet Jesus, the comforter, the real comforter.

Here the heart was being tested by the limitation of the friends. All of us likely have had similar experiences. We have appreciated everything our friends could do. But the real test of the heart meant that we, in some way, could not actually receive all the comfort that our community of friends offered to us. It can go only so far, and that's as far as a comfort of friends can go.

There's a second Approach: **The Stimulation Of Hope.**

Martha made a very strong statement when she met Jesus. She said, "Lord, if thou hadst been here, my brother had not died." Evidently, Martha believed if Jesus had been there, He would have done something so that their brother would not have died. She expressed this ray of hope. She made this statement of trust. Then she went on to say, "But I know, that even now, whatsoever thou wilt ask of God, God will give it thee."

That is a really outstanding statement of trust. Jesus said to her, "Thy brother shall rise again." Here was that stimulation of hope. Here was Jesus firing up in Martha's heart a ray of hope. She expressed herself like this, "I know that he shall rise again in the resurrection at the last day." But Jesus meant something more than that. He was helping Martha to build her hope.

The stimulation of hope is an approach to the test of the heart. Yes, "Thy brother shall rise again," Jesus said to Martha. And that was indeed a ray of hope.

The third Approach: **The Formulation Of Faith.**

Jesus said, "I am the resurrection, and the life: he that believeth in me, though he were dead, yet shall he live: And whosoever liveth and believeth in me shall never die. Believest thou this?"

I'm asking you the same question that Jesus asked Martha. Do you believe this? Jesus, in this statement, is saying much, much more than many people attribute to Him. He is more than a prophet. He is more than a good teacher. He said, "I am the resurrection, and the life." Now weigh His words carefully, dear friend, because you should follow in the same way that Martha followed with an affirmation of faith. She said, "Yea, Lord: I believe that thou art the Christ, the Son of God, who should come into the world."

Martha formulated her faith in a marvelous statement. I believe the heart is tested by this formulation of faith.

By these approaches, your heart is tested, too: by the limitation of friends, who can only go so far; by the stimulation of hope from the Lord Jesus; and by the formulation of your faith, I believe.

I urge you to follow Martha in these approaches and believe that Jesus is the Son of God who should come into the world.

Chapter Fifty-Three

Thinking Right

God made us in such a way that we can think. He made us with the power of thought. There is a right way to think, and there is a wrong way to think. No one can come to the right conclusion if he starts wrong. Just as you cannot reach your home unless you go in the right direction, so you cannot come to the right conclusion if you are thinking wrong.

Since wrong thinking will lead to wrong conclusions, we need very definitely to make an effort to think right. Our Scripture text, John 11:28-37, will help us get our bearings for **THINKING RIGHT**. This is the story of Mary and Martha, their brother Lazarus, and Jesus.

28 And when she had so said, she went her way, and called Mary her sister secretly, saying, The Master is come, and calleth for thee.

29 As soon as she heard that, she arose quickly, and came unto him.

30 Now Jesus was not yet come into the town, but was in that place where Martha met him.

31 The Jews then which were with her in the house, and comforted her, when they saw Mary, that she rose up hastily and went out, followed her, saying, She goeth unto the grave to weep there.

32 Then when Mary was come where Jesus was, and saw him, she fell down at his feet, saying unto him, Lord, if thou hadst been here, my brother had not died.

33 When Jesus therefore saw her weeping, and the Jews also weeping which came with her, he groaned in the spirit, and was troubled,

34 And said, Where have ye laid him? They said unto him, Lord, come and see.

35 Jesus wept.

36 Then said the Jews, Behold how he loved him!

37 And some of them said, Could not this man, which opened the eyes of the blind, have caused that even this man should not have died?

From our Scripture text, I bring together several **WARNINGS** to help you in thinking right.

The first Warning: **Avoid Judging Action.**

"The Master is come, and calleth for thee," Martha said to her sister, Mary. It was a secret message, and there was an immediate response. Mary arose up quickly to go and find Jesus.

The Jews misunderstood her action. When they saw Mary get up quickly to leave, they concluded that she was going to the grave, Lazarus' grave, to weep there. But, you see, they were wrong in their judgment. In judging Mary's actions, they drew the wrong conclusion because they did not know everything that was going on in her heart and mind or in the heart and mind of Martha. Because they did not know everything that was going on, they judged the action of Mary and came to the wrong conclusion.

This warning is good for us, too, because actions do not always tell us everything that is happening. Actions are an indicator. But we should avoid judging actions without all the related facts in mind.

The second Warning: **Avoid Judging Absence.**

When Mary came to Jesus, like her sister, she said, "Lord, if thou hadst been here, my brother had not died." There may be several ways to interpret Mary's word. It appears to be something of a veiled charge against Jesus for not coming when they first sent for Him. It may also be an expression of complete and utter confidence that had Jesus been there, then Lazarus would not have died.

I think Mary may be expressing something of a judgment on Jesus for not coming when they first sent for Him. In this statement is implied that Jesus' absence was the result of neglect. Had He come when they sent for Him, then their trouble would not have been so acute. She was judging the absence of Jesus.

I want you to see that Jesus did respond when He saw all this and heard the sister's remark. The Bible says He groaned in His Spirit. And then He asked, "Where have ye laid him?" He was not without deep-felt love for these sisters. But they were judging Him because He was not there, for He had been absent.

So this warning is good for us too. Absence does not necessarily mean neglect. It may be for reasons that we do not understand. These sisters needed to learn that the Lord's absence was not because He did not care.

The third Warning: **Avoid Judging Attitude.**

We have probably the shortest verse in all the Bible right here: two words, "Jesus wept." Mary was weeping. The Jews were weeping. And Jesus' heart yearned for His friends. So Jesus wept.

Now the bystanders who were looking on rendered a judgment. They said, "Behold, how he loved him!" It was in the same general community where Jesus had healed the man who was born blind recorded in John the 9th chapter. That's why they responded the way they did, "Could not this man, which opened the eyes of the blind, have caused that even this man should not have died?"

In other words, they were judging Jesus' attitude. He should have done something which He did not do. If He could have opened the eyes of the blind man, which indeed He did, He should have been able to do something for these sisters before their brother died.

This warning also is good for us because they judged the attitude of Jesus incorrectly. You see, attitude cannot be seen, and sometimes we make wrong judgments because we do not understand the attitude of the person we judge.

I lay before you these warnings so you might think right: avoid judging actions just by what you see; avoid judging absence when someone may not be there; avoid judging attitude for you cannot see everything in the heart.

Our deepest problem is we often lack the facts to think right. So I urge you, be absolutely sincere in your search.

Chapter Fifty-Four

Meeting The Impossible

Perhaps you, too, have had to meet a situation where the way through seemed almost impossible. I have had such situations. But I have learned from the counsel of another; every problem carries the clue to its own solution. It's like a stonemason. He knows how to strike the chisel to shape the stone. Just by looking at the stone, he knows where to strike it. That is learned by experience, and accomplished stonemasons do very nice work.

It is so in life. We must seek the solution by a careful examination of the problem. Jesus was especially able to meet the seemingly impossible. So I want to share with you from John 11:38-46. We will see Jesus **MEETING THE SEEMINGLY IMPOSSIBLE.**

> *38 Jesus therefore again groaning in himself cometh to the grave. It was a cave, and a stone lay upon it.*
>
> *39 Jesus said, Take ye away the stone. Martha, the sister of him that was dead, saith unto him, Lord, by this time he stinketh: for he hath been dead four days.*
>
> *40 Jesus saith unto her, Said I not unto thee, that, if thou wouldest believe, thou shouldest see the glory of God?*
>
> *41 Then they took away the stone from the place where the dead was laid. And Jesus lifted up his eyes, and said, Father, I thank thee that thou hast heard me.*

42 And I knew that thou hearest me always: but because of the people which stand by I said it, that they may believe that thou hast sent me.

43 And when he thus had spoken, he cried with a loud voice, Lazarus, come forth.

44 And he that was dead came forth, bound hand and foot with grave clothes: and his face was bound about with a napkin. Jesus saith unto them, Loose him, and let him go.

45 Then many of the Jews which came to Mary, and had seen the things which Jesus did, believed on him.

46 But some of them went their ways to the Pharisees, and told them what things Jesus had done.

Here Jesus meets the seemingly impossible. As He does, the several **STAGES** of His plan emerge. These will strengthen our faith in Him.

The first Stage: **The Command.**

"Take away the stone." Preparation had to be made for what was about to follow. Therefore Jesus gave the command to take the stone away. But Martha's objection opened her heart wide, didn't it? She said, "Lord, by this time he stinketh." The decomposition, the rotting of his body had already begun. It's too late, Lord.

Oh, how many times we object to the clear command of the Lord because we think we know better. So it was with Martha. But Jesus had given the command to take away the stone, and He replied to her, "If thou wouldest believe, thou shouldest see the glory of God!" Don't argue. Obey, believe, do what the Lord says. When the command is clear, do not falter. Proceed.

The second Stage: **The Commitment.**

So they removed the stone. The preparation was made. Not all of it because Jesus made a commitment unto God in His prayer. Notice carefully in the Scripture just how Jesus prayed. Read the prayer again, "Father, I thank thee that thou hast heard me. And I knew that thou hearest me always: but because of the people which stand by I said it, that they may believe that thou hast sent me."

Right there, my friend, is a real commitment on the part of Jesus. His prayer, first of all, contains thanksgiving to God. Then it contains trust because Jesus said, "I knew that thou doest hear me always." Then there is a petition for the people. I'm saying this so that the people standing around here may believe.

Oh yes, I am impressed with this second stage of meeting the seemingly impossible. Because, you see, Jesus committed it all to the Father so that when He was facing this seemingly impossible situation, He made it clear that He was trusting in God.

The third Stage: **The Call.**

Now notice the preparation: the stone has been taken away; the prayer has been offered; the commitment has been made. Then the call came to Lazarus, the dead man. The Bible tells us that Jesus called with a loud voice saying, "Lazarus, come forth." And the dead man came forth. What else could He do? The Creator had called him forth. Because the Creator had called him forth, he responded. And he came, bound with grave clothes, hand and foot, with a handkerchief about his face. He came like they had placed him there. Come he must because the Creator had called him.

Then to the people, Jesus said, "Loose him, and let him go." The result of this was that many believed on Him.

The call came to Lazarus, the dead man. The command to untie him came to those who stood by. But many believed when they saw what Jesus had done. Jesus, the Son of God, met the seemingly impossible with great power, even overcoming death.

We can trust Him today, as well. These stages tell us He can do as He wills: the command, "Take away the stone;" the commitment, "Father, I thank thee;" the call, "Lazarus, come forth."

Complete trust in Jesus will help you meet what seems impossible. I am not suggesting that Jesus will raise the dead for you. But, He is able to see you through what appears totally impossible. I urge you to trust Him.

Chapter Fifty-Five

Facing The Facts

God wants us to rejoice in Him. One of the writers of the Psalms urged us to praise the Lord like this: "Let all the people praise thee, O God, let all the people praise thee. Oh let the nations be glad and sing for joy." Psalm 67:3,4a

Do you know that kind of joy? God intends for you to be joyful. But that is possible only when you know Him as a personal God, your personal God. That is one of the basic facts of life.

It is right that we demand to have the facts in hand. We must be careful not to call facts mere rumors and not to call mere rumors the facts. When we have brought the facts, we must then face them with honesty and not try to avoid them.

It is also important that we go to the right source in the search for the facts. Especially this is true for the facts about Jesus Christ. John 11:47-57 gives some insights about **FACING THE FACTS**.

47 Then gathered the chief priests and the Pharisees a council, and said, What do we? For this man doeth many miracles.

48 If we let him thus alone, all men will believe on him: and the Romans shall come and take away both our place and nation.

49 And one of them, named Caiaphas, being the high

priest that same year, said unto them, Ye know nothing at all,

50 Nor consider that it is expedient for us, that one man should die for the people, and that the whole nation perish not.

51 And this spake he not of himself: but being high priest that year, he prophesied that Jesus should die for that nation;

52 And not for that nation only, but that also he should gather together in one the children of God that were scattered abroad.

53 Then from that day forth they took counsel together for to put him to death.

54 Jesus therefore walked no more openly among the Jews; but went thence unto a country near to the wilderness, into a city called Ephraim, and there continued with his disciples.

55 And the Jews' passover was nigh at hand: and many went out of the country up to Jerusalem before the passover, to purify themselves.

56 Then sought they for Jesus, and spake among themselves, as they stood in the temple, What think ye, that he will not come to the feast?

57 Now both the chief priests and the Pharisees had given a commandment, that, if any man knew where he were, he should shew it, that they might take him.

Jesus of Nazareth is a different person. As we face the facts of His life, we must analyze with care these several **CONSIDERATIONS.**

The first Consideration: **The Evidence Of His Miracles.**

Consider the evidence of His miracles. When the leaders gathered together in that council, they consented to the fact that He did perform miracles. Now these were not His friends. No, these were His opponents. They admitted that Jesus did many miracles. Indeed, they were greatly concerned about it because they said, "If we let things go, all men will believe on Him, and He will have a great following, and then the Romans will come and destroy us."

Now take it from those who lived when He did. They said, "He performs many miracles." Someone has counted them in the Gospel record and found recorded that thirty-eight specific miracles were performed by Jesus. He did many miracles, and you must consider the evidence of His miracles.

A second Consideration: **The Purpose Of His Mission.**

Jesus was not merely a worker of miracles. Even Caiaphas, the high priest, understood that. No, he really didn't understand it, but he spoke it. We are told in this text that Caiaphas, being high priest that year, prophesied. He spoke more than he knew when he said, "It is expedient for us that one man should die for the people, and that the whole nation perish not."

He was expressing in these words a great Biblical truth already stated by Isaiah the prophet in the 53rd chapter of his book: one would be sacrificed for the people. The prophecy that Caiaphas, the high priest, spoke unknowingly predicted that Jesus should die.

Our Scripture text says that not only would one die for that nation, "but also that He would gather together in one all the children of God who are scattered abroad." I am really thankful for that, my dear friend, because that includes you and me.

Now consider the purpose of His mission. He came for that express reason. Not merely as a worker of miracles, but that He would die for the nation and for all who are the people of God scattered abroad.

Now take it from this high priest, Caiaphas. He predicted that one man should die for the nation.

There's a third Consideration: **The Restraint Of His Movements.**

When Jesus understood this He retired to a remote place. We are told that He withdrew to the wilderness into a city called Ephraim. There He taught His disciples. Away from all the rest so that He would not be distressed or disturbed.

I get the impression that Jesus has a sense of timing. So He operated that way. His movements were restrained so that the outcome would be exactly what the Heavenly Father had determined.

Now, when the others came to the Passover early, in order to purify themselves for the Passover, they talked among themselves and said, "Will he come to the feast?" He was the subject of their conversation. The Pharisees had told them that anyone who knew His whereabouts should reveal Him so they could take Him.

But Jesus understood this, and He walked and directed His movements in such a manner that He wasn't taken before the time. Take it from the situation. He knew what was coming.

In facing the facts of Jesus' life, you must consider the evidence of His miracles; those who lived then admitted His miracles. You must consider the purpose of His mission; the high priest prophesied it. You must consider the restraint of His movements; Jesus knew what was coming.

These are compelling considerations. Now the decision is up to you. Believe on Him as some did when He lived.

Studies from John 12

Chapter Fifty-Six

Jesus And True Love

The word love is difficult to define. We don't really know how to express ourselves with respect to love. Let me try.

Love is the response of the heart. Love grows by the association of the object of love with the lover: the closeness of the lover and the object. We do not need to try to think out love, that is, to analyze it scientifically or technically, because it is an emotion, an expression and response of the heart more than of the mind.

However, to be proper, love needs control and direction. Because we are made in the image of God, our first and basic expression of love should be directed toward God. Even though we cannot see Him, we need to direct our first and basic love toward God. Then we need to direct our love toward our families and neighbors.

You know, Jesus said it once like this, "The first and great commandment is, Thou shalt love the Lord Thy God with all thy heart, soul, mind and strength. And the second is like unto it, Thou shalt love thy neighbor as thyself." (Matthew 22:37-38)

The Bible further counsels us in these words, "We love Him because He first loved us." That means that true love is a sharing experience.

I am going to talk to you about **JESUS AND TRUE LOVE** from John 12:1-11.

1 Then Jesus six days before the passover came to Bethany, where Lazarus was which had been dead, whom he raised from the dead.

2 There they made him a supper, and Martha served: but Lazarus was one of them that sat at the table with him.

3 Then took Mary a pound of ointment of spikenard, very costly, and anointed the feet of Jesus, and wiped his feet with her hair: and the house was filled with the odour of the ointment.

4 Then saith one of his disciples, Judas Iscariot, Simon's son, which should betray him,

5 Why was not this ointment sold for three hundred pence, and given to the poor?

6 This he said, not that he cared for the poor; but because he was a thief, and had the bag, and bare what was put therein.

7 Then said Jesus, Let her alone; against the day of my burying hath she kept this.

8 For the poor always ye have with you; but me ye have not always.

9 Much people of the Jews therefore knew that he was there: and they came not for Jesus' sake only, but that they might see Lazarus also, whom he had raised from the dead.

10 But the chief priests consulted that they might put Lazarus also to death;

11 Because that by reason of him many of the Jews went away, and believed on Jesus.

This experience provides us with several **INSIGHTS** into the nature of true love. Let's think about them.

The first Insight: **Love Expresses Devotion.**

Take a look at Mary's gift. It was very costly, we are told. It was precious ointment: a pound of ointment of spikenard very costly.

We do not know how expensive this ointment was, but some Bible students have suggested it may well have been that Mary spent all her life time saving to get this precious ointment.

Then she brought it and poured it on Jesus' feet. This act of Mary was an act of deep love. She expressed her devotion to Jesus by bringing this very expensive ointment and anointing His feet with it, and wiping them with her hair. Love, true love, expresses devotion.

The second Insight: **Love Endures Suffering.**

Notice Judas' reaction. He looked at what Mary did and considered it a terrible waste. He said, "Why was not this sold and the money given to the poor." He scorned Mary. He ridiculed her. He thought she lacked good judgment.

We are told further why Judas said what he did. It was not that he cared for the poor, but he was greedy. He was a thief. He liked the feel of money in his hands. He wanted more money. So he heaped suffering onto Mary.

In my words, he was saying she should have known better than waste all this money on this ointment. Mary's love endured that kind of suffering.

The third Insight: **Love Enjoys Approval.**

Did you notice how Jesus responded to Judas? He rebuked him, we might say. He said, "Let her alone. For the day of my burial she has kept this."

Jesus understood Mary's motive. Judas did not. But Jesus understood why she came and why she had spent her lifesaving. He understood, and He approved her in it.

Then He gave Judas a bit of council, "You have the poor always with you; but me you do not have always."

I learn another lesson from this: whatever you are going to do for the Lord, you should do now. Some of these other things can wait, but not what you do for Jesus. Jesus approved Mary's act of love. So Mary's love enjoyed Jesus' approval.

The forth Insight: **Love Encourages Belief.**

Many Jews came to the house of Mary, Martha, and Lazarus.

They came not so much to see Jesus but to see Lazarus, whom the Lord had raised from the dead. Because of this miracle of Lazarus, they came.

Let us also notice that Mary's love encouraged them to believe. Her expression of devotion surely must have had an influence on those who came and left believing.

When they saw Lazarus, when they saw Mary, they were convinced. Mary's love encouraged them to believe.

Jesus and true love should arouse you and me to consider our attitudes. Mary's love expressed devotion, endured ridicule, enjoyed approval, and encouraged belief.

Let me tell you, friend, Jesus is worthy of your true love.

Chapter Fifty-Seven

Jesus Is King

Rulers of countries claim their authority. They believe they have the right to rule. And they do, but only under the sovereign rule of Almighty God. The Bible explains through the Prophet Daniel that God sets up and puts down whom He wills in the kingdoms of men.

Many students of the Bible examine the life of Jesus and see only His works in the miracles He performed or His teachings in the words that He spoke. There is more, much more, to Jesus of Nazareth than His works or His words. In the purpose of God, Jesus came as a King, the King of Israel.

In Matthew's Gospel, we read that when the wise men came from the East in search of Him, they asked Herod, the king in Jerusalem, "Where is He that is born King of the Jews?" Were you to take the time to research it, you would find that His birth has all the qualities for His kingship.

Several times during His teaching career, the crowds would have supported any claim He might have made for the crown. On one occasion, at least, they were about to crown Him, but He refused it.

In John 12:12-19, we have an experience that is quite the opposite. On this occasion, Jesus accepted the applause of the crowd.

12 On the next day much people that were come to the feast, when they heard that Jesus was coming to

Jerusalem,

13 Took branches of palm trees, and went forth to meet him, and cried, Hosanna: Blessed is the King of Israel that cometh in the name of the Lord.

14 And Jesus, when he had found a young ass, sat thereon; as it is written,

15 Fear not, daughter of Sion: behold, thy King cometh, sitting on an ass's colt.

16 These things understood not his disciples at the first: but when Jesus was glorified, then remembered they that these things were written of him, and that they had done these things unto him.

17 The people therefore that was with him when he called Lazarus out of his grave, and raised him from the dead, bare record.

18 For this cause the people also met him, for that they heard that he had done this miracle.

19 The Pharisees therefore said among themselves, Perceive ye how ye prevail nothing? Behold, the world is gone after him.

From these verses I can establish the **AFFIRMATIONS** that **JESUS IS KING.**

The first Affirmation: **By The Procession Of The People.**

Our Scripture informs us that the people, when they heard that Jesus was coming, prepared a procession. They went out to meet Him, waving branches of palm trees. What is the significance of branches of palm trees? Branches of palm trees always signified victory. Earthly rulers, warriors, generals, when they came back from a victorious campaign, marched into town bearing palm branches. Palm branches in this procession meant victory.

Then there was a proclamation the people used. They cried, "Hosanna! Blessed is the King of Israel that cometh in the name of the Lord." The word Hosanna means "Save now!" It was a word of exaltation, a word of praise to Jesus. They cried, "Blessed is the King of Israel," and added, "who comes in the name of the Lord."

So by the procession of the people, we have the affirmation established, He is King. But there is more.

The second Affirmation: **By The Prediction Of The Prophet.**

There's a quotation here from the Prophet Zechariah. He predicted this exact event six centuries before Christ. Jesus found a young donkey and sat upon it, fulfilling the prediction of the Prophet, which reads, "Fear not, daughter of Zion: behold, thy King cometh, sitting on an ass's colt."

By the prediction of the Prophet, we establish the affirmation that He is King. What the Prophet predicted, Jesus did.

There was also the witness of the disciples. They did not understand what they were doing until it was all over. After Jesus was crucified and rose from the dead, then they remembered that they had done these things to Him.

Jesus came to fulfill all that the prophets spoke about Him. That's really wonderful! Jesus is King by the prediction of the Prophet.

The third Affirmation: **By The Proof Of The Pharisees.**

The people who welcomed Him to the Holy City bore witness. They believed on Him. The miracle of raising Lazarus from the dead assured them that here is the King of Israel.

The opposition admitted there wasn't much they could do. They said among themselves, "You see, the world has gone after Him."

Yes, even today, many people follow Jesus. They are recognizing Him, all that He claimed to be and all that was ascribed to Him. Even these of the opposition acknowledge that He is more than just a man among them. Yes, Jesus is King.

These affirmations have never been set aside. The people acclaimed Him the King of Israel. The Prophet predicted Him to be the King of Israel, referring to the daughter of Zion. The Pharisees admitted Him to be King when they said, "The whole world is gone after him."

Now, my friend, what do you do about Him? Those who lived when He lived on earth said He is King. Do you?

Chapter Fifty-Eight

Jesus—The One For All

Because we live in this world of people, our lives are influenced by others. By that, I mean changed or directed. In some areas, those changes come in ways we do not understand, and at times we do not even know we are being affected. Later we learn how a friend helped us be a better person. It may take months for us to understand what happened or how it happened.

It may also be that someone we have never known or met may influence our lives by the way other people have been changed by knowing that person. Every week by radio I can talk to people in many lands. Hopefully, our time together helps them become better followers of Christ.

Above what we can do to help each other, there is One who can influence all of us as we come to know Him. We can say He has influenced more people than anyone else.

Do you say, "No, I have not been affected by him in any way?" But, my friend, Jesus has influenced your life. He has influenced your community. He has influenced your family more than you are aware of. I can show you how this happened from John 12:20-33.

> *20 And there were certain Greeks among them that came up to worship at the feast:*
> *21 The same came therefore to Philip, which was of*

Bethsaida of Galilee, and desired him, saying, Sir, we would see Jesus.

22 Philip cometh and telleth Andrew: and again Andrew and Philip tell Jesus.

23 And Jesus answered them, saying, The hour is come, that the Son of man should be glorified.

24 Verily, verily, I say unto you, Except a corn of wheat fall into the ground and die, it abideth alone: but if it die, it bringeth forth much fruit.

25 He that loveth his life shall lose it; and he that hateth his life in this world shall keep it unto life eternal.

26 If any man serve me, let him follow me; and where I am, there shall also my servant be: if any man serve me, him will my Father honour.

27 Now is my soul troubled; and what shall I say? Father, save me from this hour: but for this cause came I unto this hour.

28 Father, glorify thy name. Then came there a voice from heaven, saying, I have both glorified it, and will glorify it again.

29 The people therefore, that stood by, and heard it, said that it thundered: others said, An angel spoke to him.

30 Jesus answered and said, This voice came not because of me, but for your sakes.

31 Now is the judgment of this world: now shall the prince of this world be cast out.

32 And I, if I be lifted up from the earth, will draw all men unto me.

33 This he said, signifying what death he should die.

In this Scripture, I find those **PARTICULARS** which should lead us to see **JESUS—THE ONE FOR ALL**.

The first Particular: **The Sincere Desire.**

This was expressed by some Greeks who had come to worship.

They had come from a distant land to Jerusalem. Their wish was to see Jesus. How had they learned about Him? Of course, people everywhere were talking about Him. There was continual conversation about this man who moved among them as a teacher, as a miracle worker, and as the King of Israel.

These men from Greece came to Philip and made a request of him, "Sir, we would see Jesus." Philip and Andrew brought these Greeks to Jesus. There was a sincere desire.

That is very important right now in your life. Wouldn't you like to see Jesus? Wouldn't you like to know Him? These Greeks had a sincere desire to see Jesus, and the disciples brought them to Him.

The second Particular: **The Serious Decision.**

As they came to Jesus, He began a brief lecture. He said a grain of wheat, in order to bear more grain, must fall into the ground and die. As long as it does not fall into the ground and die, it simply abides alone.

The secret of multiplication of a grain of wheat is for it to die so the plant can come up and bear fruit. Jesus said that is the way it is in your life and mine. The person who wants to save his life loses it. The person who would lose his life shall save it. In other words, a person must be somewhat like that grain of wheat. A person must give up to gain.

He said, "If any man serve me, he must follow me." He further said, "If you follow me, then you'll be with me where I am, and you'll have the honor of the Father." That is a serious decision. When you look around, you may see all kinds of attractive conditions. As long as you want to hang on to your life, you will abide alone; you will be without fruit. Once you are willing to give up, then you can gain.

It makes a great deal of difference which way you go. The serious decision has to do with following Jesus.

There is a third Particular: **The Specific Designation.**

Jesus prayed and asked the Father to save Him from that hour. He knew He had perfect understanding as to the purpose of His coming and what it was all going to mean. So after He had prayed, He then said, "But for this cause came I unto this hour."

I see what Jesus is telling these Greeks and these disciples. He is going to be like the grain of wheat, fall into the ground, give up to gain. And there is no other way. This is the specific designation.

Jesus went on to say, "When I am lifted up, I will draw all men unto me." From this statement, I gather a very significant point. Jesus is affirming that He is the only One. He is the One for all. His death is the only way. That is very specific. And Jesus points this out to us.

The cross is more than a way to die. Hundreds of people died on crosses during the Roman period. His was the only cross of specific designation. He said, "When I am lifted up from the earth, I will draw all men unto me."

That cross was more than a place to die, I reflect. It was a means to life. For as a grain of wheat fell into the ground, it died to bear fruit. That designation which Jesus made still holds today. It's the same today as when He spoke it.

From this account, we conclude, Jesus is the One for all. No one else will do. I come to you and emphasize and urge you, do what the Greeks did: ask to see Jesus. Then do what Jesus said: decide to follow Him. Then accept what Jesus affirmed: the lifted up way.

How do you accept it? You accept it by believing that when He died on the cross, He died for you. He said, "When I am lifted up, I will draw all men unto me.

Chapter Fifty-Nine

Jesus—The Son Of Man

In wisdom, God made us so we can think. Our minds are wonderful machines. We can store many different ideas in our minds. We are told there is no limit to what we can learn, if we set our will to learn it.

Our minds are so made that we can receive or reject an idea. The reason is our wills control our minds. Because of this fact, we should carefully examine every idea or thought to make sure it is true before we accept it to store in our minds.

When we are examining an idea, we often ask questions in order to evaluate it. That is a good way to make sure of the truth of what we are considering.

I want to discuss **JESUS—THE SON OF MAN.** People in Jesus' day often had questions about Him. They knew what Moses had written. They understood the Bible. But their teachers had given them additional teaching, which didn't always correspond with what Jesus was doing or teaching. This raised doubts like men have today. They really many times wanted to know. But those doubts were serious barriers.

John 12:34-43 gives some insights about recognizing Jesus.

34 The people answered him, We have heard out of the law that Christ abideth for ever: and how sayest thou,

The Son of man must be lifted up? Who is this Son of man?

35 Then Jesus said unto them, Yet a little while is the light with you. Walk while ye have the light, lest darkness come upon you: for he that walketh in darkness knoweth not whither he goeth.

36 While ye have light, believe in the light, that ye may be the children of light. These things spake Jesus, and departed, and did hide himself from them.

37 But though he had done so many miracles before them, yet they believed not on him:

38 That the saying of Esaias the prophet might be fulfilled, which he spake, Lord, who hath believed our report? And to whom hath the arm of the Lord been revealed?

39 Therefore they could not believe, because that Esaias said again,

40 He hath blinded their eyes, and hardened their heart; that they should not see with their eyes, nor understand with their heart, and be converted, and I should heal them.

41 These things said Esaias, when he saw his glory, and spake of him.

42 Nevertheless among the chief rulers also many believed on him; but because of the Pharisees they did not confess him, lest they should be put out of the synagogue:

43 For they loved the praise of men more than the praise of God.

From our text, I wish to expose several **BARRIERS** which often keep people from seeing **JESUS—THE SON OF MAN**.

The first Barrier: **The Darkness Of Mind.**

Didn't you hear Jesus say, "Walk while you have the light, because when you are in the darkness, you cannot see"? There's a real danger in the darkness of the mind. It keeps us from seeing the relations of truth. It is very depressing. And it is very confining.

But then Jesus spoke about light. Light comes and shows the way. Jesus urged, "Walk while you have the light." He said, "I am the light of the world. He that followeth me shall not walk in darkness, but shall have the light of life." Where there is light, darkness is dispelled. It is driven away.

But I want you to feel what Jesus was talking about in the darkness of the mind. When men are compassed by their own willful ignorance, the darkness of the mind is most oppressing and most distressing. Jesus calls our attention to that barrier of seeing Jesus as the Son of Man.

Now, my friend, don't let the darkness of your mind keep you from seeing Jesus as He truly is.

The second Barrier: **The Blindness Of The Heart.**

The evidence was clearly there. He had done many miracles. But even though He had done many miracles, they did not believe on Him. The evidence was there. They had seen His miracles. They had heard His teachings. But they refused to believe, and that refusal led to terrible blindness.

The Prophet Isaiah spoke of this as Jesus quoted from Him. He said, "Who hath believed our report? And to whom hath the arm of the Lord been revealed?" It had been revealed. They did see it. They knew that Jesus had performed more miracles than anybody else had. But they refused to believe. That is what I have called blindness of the heart; it is an awful blindness. When there is sight, truth can be perceived. But when there is blindness, truth cannot be perceived.

My dear friend, don't let blindness of the heart keep you away from Jesus. The evidence is there. He performed the miracles. Now, open your eyes and see. Don't let the blindness of the heart keep you from Jesus.

The third Barrier: **The Praise Of Men.**

That pressure is very hard. It comes upon people and moves them to improper action. Just to be well received by those around us is often a very serious barrier. It was so in this case. Many believed, we are told. But they would not confess Him because they loved the praise of men more than they loved the praise of God.

Yes, this is a solid barrier, even today. It will stop you and turn you aside just because you want the acceptance of your neighbors, your friends, people in high places. You too, are not willing to confess Him because you love the praise of men more than the praise of God. Where concern is found, proper action will follow. So I appeal to you, do not let the praise of men keep you from Jesus.

These barriers need not keep you from seeing Jesus as the Son of Man. But they are serious barriers: the darkness of the mind, the blindness of the heart, and the praise of men.

In their place, you can have light so you can see where you are going. You can have sight so you can understand the truth. You can have the joy of knowing that you belong to Jesus. He is the Son of Man. Why not come to Him now?

Chapter Sixty

Jesus—The Sent One

A certain captain in the Roman Army once had a dear servant who was sick. When the Captain heard that Jesus was coming to his town, he sent some of the Jewish leaders to ask Jesus to heal the sick servant. As the Lord came near the house, the Captain sent friends to tell Jesus how he felt completely unworthy that Jesus should come to his house. He said, "For I am also a man set under authority, having under me soldiers, and I say to one, Go, and he goeth; and to another, Come, and he cometh; and to my servant, Do this, and he doeth it" Luke 7:8.

Jesus was surprised at the Captain's words, and He said, "I have not found so great faith, no, not in Israel." You see, the Captain knew what it meant to be sent. He also knew what it meant to issue orders to his men. He expected each one to obey and do what he was told. Anyone who has been sent should do what he has been sent to do.

In the highest order of authority, we see **JESUS—THE SENT ONE**. His birth was not an accident of history. He was the Sent One. He knew He came for a reason. He spoke different times of His hour not being as yet. Then He spoke on other occasions that the hour had come. He spoke of being sent by the Father. From the Biblical record in the Gospels, we must conclude His life was under divine direction. God was directing His life. This becomes evident in the text of this message in the Gospel of John 12:44-50.

44 Jesus cried and said, He that believeth on me, believeth not on me, but on him that sent me.

45 And he that seeth me seeth him that sent me.

46 I am come a light into the world, that whosoever believeth on me should not abide in darkness.

47 And if any man hear my words, and believe not, I judge him not: for I came not to judge the world, but to save the world.

48 He that rejecteth me, and receiveth not my words, hath one that judgeth him: the word that I have spoken, the same shall judge him in the last day.

49 For I have not spoken of myself; but the Father which sent me, he gave me a commandment, what I should say, and what I should speak.

50 And I know that his commandment is life everlasting: whatsoever I speak therefore, even as the Father said unto me, so I speak.

From these words of Jesus, I set forth several basic **STATEMENTS** for an understanding that Jesus is The Sent One.

The first Statement: **There Is The Light Of Faith.**

Some things can not be reasoned out. Some experiences in life are beyond our reason. They must be believed. Jesus said, "He who believes on me does not believe only on me, but he also believes on him who sent me."

We are not asked to abandon our thought. We are only asked to harness it, to bring it into proper focus, so what we believe is what we ought to believe. And there is the light of faith. It is beyond reason. By faith, the Bible says, we understand that the worlds were framed by the Word of God.

Now, we cannot understand this in any other way. There's only one way that we can understand the origin of the universe. By faith we understand that the worlds were framed by the word of God. You see, there is the light of faith.

The light of faith in Jesus is to connect with faith in God. Here then, is a basic statement: there is the light of faith.

One of the great church fathers years ago, by the name of Tertullian, once said, "I believe because it is ridiculous." He was saying, because I cannot reason it out, I will, therefore, accept it by faith. There is the light of faith.

The second Statement: **There Is The Locus Of Judgment.**

Now, every judgment must rest upon some fact. The judge must know the law. He cannot create the law as he goes. He must relate his decision and judgment to existing law, what has been written and what has been practiced. There is the locus of judgment.

It is so in our courts of the land. It is so, also, in the courts of God. Divine judgment also rests upon fact. Jesus said, "It rests upon my words." He said, "I did not come to judge; I came to save the world." At the same time, He said, "The words that I have spoken, they will judge you in the last day."

Surely it is true: His words are saving words. But His words are also judging words. So He said the locus of judgment rests on His words. There is a definite connection between His word and the final day of judgment, my friend. Isn't it wonderful that He has told us beforehand so that we can understand how to prepare for that appearance in the court of God?

Here then, is a basic statement. There is the locus of judgment: His Words.

The third Statement: **There Is The Line Of Authority.**

Many claims have been made for final and divine authority. But there is only one that is absolutely true and sure. It is the claim that Jesus made here. He said, "I have what I have from the Father. I understand his commandment, and his commandment is everlasting life. I am saying what I am saying because he has told me."

You see, there is a direct connection, a direct line of authority. The claim that Jesus made is absolutely correct. He was God in the flesh. He was the Sent One. He did and said what He was to do and say. He came to bring everlasting life. "For God so loved the world that he gave his only begotten Son, that whosoever believeth in him should not perish, but have everlasting life."

There is the line of authority. As God in the flesh, He was the Sent One. He had a direct connection with the Father. He understood what God the Father wanted Him to do. And He did it. Here then is another basic statement: there is the line of authority right to God the Father. Jesus is the Sent One.

You will have a fuller understanding of Jesus as the Sent One by accepting these statements. There is the light of faith; Praise God! There is the locus of judgment; we know His Word beforehand. There is the line of authority right to God the Father. Jesus is the Sent One.

Studies from
John 13

Chapter Sixty-One

Love Symbolized

Many years ago, an Englishman affirmed, "Love is the greatest force in the world." But long before that, the Apostle Paul wrote what has been called the greatest dissertation on love. It is recorded in I Corinthians 13. Paul concluded his dissertation with these words, "And now abide faith, hope, love, these three; but the greatest of these is love."

A listener once wrote to me to tell me he had discovered a whole new body of literature when he read the New Testament. As he read the Gospels, he saw that Jesus is the True Love. The golden text of the Bible is still true, "For God so loved the world that he gave his only begotten Son, that whosoever believeth in him should not perish, but have everlasting life." (John 3:16)

I want to talk to you about **LOVE SYMBOLIZED** from John 13:1-11. This is likely one of the most misunderstood acts of Jesus.

> *1 Now before the feast of the passover, when Jesus knew that his hour was come that he should depart out of this world unto the Father, having loved his own which were in the world, he loved them unto the end.*
>
> *2 And supper being ended, the devil having now put into the heart of Judas Iscariot, Simon's son, to betray him;*
>
> *3 Jesus knowing that the Father had given all things into*

his hands, and that he was come from God, and went to God;

4 He riseth from supper, and laid aside his garments; and took a towel, and girded himself.

5 After that he poureth water into a basin, and began to wash the disciples' feet, and to wipe them with the towel wherewith he was girded.

6 Then cometh he to Simon Peter: and Peter saith unto him, Lord, dost thou wash my feet?

7 Jesus answered and said unto him, What I do thou knowest not now; but thou shalt know hereafter.

8 Peter saith unto him, Thou shalt never wash my feet. Jesus answered him, If I wash thee not, thou hast no part with me.

9 Simon Peter saith unto him, Lord, not my feet only, but also my hands and my head.

10 Jesus saith to him, He that is washed needeth not save to wash his feet, but is clean every whit: and ye are clean, but not all.

11 For he knew who should betray him; therefore said he, Ye are not all clean.

From this text, we shall see the several **SITUATIONS** in which Jesus symbolized love.

The first Situation: **The Occasion.**

It was the feast of the Passover. It was an important feast given to Israel by the Lord when they came out of Egypt in the time of Moses. It commemorated their Exodus from Egypt. It was to be kept perpetually. Actually, the observance of the Passover commemorated the salvation of the firstborn son. In every family that carefully obeyed the instruction, the first-born was delivered from death.

The Passover was observed in Jesus' day. In fact, He first observed the Passover in Jerusalem when He was twelve years of age. We read in the Gospel of Luke that Jesus went with Joseph and Mary and others from Nazareth to Jerusalem to observe the Passover when He was twelve.

Now in John 13, Jesus is observing the Passover for the last time before He was crucified. As the occasion is introduced, John, by the Holy Spirit, states that Jesus loved His own which were in the world, and He loved them unto the end. I want to explain that for you. I noticed in my Greek New Testament that the phrase, to the end, is *eis tetos*. That means to the uttermost, to the end of love, as far as love could go.

So He put water into a basin. It was a ceremonial washing when He would normally, as governor of the Passover, wash His hands. But He began to wash the disciples' feet. The occasion was the celebration of the saving of the firstborn from death in the bondage of Egypt.

Jesus went from one to another of His disciples reclining about the Passover meal, coming last to Peter.

The second Situation: **The Objection.**

Peter made a strong objection. He said, "You are not going to wash my feet." It was a washing procedure, and Jesus was washing the disciples' feet, but Peter objected very strenuously when He came to him.

I think Peter must have been the last of the twelve disciples as Jesus had washed their feet. He very emphatically said, "You are not going to wash my feet." Then Jesus answered, "If I do not wash you, you have no part with me.

Now notice Peter's response. When he understood that the washing was absolutely necessary, then he said, "Not only my feet, but also my hands and my head." Yes, Peter then was very anxious that he should have complete fellowship with Jesus.

The objection was overridden. He had first said you'll never do it. Then he said to do it well, thoroughly, "Wash not only my feet, but also my head and my hands."

The third Situation: **The Orders.**

Here's the third situation. He said, "Once you have been bathed, or cleansed, all you need then is to wash the feet in order to be

273

clean." The symbolism of this, of course, can be taken to the times in which Jesus lived. They had the central bathhouse in the village or the town. To prepare for the Sabbath Day, for example, the Jewish men would go to the bathhouse, and bathe. After they had walked home, they would wash their feet, and then they would be clean. Jesus said, "Once you have been cleansed, then all you need to do is wash the feet."

I want you to notice that Jesus was here symbolizing real cleansing, the cleansing of His love. I just showed you from the first verse that Jesus loved His own unto the uttermost. And Jesus symbolized His love by washing their feet. Even the one who was not clean. He told Peter, "You are clean, but not all," because He knew which one was going to betray Him. So He said, "You are not all clean."

This washing was not to cleanse the feet. It was to symbolize forgiving, cleansing love for them even to the uttermost. His love was enough to take them all in, forgive them all, varied as they were. Even the one who would betray Him, Jesus was willing to cleanse. Now that's what I call surpassing love.

Chapter Sixty-Two

Love Exemplified

Have you ever watched someone working, and it looked so simple and so easy? Every move seemed to count and the material was easily brought together. Then did you ever try to do what your friend was doing and found that when you tried it, it wasn't so easy? Because you did not actually know how. That's the reason. If you had been shown how, it would have been much easier.

Usually, there are instructions for any job that you might undertake. There are certain ways to do certain jobs. It's often much better, though, if you have someone to show you how, more than just looking at instructions or trying to find and figure out your own way.

Now Jesus' love to the disciples was to the uttermost. But to show the disciples what He meant, He washed their feet. He symbolized love. The washing was the symbol of His forgiving, cleansing love freely offered to them all.

Now, let's see how this portion, John 13:12-20, will illustrate for us **LOVE EXEMPLIFIED.**

12 So after he had washed their feet, and had taken his garments, and was set down again, he said unto them, Know ye what I have done to you?

13 Ye call me Master and Lord: and ye say well; for so I am.

14 If I then, your Lord and Master, have washed your feet; ye also ought to wash one another's feet.

15 For I have given you an example, that ye should do as I have done to you.

16 Verily, verily, I say unto you, The servant is not greater than his Lord; neither he that is sent greater than he that sent him.

17 If ye know these things, happy are ye if ye do them.

18 I speak not of you all: I know whom I have chosen: but that the scripture may be fulfilled, He that eateth bread with me hath lifted up his heel against me.

19 Now I tell you before it come, that, when it is come to pass, ye may believe that I am he.

20 Verily, verily, I say unto you, He that receiveth whomsoever I send receiveth me; and he that receiveth me receiveth him that sent me.

We must follow closely the **TEACHINGS** of Jesus to see how love is exemplified.

Jesus gave them: **The Comforting Supposition.**

He said, "Do you know what I have done to you? You call me Master and Lord: and you say well; for so I am." He must have paused, then continued, "Since I am your Lord and Master, and I have washed your feet; you also ought to wash one another's feet."

That's what I call a comforting supposition. You call me Master and Lord, and I have exemplified my love to you. So you are to exemplify your love as I have done to you. I want you to catch the full impact of that word *ought*, as Jesus said it. "You ought also to wash one another's feet. As I have done, so you ought to do."

That is a powerful word, ought. Now don't dilute it, my friend. Don't dodge it! Just take it as Jesus gave it. "You call me Master and Lord: and you say well; for so I am. Since I am your Master and Lord, you ought to wash one another's feet as I have washed yours."

Surpassing love goes beyond what seems to be reasonable. So Jesus washed their feet and exemplified His love.

Jesus then gave them: **The Careful Stipulation.**

He is the model. He said, "As I have done, so you should do." He led the way; He showed them. Now notice carefully the words of Jesus which followed. He said, "The servant is not greater than his master; nor the one who is sent greater than he who sent him."

We ought to know something about that, surely. The master is always the responsible person. When the master gives instruction to the servant, the servant should do what he is asked to do. In some ways, we have much to learn of that these days, don't we? But it is always true, and Jesus said it emphatically.

That's what I call a careful stipulation. The one who follows the instructions of the master is going to be a happy person. He promised, "If you know these things, happy are you if you do them." This teaching is the careful stipulation to exemplify love, His kind of love.

And then Jesus gave them: **The Cutting Specification.**

He tells them of an exception. He said, "I know all of you, and I know that not all of you are with me." "Not all," He said. I wonder how that betrayer must have felt when Jesus began to point him out. He said, "The one who has had his hand on the table to eat bread with me is going to lift up his heel against me." I wonder how he must have felt. I call that a cutting specification.

Then Jesus gave them some hope with a prediction, "Now I tell you before it comes, so that, when it is come to pass, you will know that I am he." I am constantly impressed with the foreknowledge of Jesus, how He was able to understand what was before. We often say that we can understand better when we look back than when we look ahead. So Jesus made the prediction so they would understand clearly that He was the One.

But I want you to notice right at the end of our Scripture text how Jesus put it, "He who receives whomever I send receives me. And he who receives me receives him who sent me." Isn't that beautiful? That unification, that connection, so clearly set forth. But here is the teaching in a cutting specification to exemplify love. Jesus pointed it out beforehand to give hope and assurance.

Love is exemplified by Jesus' comforting supposition, the disciple should be like his lord; the careful stipulation, the servant is not above his lord; and the cutting specification, the betrayer is responsible to his lord. Surely that is surpassing love.

Where do you find yourself in this situation?

Chapter Sixty-Three

Love Petrified

Some substances, when they become cold, become very hard. To become pliable, they must be warmed. Certain precious metals, like gold and silver, have a low melting point compared to steel. We are told that a dead tree under proper conditions will petrify, become like rock. After that, it has no function, no particular use, except a museum piece.

Now, even in our human relations, sometimes love gets cold and hardens. It loses its warmth. Even love toward God can cool off and get somewhat hard. Here in John 13:21-30, we have demonstrated for us what happened when **LOVE PETRIFIED.**

21 When Jesus had thus said, he was troubled in spirit, and testified, and said, verily, verily, I say unto you, that one of you shall betray me.

22 Then the disciples looked one on another, doubting of whom he spake.

23 Now there was leaning on Jesus' bosom one of his disciples, whom Jesus loved.

24 Simon Peter therefore beckoned to him, that he should ask who it should be of whom he spoke.

25 He then lying on Jesus' breast saith unto him, Lord, who is it?

26 Jesus answered, He it is, to whom I shall give a sop, when I have dipped it. And when he had dipped the sop, he gave it to Judas Iscariot, the son of Simon.

27 And after the sop Satan entered into him. Then said Jesus unto him, That thou doest, do quickly.

28 Now no man at the table knew for what intent he spake this unto him.

29 For some of them thought because Judas had the bag, that Jesus had said unto him, Buy those things that we have need of against the feast; or, that he should give something to the poor.

30 He then having received the sop went immediately out: and it was night.

Our Lord gave several **WORDS** which show us how love can be petrified.

Love hardens under: **The Piercing Word.**

I want you to reflect upon what Jesus said, "One of you shall betray me." Can you create the picture in your mind? Can you see Jesus with His twelve disciples; those who had been closest to him; those who had heard all His teachings; those whose feet He had just washed to demonstrate His endless, matchless love? Those were the ones that were gathered with Him now at the table when He said, "One of you shall betray me."

One of you, He said. They had not yet known what that meant. It must have pierced each one of them to the heart, "One of you shall betray me." That is a piercing word; it is a word that cuts to the quick, cuts deep in the heart. That's one word from Jesus to demonstrate how love can petrify.

When the piercing word revealed a betrayer, there had to follow: **The Identifying Word.**

John, who was lying on Jesus' bosom, asked the question, "Who is it, Lord?" Of course they wanted to know. Jesus had made it specific enough that one of them was going to do this awful deed. And John said, "Who is it, Lord? Tell us who it is."

Now watch how Jesus answered. He said, "He it is, to whom I will give the morsel when I have dipped it." I understand from reading the Jewish encyclopedia that the observance of the Passover had in it the dipping of a morsel of bread, then eating it as some symbol of the deliverance from the land of Egypt.

Jesus, as the host of that Passover feast, took this morsel and dipped it, and gave it to Judas Iscariot. Now he was marked out by the identifying word, "He it is to whom I shall give the morsel when I have dipped it."

I don't see any other conclusion to draw but that the love Judas had hardened; it was petrified. Jesus' identifying word brought it into the open when He gave the morsel to Judas Iscariot, Simon's son. That was the identifying word.

What followed was not a happenstance, for Jesus gave: **The Commanding Word.**

We are informed in this text that as soon as Judas had received the morsel, Satan entered into his heart. Then Jesus said, "Whatever you do, do it quickly," do not hesitate; the time has now come for you to act.

This may well have been brooding in Judas' mind. Earlier in John's Gospel, we learn that Judas was the one who said, "Why was not this sold for three hundred pence and given to the poor?" That was when Mary anointed the feet of Jesus with that box of precious ointment. He must have been brooding over this for some time.

Now Jesus said to him, "What you do, do quickly." It was not clear to the others. We would think that they should have now understood what Jesus was predicting, pointing out to them and giving the command that it be accomplished. It was clear to Judas, because the Bible tells us here that he went out immediately. He went out into the darkness of the night.

There is something rather foreboding about that. Here was a man whose love had petrified. When Jesus said, "Do it quickly," Judas went out into the night. The darkness of night surrounded him.

Thus, in this experience of Judas, love petrified. It hardened; it lost its warmth. Now Jesus' words show us how that can be possible:

it was the piercing word, "One of you;" it was the identifying word, "He it is to whom I will give the morsel when I have dipped it;" and it was the commanding word, "Do it quickly."

My friend, love needs to be kept alive. Don't let your love die or petrify. Even in this, Jesus loved him. And He loves you.

Chapter Sixty-Four

Love Clarified

Are you like me? I often wish I knew more. I wish I had more time to study. There is so much to learn, and it seems as though I have so little time to learn it. Some things I know I could have a better knowledge of. Some things I wish I could study deeper and get a fuller grasp on them.

In my relation to the Lord, I always want to know more, don't you? There is only one source of information on that subject, and that's the Bible. I turn to it often, every day, in fact. Mrs. Yoder and I usually read a chapter from the Bible each morning and pray together. The Heralds of Hope staff meet every workday for Bible study and prayer.

In this relation of love, we all need to know more. This calls for much more clarification. We need help to understand better the whole nature of love. In John 13:31-38, there is much help in understanding how Jesus **CLARIFIED LOVE**.

> *31 Therefore, when he was gone out, Jesus said, Now is the Son of man glorified, and God is glorified in him.*
>
> *32 If God be glorified in him, God shall also glorify him in himself, and shall straightway glorify him.*
>
> *33 Little children, yet a little while I am with you. Ye shall seek me: and as I said unto the Jews, Whither I go,*

ye cannot come; so now I say to you.

34 A new commandment I give unto you, That ye love one another; as I have loved you, that ye also love one another.

35 By this shall all men know that ye are my disciples, if ye have love one to another.

36 Simon Peter said unto him, Lord, whither goest thou? Jesus answered him, Whither I go, thou canst not follow me now; but thou shalt follow me afterwards.

37 Peter said unto him, Lord, why cannot I follow thee now? I will lay down my life for thy sake.

38 Jesus answered him, Wilt thou lay down thy life for my sake? verily, verily, I say unto thee, The cock shall not crow, till thou hast denied me thrice.

My friend, with these words, Jesus defined the several **AREAS** where love must be clarified.

The need arises in: **The Area Of Conflict.**

The opening words of this text are these: "Then, when he had left." The reference is to Judas, who had gone to finish his negotiations with the high priest to betray Jesus for thirty pieces of silver. Satan had entered into him, and Judas became a tool of Satan.

On other occasions, Jesus had cast out demons and released the one who was in bondage to that demon or demons. This time Satan took such complete control of Judas that there seemed to be something of a release after he left, because then Jesus said, "Now, the Son of man is glorified. And God will glorify Him very shortly." God will do it.

There is the area of conflict where love must be clarified. You see, it appears as though Jesus was distressed, oppressed, by the fact that Satan had taken over one of His disciples. It was not until he had gone that Jesus could say, "Now is the Son of man glorified."

Then He further said to the disciples, "I am going away, and you cannot come." There was a kind of conflict as well, between where He was going and where the disciples would be. We must somehow respect that difference, "You cannot come." But we must know what the conflict is, and we must keep our love clear. Conflict is one area calling for love to be clarified.

The need is found in: **The Area Of Conformity.**

Jesus said, "I am giving you a new commandment. I want you to love one another as I have loved you." I am quite certain there must have been a difference. Jesus was presenting to them a much higher level of love than they had ever experienced among themselves. He had demonstrated it, exemplified it, and symbolized it when He washed their feet and then said to them, "What I have done to you, you ought to do to each other."

In the light of His actions, He said to them, "A new commandment I am giving you, that you love one another as I have loved you." He then explained the result, that such love would create a new condition. All men would then know they were His disciples because of the love that they had for one another.

I apologize, I confess before God that too many Christian people have not lived up to the ideal that Jesus gave them here. It has been a scandal that professed disciples have not loved each other like Jesus has loved us. Here is the area of conformity, conforming our love to be like His love. Our love needs to be clear. It is really not possible to have this kind of love until one is truly His disciple. That is the area of conformity, to be like Him because we belong to Him.

The proof of that love is expressed in: **The Area Of Commitment.**

Jesus said, "You can't go now." Peter said, "Why not? Where are you going?" Jesus answered, "You can't come now, but you will come later on." And then Peter had a tremendous aspiration. He said, "Why can't I come now? I will lay down my life for thy sake."

Oh, what an aspiration that was for Peter! But Jesus gave Him a sober, solemn revelation: "The cock shall not crow until you have denied me three times." Peter had just said, "I will lay down my life for Thy sake." Jesus responded, "You will? Here's what you really will do; you will deny me three times." Well, Peter had quite an aspiration, but his aspiration evaporated when Jesus told him what he would really be doing.

In the area of commitment, my friend, our love needs to be clear, absolutely clear. Our frailty often breaks out, and we find that we can't do what we would like to. That was Peter's problem in the area of commitment.

Thus, Jesus clarified love in three areas: conflict with the enemy, conformity to the Lord, and commitment to loyalty.

I urge you, my friend, to find such love in Jesus.

Studies from John 14

Chapter Sixty-Five

Faith—The Cure For Fear

We all have some fears. We are told by the doctors that we are born with this emotional response, fear. Then we have also developed some fears. Some are good fears, and some are not good. The good fears protect us from accidents. The not-so-good fears prevent us from enjoying life. Many of our fears are without foundation. Often we are afraid of what will happen, which never happens.

One of our most basic fears is stated in the question, "What will happen to me when I die?" That is a good fear, a fear you ought to listen to. I am glad to tell you that fear can be cured. Jesus has a word for us about such fear in John 14:1-6.

> *1 Let not your heart be troubled: ye believe in God, believe also in me.*
>
> *2 In my Father's house are many mansions: if it were not so, I would have told you. I go to prepare a place for you.*
>
> *3 And if I go and prepare a place for you, I will come again, and receive you unto myself; that where I am there ye may be also.*
>
> *4 And whither I go ye know, and the way ye know.*
>
> *5 Thomas saith unto him, Lord, we know not whither thou goest; and how can we know the way?*

6 Jesus saith unto him, I am the way, the truth, and the life: no man cometh unto the Father, but by me.

Yes, faith can cure fear. In this text, Jesus defined the several **QUALITIES** of **FAITH—THE CURE FOR FEAR.**

The first Quality: **The Reality Of Faith.**

Faith is a common reality to all of us. We all have faith, faith in something or somebody. It is a part of our person; we are made with the capability of believing. The Apostle Paul, when writing to the Romans, said, "God hath given to every man a measure of faith."

So faith is a fact. This reality is a part of our being. The important thing about it is that it needs direction. Just any kind of faith will not be the kind that can cure fear. Faith needs direction. And it is a common reality to all of us.

There must be then a certain reality. I am sure you will agree with me there is a Supreme Being. We all know this to be a fact, a reality. What we need to accept further is the fact of the True God. I don't know what kind of god you worship. Some of my listeners write to me and ask, "Who is God? How can I know Him?"

I want to point out to you that faith needs direction and that a certain reality must come through to us. We must accept the fact of the True God.

Now, even though you may not know very much about God, I want to insist, my friend, that you must accept this fact; the reality of the True God. This is the first quality of faith to help you cure fear: the reality of faith.

But, beyond the fact of the true God, there is a companion reality which is Jesus Christ. The words from John 14:1-6 are the words of Jesus. Here He said, "You believe in God, believe also in me." We also need this fact: the reality of Jesus. My friend, that must be according to the Bible. You may have your thought or idea about Jesus, but if that does not agree with what the Bible says, it is of little value to you.

Very often, right at this point, we divide. We come to the parting of the way. The reality of faith, my friend, must take in a belief in God and a belief in Jesus to cure the fear of death. That reality can be experienced by believing these words of Jesus.

The second Quality: **The Durability Of Faith.**

I note that Jesus referred to God's dwelling place. Perhaps that sounds strange to you, but I want to make sure you understand that God is more than an idea. Some have argued for this. But Jesus speaks of God as having a dwelling place. He calls it "My Father's house." There is a sense in which God can be localized; that is, He has a dwelling place.

The Bible, in other places, refers to heaven being God's throne and the earth His footstool. Please don't take this only in a symbolic or poetic sense. Jesus referred to His Father's house having many mansions. That means, God is in a place, an eternal place.

Then there is the declared promise of Jesus, "I go to prepare a place for you." That is His purpose to do for us. How precious this is to us! How wonderful to know an enduring faith in this declared promise of Jesus! He said, "I am going to prepare a place for you, and then I will come again and receive you unto myself."

The promise includes the desired presence of Jesus, because He said, "Where I am, there ye may be also." What a precious, precious promise that is to us. This kind of faith can cure your fear of that serious question, "Where shall I go when I die?"

The third Quality: **The Personality of Faith.**

This is the most effective Quality of faith.

Here we are getting right down there where it will indeed serve as the cure for fear. There is the sureness of the way, for Jesus said, "You know where I'm going, and you know the way." That tells me, friend, that we are to follow Him. We cannot find our way. The only way we can know where we are going is when we are following Jesus.

But Thomas, one of His disciples, responded, "Lord, we know not where you are going and how can we know the way?" Ah yes, Thomas expressed much of my thought, my thought before I came really to know Jesus. Perhaps Thomas expressed your thought, too.

How can we know the way? Now listen, and you will get the security that Jesus gives us by the personality of faith. He answered

Thomas, "I am the way, the truth, and the life: no man cometh unto the Father, but by me." There you have faith clothed in a person. That's why I have called it the personality of faith.

The affirmation of Jesus is, "I am the way, the truth, and the life." Nothing is more needed than this focus of faith on Jesus. He is the way to the Father's house. Because He is one with the eternal Word, He is truth. We have real life only when we receive Jesus as our Saviour and Lord. To cure fear, we need the personality of faith in Jesus.

Faith cures fear when it knows these qualities: reality, durability, and personality. Does your faith have these qualities?

Chapter Sixty-Six

How To Experience God

Many long for God. But where can He be found? Is God real or is He only an idea—perhaps even an escape idea?

I'm glad to tell you God is real. We can see the facts about God all around us. The Apostle Paul writing to the Romans, said, "For the invisible things of him from the creation of the world are clearly seen, being understood by the things that are made, even his eternal power and Godhead, so that they are without excuse:" Romans 1:20.

God has not left Himself without evidence of the fact that He is real, so much so that the Apostle argued that the invisible things are understood by the things that one can see.

Now, let's talk about **HOW TO EXPERIENCE GOD.** When God created the first man, Adam, the Bible tells us that He breathed into his nostrils the breath of life, and Adam became a living soul.

The Bible further tells us that when God created Adam, He created him in His image and likeness. That means that the first man, Adam, was fit for fellowship with God. That means something else too. It means that every child of Adam has been born with the capacity to fellowship with God. That is why every person has a longing for God. Even those people who claim to be atheists, by the very fact that they deny God, admit His existence. Every effort to get rid of the idea of God is proof that, that person thinks God must, after all, be. He is there. He must be there, or there would be no need to get rid of Him.

That restlessness can be changed to an experience with God. A great African Bishop of the church many years ago made this statement, "Our souls are restless until they find their rest in Thee," speaking of the true God.

From the words of Jesus in John 14:7-12, we can learn how to experience God.

> 7 *If ye had known me, ye should have known my Father also: and from henceforth ye know him, and have seen him.*
>
> 8 *Philip saith unto him, Lord, shew us the Father, and it sufficeth us.*
>
> 9 *Jesus saith unto him, Have I been so long time with you, and yet hast thou not known me, Philip? he that hath seen me hath seen the Father; and how sayest thou then, Show us the Father?*
>
> 10 *Believest thou not that I am in the Father, and the Father in me? the words that I speak unto you I speak not of myself: but the Father that dwelleth in me, he doeth the works.*
>
> 11 *Believe me that I am in the Father, and the Father in me: or else believe me for the very works' sake.*
>
> 12 *Verily, verily, I say unto you, He that believeth on me, the works that I do shall he do also; and greater works than these shall he do; because I go unto my Father.*

When we really desire to experience God, we must accept the **CERTAINTIES** which are set forth in this text.

We must first accept as Certain: **The Universal Search.**

Jesus made an affirmation when He said, "If ye had known me, ye should have known my Father." Here is a direct route from Jesus to God. He made it positively clear that that is the route you must take if you want to experience God. Philip raised the question, the problem all of us face, when he said, "Lord, show us the Father, and it will satisfy us." The very fact that Philip would make this statement proves there is what I have called a God-echo in the soul of every man. Because you and I are like Philip, we would like so much to see God. If somehow He would only make His appearance.

I remember reading when Moses was up on the mountain with God, he had the same problem. He said to the Lord, "Show me thy face." But God said, "No, you cannot see my face."

There is that certainty of the universal search. It proves that there is a God-echo in the soul of every man. Don't you agree, the real search is to experience God?

Then we must accept as Certain: **The Unusual Statement.**

Jesus, first of all, established a condition as He replied to Philip in these words, "Have I been so long time with you, and you have not known me, Philip?" Philip had overlooked the evidence. It was right there. He was associated with the evidence. It should have been clear to him. So Jesus wondered why Philip had not been able to understand this. Jesus was there. Philip had seen Him. Then Jesus said clearly, "He that hath seen me hath seen the Father." That must have been a rather severe rebuke to Philip.

Jesus further instructed Philip, "You must recognize, Philip, that I am in the Father and the Father is in me." This brings me to the truth that belief goes beyond mere flesh. Philip saw a man in the flesh. He should have been able to see beyond that and see God in the flesh.

Jesus went on to say, "The works that I do and the words that I speak are the works and words of the Father who dwells in me." Yes, there is another certainty here: God-unity is a necessary fact.

Now, this idea is very difficult to come by just in your mind. But Jesus made it clear to Philip, the way to experience God is to accept the unusual statement that Jesus made of the unity between Him and God.

Finally, we accept as Certain: **The Unqualified Situation.**

Jesus placed the foundation for this certainty in these words: "Believe me that I am in the Father and the Father in me." If that is more than you can do, He went on to say, "believe me for the very works' sake."

My friend, to experience God, there is no escape from believing in Jesus. This is the unqualified situation. Many people would like to sidestep this. But you can't. If you want to experience God, then here is what Jesus said must be, "Believe me that I am in the Father, and the Father in me."

The realization of this unqualified situation becomes clearer as we listen when Jesus also said, "He that believeth on me, the works that I do shall he do also; and greater works than these shall he do; because I go unto my Father." There is a God-connection here, a beautiful God-connection.

One who believes in Jesus will be doing the same kind of works that He did and even go beyond the works that He did. Well, right now, I am talking with you in a way that Jesus could not do when He was here on earth. I am coming to you by way of the radio, and you are listening. Praise God! We are having fellowship together in the words of God, the words of Jesus. Jesus said, "He that believes on me will do greater works than I do because I go to my Father."

To experience God, you must realize there is that God-echo in the soul; there is that God-unity between Father and Son; there is that God-connection between God and us.

There is a longing in the human soul for God! To experience Him, you must consent to these certainties: the universal search, the unusual statement, the unqualified situation. These are certainties which are appropriated by faith. Take your step of faith now. Reach out and receive them. Know what that God-echo means in your soul, what that God-unity means between Father and Son, and what that God-connection can mean between God and you.

Chapter Sixty-Seven

Personal Possibilities In Prayer

Have you wished you could make contact with God? Have you ever felt deserted by all your friends? Have you ever wished for help, and there seemed to be no one who could or would help you?

King David knew what it was to need help. Once, he wrote these words, "The sorrows of death compassed me, And the pains of hell gat hold upon me: I found trouble and sorrow. Then called I upon the name of the LORD; O LORD, I beseech thee, deliver my soul." Psalm 116:3, 4. And David found help.

Do you know that help for you is as close as a prayer? We all have times of distress. We often need help. Where we go for help is very, very important. Jesus understood what our needs would be.

The disciples were expressing sorrow because Jesus told them He was going away. They were quite distressed because they were sure they would lose Him. Never again would they be able to make contact with Him. They were wrong, for Jesus showed them a new way. It was the way of prayer. In this way, they could have immediate contact with Him. Listen to the words of Jesus from John 14:13-15.

> *13 And whatsoever ye shall ask in my name, that will I do, that the Father may be glorified in the Son.*
>
> *14 If ye shall ask any thing in my name, I will do it.*
>
> *15 If ye love me, keep my commandments.*

Here the Lord Jesus lays down certain necessary **DIRECTIVES** by which we may reach the highest **PERSONAL POSSIBILITIES IN PRAYER**. This holds great opportunities and challenges for you and me.

Jesus said we must: **Connect With God.**

Notice the invitation in verse 13, "Whatever you ask." This is a large invitation. Please notice that Jesus did not say, whatever you demand. He said, "Whatever you ask." Asking assumes humility. This is very important if we are to reach the possibilities of prayer. The asking can be anytime, immediately, right now, without any delay—whatever and whenever you wish to ask.

Notice the connection as Jesus said, "Whatever you ask in my name." Our names do not really count very much in heaven. Our names are useless. We are sinners. We need first of all to come to the Saviour, then we can ask in His name. No name but His name. Be very sure that you catch that in the words of Jesus. We don't go any other route. We have no other name that we can use in prayer to get through to God. Jesus said, "Whatever you ask in my name." It makes no difference how holy anyone else may have been; nobody's name can take the place of Jesus' name in this directive He gave us.

There is an object or goal in making contact with God: His glory. Jesus said that He would answer the prayer in His name that the Father may be glorified. The glory of God is the object of prayer. So when you connect with God, be sure that you pray for His glory.

I learned once of a lovely home high in the mountains in Europe where needy people could find help. It was built especially to care for missionaries and Christian workers. Some were broken in spirit ,and some broken in body. The testimony reported many wonderful answers to prayer because they prayed for the glory of God. When they prayed for the healing of the broken spirit or the broken body, they would simply ask the Lord to do what would be for His highest glory. Many of them were wonderfully healed.

"Whatever you ask in my name," Jesus said, "that I will do that the Father may be glorified in the Son." So connect with God, my friend, for your possibilities in prayer.

Then Jesus said we must: **Accept The Limit.**

There is a restriction in verse 14, "If you ask anything in my name." We found that phrase in verse 13, too, "in my name." Let us think about that again. When Jesus prayed to God before He was crucified, He prayed, "Not my will, but thine be done." I wonder whether this phrase, "in my name," may not reflect something of that same attitude. When we ask according to our needs, we must do so in the name of Jesus. That means that we will submit ourselves to whatever He knows is best.

I learned when I studied verse 14 that there is a condition attached to the asking, "If you shall ask anything." Our dependence on the Lord is expressed in that way. We do not order God around. We do not issue commands. We make requests. We ask the Lord in His name. Then we get the answers to our prayers.

This directive means that in order to do business with God in the name of Jesus, our requests must be in harmony with His will. Be sure you understand this; accept the limit.

Jesus also said we must: **Reflect His Love.**

Again there is a condition expressed, "If you love me." The word love used in verse 15 is the word for divine love, called in Greek, *Agape*. It's that love that does not really require response to be exercised. The expression of this kind of love simply pours itself out.

Jesus is here really saying, "If you keep on loving me," as though the act was already in progress. The evidence of that love will be keeping His commandments. It will be love in action: the action of obedience. Listen, my friend, don't pray what you don't do. Obedience to the commandments of Jesus expresses our love, reflects His love ,and relates to prayer.

These directives carefully followed will bring you great possibilities in prayer: first, connect with God; second, accept the limit; third, reflect Jesus' love.

We all need the help of meaningful prayer. Here are great possibilities for you in your personal prayer life. What does prayer mean to you? I challenge you to operate on these directives so you will achieve real possibilities in personal prayer.

Chapter Sixty-Eight

Deliverance From Doubt

Do you have questions about God? Have you been searching for answers, and for some reason, you are not able to find those answers? I know many people struggle with unanswered questions about God until they begin to doubt the truth. Doubt is a tool of the devil. He used it successfully in his deception in the Garden of Eden. It has tormented men in every age. It is the exact opposite of trust and faith. Doubt is destroying not only to our inner peace, but also to our thought patterns and physical welfare.

To struggle with unanswered questions is not wrong if they are honest questions. It is no sign of great intelligence to ask unanswerable questions. It is a sign of greater intelligence to find answers. Unanswered questions need not nurture doubt, and when they do, it does not mean that you cannot be delivered.

John 14:16-26 provides **DELIVERANCE FROM DOUBT.**

16 And I will pray the Father, and he shall give you another Comforter, that he may abide with you for ever;

17 Even the Spirit of truth; whom the world cannot receive, because it seeth him not, neither knoweth him: but ye know him; for he dwelleth with you, and shall be in you.

18 I will not leave you comfortless: I will come to you.

19 Yet a little while, and the world seeth me no more; but ye see me: because I live, ye shall live also.

20 At that day ye shall know that I am in my Father, and ye in me, and I in you.

21 He that hath my commandments, and keepeth them, he it is that loveth me: and he that loveth me shall be loved of my Father, and I will love him, and will manifest myself to him.

22 Judas saith unto him, not Iscariot, Lord, how is it that thou wilt manifest thy self unto us, and not unto the world?

23 Jesus answered and said unto him, If a man love me, he will keep my words: and my Father will love him, and we will come unto him, and make our abode with him.

24 He that loveth me not keepeth not my sayings: and the word which ye hear is not mine, but the Father's which sent me.

25 These things have I spoken unto you, being yet present with you.

26 But the Comforter, which is the Holy Ghost, whom the Father will send in my name, he shall teach you all things, and bring all things to your remembrance, whatsoever I have said unto you.

In our text, Jesus tells us by what **MEANS** we can be delivered from doubt. Praise the Lord! You do not need to be whipped or tormented by doubt, because Jesus gives us the means by which we can be delivered from doubt.

The first Means: **By The Abiding Presence Of The Spirit.**

Observe that the Spirit comes from the Father and that He is going to be present with us forever! He is the Spirit of truth. How we search without finding! But when the Spirit of truth comes and abides with us, then we no longer need to search for truth because He ministers the truth to us. He is the Spirit of truth because He comes from the Father.

Notice that Jesus says He is going to send another Comforter. The Father is going to give us another Comforter. The word comforter has a great meaning in it. It means one who is called alongside, like an attorney or advocate. In one Scripture text, Jesus is called our Comforter or Advocate. We have an Advocate with the Father, Jesus Christ. So Jesus is our Advocate with the Father, and the Spirit of truth is our Advocate from the Father.

This, of course, is only true for believers. This is a fact that only believers can claim. The Spirit comes along side of those who believe in Jesus, to be that divine abiding presence. Yes, He comes to abide. He comes to live. He lives with us and in us: very real but not visible. This need not trouble us because we work daily with elements that we cannot see. Here is the Holy Spirit, the Spirit of truth, whom we can experience even though we cannot touch or feel Him with our normal sense of touch.

I point out to you the first sure means by which you can be delivered from doubt: through the abiding presence of the Spirit.

The second Means: **By The Assuring Promise Of Jesus.**

Oh, this blesses my heart, my friend, because Jesus said, "Because I live, you shall live also." Here before His crucifixion, He was anticipating the resurrection. He knew that the grave would not be able to hold Him, so He assured the disciples and us with this precious promise that because He lives, we also will live. This should surely help you overcome any doubt.

Then I noticed also the very beautiful union that Jesus talked about, a union with us, and not only with us but with the Father. He said, "I am in the Father, and you are in me, and I am in you." I will very frankly tell you, I don't understand all this. But I'm going to accept what Jesus said, and I'm going to believe that He knew what He was talking about. I am going to claim the promise that Jesus made that He is in the Father, and I am in Him, and He is in me. You can claim that promise too, by faith.

In addition, He is going to manifest Himself to us, not to the world. Judas asked, "Why not to the world?" Jesus answered, "If a man love me, he will keep my words: and then my Father will love him, and we will come unto him, and make our dwelling place with him." The world does not love and so cannot receive.

So we now have the Father, the Son, and the Spirit living with us. Jesus said the Spirit would dwell with us. Then when we walk in His commandments and do those things that He has asked us to do, He and the Father will come also and live with us. They will be at home with us.

So here then is the second certain means by which you can be delivered from doubt. You can be delivered from your doubt by the assuring promise of Jesus.

And the third Means: **By The Exciting Possibility Of Learning.**

Jesus said, "My words are not mine, but they are the Father's, who sent me." This is very clear: the authority of Jesus goes back to God the Father.

He commented again about the Comforter coming. The Father is going to send Him. We will be receiving the gift of the Holy Spirit. Now watch very carefully what this means to us. I discovered that the word spirit in the first part of our Bible, called the Old Testament, is the Hebrew word, *ruach*. It is first used in Genesis 1:3 when the *Ruach Elohim*, the Spirit of God, brooded upon the face of the deep in the creation of the world.

The New Testament word is *pneuma*. Both of these words are, in essence non-material; that means we cannot feel and touch them. But the gift of the Spirit of God is our exciting possibility. He has a teaching position. Jesus said, "He shall teach you all things, and bring all things to your remembrance, whatever I have said unto you." What an exciting possibility of learning! The Holy Spirit is going to teach us the things we ought to know.

I want you to notice that Jesus said, "Whatever I have said unto you." Some people, I'm sorry, claim to have such a special relationship with the Holy Spirit that they don't need to give attention to the Bible. That is wrong. When Jesus said, "The things I have said unto you," He meant the Spirit would teach us by the Word.

So here, then, is the third means by which you can be delivered from doubt, by the exciting possibility of learning. The Holy Spirit shall be the teacher.

By these means, we can be delivered from doubt: by the abiding presence of the Spirit, the assuring promise of Jesus, and the exciting possibility of learning. I urge you to use these means which Jesus has given and meet your need to be delivered from doubt.

Chapter Sixty-Nine

True Peace

I have observed that the longing for peace is expressed today in many ways. Some people act as though the only way to get peace is to fight. Does that not seem to you to be a contradiction? It does to me. The Prophet Isaiah, 700 years before Christ, wrote these words, "Thou wilt keep him in perfect peace, whose mind is stayed on thee, because he trusteth in thee," Isaiah 26:3.

In another place in the prophecy of Isaiah, he called Jesus the Prince of Peace. He said that a son would be given, a child would be born, and one of His names would be the Prince of Peace.

Because there has been very little peace since Jesus was born in Bethlehem, some people think He is not really the Prince of Peace, but He is. This meditation is about true peace as Jesus spoke about it.

Men of our world are searching for peace, peace between nations. That is a worthy goal, a worthy objective. I hope they will be able to establish peace.

But even more important than peace between nations is the peace in your heart. Could it be that inner peace must come first before outer peace can be attained? Well, I know this one thing: if you have inner peace, peace in your heart, at least your problem is solved. I'm sure that is what you want.

To see what Jesus had to say about true peace, we are going to

John 14:27-31.

> *27 Peace I leave with you, my peace I give unto you: not as the world giveth, give I unto you. Let not your heart be troubled, neither let it be afraid.*
>
> *28 Ye have heard how I said unto you, I go away, and come again unto you. If ye love me, ye would rejoice, because I said, I go unto the Father: for my Father is greater than I.*
>
> *29 And now I have told you before it come to pass, that, when it is come to pass, ye might believe.*
>
> *30 Hereafter I will not talk much with you: for the prince of this world cometh, and hath nothing in me.*
>
> *31 But that the world may know that I love the Father; and as the Father gave me commandment, even so I do. Arise, let us go hence.*

From these words of Jesus, I aim to set forth those certain **ELEMENTS** found in **TRUE PEACE**.

There is so much in the world today that is not really true peace. What Jesus spoke about is true peace. I want to show you what those elements are so that you can find true peace.

The first element of peace: **The Special Type.**

His peace is a special type. There is more than one type of peace. There is the world peace. Jesus spoke about that. But that is fleeting. It is gone tomorrow. World peace does not last. His peace lasts. His peace is secure.

His peace is a gift. He said He is going to give us His peace. That means there is no point in struggling for it. There is no point in working so hard for it because His is a special type of peace that He gives. It is inner peace. He said, "Let not your heart be troubled, neither let it be afraid." Inner peace is not affected much by the outside. It is in the heart, right there, where all the thought processes are. Peace of the heart the world knows nothing about.

I know that you are craving that inner peace. Maybe you don't know where to find it or how to get it. Just open your heart and receive it. It is the type of peace that Jesus gives. It is the kind of peace that is secure, that lasts, that doesn't pass away like world peace does. He said He is going to give it. So you have to receive it because it is a special type of peace.

The second element of peace: **The Special Time.**

The peace He spoke about depended upon His departure. He said, "I am going away." What did He mean? He meant that He was going to die on the cross. He was not going to be with them anymore like He had been those three and one half years of His ministry. By His departure, He meant the death on the cross and more.

He was referring to His return to His Father in heaven when He would leave earth for His heavenly glory. That time was very important because He said to them, "And now I have told you before it come to pass that when it is come to pass, you might believe."

For us, this is now a reality. He has been crucified, He did rise from the dead, and He has ascended to glory. So the time for us to receive the peace is now. But when He was talking to the disciples it was a special time to which He referred. It had to do with His crucifixion and return to God.

He said He was going to the Father, and they should really rejoice over that because the Father was greater than He. This special time has come. So now, my friend, you and I can receive that true peace, the type that Jesus spoke about, because the time has come for you and me to receive that peace.

The third element of peace: **The Special Tension.**

He said, "The prince of this world is coming, and has nothing in me."

Here is an important truth. There are two princes: the prince of this world and the Prince of both worlds. Jesus certainly stands over the prince of this world. He is much, much more than the prince of this world. With Jesus, he has no common ground. The prince of this world is the devil, Satan. Jesus and Satan have no agreement.

Jesus emphasized that He had a particular purpose. What He was doing was to show the world God's love. "That the world may know that I love the Father; and as the Father gave me commandment, even so I do," were His words. I see immediately the tension between the prince of this world and Jesus. They have no agreement. They agree on nothing. But Jesus and the Father do agree. Peace only comes through Jesus. Peace does not come by the prince of this world. Remember that, Jesus gives the true peace.

These certain elements of true peace call you and me to faith in Jesus, because His peace is a special type, it has a special time, and creates a special tension. To receive true peace, then, we must believe in Jesus. That's my word to you, my friend. To get true peace in your heart, you must believe in Jesus; then you can receive the gift of true peace from Him.

Studies from John 15

Chapter Seventy

How to Live Right

Everybody has the same problem. The thrust of this message is of universal interest. It is absolutely true: we know there is a right way and there is a wrong way. But the problem is how to find out which is the right way and which is the wrong way, **HOW TO LIVE RIGHT.**

All of us want to do better. We try, but we often fail. New years remind us of the need to amend our ways. Whether in your calendar it is a new year or not, it is good to think about what we have done in the past year and how we can improve in the year to come.

Jesus knew we would have the problem of finding the right way, so He taught us as given in John 15:1-8.

1 I am the true vine, and my Father is the husbandman.

2 Every branch in me that beareth not fruit he taketh away: and every branch that beareth fruit, he purgeth it, that it may bring forth more fruit.

3 Now ye are clean through the word which I have spoken unto you.

4 Abide in me, and I in you. As the branch cannot bear fruit of itself, except it abide in the vine; no more can ye, except ye abide in me.

5 I am the vine, ye are the branches: He that abideth in me, and I in him, the same bringeth forth much fruit: for without me ye can do nothing.

6 If a man abide not in me, he is cast forth as a branch, and is withered; and men gather them, and cast them into the fire, and they are burned.

7 If ye abide in me, and my words abide in you, ye shall ask what ye will, and it shall be done unto you.

8 Herein is my Father glorified, that ye bear much fruit; so shall ye be my disciples.

From these words of Jesus, we can learn how to live right. He presented several **HELPS** that will lead us to a life that is right.

Help number one: **Allow The Father's Pruning.**

Jesus framed the setting, "I am the vine, my Father is the husbandman." In other words, God, the Father, is the caretaker. He looks over the vine and the branches. He inspects and cultivates as the caretaker. "Everyone in me," Jesus explained, "that does not bear fruit he takes away: and everyone that does bear fruit, he prunes it so that it will bring forth much fruit and more fruit."

Pruning is a simple act that God does, for Jesus further explained that we are made clean by the word which He has spoken unto us. The Bible says of itself in Hebrews 4:12 that the word of God is quick, and powerful, sharper than any two-edged sword, dividing the thoughts and intents of a man's heart. No wonder Jesus could say, "You are clean through the word that I have spoken to you."

So one help in living right is to allow the Father's pruning through the Word. He knows very well how that should be done.

Help number two is: **Admit Your Inability.**

Jesus expressed an evident truth when He told His disciples a branch cannot bear fruit unless it is attached or abides in the vine. Anybody who has observed the growth of vines or trees knows that to be true. It is impossible for a branch that is broken off to bear any kind of fruit because the nourishment comes from the vine, not from the branch.

Jesus made the analogy: like the branch must abide in the vine, so we must abide in Him if we are going to bear fruit. There is no fruit without Him. He said, "Without me, you can do nothing." So, there's no room really for self-effort. Admit your own inability. That's a help to live right because it makes you alert and aware of the help He supplies.

A third Help is: **Aspire To Glorify God.**

Jesus stated, "In this is my Father glorified, that you bear much fruit." He spoke of bearing fruit, then more fruit, and finally much fruit, all the result of abiding.

But He also said that if one does not abide in Him, he is taken away like a branch that doesn't bear fruit, and that branch is gathered and thrown into the fire. You see, Jesus is talking here; I'm only telling you what He said, and He said, "If anyone does not abide in me, he is cast forth as a branch and is withered. And men gather them and cast them into the fire." Fruitlessness means the fire.

Abiding in Jesus and doing His commandments means the glory of God; it means receiving. He said, "If you abide in me, and my words abide in you, you shall ask what you will, and it shall be done unto you." That way, the Father is glorified.

Much fruit is to God's glory. So aspire to glorify God. Fix your mind on God. Abide in Him. Admit your own inability and aspire to glorify God. My friend, it will make a difference, a big difference.

I challenge you to accept these three helps which Jesus offered His disciples. They are all important if you are going to live right: allow the Father's pruning; admit your own inability; then aspire to glorify God.

Chapter Seventy-One

More Than Servants

The Lord wants us to be better people. He longs for us to have a higher life, a better life. Man was made in the image of God, for fellowship with God, and for His pleasure. Then came sin bringing suffering and separation from a holy God. So God moved in redemption and sent Jesus to restore us to the Father.

But too many people are satisfied where they are. For some reason, they believe everything is locked in. Some religions claim there is nothing you and I can do. The Christian faith holds out the possibility of rising, of being **MORE THAN SERVANTS.**

The Bible says that to be a Christian will put a totally new outlook in your mind. In John 15:9-17, Jesus explained to His disciples about being more than servants.

> *9 As the Father hath loved me, so have I loved you: continue ye in my love.*
>
> *10 If ye keep my commandments, ye shall abide in my love; even as I have kept my Father's commandments, and abide in his love.*
>
> *11 These things have I spoken unto you, that my joy might remain in you, and that your joy might be full.*
>
> *12 This is my commandment, That ye love one another, as I have loved you.*

13 Greater love hath no man than this, that a man lay down his life for his friends.

14 Ye are my friends, if ye do whatsoever I command you.

15 Henceforth I call you not servants; for the servant knoweth not what his lord doeth: but I have called you friends; for all things that I have heard of my Father I have made known unto you.

16 Ye have not chosen me, but I have chosen you, and ordained you, that ye should go and bring forth fruit, and that your fruit should remain: that whatsoever ye shall ask of the Father in my name, he may give it you.

17 These things I command you, that ye love one another.

Oh yes, more than servants, that's what Jesus said: "You are no longer servants, you are my friends." Jesus' words to the disciples contain some encouraging **STATEMENTS** for us to attain to the level of being more than servants.

Jesus's first statement: **Obedience Brings Love.**

Jesus said, "Continue in my commandments, keep my commandments and then you will abide in my love." Then He suggested how, "That's the way I did; I kept my Father's commandments, and so I am abiding in His love. And if you keep my commandments, you will abide in my love."

So continue in love. It's the Father, it's Jesus, and you. His commandments are a way of life. They get right there on the inside, where attitudes are made. It's the basic heart attitude of following in the commandments of Jesus. He said, "That's the way your joy is going to be full." Joy comes from such obedience. No one can love the loving Saviour without obeying Him.

Jesus, at another time, asked this question, "Why do you call me Lord, Lord, and do not the things that I say?" Ah yes, obedience brings love. He encouraged them, "Continue in my commandments, keep on doing them, and then you will continue to abide or live in my love." So, obedience brings love.

Jesus's second statement: **Love Brings Friendship.**

What is His commandment? He said, "This is my commandment, that you love one another as I have loved you." That is a very high standard. To love one another as Jesus loved us is, I say, a very high standard. He said, "No greater love has anyone than this, that a man would lay down his life for his friends." That is love's greatest act, a self-sacrificing act.

To be a friend of Jesus is to follow Him without any question or argument. If you want to be above a servant, then your friendship must respond to Jesus in unqualified, unquestioning following of what He said. He said, "This is my commandment, that you love one another as I have loved you." That kind of love brings friendship. Listen to Him, "I do not call you servants anymore; I call you friends." I call you friends.

My dear friend, I would like to introduce you to the most wonderful friend there is, Jesus. Love for Him brings friendship.

Jesus's third statement: **Friendship Brings Fellowship.**

A new kind of relation, a very close relationship. Jesus spoke to the twelve, "I don't call you servants anymore because I have shared with you everything my Father has made known to me." Just ponder that, "Everything I have heard from my Father, I have made known unto you."

Then He went on to say, "You have not chosen me, but I have chosen you." That is a most wonderful relationship, to realize that Jesus is so much interested in you that He chose you. Yes, I think we can make that application. I know He's talking to the disciples here, but I believe we can apply that to you and me. Jesus has chosen you.

The question is, have you responded to that choice? Have you found that friendship brings fellowship? That kind of fellowship is very real and close and intimate.

Then there's a new result. He said, "You are going to bear fruit, and your fruit is going to remain because I have chosen you and ordained you and sent you out to bear fruit." My friend, I would like to help you be more than a servant. I want you to be a friend of Jesus.

These statements can help so much: obedience brings love, and love brings friendship, and friendship brings fellowship.

Jesus wants us to be His friends. For that reason He tells us what He did. Do you know Him as your own very intimate friend? To add this new dimension to your life, these statements are highly important. You can be more than a servant, but what have you done about becoming Jesus' friend?

Chapter Seventy-Two

Why Christians Suffer

Do you have any hardships that really bother you? Are they puzzling to you? Are there days when you don't know why things happen as they do? Let me help you. I bring you hope based on God's word, the Bible. I believe the Bible is the only real foundation for hope. In it, we can find the answers to our most puzzling questions. One of those questions is, why do good people suffer? Or **WHY CHRISTIANS SUFFER?**

The problem of suffering is common to mankind. Even people who do not believe in God have sufferings. We all face hardships, difficulties in life. I'm sure it has affected you. Sometimes Christians suffer greatly. I know there are places where that is happening. The conditions are far from favorable, and we sometimes wonder, what can we do? We raise the question, why? And sometimes, we may be inclined to put the blame on God.

My friend, I want to share with you from John 15:18-27 where Jesus takes up this problem: why good people suffer.

> *18 If the world hate you, ye know that it hated me before it hated you.*
>
> *19 If ye were of the world, the world would love his own: but because ye are not of the world, but I have chosen you out of the world, therefore the world hateth you.*

20 Remember the word that I said unto you, The servant is not greater than his lord. If they have persecuted me, they will also persecute you; if they have kept my saying, they will keep yours also.

21 But all these things will they do unto you for my name's sake, because they know not him that sent me.

22 If I had not come and spoken unto them, they had not had sin: but now they have no cloak for their sin.

23 He that hated me hated my Father also.

24 If I had not done among them the works which none other man did, they had not had sin: but now have they both seen and hated both me and my Father.

25 But this cometh to pass, that the word might be fulfilled that is written in their law, they hated me without a cause.

26 But when the Comforter is come, whom I will send unto you from the Father, even the Spirit of truth, which proceeded from the Father, he shall testify of me:

27 And ye also shall bear witness, because ye have been with me from the beginning.

In this text, Jesus gives us answers to the question of suffering by several decisive **INSIGHTS**.

The first insight is: **Suffering Compared.**

Suffering is not new. He suffered before us. He said, "Don't be surprised if you have problems because I have had problems before you have." It is not unusual, He said, to get this kind of response from the world. It is not really avoidable; you can't avoid it. "What they did to me, they will do to you."

So, my friend, this matter of suffering is of long standing. Jesus said it should not be surprising to us if His followers suffer like He suffered. That is what people do not understand; they can't really follow; they don't know why, in some cases, that the sufferings come from others. But they do. So, in some ways, as He suffered, we suffer. He said, "I have chosen you out of the world, therefore the world hates you."

You see, as Christians, we are different from people who do not believe and follow Jesus. It is that way, my dear friend. It is important for us to remember that.

The next insight is: **Suffering Laid Bare.**

He said, in a very straightforward statement, the reason why people inflict suffering on the good is they do not know God. It's a very straightforward statement, but that's what He said, "They do not know Him who sent me." That's why they act like they do. His words had revealed their sin. Instead of changing them, they lashed out against Him.

Now let's put it back there in the setting where Jesus was talking. He came and told people what their problems were, and He told them how to solve those problems by coming to God and really following His words. Jesus' words left them with no covering. He said, "I did a work among them that nobody else ever did. And because I did this work among them, they now have no covering for their sin." Because they had no covering for their sin, they lashed out against Him.

From this statement of Jesus, I must conclude that it still works the same way. I say this very guardedly, my friend, but I believe Jesus is teaching us that persecutors of good are ignorant of God.

The final insight is: **Suffering Shared.**

He says innocence is vindicated. He quotes from the Old Testament and says, "They hated me without a cause." I am sure it is very difficult for people today to accept: to be hated, to suffer without a reason is very oppressive. It hits us, without a cause.

But I want to comfort you because Jesus said, "When the Comforter is come, whom I will send to you from the Father, He shall testify of me, and you also shall bear witness." I like this word from Jesus because the word Comforter is such a blessed truth. When the Spirit of truth has come, He will be right there alongside of us. Church history is full of examples of great suffering by Christians who remained faithful in suffering, for the Holy Spirit held them up and enabled them.

I want to comfort you with these words from Jesus, "The Comforter will come, and He will be right there beside you to sustain you and witness to you so you will be able to witness as well."

These insights do not remove suffering, but they tell us why. Unbelievers do not know God. That is why they inflict suffering. If they knew God, they would not inflict suffering. If you are undergoing suffering, be encouraged. Jesus knows your need, and He wants to help you in that need.

Remember, He suffered before we suffer. And I shall add, He suffers when we suffer. Praise the Lord for this great truth!

Studies from John 16

Chapter Seventy-Three

Think Right

Isn't it wonderful that God has made us so that we can think? Oh, how thankful we should be that we are not like the animals that can't think. They have only one way that they can do anything. They are programmed by nature to do certain things which they cannot change by thinking.

But God has given us the right and ability to think. He has never violated that right and ability. It, therefore, becomes a high privilege to be able to think. And I should add, our thinking may well be like God's thinking. It can be as we think God's thoughts after Him. The Bible tells us that God made us in His image and after His likeness, which includes the ability to think and the power to choose. But then, for us, there is a right way and a wrong way to think. Since God has given us the ability to think, He surely wants us to **THINK RIGHT**, to think the right way.

Jesus was concerned about His disciples and about us. This concern is expressed as He spoke to the disciples in John 16:1-6.

1 These things have I spoken unto you, that ye should not be offended.

2 They shall put you out of the synagogues: yea, the time cometh, that whosoever killeth you will think that he doeth God service.

3 And these things will they do unto you, because they have not known the Father, nor me.

4 But these things have I told you, that when the time shall come, ye may remember that I told you of them. And these things I said not unto you at the beginning, because I was with you.

5 But now I go my way to him that sent me; and none of you asketh me, Whither goest thou?

6 But because I have said these things unto you, sorrow hath filled your heart.

From Jesus' words to His disciples, we should find two **DIRECTIVES** for how we think.

The first Aspect to the Directive: **Of Preparation.**

He said, "I have spoken these things unto you, that you should not be offended." To think right, we need the preparation against offenses. To be offended means to be shocked or to be scandalized, to be greatly distressed, troubled, or hurt. But to know beforehand what is going to happen will be a great help when that time comes. So Jesus gave these words to the disciples to prepare them so that they would not be shocked and would be able to understand better.

There is the preparation against mistreatment, because He said, "They will separate you, they will put you out of their worship places, their synagogues. And, in fact, they will think that when they kill you, they are doing God service."

I have learned through my study of religions that religion is a mighty force. That is why it is so important, my friend, for you to be sure that you are right in the kind of religion that you have. Because Jesus said it could even get to the place that when people kill you, they will think they are doing God service. It surely seems that would be a seriously distorted conclusion, wouldn't it?

Then He said also we need preparation against partial knowledge. When He was commenting about these people who would think they were doing God service when they killed believers, He said, "They do that because they do not know the Father, and they do not know me." That means they have only partial knowledge: not enough knowledge, just some knowledge. They don't know the Father, because the Father would not tell them to take life, you see.

So to think right, we must take seriously this matter of preparation, so we know what is coming, and will not be shocked, but will be able to understand more clearly.

The second Aspect to the Directive: **Of Consolation.**

Jesus said to the disciples that He was telling them these things beforehand so that they could remember them later. They were to remember Jesus' words, and they were to think of the good things that had happened. He said, "I couldn't tell you this in the beginning, because I myself was with you. But since I'm going away, I'm telling you these things so that you will be able to remember them." They could not remember what they had not known.

All of us, I'm sure, have some very precious memories. We like to remember the good things in life. These words from Jesus to the disciples would surely be good things to remember. It would bring consolation to their hearts to remember these words of Jesus.

In addition, there is a consolation in separation because Jesus said, "I am going away. I'm going to the One who sent me and I want this to be a consolation to you. Many of you ask me, "Where are you going?" That's why He was telling the disciples that He was going back to the One who had sent Him.

They also had Jesus' consolation in sorrow because He said sorrow had filled their hearts because He had told them these things. I was trying to imagine how the disciples must have felt when all of this was going on. It must have been a real consolation to them to know that they could have the words of Jesus to think about after He had gone. And so Jesus told them that the sorrow would be only for a short while. They would then be able to rejoice and be glad.

So to think right, read this consolation from Jesus. I believe that thinking right is surely connected with Jesus and our relationship to Him. His Words give us helpful guidance. We should be prepared so we will not be shocked when some of these experiences come. And we can be consoled because we can remember the words of Jesus.

Chapter Seventy-Four

The Comforter

God made us so we can think. He made us with minds, and we can, in a large measure, think like He thinks. Even though we can think, and in some measure, think like God thinks, we will never know everything. Especially not just by thinking.

Because we can not know everything, it is necessary for us to have somebody to help us, somebody to guide us. Now the Lord knew that. God knew our need. So in His plan, He sent a helper whom He called **THE COMFORTER**, somebody who could guide and help us. Jesus told His disciples about that part of God's plan in John 16:7-11.

> *7 Nevertheless I tell you the truth; It is expedient for you that I go away: for if I go not away, the Comforter will not come unto you; but if I depart, I will send him unto you.*
>
> *8 And when he is come, he will reprove the world of sin, and of righteousness, and of judgment:*
>
> *9 Of sin, because they believe not on me;*
>
> *10 Of righteousness, because I go to my Father, and ye see me no more;*
>
> *11 Of judgment, because the prince of this world is judged.*

The Comforter: that is exactly what Jesus called Him in the first verse of this text. Jesus gives us two **CLARIFICATIONS** regarding this Comforter.

The first clarification is: **The Promise Of His Coming.**

The Comforter will work. He will reprove the world of sin. Jesus is speaking to the disciples in one of those last discourses before His leaving them. Jesus said, "For if I go not away, the Comforter will not come to you." It was necessary for Jesus to go back to the One who sent Him, as He earlier had told them, in order for the Comforter to come. He said if He did go back, then He would send the Comforter unto them.

The Comforter is the name of the One who was to come to follow Jesus, to be with the disciples, and to do the work that Jesus had begun.

When Jesus went back to the Father, the Father sent the Comforter just like He promised Jesus He would do. Jesus spoke of the close connection between the Comforter and Him. While we may not understand all that Jesus intended by this statement, we can understand that He said, "The Comforter will come when I go away." That surely is a clarification regarding the Comforter.

The second clarification is: **The Purpose Of His Coming.**

We want to think about this and try to follow just what Jesus said, "When he (that is the Comforter) has come, he will reprove the world of sin, of righteousness, and of judgment."

Let us examine this word reprove. It means He will convict; He will accuse; He will stand in judgment over the world because of sin, of righteousness, and of judgment. Make a careful note of the relation; Jesus is referring to the Comforter's relationship to the world. Jesus always made a difference between the world and the disciples, you see. So, He was saying to the disciples that when the Comforter has come, then He will have a work to do with respect to the world.

What is the purpose of His coming? To convict, accuse the world. There are three particular areas in which the Comforter will work. He will reprove the world of sin, Jesus said.

Now notice in verse 9 why He will do that. He will <u>reprove the world of sin</u> because they do not believe on Jesus. That is so important. Lack of faith in Jesus will bring the accusing of the Comforter to the world and His reproving in the world.

People make up the world, and the Comforter will convict and accuse them because they do not believe on Jesus.

One time Jesus said to those around Him, "You will not come to me that you might have life." They did not come because they did not believe on Jesus. The Comforter is going to reprove and bring an accusation against those people who do not believe in Jesus. Do you believe in Jesus? What do you believe about Him?

He will also <u>accuse the world because of righteousness.</u> "Of righteousness," Jesus said, "because I go to my Father, and you see me no more." What righteousness do you think Jesus had reference to? Certainly not our righteousness, because the Prophet Isaiah seven hundred years before said that our righteousnesses are as filthy rags. So it must be that the Comforter is going to accuse the world of the righteousness of Jesus. That seems to be exactly what He meant when He said, "Because I go to my Father and you see me no more."

Believe me, my friend, every record we can find about the life of Jesus tells us that He lived without sinning. He did not have any sin. He was absolutely righteous. That is the reason why He could go to the Father without anybody ushering Him into His presence. That is not true of us; that is not true of anybody else except Jesus. So, the Comforter is going to accuse the world of righteousness to show how we need help.

Then the third area where He is going to work is to <u>accuse the world of judgment.</u>

The reason is the prince of this world is judged. Who is the prince of the world? The devil, Satan, is the prince of this world. Yes, Jesus said so, and so did the Apostle Paul. Jesus said that the Comforter is going to accuse the people of the world that are not disciples of Jesus. He is going to accuse them of judgment because the prince of this world already stands under the judgment of God. It is not a question of having a trial. The trial has already been held, and Satan is under the judgment of God. That would mean, of course, that anyone who follows Satan would also be under the judgment of God; the decision, the sentence, has already been passed.

Now, you see how important an understanding of the Comforter is for us. Jesus was gracious to give us these two clarifications about the Comforter: the promise that He will come and the purpose of His coming. He came to convict and accuse the world: of sin because they believe not on Jesus; of righteousness, because Jesus is the only righteous one and He has gone to the Father; of judgment, because the prince of this world is judged.

There you have the truth from Jesus about the Comforter. He has come, my friend. Yes, and He is working. He is doing exactly what Jesus said He would do. Has He spoken to you in any way about your sin, about the righteousness of Jesus, about the judgment of the prince of this world?

Chapter Seventy-Five

The Spirit Of Truth

We all know there are two areas of thought, the area of the true and the area of the false. It is not always easy to decide between these two. Sometimes the false may sound, oh, so nearly true. Then sometimes, the true may be mixed with the false. But actually, when the true is mixed with the false, it is not true; it is false. So it is sometimes rather difficult to be able to see the line between the false and the true. For that reason, we all need help to draw the lines.

God is always faithful to fulfill the needs of mankind. We need to know truth to order our lives for His glory. We do not need to grope around to find it. Jesus said He was the truth. He prayed the Father to sanctify the disciples by His Word, which is truth.

Oh, let us praise the Lord that in wisdom He sent **THE SPIRIT OF TRUTH**, as Jesus promised the disciples, in order that we might be able to see that line between the true and the false. John 16:12-15 brings us the words of Jesus talking to His disciples.

> *12 I have yet many things to say unto you, but ye cannot bear them now.*
>
> *13 Howbeit when he, the Spirit of truth, is come, he will guide you into all truth: for he shall not speak of himself; but whatsoever he shall hear, that shall he speak: and he will shew you things to come.*

14 He shall glorify me: for he shall receive of mine, and shall shew it unto you.

15 All things that the Father hath are mine: therefore said I, that he shall take of mine, and shall shew it unto you.

Here Jesus tells us the **RELATIONSHIPS** the Spirit of Truth will have with His disciples. While Jesus spoke these words to the disciples, we follow them. He spoke of the relationships the Spirit of Truth would have with them.

The first relationship is: **He Will Guide Them.**

There was more to tell, more than He could tell them then. He said, "You cannot bear them now." They would need to wait until the final acts of redemption were completed to be able to understand the things that they were to know. He said, "You can't stand it now, but when the Spirit of truth has come, He will guide you." That will help very much! The relationship will be that the Spirit of Truth will guide the disciple.

Now notice He will do more than just guide. He will guide into all truth. We do need help to see the fine line between the true and the false. We will find that the Spirit of Truth will guide the disciples into all truth.

And, He will not speak of Himself, but rather He will speak whatever He hears. That means to me that the Spirit will be a transmitter; that is, He will only tell the disciples what He has heard. He will not be the source of information, but rather He will be a bearer of information. So He will not speak of Himself at all.

The Spirit of truth, Jesus promised to His disciples, will guide them by taking the things of Jesus, the words of Jesus, and showing those words to the disciples. Then He also will show them things yet to come.

Disciples can be sure that the Spirit of truth will come because Jesus promised. He will come, He will guide them, and He will show them things to come.

The second relationship is: **He Will Glorify Jesus.**

How will He glorify Jesus? He will receive from Jesus and will give to the disciples. The disciples' experience after Pentecost was exactly what Jesus said it would be. They received the things from the Spirit and were able to give them to others. Because the Spirit had received them and had given them to the disciples, you see. In that way, He was glorifying Jesus.

He would further show them that everything that Jesus had, came from the Father. Because Jesus told them that, "All things that the Father hath, are mine." Therefore, the Spirit would take the things of Jesus and show them to the disciples. In doing so, He was taking the things of the Father and showing them to the disciples.

Here is a kind of central abiding truth. It is not easy sometimes to understand the relationships between the Father, the Son, and the Spirit. Jesus clarified this for us and pointed out that there is a very close relationship between them.

I know when I speak like this, some people think that I am talking about three Gods. But no, I am talking about the mystery of the person of God. Jesus said the Spirit of truth is going to take the things of the Father, which also belong to the Son, and show them to His disciples.

I must freely say to you that this is not easy to understand. It becomes easier as we believe and accept what Jesus said. We know that Jesus never lied to anyone; God has never lied to anyone. So there is complete unity here in the Father, Son, and Spirit because the Spirit of Truth is going to glorify Jesus by showing the disciples what the Father has.

I am so glad the Bible is the Book for all people everywhere. God means that you and I shall receive help from the experience of the disciples. Jesus' teachings are for us today. That is why God gave us the Bible, and that is the reason He kept it for us until this very day.

These words were spoken not only to the disciples right there with Jesus. But as disciples today, we are followers of Jesus, so this truth comes to us, too. The Spirit guides us into truth and glorifies Jesus to us.

Chapter Seventy-Six

How To Cure Worry

All of us are alike. We wonder what is going to happen tomorrow. We make our plans, but we cannot always carry out our plans. They do not always work. And then, because they do not work, we have a tendency to worry. That is, we get distressed; we are unsure what the end will be. Sometimes we really get quite upset, don't we?

I wish to show you **HOW TO CURE WORRY** from Jesus' teaching to the disciples in John 16:16-27.

> *16 A little while, and ye shall not see me: and again, a little while, and ye shall see me, because I go to the Father.*
>
> *17 Then said some of his disciples among themselves, What is this that he saith unto us, A little while, and ye shall not see me: and again, a little while, and ye shall see me: and, Because I go to the Father?*
>
> *18 They said therefore, What is this that he saith, A little while? we cannot tell what he saith.*
>
> *19 Now Jesus knew that they were desirous to ask him, and said unto them, Do ye inquire among yourselves of that I said, A little while, and ye shall not see me: and again, a little while, and ye shall see me?*
>
> *20 Verily, verily, I say unto you, That ye shall weep and*

lament, but the world shall rejoice: and ye shall be sorrowful, but your sorrow shall be turned into joy.

21 A woman when she is in travail hath sorrow, because her hour is come: but as soon as she is delivered of the child, she remembereth no more the anguish, for joy that a man is born into the world.

22 And ye now therefore have sorrow: but I will see you again, and your heart shall rejoice, and your joy no man taketh from you.

23 And in that day ye shall ask me nothing. Verily, verily, I say unto you, Whatsoever ye shall ask the Father in my name, he will give it you.

24 Hitherto have ye asked nothing in my name: ask, and ye shall receive, that your joy may be full.

25 These things have I spoken unto you in proverbs: but the time cometh, when I shall no more speak unto you in proverbs, but I shall shew you plainly of the Father.

26 At that day ye shall ask in my name: and I say not unto you, that I will pray the Father for you:

27 For the Father himself loveth you, because ye have loved me, and have believed that I came out from God.

In this text, Jesus tells us the real **SECRETS** of how to cure worry. Would you like to know what those secrets are?

These Secrets do not need to be whispered.

The first: **Trust The Promise.**

Jesus said, "I am going to the Father." That was very important. But the disciples got worried. They could not understand what Jesus meant. Because they could not understand what He meant, it gave them much trouble in their hearts. They did not yet know His purpose and work.

Some people are like those disciples. When they can't understand something, they let it trouble them, creating great moments of distress, unrest, worry. They do not trust the promise of Jesus. Jesus made a promise, but they did not believe that promise because they couldn't understand it.

My friend, our failure to understand is no call for worry. Perhaps our worry should rather be when we fail to believe or trust the promise. That should give us cause to worry. So the first secret to cure worry is to trust the promise.

The second Secret is: **Enjoy The Presence.**

Each experience in life must be kept in its place. God desires good for us. He doesn't want us to go through distressing moments. He wants us to have joy, real joy. Jesus used the illustration of a woman giving birth to a child: when the time comes, she has much sorrow because of the pain of delivery; but once the child is born, she forgets about the pain, and she rejoices that her son is born. Oh yes, if you are a mother, you know what Jesus was talking about.

Jesus is surely right; after the moment of sorrow, joy comes. So He told the disciples that sorrow is only passing, only passing because of the situation at the moment. He said, now you are sorrowful, but you will rejoice. When you see me again, your heart will rejoice. I recommend this secret of enjoying the presence of Jesus.

Now quite certainly, you and I do not experience the presence of Jesus like those early disciples did. He is not here with us in bodily form. But by faith, we can experience the presence of Jesus. That is an effective secret to cure worry. I wish I could explain it better for you. But I'll tell you what you can do. You can experience it if you follow on the way with Jesus.

The third Secret is: **Learn To Pray.**

Sometimes I get a request from a listener to send him or her a prayer book. From this counsel of Jesus, it should be clear to us that we don't need a prayer book. What we need is to make our prayers to God the Father in the Name of Jesus.

Friend, you can talk to God, our Father, just like you talk to a neighbor. He can be just as real as that to you. So learn to pray. Jesus said, "You ask in my Name, and the Father knows exactly what your needs are." Be simple, be straightforward. Tell God, the Father, what your needs are, and ask in the Name of Jesus. That is what He said we should do. He said, "I do not say that I am going to pray to the

Father: because the Father loves you because you love me." For that reason, He will answer you, and joy will come when answers come.

So learn to pray. That is a wonderful way to cure worry. Prayer is simply talking to our heavenly Father. Jesus said, when we ask, we make our requests in Jesus' Name: "Whatsoever ye shall ask the Father in my name, he will give you. Hitherto have ye asked nothing in my name:... At that day, ye shall ask in my name."

God desires that we have joys. Jesus used the illustration of a woman to illustrate how joy can come to us. He has made us that way, to have joy. You can cure worry by using these secrets that Jesus gave us: trust the promise, enjoy the presence, and learn to pray.

Chapter Seventy-Seven

Plain Speech

For the disciples, Jesus' words were often above their understanding. They puzzled over them. There are people today who still puzzle over the words of Jesus. They are unsure what they mean.

Well, we all want **PLAIN SPEECH**. We say, make it simple; take it out of the complex and make it simple. That's what I try to do when I come to you each week; I try to make it simple. It is more important to be understood by people than to baffle them.

We learn from the Gospel records that the common people in Jesus' day heard Him gladly, and it is amazing how simple many of His teachings were. Let's see what happens in John 16:28-33, where we have the disciples saying, "He now speaks plainly."

> *28 I came forth from the Father, and am come into the world: again, I leave the world, and go to the Father.*
>
> *29 His disciples said unto him, Lo, now speakest thou plainly, and speakest no proverb.*
>
> *30 Now are we sure that thou knowest all things, and needest not that any man should ask thee: by this we believe that thou camest forth from God.*
>
> *31 Jesus answered them, Do ye now believe?*
>
> *32 Behold, the hour cometh, yea, is now come, that ye*

shall be scattered, every man to his own, and shall leave me alone: and yet I am not alone, because the Father is with me.

33 These things I have spoken unto you, that in me ye might have peace. In the world ye shall have tribulation: but be of good cheer; I have overcome the world.

In this talk, Jesus made several **STATEMENTS** which the disciples could understand. Let's talk about this plain speech.

His first Statement: **"I Leave The World."**

My friend, I have often been impressed how Jesus lived with a sense of purpose. He lived with the end in view. He knew why He was here. He knew where He was going. So, He could say to the disciples, "I came from the Father, and now I go to the Father; I leave the world."

His disciples then seemed to understand, and they confessed their faith in Jesus. They said, "Now we know, now we believe."

The Bible clearly tells us that Jesus, the Son of God, came into the world and went back to heaven. He said here to the disciples, "I leave the world, and I go back to the Father." There is some mystery about this. In some respects, it is difficult, but still, when Jesus made that statement the disciples said, "Now we understand clearly, and we believe that thou art from God."

My friend, I would like to tell you that this is a very important position to come to: to understand what Jesus meant when He said, "I leave the world, and go to the Father," because going back to the Father meant that His work was being finished.

His second Statement: **"I Am Not Alone."**

He said, "You are going to leave me, you are going to run away, you are going to be scattered, you are going to your own homes, but I will not be alone; I am not alone." In distress, many often desert. The records of history show many people who have turned traitor at the most difficult moment. Jesus predicted that the disciples would run away and leave Him. And they did. Yes, they did. But He said God would not leave Him. He said, "I am not alone, because the Father is with me."

God never forsakes the trusting soul. Jesus expressed His assurance that God would not leave Him, even though everybody else would leave Him. That comes to me as a great comfort. I hope it comes to you as a great comfort. This is what I call plain talking. Jesus said, "I am not alone, because the Father is with me."

I would like to say to you, my friend, that you and I can have a similar experience with Jesus. God will not forsake the trusting soul. This can come to us as a great comfort. I hope you understand this plain speech.

His third Statement: **"I Have Overcome The World."**

That's the last sentence in the text which I read. The world is not friendly toward people who believe in God. We all have our oppositions. It seems that there's always somebody to stand in our way, to make it hard for us.

Jesus said to His disciples, "I am going to give you peace. I have spoken these things to you so that you might have peace in me." Then He added, "I have overcome the world." I want to make sure you understand that peace in your heart is a gift from Jesus. He said it is a gift, "I give you peace."

His victory assures us of victory. He said, "I have overcome the world." So we can be of good cheer. The opposition has been put down. We no longer have the force of the opposition because Jesus has overcome the world. We can find great hope in His victory. My friend, I want to make sure that you understand the plain speech of Jesus when He said, "I have overcome the world."

These statements arrest our attention because they tell us Jesus must be more than an ordinary man: He said, "I have overcome the world;" "I am not alone;" "I leave the world." These statements tell us of His purpose, His assurance, and His victory. He can encourage you, but He cannot help you until you believe on Him.

Studies from
John 17

Chapter Seventy-Eight

The Difference In Jesus

There are no two people who are exactly alike. Sometimes we may see someone who reminds us of a friend, but we are all a little different. Yet, we can say Jesus has no one nearly like Him, no. The Bible calls Him the only one of God. That may be a little hard to grasp, to really understand, but the Bible calls Jesus the only one of His kind.

The mystery of God in the flesh cannot be simplified. We must say that is a miracle and miracles, cannot be simplified. But our hope lies in the fact that He is different.

That Jesus is different is well shown in His prayers. In our study of the Gospel of John, we come to one of the prayers Jesus prayed. John 17 is the longest recorded prayer of Jesus. The others we have in the record are quite short, although we know from the Gospels that Jesus sometimes spent whole nights in prayer. On one occasion He fasted for forty days and surely spent much of that time in prayer.

THE DIFFERENCE IN JESUS can be understood from the first part of this revealing prayer in John 17:1-8

1 These words spake Jesus, and lifted up his eyes to heaven, and said, Father, the hour is come; glorify thy Son, that thy Son also may glorify thee:

2 As thou hast given him power over all flesh, that he

should give eternal life to as many as thou hast given him.

3 And this is life eternal, that they might know thee the only true God, and Jesus Christ, whom thou hast sent.

4 I have glorified thee on the earth: I have finished the work which thou gavest me to do.

5 And now, O Father, glorify thou me with thine own self with the glory which I had with thee before the world was.

6 I have manifested thy name unto the men which thou gavest me out of the world: thine they were, and thou gavest them me; and they have kept thy word.

7 Now they have known that all things whatsoever thou hast given me are of thee.

8 For I have given unto them the words which thou gavest me; and they have received them, and have known surely that I came out from thee, and they have believed that thou didst send me.

We are in the prayer room with Jesus. From this part of Jesus' prayer we are shown that He had certain outstanding **POSSESSIONS** which made Him different.

The first Possession is: **His Eternal Life.**

He had received as a gift from the Father the power to give that life to others. "Thou hast given him power over all flesh, that he should give eternal life to as many as thou hast given him." Eternal life, my dear friend, is a gift; it is not earned. There would be no way that you or I could earn eternal life. We do not receive it for wages, for work done. No, Jesus possessed eternal life to give to those whom the Father had given Him, to those whom the Father knew. To them, Jesus gave eternal life. I can add, to them, Jesus now gives eternal life.

Well, what is eternal life? Jesus prayed, "This is eternal life, that they might know thee the only true God, and Jesus Christ, whom thou hast sent." That is eternal life. Now that is not so difficult. No, not when we have the Bible and when I can come to you like I am and explain to you that Jesus gives eternal life because He possessed eternal life, and the Father gave Him the right to give it to those whom God had given Him. Oh, praise the Lord for that!

The next Possession is: **His Eternal Glory.**

Here in His prayer He asked the Father to glorify Him with the same glory that He had before the world was. He said He had finished the work that God gave Him to do. In that, He glorified the Father. His work was assigned to Him. It was outlined beforehand. During His lifetime, He finished that work. Surely that brought glory to God, His Father, to have finished His work exactly like the Father had planned.

So He asked for that pre-world glory. Let me explain. He said, "Glorify me with thy own self with the glory which I had with thee before the world was." Say, that's a wonderful thought, isn't it? Jesus was with the Father before the world was ever made. That shows us that He is eternal; it shows us that He shared the Father's glory.

Jesus possessed the eternal glory, and He was asking the Father to restore to Him that same glory which He had before the world was created.

The final Possession is: **His Eternal Word.**

The Words of Jesus are the Words of God. He prayed, "I gave them the words which thou hast given me; and they have kept thy word." The Word was given to Jesus to give to the disciples, and they kept or observed to do what the Words told them to do.

It is important to note that this is the eternal Word because it comes from the eternal God. You see? To receive the eternal Word from the eternal God is an enlightening experience. Revelation is light; it pierces the darkness; it throws back our ignorance and we come into the light of understanding. So Jesus gave what He had received, and they received it from Him. And the result was, they believed that God had sent Jesus.

It still works that way. Jesus possessed the eternal Word, and when we receive His Word, we receive the Word of God. It will generate or create in us, faith, or belief.

These possessions that Jesus had set Him apart from all others.

No one else can make such claims as He made: to give eternal life, to share eternal glory, or to teach the eternal Word. He invites you to believe on Him, strengthen your faith in Him, and fasten your hope upon Him.

Chapter Seventy-Nine

Jesus's Goals For Disciples

In life, we achieve the most when we set goals for ourselves. It is usually best to set a goal that isn't reached too easily, so we must stretch, as it were, try just a little bit harder to reach that goal. Of course, we need to know our limits so as to do our best, but not to become discouraged when we cannot reach the goal.

In the spiritual life, there are also goals to be achieved. Sometimes other people set goals for us. God has set goals for us. In Romans 3:23, we read, "For all have sinned and come short of the glory of God." God has certain goals for us, and in this prayer of Jesus, I want you to notice some of the goals He set for His disciples.

This is the second of three messages based on the longest recorded prayer of Jesus. Some people call it the high priestly prayer. The other prayers we have on record are all shorter. We do know, though, that Jesus spent whole nights in prayer on different occasions. At the beginning of His ministry, He fasted forty days and forty nights. So Jesus was a person of prayer.

We go again to this sacred prayer room in John 17:9-17. Join me to meditate about **JESUS' GOALS FOR DISCIPLES.**

> *9 I pray for them: I pray not for the world, but for them which thou hast given me; for they are thine.*
>
> *10 And all mine are thine and thine are mine; and I am*

glorified in them.

11 And now I am no more in the world, but these are in the world, and I come to thee. Holy Father, keep through thine own name those whom thou hast given me, that they may be one, as we are.

12 While I was with them in the world, I kept them in thy name: those that thou gavest me I have kept, and none of them is lost, but the son of perdition; that the scripture might be fulfilled.

13 And now come I to thee; and these things I speak in the world, that they might have my joy fulfilled in themselves.

14 I have given them thy word; and the world hath hated them, because they are not of the world, even as I am not of the world.

15 I pray not that thou shouldest take them out of the world, but that thou shouldest keep them from the evil.

16 They are not of the world, even as I am not of the world.

17 Sanctify them through thy truth: thy word is truth.

In this part of Jesus' prayer, He defined those certain **GOALS** for His disciples.

The first is: **The Goal Of Unification.**

Those whom the Father had given to Him were certain ones. He prayed that those who belonged to the Father, the Father had given to Him. There was complete unity between Him and the Father as they shared together.

Notice that Jesus expressed desire for them to be one. In what way? He prayed, "So that they may be one, as we are." This is very important, my friend. It's not just to be one, but to be one like God and Jesus are one, like the Father and the Son are one. That is the goal of unification that Jesus set up for His disciples. They belonged to the Father, and the Father gave them to Jesus, and now Jesus is asking the Father that they may be one as He and God are one.

I have learned that all true believers all over the world have a sense of belonging together. That's what Jesus was talking about. He set forth this goal of unification for His disciples.

The next is: **The Goal Of Identification.**

He prayed, "I have kept them in Thy name." They belonged to Jesus, and Jesus said, "I have kept them in Thy name." This, too, is a very important idea, because the people of God belong together because they are the people of God, and they have this identification.

We don't necessarily wear anything which identifies us, and yet we do. Because we are not of this world, we have the joy of Jesus. He said, "I speak these things in the world, that they might have my joy fulfilled in themselves." So there is that joy of the Lord that is something of a badge of identity.

But then, Jesus said, "They are not of this world, even as I am not of this world." Because they were not of this world, the world hated them. You see, there is a kind of identification, a kind of separation, you might say, that Jesus has set as a goal for His disciples. You can't be both, my friend. You cannot be a disciple of Jesus and a friend of the world. Jesus made that very clear here, didn't He? The goal of identification for the Lord's disciples is separation from the world, like He was not of this world.

The final is: **The Goal Of Sanctification.**

Here Jesus prayed that God would keep them from the evil, not take them out of the world, but keep them from the evil. They were in the world; they lived in a certain location in the world. Jesus prayed to the Father that they might be kept from the evil that is in the world, and that they might follow Him as being not of the world. I believe you can call that a process and a position, to be kept from the evil and to be like Jesus, not a part of the world.

But Jesus further prayed for the special means by which this sanctification might be effected in the lives of the disciples. He asked the Father, "Sanctify them through thy truth; thy word is truth." My friend, how thankful I am that we have God's Word, the Holy Bible. Do you see what Jesus says it will do? It will sanctify His disciples because God's Word is truth.

Praise God for these goals that Jesus desired for His disciples. They are possible because Jesus prayed to God the Father with specific requests. Let me repeat them for you: the goal of unification, that we might be one as He and the Father are one; the goal of identification, that we might truly understand that we belong to God and not to the world; and the goal of sanctification, that we might apply the word of truth to our hearts which will sanctify us unto God.

As believers, we have unique goals to reach. Because Jesus prayed, we can reach them. For this, we give thanks unto the Lord.

Chapter Eighty

The High Calling

Very few, if any, people live up to their full potential. We are doing less than we are capable of doing. That's true in many respects. Our minds are capable of much more than we engage them with. Bodily, physically we probably could do much more than we are doing if we were doing all we could. The real sin is when we are satisfied with less than the possible. To be the best we can, we should reach for more every day. We need to know then what is expected of us.

In the two preceding chapters, we focused on the prayer of Jesus just before He was arrested and crucified. Jesus prayed other prayers, but the ones that were recorded in the Gospels are mostly short prayers. We do know, though, from the Gospel records that Jesus spent whole nights in prayer at times, and on one occasion, He fasted for forty days. So Jesus was a person of prayer. But not many of His prayers are recorded. This one in John 17 is what some people call the high priestly prayer.

Let us think about **THE HIGH CALLING** of being a disciple from the prayer of Jesus in John 17:18-26.

> *18 As thou hast sent me into the world, even so have I also sent them into the world.*
>
> *19 And for their sake I sanctify myself, that they also might be sanctified through the truth.*

20 Neither pray I for these alone, but for them also which shall believe on me through their word;

21 That they all may be one; as thou, Father, art in me, and I in thee, that they also may be one in us: that the world may believe that thou hast sent me.

22 And the glory which thou gavest me I have given them; that they may be one, even as we are one:

23 I in them, and thou in me, that they may be made perfect in one; and that the world may know that thou hast sent me, and hast loved them, as thou hast loved me.

24 Father, I will that they also, whom thou hast given me, be with me where I am; that they may behold my glory, which thou hast given me: for thou lovedst me before the foundation of the world.

25 O righteous Father, the world hath not known thee: but I have known thee, and these have known that thou hast sent me.

26 And I have declared unto them thy name, and will declare it: that the love wherewith thou hast loved me may be in them, and I in them.

In this final part of Jesus' prayer, He set forth the distinctive **RIGHTS** His disciples are to enjoy.

The first Right of disciples is: **To Be Sent Like Jesus.**

He prayed, "As thou hast sent me, even so I have sent them." That is a distinct mission. What a calling we have to be in the world like Jesus was in the world. This is a right which many disciples have missed, I fear. The purpose is so that others will believe. That is what we are existing for as disciples, to tell others so that there will be more disciples, that the world may know. Jesus prayed, "That the world may know thou hast sent me," that the Father sent the Son.

Yes, this is a very high calling, a right that too few disciples even care to think about. The world will know who Jesus is when we take our places, understanding that we have been sent into the world like Jesus was sent into the world. Nothing turned Him aside.

Oh, my friend, let me challenge you with this. If you are a believer, then understand that Jesus said that we are in this world like He was in this world. May the Lord help us to understand this.

The second Right of disciples is: **To Be Glorified With Jesus.**

Oh, I rejoice in this! Jesus prayed that He had taken the glory which God had given Him and had showed it unto them or given it unto them. He had expressed His desire to have His disciples enjoy the kind of oneness that He and the Father experienced. Several times in this prayer, He said, "That they may be one as we are one." That is a beautiful idea and one that we certainly should rise to. It is a right, a high calling of our discipleship.

But it is to me, I would say, even more wonderful to share Jesus' glory. He said He wants them whom the Father has given to Him to share His glory, "I want them to be with me where I am that they may behold my glory."

Right now, our eyes are not equipped to see glory. Some day when we have our new bodies, our resurrected bodies, we are going to be able to see glory. At that fulfilling time, we are going to have the wonderful experience of sharing the glory of Jesus. That is our high calling, that is our right, to be glorified with Jesus.

The third Right of disciples is: **To Be Taught By Jesus.**

He prayed, "I have declared Thy name to them and will declare it." Jesus was a wonderful teacher, the best teacher. Many people look at the teachings of Jesus and say, this is outstanding; this is better than any teaching we have seen anywhere. The disciples knew that God had sent Jesus. They could understand from His teachings that He was more than an ordinary teacher. So He is, and He always has been, you see. Jesus taught them about God. He could pray, "I have told them, so that the love which thou hast loved me with, may be in them, and I in them." There is a kind of personal instruction here. Yes, Jesus taught them, and to be taught by Jesus is a right, a distinct right of disciples.

I'm glad to testify to the fact that Jesus does teach the believer, the disciple who is willing to be really a disciple. Many believers do not live up to their rights. What a high calling we have, to be sent like Jesus into the world, to be glorified with Jesus in the future, and now to be taught by Jesus.

I appeal to you, if you are a believer, attain to your rights.

Studies from John 18

Chapter Eighty-One

Judas—The Betrayer

One of the most outstanding events in all of history is the death of Jesus of Nazareth. The records in the Bible clearly report his birth and report His death in even more detail. We must pay close attention to what the record says.

Certain Bible passages predicted His death many centuries before He was born. There was King David, for example, when he wrote Psalm 22. In it, he describes a kind of death that is most clearly a death by crucifixion. The Prophet Isaiah, in chapter 53 of his book, seven hundred years before Christ, also spoke about One who would bear the sins of many in His death.

The writers of the New Testament Gospels give us the actual account of the events that surrounded Jesus' death. In this meditation I choose to focus attention on the betrayal of Jesus by His disciple called Judas in John 18:1-9.

> *1 When Jesus had spoken these words, he went forth with his disciples over the brook Cedron, where was a garden, into the which he entered, and his disciples.*
>
> *2 And Judas also, which betrayed him, knew the place: for Jesus ofttimes resorted thither with his disciples.*
>
> *3 Judas then, having received a band of men and officers from the chief priests and Pharisees, cometh thither with*

lanterns and torches and weapons.

4 Jesus therefore, knowing all things that should come upon him, went forth, and said unto them, Whom seek ye?

5 They answered him, Jesus of Nazareth. Jesus saith unto them, I am he. And Judas also, which betrayed him, stood with them.

6 As soon then as he had said unto them, I am he, they went backward, and fell to the ground.

7 Then asked he them again, Whom seek ye? And they said, Jesus of Nazareth.

8 Jesus answered, I have told you that I am he: if therefore ye seek me, let these go their way.

9 That the saying might be fulfilled, which he spake, Of them which thou gavest me have I lost none.

I said one of the most outstanding events in history is the death of Jesus. Our text explains the **FACTS** of how Judas betrayed Jesus.

Fact number one: **There Was The Secret.**

We are told that Jesus and His disciples crossed over the brook Kidron. The Kidron Valley separates Mt. Moriah, the temple area, and the Mt. of Olives to the east of the city. In those days, a path led from the Eastern Gate through the valley across the brook and into the garden which was called the Garden of Gethsemane.

I understand that the word Gethsemane actually implies an oil press. There were olive trees on the slopes of the mount which gave it the name, Mount of Olives. They most likely had an olive press in a nearby place. You can still see the remains of an ancient olive press on the eastern slope of the Mount of Olives in Bethany.

Well, Judas knew the place in this garden because Jesus had often gone there with His disciples. It must have been a kind of secret place where He could spend time alone with His disciples. There was then the secret garden.

Fact number two: **There Was The Security Guard.**

We noted as we read that Judas had received a band of men and officers. By examining the English word, band, in the Greek New Testament, we find that it is pronounced *speira*, which means a Roman cohort of as many as 600 men. Now whether he had the whole battalion or not, we do not know. But the word actually implies that he had 600 men plus the officers or temple guards.

Why would he bring that many soldiers to take one man? Most likely, they expected some resistance, and they prepared to overcome any resistance that His disciples might offer. They came with lanterns, torches, and weapons.

Jesus was very popular. Only a few days before this, large crowds had escorted Him into Jerusalem and had shouted, "Hosanna to the Son of David." Just in case He might be surrounded by these crowds, Judas came with this great band of soldiers and officers with lanterns, torches, and weapons.

But Jesus, unafraid, stepped forward and asked, "Whom do you seek?" And they said, "Jesus of Nazareth." Immediately Jesus identified Himself by saying, "I am he." I want you to observe a very clear statement in verse 5. It reads like this, "And Judas also, who betrayed him, stood with them." Get that clear from this record. Judas was with them, not with Jesus.

Fact number three: **There Was The Shocking Discovery.**

They surely did not expect Him to step out and identify Himself like He did. When He did identify Himself, fear seized them, and they fell backward to the ground. It was an unexpected easy capture. They had come with a large band of soldiers and their weapons to make what they imagined to be a difficult capture. But He stepped out and gave Himself over to them.

When they had somewhat revived from this shocking discovery, He asked them again, "Whom do you seek?" They answered, "Jesus of Nazareth." He said, "I told you I am he, and since you are seeking me, let these go their way." In other words, Jesus said the disciples are not prepared, nor do they intend to offer any resistance. So He said, "Take me and let them go."

I want you to refer to verse 9. Jesus asked that His disciples be permitted to go their way and not share in His arrest so that the statement He had made earlier would be fulfilled. In His prayer, He had prayed that He had kept all of them except the son of perdition. He was asking the officers to let His disciples go, and the Scripture was fulfilled which He spoke, "Of them whom thou gavest me I have lost none." That was part of His prayer that He prayed before He went to the garden.

Thus, we see how Judas carried out His evil intent: first, by invading the secret garden where Jesus had gone with His disciples; second by involving the security guards with a great band of soldiers; and then, to their amazement, they made a shocking discovery which they were hardly prepared for when Jesus volunteered to be arrested.

Do you see that Jesus did not resist arrest even though He knew what the outcome would be? He said one time, referring to His life, "No man takes it from me; I lay it down of myself; I have power to lay it down, and I have power to take it again." Do you understand? He willingly died for us, for you and me.

Chapter Eighty-Two

Peter—His Failure

The very heart of the Gospel comes into focus in the study of these chapters in the Gospel of John. The word Gospel means "good news." At the same time, the events which we are studying are surrounded with sorrow. Some great aspirations end in sorrow.

Peter, a disciple of Jesus, once told Jesus he would lay down his life for Him. When Peter made that boast, Jesus replied he would instead deny Him even before the cock would crow. But Peter insisted he would never deny his Lord.

I admire Peter for his good intentions. Good intentions are noble and right. But to have any real value, they must be backed by loyal actions. That is what we are now going to consider from John 18:10, 11; 15-18; 25-27, **PETER—HIS FAILURE.**

> *10 Then Simon Peter having a sword drew it, and smote the high priest's servant, and cut off his right ear. The servant's name was Malchus.*
>
> *11 Then said Jesus unto Peter, Put up thy sword into the sheath: the cup which my Father hath given me, shall I not drink it?*
>
> *15 And Simon Peter followed Jesus, and so did another disciple: that disciple was known unto the high priest, and went in with Jesus into the palace of the high priest.*

16 But Peter stood at the door without. Then went out that other disciple, which was known unto the high priest, and spake unto her that kept the door, and brought in Peter.

17 Then saith the damsel that kept the door unto Peter, Art not thou also one of this man's disciples? He saith, I am not.

18 And the servants and officers stood there, who had made a fire of coals; for it was cold: and they warmed themselves: and Peter stood with them, and warmed himself.

25 And Simon Peter stood and warmed himself. They said therefore unto him, Art not thou also one of his disciples? He denied it, and said, I am not.

26 One of the servants of the high priest, being his kinsman whose ear Peter cut off, saith, Did not I see thee in the garden with him?

27 Peter then denied again: and immediately the cock crew.

Good intentions are noble and right. To have any real value, they must be backed up with loyal actions. From these verses, we can understand the **WAYS** Peter was led into failure.

The first Way: **Peter's Futile Defense.**

In the garden, faced by a military guard, Peter drew his sword. Peter meant to carry out his boast to lay down his life for Jesus. He was ready to take his sword and defend his Lord. He must have meant to cut Malchus down, to cut off his head. Apparently, the servant ducked, and Peter simply sliced off his ear.

Now listen to Jesus rebuke Peter, "Put up your sword, Peter." This was not the way to defend his Lord. Peter had it wrong. Jesus gave him a reason, saying His Father has a plan which He will carry out. Peter misunderstood what this was all about. He failed.

The second Way: **Peter's First Denial.**

As Jesus was led off to be tried, Peter was following all right. That in itself is worthy. He could not get inside the courthouse because he did not know the right people. So another disciple brought him in. We conclude it must have been John, the disciple of our Lord. He was known by the high priest and could go to the doorkeeper and request the maid to let Peter in, which she did.

But then, when this girl looked upon Peter, she asked him a burning question. "You are not one of this man's disciples, are you?" That is exactly the way she asked the question so as to anticipate Peter saying, "No." We have ways to anticipate answers when we ask questions, and this girl asked the question in such a way that it was easy for Peter to say no. "You are not one of this man's disciples, are you?" And Peter said, "I am not." In that answer, he was denying his Lord just as Jesus said he would.

Then Peter stepped up to the fire which the servants and officers had made and warmed himself. It appears that Peter was trying to be unknown. He was trying to hide there among those officers and servants so as to be undetected. That was his first denial.

The third Way: **Peter's Final Denial.**

Those servants and officers were not friends of Jesus. But Peter stood there with them anyway. That means Peter identified himself with the enemies of Jesus. That was the wrong thing to do, but there he was. They asked him the same question in the same way that girl had asked, which meant they were expecting Peter to say no. It made it easier, I suppose. Anyway, Peter did say, "I am not."

Now notice what happened next. There was there a kinsman of the servant whose ear Peter had cut off. We may be sure this kinsman had looked very carefully when Peter cut off that ear. So he said, "I saw you in the garden with him, did I not?" It's a different kind of question this time. This man expected yes as an answer, and a good reason. Most likely, he had watched Peter very carefully, and now here he was, facing him. "I saw you in the garden with him, didn't I?" expecting yes as an answer.

But since Peter had already denied the Lord twice, he found he could do nothing else, and Peter denied again. But then, the cock crowed. Peter did exactly what Jesus predicted he would do. He denied Jesus before the cock crowed. We feel deeply for Peter, because we know what failure means. Our high aspirations often lie shattered when we face testing.

Now, my friend, has Jesus been calling you to a loyal walk with Him? Remember, His sacrifice was the greatest event of history. Guard against a futile defense of Jesus, a first step in denying your Lord, and hiding among His enemies. Back your devotion to Jesus by loyal actions and failure will not be yours.

Chapter Eighty-Three

The High Priest

In tracing out the death of Jesus, I take the records in the Bible as reliable. I believe those records are a true report. He was arrested by the security guard and first brought before the religious court headed by the high priest.

Some of Jesus' teachings clashed with the interpretation of the religious leadership. He had encountered them on different occasions. It is not surprising, then, that after His arrest, He would be brought first before the religious court. The recorder was careful to give the essential details in each of the events which led up to Jesus' death. Remember, the death of Jesus is the most important event of history.

In John 18:12-14, 19-24, the role of **THE HIGH PRIEST** in the trial of Jesus comes plainly into view.

> *12 Then the band and the captain and officers of the Jews took Jesus, and bound him,*
>
> *13 And led him away to Annas first; for he was father-in-law to Caiaphas, which was the high priest that same year.*
>
> *14 Now Caiaphas was he, which gave counsel to the Jews, that it was expedient that one man should die for the people.*
>
> *19 The high priest then asked Jesus of his disciples, and of*

his doctrine.

20 Jesus answered him, I spake openly to the world; I ever taught in the synagogue, and in the temple, whither the Jews always resort; and in secret have I said nothing.

21 Why askest thou me? ask them which heard me, what I have said unto them: behold, they know what I said.

22 And when he had thus spoken, one of the officers which stood by struck Jesus with the palm of his hand, saying, Answerest thou the high priest so?

23 Jesus answered him, If I have spoken evil, bear witness of the evil: but if well, why smitest thou me?

24 Now Annas had sent him bound unto Caiaphas the high priest.

From this record, we highlight the several **PROCEDURES** that were used in this religious court led by the high priest.

The first Procedure: **The Court Is Examined.**

Going back into the history of the high priesthood, I find that the first high priest in the days of Moses was his brother, Aaron. God had established this priestly line by selecting the tribe of Levi to be the priestly tribe. Both Moses and Aaron were of that priestly tribe, Levi. God had said to Moses that the sons of Aaron should follow him in the office of high priest.

Some years before the Christian era, the appointment of the high priest was made by the Roman government instead of being selected and anointed by the religious leaders in Israel. This man, Annas, was appointed in his thirty-seventh year to be high priest by the Roman government.

Caiaphas, his son-in-law, however, was the functional high priest. From other records, we learn that his name was Joseph Caiaphas. He was the one who had spoken like this: "It is expedient that one man die for the people and that the whole nation perish not." He had said this after Jesus had raised Lazarus from the dead. He had said it because he feared the revenge of Rome, as he saw how everybody was following after Jesus. He was really afraid that Rome would come and destroy the nation. But he said more than he knew when he said, "It is expedient that one man die for the people." Yes, he said more than he knew.

The court then was a religious court with the high priest in charge. They gathered to investigate the problem of Jesus.

The second Procedure: **The Problem Is Explained.**

First of all, the problem needed to be stated. The high priest asked Jesus of His disciples and of His doctrine. Reading through the Gospel of John, we have learned that Jesus had many disciples. They came to Him from many different areas. People enjoyed His teaching. We are told on one occasion that even the officers of the temple had said, "Never man spoke like this man." Others had said about Him that He taught with authority. So, this high priest's court wanted to know about Jesus' disciples.

They also wanted to know about His doctrine. You recall some of Jesus' teachings were opposite to the interpretation of the religious leaders of His day. Jesus simply reminded them that He had never taught in secret; His teaching had always been in the open. He had taught in the synagogues and the temple where the Jews always resorted. If they wanted to know what He had taught, the most practical thing to do would be to call in those who had heard Him. He assured them, "They know what I said."

Here is a very important consideration: the result of the teaching. I have observed even today that what happens to people who accept the teaching of Jesus is something to observe, to watch, to analyze. Jesus faced the problem very well, "Ask those who heard me; they can tell you what I taught." So the problem is explained.

The third Procedure: **The Criticism Is Exposed.**

That officer standing by drew a conclusion which was not valid. Instead of listening, he quickly struck Jesus because he interpreted what Jesus said to be an insult to the high priest. But he violated the very law he wanted to defend, for Moses' law declared a man innocent until convicted. The trial was not over. He took justice in his own hands, and it didn't turn out well.

Jesus exposed him very quickly, saying, "If I have spoken evil, then bear witness of the evil." In other words, tell me where I was wrong. If I answered incorrectly, I will accept the justice, but if I have answered well, you have smitten me illegally. Justice was the purpose of the trial, and Jesus exposed this officer's violation. It is important that we catch that truth.

The religious court had their hearing. I would say, it was proper that they did. One fault comes to the surface, though: the sentence was implied before the trial was completed. We now know that Jesus was destined to die. Yet, it must be clear; justice was not carried out with respect to Him in this trial. Why wasn't it? Because, to bring about peace with God for us, for you and me, the death of Jesus was the only way.

Men still bring Jesus to their courts of judgment to be examined; they still have a problem explaining Jesus; and He can expose unjust criticism today as He did then, by His Word. Remember, He came to die. Accept His gift of eternal life.

Chapter Eighty-Four

Pilate—The Roman Governor

The first court before which Jesus stood trial was a religious court. It was proper for that to happen. From the religious court, Jesus' case was transferred to the civil court. This was headed by Pilate, the Procurator. He had been appointed in the year 26 in the common era.

Rome had such governors in various parts of the empire, but the governing of Palestine seemed to be so difficult that Pilate, the Governor, was responsible directly to the Emperor in Rome. Several years ago, a pillar was found in the ruins of Caesarea along the sea coast. In the inscription on that pillar was the name *Pilatus*, that is Latin for Pilate. So there is no question but that Pilate was a Roman Governor in Palestine. The Bible record states he was there at this time and was to render a judgment about Jesus. They brought Him to Pilate's judgment hall early in the morning. The Governor expected to sit in judgment then.

John, the beloved disciple, in his report of that scene, pictures the captain and his soldiers, the religious leaders with the mob which had gathered and **PILATE—THE ROMAN GOVERNOR**. The text is found in John 18:28-40.

> *28 Then led they Jesus from Caiaphas unto the hall of judgment: and it was early; and they themselves went*

not into the judgment hall, lest they should be defiled; but that they might eat the passover.

29 Pilate then went out unto them, and said, What accusation bring ye against this man?

30 They answered and said unto him, If he were not a malefactor, we would not have delivered him up unto thee.

31 Then said Pilate unto them, Take ye him, and judge him according to your law. The Jews therefore said unto him, It is not lawful for us to put any man to death:

32 That the saying of Jesus might be fulfilled, which he spake, signifying what death he should die.

33 Then Pilate entered into the judgment hall again, and called Jesus, and said unto him, Art thou the King of the Jews?

34 Jesus answered him, Sayest thou this thing of thyself, or did others tell it thee of me?

35 Pilate answered, Am I a Jew? Thine own nation and the chief priests have delivered thee unto me: what hast thou done?

36 Jesus answered, My kingdom is not of this world: if my kingdom were of this world, then would my servants fight, that I should not be delivered to the Jews: but now is my kingdom not from hence.

37 Pilate therefore said unto him, Art thou a king then? Jesus answered, Thou sayest that I am a king. To this end was I born, and for this cause came I into the world, that I should bear witness unto the truth. Every one that is of the truth heareth my voice.

38 Pilate saith unto him, What is truth? And when he had said this, he went out again unto the Jews, and saith unto them, I find in him no fault at all.

39 But ye have a custom, that I should release unto you one at the passover: will ye therefore that I release unto you the King of the Jews?

40 Then cried they all again, saying, Not this man, but Barabbas. Now Barabbas was a robber.

From this Scripture, we obtain insights into the **PROCEEDINGS** employed by Pilate—the Roman Governor.

The first proceeding was: **The Accusation Was Required.**

It was early when they brought Jesus to Pilate. He had the right to ask His accusers to state their case, "What accusation do you bring against this man?" In reply, they simply said, "If He were not a malefactor, we would not have brought Him to you." In other words, we do not bother you with the innocent, Governor. He is an evildoer. Malefactor means evildoer or a doer of evil. They answered, we brought Him here because He is an evildoer, and He must stand judgment before you.

But Pilate tried to turn the case back to them by saying, "You have a law; judge him by your law." But they replied, "It is unlawful for us to execute a man." Rome had denied them this right, and they were correct in saying it.

However, I want you to notice carefully verse 32. It reads like this: "That the saying of Jesus might be fulfilled, which he spoke, signifying what death he should die." You see, the Jewish system of execution was by stoning. The Roman system of execution was by crucifixion. Jesus had said (it is recorded in John 12:32), "And I, if I be lifted up, will draw all men unto me." He said that to signify what death He should die. When Jesus had spoken to Nicodemus early in His ministry, He had said, "As Moses lifted up the serpent in the wilderness, even so, must the Son of man be lifted up." So their request that Pilate try Him and sentence Him was in harmony with the divine purpose.

The second proceeding was: **The Investigation Was Conducted.**

Pilate asked Jesus four questions. The first one was right on target, "Are you the King of the Jews?" That was a very touchy question. It was basic to the trial. If Jesus had said "yes," He would immediately have run into the problem of the Roman over-lordship. I would have you note, however, that Jesus did not deny it; He only raised the question, "Do you say this of yourself, or did somebody else tell you?" He did not deny it. At the moment, He did not admit it.

Pilate's second question was logical, "What have you done?" He was searching for evidence: Pilate needed to know why the nation had delivered Him. But that was a loaded question. It was hardly a fair question because He would convict Himself. If indeed He was a malefactor, doer of evil, as they said He was, He would have convicted Himself. It was hardly a fair question.

Then Jesus replied, "My kingdom is not of this world order." Pilate immediately caught the note and asked Him the third question, "Are you a king then?" Jesus answered, "You say that I am a king. I really came to bear witness to the truth. And everyone who is of the truth hears my voice."

Then Pilate asked the fourth question, "What is truth?" It was an easy way to avoid a responsibility. Pilate hadn't heard Jesus once declare, "I am the way, the truth, and the life." What is truth? Jesus is truth. That, Pilate missed in investigating the case.

The third proceeding was: **The Summation Was Offered.**

Pilate's first statement to the Jews was courageous, "I find no fault in Him." That is a clear statement, a clear summation of the case, "I find no fault." But instead of carrying through with that, he responded, "I am willing to honor your custom that at Passover I release some prisoner to you. Now, will you, therefore, that I release unto you the King of the Jews?"

That must have been an insult to them. They immediately responded by rejecting his proposal in these words, "Not this man, but Barabbas." The comment is that Barabbas was a robber. He was an insurrectionist, a criminal. But they chose a criminal for release rather than an innocent man. Pilate offered the summation, but they rejected it.

The trial before Pilate was not based on facts but on feeling. They chose to free a wicked man and crucify an innocent one. But, my friend, only an innocent one could die for us. Pilate verified His innocence. He said, "I find no fault in Him."

Again, I raise the question, "Why?" God knew that only in that way would it be possible for us to be forgiven. Peace with God is possible only by His way. Your way or my way will not bring peace.

In every land, the government has some process by which to administer justice. There is surely in all countries a system of courts. They are not all the same, but there are processes to deal with lawbreakers. The tragedy is when innocent people are assumed to be guilty before evidence of guilt has been established.

Studies from John 19

Chapter Eighty-Five

Who Is Guilty?

In the trial of Jesus, we must raise the question, **WHO IS GUILTY?** His life was full of loving acts of kindness, healing the sick, and teaching the people. Because He was misunderstood, He had to stand trial before the Roman court.

As John reports what happened during Jesus' trial before the Roman ruler, we wonder really who was on trial. We will consider John 19:1-7 in this meditation.

1 Then Pilate therefore took Jesus, and scourged him.

2 And the soldiers platted a crown of thorns, and put it on his head, and they put on him a purple robe,

3 And said, Hail, King of the Jews! and they smote him with their hands.

4 Pilate therefore went forth again, and saith unto them, Behold, I bring him forth to you, that ye may know that I find no fault in him.

5 Then came Jesus forth, wearing the crown of thorns, and the purple robe. And Pilate saith unto them, Behold the man!

6 When the chief priests therefore and officers saw him, they cried out, saying, Crucify him, crucify him. Pilate saith unto them, Take ye him, and crucify him: for I find no fault in him.

7 The Jews answered him, We have a law, and by our law he ought to die, because he made himself the Son of God.

Who is guilty? To answer this question, I submit we must weigh carefully several searching **OBSERVATIONS**.

The first Observation is: **He Was Scourged By The Soldiers.**

Yes, He was beaten. Perhaps they beat Him to force a confession of wrong. That is a method often used to bring a forced confession: whip him, torment him, hurt him, and perhaps he will say something that will give an occasion to pass sentence against him. It may well be that Pilate planned that kind of an approach. So He was scourged by the soldiers.

It may also be that it was simply to humiliate the prisoner. We are told that in the time the Romans ruled, the soldiers had a game they played with the prisoner. They called it "the game of the king." Even today, in the city of Jerusalem under the Church of the Ecce Homo there is the Pavement, the courtyard of Antonia, the Roman fortress paved with huge stones. The game is laid out on the pavement, cut in the stones, exactly where and what these soldiers did. It was "the game of the king." They plaited a crown of thorns and put it on His head. They took off His own garment and put on Him a purple robe to mock Him, to humiliate Him. With open hand, they smote Him. Others of the Gospels report that they spit upon Him.

I raise the question, "who is guilty?" This whipping, scourging by the soldiers, the mocking and humiliation, does this indicate who is guilty?

The second Observation is: **He Was Faultless Before Pilate.**

After the soldiers had done their awful work of beating Jesus, Pilate brought Him forth to the people. Ah, but Pilate had violated due process of the law, because he had punished a man before his guilt had been established. He had him beaten before there was any evidence of guilt. Every civil court should protect the innocent instead of bringing punishment upon him. Pilate, I tell you, violated the due process of Roman law.

It may be that Pilate needed to satisfy the accusers of Jesus. By having Jesus beaten, he could bring Him out and show them that he had taken stern measures against Him. This might satisfy them. The evidence of His humiliation might satisfy the accusers.

I can almost see Jesus right now standing there beside the Roman governor: Jesus with His crown of thorns and purple robe. Pilate declared, "I find no fault in him." He called their attention to Him standing there with the crown of thorns and purple robe by announcing, "Behold the man!" Did this answer the question, who is guilty? Pilate concluded, "I find no fault in him." Who then is guilty? That is my question.

I'm making some observations, some searching observations from this account: He was scourged by the soldiers; He was faultless before Pilate.

The third Observation is: **He Was Condemned By The Crowd.**

When they saw Him crowned with thorns and decked with a purple robe, they cried out, saying, "Crucify him, crucify him." A mob spirit prevailed. Justice could not be carried out and seldom is when a mob spirit prevails.

Pilate responded by a most carefully stated proposition, "You take him and crucify him, because I find no fault in him." I would think, and so would you, that an innocent person should not be punished. Twice now, we have heard Pilate declare he had found nothing in Jesus worthy of death: "I find no fault in him."

They then responded by referring to one of their laws. Here before the civil court, these people bring up a religious law. They say, "Our law calls for his death because he made himself the Son of God."

They were right. Anyone who blasphemed the Name of God, according to their law, was to be executed. But just suppose that this One who is on trial is, indeed, the Son of God.

Now our question of who is guilty begins to focus. Suppose they are wrong, that He is really the Son of God. How shall we answer the question, who is guilty?

I have answers. The soldiers are guilty for tormenting and beating an innocent person. Pilate is guilty for punishing before guilt was established; he did not live up to his oath of office as a Roman governor. The people are guilty for condemning when there was no conclusive evidence. Just suppose He is the Son of God. Then all the world is guilty. That means you and I are guilty, too.

Chapter Eighty-Six

The Final Choice

All of us face choices every day. Some choices are very serious. Some may be rather trivial. But each decision requires the will to carry it out. The serious choices can mean the difference between life and death. The most far-reaching choice I submit to you is the choice we make for or against Jesus Christ because that has to do with the destiny of this life.

At the time when our decision is focused upon Jesus Christ, we are subject to influences affecting our reasoning. There are several ways power can be used to influence that choice. In John 19:8-15, we get the setting for **THE FINAL CHOICE**.

> *8 When Pilate therefore heard that saying, he was the more afraid;*
>
> *9 And went again into the judgment hall, and saith unto Jesus, Whence art thou? But Jesus gave him no answer.*
>
> *10 Then saith Pilate unto him, Speakest thou not unto me? knowest thou not that I have power to crucify thee, and have power to release thee?*
>
> *11 Jesus answered, Thou couldest have no power at all against me, except it were given thee from above: therefore he that delivered me unto thee hath the greater sin.*
>
> *12 And from thenceforth Pilate sought to release him: but*

the Jews cried out, saying, If thou let this man go, thou art not Caesar's friend: whosoever maketh himself a king speaketh against Caesar.

13 When Pilate therefore heard that saying, he brought Jesus forth, and sat down in the judgment seat in a place that is called the Pavement, but in the Hebrew, Gabbatha.

14 And it was the preparation of the passover, and about the sixth hour: and he saith unto the Jews, Behold your King!

15 But they cried out, Away with him, away with him, crucify him. Pilate saith unto them, Shall I crucify your King? The chief priests answered, We have no king but Caesar.

When faced with the final choice, we should be aware of the **USES** of power in arriving at our decision.

The first use of power is: **The Power Of Silence.**

Pilate was seized with fear when he heard that the Jews said Jesus made Himself the Son of God. Pilate realized then that he was dealing with more than an ordinary person. You can be quite sure that Pilate was not a believer in the God of the Jews. By no means! He was an idol worshipper. But, nonetheless, he was seized with fear and put the question to Jesus like this, "From where are you?"

There seemed to be a mystery about Jesus. Pilate realized that he was dealing with someone more than his equal. But I want you to notice how Jesus used the power of silence. He knew how to use it. He just kept quiet; He said nothing; He did not answer Pilate at all. Few people know how to use the power of silence, but Jesus knew how, so He was forcing Pilate to make a decision.

The second use of power is: **The Power Of Rulers.**

When Jesus refused to speak, Pilate attempted to bring the power of Rome down on His head. He said, "Do you not know that I have power to crucify you and power to release you? My word can mean your life, or my word can mean your death." He was at the mercy of the ruler. That is the kind of power Pilate had as a Roman ruler. That was Roman power, the power of rulers. With a whim and a word, they could pronounce life or death.

But Jesus answered him something like this, "You have no power at all. There is a divine power that you do not recognize." Now here is exactly what He answered, "You would have no power at all against me except it were given you from above." Roman power, Jesus informed Pilate, is subject to divine power. The power of the state is not absolute. Jesus made that very clear to Pilate.

There was that political power that the accusers of Jesus began to employ, the power of rulers. Rome allowed no rival. Therefore, the appeal was made to Pilate that unless He would crucify Jesus, he would get himself into trouble with the emperor, Caesar.

Now Jesus had set Pilate straight. But the accusers of Jesus threatened him with political power. He had to make a choice. Pilate had to make a choice. Many rulers like Pilate do not realize their power is not absolute.

The third use of power is: **The Power Of The Public.**

So Pilate sat upon his judgment seat in the place called the Pavement. It was simply a mockery. He put on his Roman robes and sat, most likely looking very stern, upon the seat of judgment. He then announced the accusation, "Behold your king." But the power of the public moved in. It was a mob movement. They passed sentence without law. They cried out, "Away with him, away with him, crucify him." And thus, the innocent One was sentenced to death by the power of the public.

Mobs are seldom rational. They can be led. And that's what we have here. Jesus became subject to the power of the public.

The final choice was between Caesar and Jesus. For Pilate, it meant his political future. And here, he failed to understand wherein true power lies. He was influenced by the power of the public.

Chapter Eighty-Seven

The Crucifixion

The most solemn event of human history recorded is the crucifixion of Jesus of Nazareth. His life has challenged many men to live right all down through the centuries. Many have suffered death because of their faith in Him. The Bible records leave no room to doubt that He was actually crucified. It is to that solemn event we give attention in this meditation.

There are records outside of the Bible which also testify to **THE CRUCIFIXION** as a historical event. This is no idle tale or story. This is history, well-validated by the record in John 19:16-22.

> *16 Then delivered he him therefore unto them to be crucified. And they took Jesus, and led him away.*
>
> *17 And he bearing his cross went forth into a place called the place of a skull, which is called in the Hebrew Golgotha:*
>
> *18 Where they crucified him, and two other with him, on either side one, and Jesus in the midst.*
>
> *19 And Pilate wrote a title, and put it on the cross. And the writing was, JESUS OF NAZARETH THE KING OF THE JEWS.*
>
> *20 This title then read many of the Jews: for the place where Jesus was crucified was nigh to the city: and it was*

written in Hebrew, and Greek, and Latin.

21 Then said the chief priests of the Jews to Pilate, Write not, The King of the Jews; but that he said, I am King of the Jews.

22 Pilate answered, What I have written I have written.

When we study what happened when Jesus was crucified, we must examine the vital **FACTS.** Let us picture them in our minds so the Holy Spirit can give us understanding.

The first Fact is: **The Character Of The Companions.**

You read, "Then delivered he him therefore unto them to be crucified. And they led him away." Undoubtedly, reference is made here by "they" to the soldiers and the people. Roman soldiers were framed in such heartless actions. They led Him to the common place of execution, Golgotha. That hill of the skull, my friend, is still visible today. Oh yes, I've stood at the foot of Calvary, and in my mind have pictured Him there on the cross.

What is the character of His companions that were crucified with Him? There were two others, we are told. Mark's Gospel reports that they were thieves. Luke's Gospel calls them malefactors. The Prophet Isaiah, 700 years before Christ, predicted, "He was numbered with the transgressors." Yes, one, two, three. These two others, crucified with Him, were sinners, serious sinners, men upon whom the law had a claim, for they had broken it. His companions in crucifixion were sinners.

The second Fact is: **The Intention Of The Title.**

Pilate, we are told, wrote a title and put it on the cross of Jesus. This is what it read: "Jesus of Nazareth, the King of the Jews." I imagine that Pilate did that to humiliate Jesus. It would be a sorry end for a political aspirant, someone who wanted to rise on the political scale. To end up on the cross would be a humiliating experience. It would be a way for Pilate to dispose of a political enemy. It most likely was intended to give a blow to Jesus.

I suspect that the intention of the title was to humiliate the Jews. It was to remind them that they were securely under Rome. Here the King of the Jews was suspended between heaven and earth on the cross. He supposed all their hopes were dashed. Pilate hoped, yes, that he could humiliate the Jews this way.

He did not know, of course, that Jesus had told Peter in the garden that He could pray to the Father, and the Father would send Him twelve legions of angels that He might be delivered. But the Lord had added, "But how then shall the scripture be fulfilled?"

"Jesus of Nazareth, King of the Jews," was written in three languages and put above Him on the cross. The languages were Hebrew, Greek, and Latin. Everybody passing by could read it. The intention of the title must have been to put a stop to any idea that Jesus was a King.

The third Fact is:: **The Inflexibility Of The Verdict.**

The leaders of the Jewish people came to Pilate and objected to the title. They said, "Write not, The King of the Jews; but that he said, I am King of the Jews." Jesus never said that. Really Pilate had tried to extract it from Him. They did not know that Gabriel, when he told Mary she would give birth to Jesus, promised her that God would give to Him the throne of His father David and He would rule over the house of Jacob forever. This is what the angel said to Mary. But they did not know that.

Pilate, with a show of power, refused to change it. He said, "What I have written, I have written." Could he have remembered that Jesus had told him shortly before that he had no power except that which was given to him? Beyond this title that Pilate gave to Jesus, the Bible refers to Jesus as King of Kings and Lord of Lords. Yes, my friend, Pilate's inflexibility regarding the verdict may have showed more power than he himself possessed.

It cannot be doubted that Jesus was crucified. All records agree. The facts support the truth: He was crucified. But before any benefit can come to you, you must acknowledge those facts associated with His crucifixion and receive Him as your sacrifice for sin.

Chapter Eighty-Eight

The Completed Act

I'm sure that you, like I, realize that our human existence is full of many uncertainties. Each day brings its changes, and many of them are unpredictable. Only one person knew how His days would end. Even during the last week of His life, Jesus explained to the disciples exactly what was going to happen. He lived with the end in view.

We are not blessed like that. The only certainty we have is the fact of the end. The time of the end is hidden from us. Not so with Jesus. The record contained in John's Gospel shows us how Jesus came to His death. I want you to notice from John 19:23-30, that He clearly understood what was happening; He was aware of **THE COMPLETED ACT.**

> *23 Then the soldiers, when they had crucified Jesus, took his garments, and made four parts, to every soldier a part; and also his coat: now the coat was without seam, woven from the top throughout.*
>
> *24 They said therefore among themselves, Let us not rend it, but cast lots for it, whose it shall be: that the scripture might be fulfilled, which saith, They parted my raiment among them, and for my vesture they did cast lots. These things therefore the soldiers did.*
>
> *25 Now there stood by the cross of Jesus his mother, and*

his mother's sister, Mary the wife of Cleophas, and Mary Magdalene.

26 When Jesus therefore saw his mother, and the disciple standing by, whom he loved, he saith unto his mother, Woman, behold thy son!

27 Then saith he to the disciple, Behold thy mother! And from that hour that disciple took her unto his own home.

28 After this, Jesus knowing that all things were now accomplished, that the scripture might be fulfilled, saith, I thirst.

29 Now there was set a vessel full of vinegar: and they filled a sponge with vinegar, and put it upon hyssop, and put it to his mouth.

30 When Jesus therefore had received the vinegar, he said, It is finished: and he bowed his head, and gave up the ghost.

My friend, from the array of evidence, I have selected three remarkable **PARTICULARS** which should convince anyone that Jesus died.

There will be no more room for doubt.

The first Particular: **The Disposal Of His Clothes.**

There were the soldiers, the ones who had crucified Him. It may well be that their each receiving a part of His clothing was a reward for their act. A reward for their act? Well, perhaps that was the only way they got paid for it, a little bonus, perhaps. At any rate, they made equal parts, then cast lots for the inner garment, the vestment, the seamless tunic. It was not the outer garment; it was the inner garment for which they cast lots because it was woven from the top to the bottom throughout.

Isn't it striking that the disposal of His clothes had been predicted years before by King David in the 22nd Psalm? "They parted my raiment among them, and upon my vesture did they cast lots." The soldiers did not know what they were doing. They were not aware that they were fulfilling Scripture. But they were. Isn't that remarkable? The disposal of His clothes was a particular which cannot be ignored. It seems like a very insignificant act, and yet, the Bible predicted that this was exactly what they would do when they crucified Jesus.

The second Particular: **The Disclosure Of His Concern.**

We are informed that there were four women standing near the cross. It was His mother, his mother's sister, Mary the wife of Cleophas, and Mary Magdalene. These four women, most likely, were very close to Him. More than likely, the other women were close friends of His mother's. She was there. At the time of the birth of Jesus, Simeon, as a prophet, had said that a sword would pierce through her own heart. Here she was by the cross of Jesus, witnessing His death.

Besides these four women, there was the disciple whom Jesus loved. Most students of the Bible identify him as John the Apostle.

While they were there, Jesus from the cross disclosed His concern and said to His mother, "Woman, behold thy son." Then to John, He said, "Behold thy mother." Thus, His last earthly concern was to make sure that His mother was cared for by loving hands, John's hands. Such a loving act is a particular that cannot be ignored. The disclosure of His concern is clear, is it not?

The third Particular: **The Distinction Of His Cry.**

Now read again verse 28, "After this, Jesus knowing that all things were now accomplished." I mentioned earlier that Jesus knew when the end would be. Here we are informed that He was completely knowledgeable. He knew the end was coming. So He asked for something to drink by saying, "I thirst." He had full knowledge of it. The Prophet David had predicted that His tongue would cleave to the roof of His mouth with thirst.

Then followed His final word, His final word. After He had taken the vinegar from the sponge, He declared as His final word, "It is finished." Praise the Lord! It will never be altered; it cannot be changed. He said clearly, "It is finished," then bowed His head and gave up His spirit.

My dear friend, no amount of reasoning can change the record.

Our Lord's distinctive cry settles that. Such a far-reaching act, such a word from the Saviour is a particular which cannot be ignored.

From these remarkable particulars, we are brought to the unshakable conclusion: He died. He gave His innocent life, the innocent for the guilty. When I survey the wondrous cross, I see God's great completed act!

Chapter Eighty-Nine

The Wonder Of It All

Some people in Jesus' day thought they crucified a dangerous criminal. Some people thought He was a powerful rival. So in some way, they knew they must get rid of Him. Few knew then what the crucifixion really meant. Even though Jesus had spoken about His crucifixion to His disciples, yet, even they hardly knew what He was talking about.

The Gospel of John gives us insights beyond the event itself through a carefully written record. I affirm the death of Jesus is a momentous event. That is why it will be good for us to think together about **THE WONDER OF IT ALL** from John 19:31-37.

> *31 The Jews therefore, because it was the preparation, that the bodies should not remain upon the cross on the sabbath day, (for that sabbath day was an high day,) besought Pilate that their legs might be broken, and that they might be taken away.*
>
> *32 Then came the soldiers, and brake the legs of the first, and of the other which was crucified with him.*
>
> *33 But when they came to Jesus, and saw that he was dead already, they brake not his legs:*
>
> *34 But one of the soldiers with a spear pierced his side, and forthwith came there out blood and water.*

35 And he that saw it bare record, and his record is true: and he knoweth that he saith true, that ye might believe.

36 For these things were done, that the scripture should be fulfilled, A bone of him shall not be broken.

37 And again another scripture saith, They shall look on him whom they pierced.

As we think about the death of Jesus, we ought to give special attention to certain serious CONSIDERATIONS regarding that momentous event. **THE WONDER OF IT ALL!**

Consider The Holy Sabbath.

The event of Jesus' death took place at the time of one of the most holy religious days. The calendar said it was the time of the Passover. Its significance can hardly be overemphasized. It was a commemoration of the deliverance of the Jews from Egypt hundreds of years before. They were saved from death by the sacrifice of a lamb. The blood was very important, for they were instructed by Moses to catch the blood in a basin and sprinkle that blood on the doorposts and on the lintels of the houses in which they were to keep themselves.

Every faithful Jew in Jesus' day kept the Passover. It was a high day. It was a great day. It was the solemn remembrance of God's mercy back there in the time when they were brought out of the land of Egypt by the hand of Moses. It was for that reason that the Jews came to Pilate and wanted to be sure that these bodies were not left on the crosses during this high holy day. These bodies on the crosses would desecrate that holy sabbath. So we must consider the holy sabbath.

Consider The Spear-Pierced Side.

There were two crucified with Jesus, one on one side and one on the other. They were thieves; they were malefactors. So the soldiers were ordered by Pilate to break the legs of those who were crucified to hasten their death. What really happened was, they would have no further support, and they would die of suffocation because their lungs could not expand. So the soldiers came, and with one blow of the mallet, broke each leg of the thieves.

But when they came to Jesus, they discovered He was dead already, so they did not break His legs. Instead, one of the soldiers, with his spear, pierced the side of Jesus, and immediately, blood and water came forth.

Do you know what Moses said to the children of Israel many, many years before? He said, "The life is in the blood." And Moses also said, "Without the shedding of blood, there is no remission." I want you to consider the spear-pierced side of Jesus on the cross.

Consider The Fulfilled Scripture.

I am deeply impressed as I read these records that soldiers, governors, and people were fulfilling Scriptures they hardly knew had even been spoken. These are to bring us to believe. So wrote the Apostle John. He said, "My record is true." And it is true that you might believe. The truth of the Bible comes out clear, for it is further stated the Scripture was fulfilled, "A bone of Him shall not be broken." Praise the Lord! Isn't it wonderful that King David, one thousand years before Christ, would write that in Psalm 34:20? "He keepeth all his bones; not one of them is broken."

The second Scripture that was fulfilled right there is from Zechariah 12:10, "They shall look on me whom they have pierced." That tells me that Jesus bears the marks now. Yes. Isn't this a great revelation of the plan of God, that King David and Zechariah would predict, and the Scriptures would be fulfilled, that very time when Jesus died on the cross? Oh, the wonder of it all!

My friend, give serious attention to these considerations: that holy sabbath, the spear-pierced side, those fulfilled Scriptures. They bear testimony to the truth so you can believe.

Chapter Ninety

Where Did They Lay Him?

Some who read the records of the crucifixion of Jesus claim that Jesus never died. This is hardly possible if we are honest with the record. We can hardly say Jesus never died.

Then there are others who even claim that He was not crucified. But the record in the Bible leaves no doubt. When we take the words in their true sense, we are led to the conclusion: yes, He was crucified, and yes, He died. He died sooner than the thieves. His death was validated by the soldier.

Because it was a religious holiday, it was necessary to bury the bodies quickly. Two men who loved Jesus, unknown to His disciples, come upon the scene to fill that need, as recorded in John 19:38-42.

> *38 And after this Joseph of Arimathaea, being a disciple of Jesus, but secretly for fear of the Jews, besought Pilate that he might take away the body of Jesus: and Pilate gave him leave. He came therefore, and took the body of Jesus.*
>
> *39 And there came also Nicodemus, which at the first came to Jesus by night, and brought a mixture of myrrh and aloes, about an hundred pound weight.*
>
> *40 Then took they the body of Jesus, and wound it in linen clothes with the spices, as the manner of the Jews is*

to bury.

41 Now in the place where he was crucified there was a garden; and in the garden a new sepulchre, wherein was never man yet laid.

42 There laid they Jesus therefore because of the Jews' preparation day; for the sepulchre was nigh at hand.

As we watch the actions of these two men, certain **DETAILS** establish the fact of the burial of Jesus. They answer the question, **WHERE DID THEY LAY HIM?**

The first Detail: **The Permission.**

Joseph of Arimathaea was the spokesman. He went secretly to Pilate for fear of the Jews and asked him for the body. He obtained permission to take down the body of Jesus. Apparently, those who loved Him were much too frightened.

Mark's Gospel reports that Pilate was not sure that Jesus was dead already, so he asked the centurion who was in command at the crucifixion. The captain of the soldiers verified that Jesus was dead.

To get this permission, Joseph was a bold man, even though he went secretly. The Jewish feast of the Passover was near. He must act quickly to take care of the body of Jesus so that he would be able to eat the Passover. He risked his reputation, indeed. But he was willing to do it. So there was the detail of the permission.

The second Detail: **The Preparation.**

Another came to help Joseph. His name was Nicodemus. He had come to Jesus by night. We learn of this in the early part of John's Gospel. Jesus called him then a master in Israel. And once after that, Nicodemus stood in defense of Jesus when the Sanhedrin would have condemned Him before they heard Him.

He must have been a believer; he must have been. He came to help Joseph take care of the body of Jesus. He was prepared. He came with a mixture of spices, myrrh, and aloes, about 100 pound, weight (fifty kilograms). They took the body of Jesus down from the cross and wound it in linen clothes with the spices, as was the practice of the Jews, to bury.

Nicodemus was a man of forethought. He came prepared with the spices and linen because they knew they must take care of this quickly. They did not have much time. These dedicated men with loving hands did what they could to the body of Jesus. This is a beautiful detail, the preparation that they made.

The third Detail: **The Place.**

I read, "Now in the place where he was crucified there was a garden." It was near the hill of crucifixion. And there was a new tomb there, a tomb that had never been used. I have stood at the foot of Calvary, outside of Jerusalem's old city wall. The garden and the tomb: I have seen them. There they laid Him.

They acted quickly because it was the Jewish day of preparation for the feast of the Passover. The sepulchre was near at hand. Matthew wrote that Joseph used his own new tomb. So they laid His body in the tomb.

These details leave no doubt that Jesus died and was buried: the centurion acknowledged that He was dead; Pilate gave permission to remove the body from the cross; these men prepared their spices and linen to take care of His dead body. They selected a place prepared for a dead body and entombed His body in the sepulchre in which no one had ever been laid.

Studies from John 20

Chapter Ninety-One

Haunting Fear

All of us have certain fears that keep nagging us. In letters we get, some people write like this: "Please pray for me so I will have a prosperous life." Others say, "Please pray for me so that I may pass my exam." Still others ask us to pray, "So that I might find a good wife." You see, all of us have certain fears that keep nagging at us.

And fears can be very distressing. They sap our vitality. They make us tired and misdirect our lives. Why do fears come? Are fears normal? Is it possible to overcome fear? The disciples in Jesus' day also had fears. They had what I call **HAUNTING FEAR,** the kind that kept nagging at them.

In the sorrow and disappointment of the death of Jesus, fear was the normal response of those who loved Him. This is recorded in John 20:1-10.

> *1 The first day of the week cometh Mary Magdalene early, when it was yet dark, unto the sepulchre, and seeth the stone taken away from the sepulchre.*
>
> *2 Then she runneth, and cometh to Simon Peter, and to the other disciple, whom Jesus loved, and saith unto them, They have taken away the Lord out of the sepulchre, and we know not where they have laid him.*
>
> *3 Peter therefore went forth, and that other disciple, and*

came to the sepulchre.

4 So they ran both together: and the other disciple did outrun Peter, and came first to the sepulchre.

5 And he stooping down, and looking in, saw the linen clothes lying; yet went he not in.

6 Then cometh Simon Peter following him, and went into the sepulchre, and seeth the linen clothes lie,

7 And the napkin, that was about his head, not lying with the linen clothes, but wrapped together in a place by itself.

8 Then went in also that other disciple, which came first to the sepulchre, and he saw, and believed.

9 For as yet they knew not the scripture, that he must rise again from the dead.

10 Then the disciples went away again unto their own home.

In this experience of the followers of Jesus, we can discern the **REALITIES** which caused the haunting fear.

The first Reality is: **The Conclusion.**

When Mary Magdalene came to the tomb, it was the first day of the week and very early. While it was still dark, she came. What does that tell you about Mary Magdalene? It tells me she had a deep love for the Lord Jesus, which moved her to action so that nothing was too much for her to do.

She came just as soon as it was proper for her to come—on that first day of the week, very early in the morning. As she approached, she saw "the stone taken away from the tomb." Matthew's gospel reports to us that an angel rolled it away. When Mary arrived at the tomb, she saw that the stone had been rolled away from the mouth of the tomb.

Her immediate conclusion was that somebody had stolen the body. By inference, she drew the conclusion that the body of Jesus had been stolen. There were grave robbers in the community, and they had stolen the body of Jesus and carried it away. She did not stop to look. She did not stop to consider. Fear seized her, and her conclusion drove her to do something about it. Her conclusion was based on insufficient evidence, for all she had seen was the stone rolled away from the tomb.

We sometimes draw our conclusions from insufficient evidence, and they may, indeed, give rise to some of our haunting fears. It is good that fear leads to action.

The second Reality is: **The Consultation.**

She ran quickly to Simon Peter and told him what her conclusion was. She said, "They have taken away the Lord out of the tomb, and we know not where they have laid him." The body is stolen, she said to Peter.

Now you can imagine, can't you, how quickly Peter and John looked at each other and simply nodded. There wasn't a long consultation, a very brief one. They started out for the tomb, racing to arrive there. They ran to the tomb. They agreed to investigate. It seemed like it was second nature with them. They knew this needed some looking into, some verification. But Peter was outrun. The other disciple arrived there first, and he surveyed the tomb. He saw that the stone was rolled away. By stooping down, he could look into the tomb. He saw the linen clothes lying there, but he did not go in.

That consultation was very brief before they started out for the tomb. And John (we believe it was John), arriving there first, simply surveyed the situation without drawing any other conclusion than that which Mary had reported.

Well, it is a good idea to consult with someone else and to exercise some restraint. It didn't help their fear, however, their haunting fear that somebody had stolen the body of Jesus.

The third Reality is: **The Confirmation.**

Peter came and went in to examine the facts that were available. He saw the linen clothes lying there. The napkin or handkerchief that was around His head was not with the linen clothes, but was wrapped together in a place by itself. The body of Jesus was not there. That was absolutely true.

We do not know exactly how the clothes were arranged. Were

they unwound and lying in a heap? Or were they lying in the form of His body? The body was not there. He understood that the body of Jesus had disappeared.

Then the other disciple went in too and saw the same thing that Peter saw. The Bible says he saw and believed. Believed what? I think he believed what Mary told them: somebody had stolen the body of Jesus. Because verse 9 tells us, "For as yet they knew not the scripture, that he must rise again from the dead." So they must have believed what Mary reported. They had no understanding about the Lord's resurrection.

Here then was the confirmation of Mary's conclusion. There was no body there. Consequently, there was no hope there. As a result, there was no future for them. All the evidence pointed to the conclusion Mary had come to.

So much had happened that the disciples were unable to take it all in. It was His death three days before, his burial in the tomb, the great stone rolled before the mouth of the tomb, and now his disappearance. All this resulted in a haunting fear that all was lost. But Jesus had told them He would rise. Their hope was overshadowed with fear.

I want to brighten your hope. Your haunting fear can be relieved if you'll trust in Him. The tomb is empty. He arose.

Chapter Ninety-Two

Crushing Sorrow

Some happenings in life leave a deep wound of sorrow which is hard to heal. Some sorrows are soon changed to joy. But some come down on us like a crushing load. All of us have had disappointments that have turned into crushing sorrow. All of us have laid loved ones in the grave.

Mary Magdalene had such an experience when she found the tomb empty where Jesus had been buried. Jesus meant so very much to her. As the events of the last several years came crowding through her thoughts, she felt she could not give Him up. It was Jesus who had rescued her from evil spirits and had given her peace and joy.

John's Gospel tells us how she was crushed with sorrow and how her sorrow was changed to joy. It is found in John 20:11-18.

> *11 But Mary stood without at the sepulchre weeping: and as she wept, she stooped down, and looked into the sepulchre,*
>
> *12 And seeth two angels in white sitting, the one at the head, and the other at the feet, where the body of Jesus had lain.*
>
> *13 And they say unto her, Woman, why weepest thou? She saith unto them, Because they have taken away my Lord, and I know not where they have laid him.*

14 And when she had thus said, she turned herself back, and saw Jesus standing, and knew not that it was Jesus.

15 Jesus saith unto her, Woman, why weepest thou? whom seekest thou? She, supposing him to be the gardener, saith unto him, Sir, if thou have borne him hence, tell me where thou hast laid him, and I will take him away.

16 Jesus saith unto her, Mary. She turned herself, and saith unto him, Rabboni; which is to say, Master.

17 Jesus saith unto her, Touch me not; for I am not yet ascended to my Father: but go to my brethren, and say unto them, I ascend unto my Father, and your Father; and to my God, and your God.

18 Mary Magdalene came and told the disciples that she had seen the Lord, and that he had spoken these things unto her.

From Mary's **CRUSHING SORROW** we should find the **REVELATIONS** by which her sorrow was turned to joy.

The first Revelation was: **The Vision.**

The first part of the chapter informs us that she had come early to the tomb and found the stone taken away. She ran to Peter and the other disciple to tell them that somebody had stolen the body of Jesus. They came, looked in the tomb, and concluded that Mary was correct.

They went again to their own home. But Mary came back to the tomb, heartbroken. There she was by the tomb. Then she stooped down and looked in. She saw the vision of angels. There were two of them, one at the head, the other at the feet where the body of Jesus had lain. Angels are heavenly messengers, and they had a word for her. It was a question they asked her, "Woman, why do you weep?" Her response was the same as it had been to the disciples. She answered, "They have taken away my Lord, and I do not know where they have laid him."

There was the vision of the angels as the first revelation to turn Mary's crushing sorrow into joy. To be able to tell what caused her sorrow was the first revelation toward turning that sorrow into joy.

The second Revelation was: **The Voice.**

After she had this conversation with the angels, she turned herself back and saw Jesus standing there. But in her distress, she did not know it was Jesus. She supposed Him to be the caretaker of the garden. Who else would have done something with the body of Jesus if not the caretaker of the garden? So she said to Him when He asked her why she was weeping, "Sir, if you have carried him away, tell me where you have laid him, and I will take him away."

Here her loyalty showed, didn't it? She was very loyal to Jesus. She would not let the grave robbers do anything with His body. She would somehow take care of this. She supposed Him to be the gardener.

Then she heard her name in that voice. There's no sweeter sound on earth, they tell us, than one's name. And I would like to add, no one can speak your name like Jesus. It was that way with Mary. All He said to her was, "Mary," and she immediately recognized Him. His voice told her who He was, and she immediately responded. It was His voice and her name that made it real to her.

Oh, I see her crushing sorrow being turned to joy right there with the revelation of the voice.

The third Revelation was: **The Verification.**

First was the vision, then the voice, now the verification. It was His command, "Do not cling to me." My English Bible reads, "Do not touch me." I studied very carefully this statement in the Greek New Testament, and I find the idea is, "Stop hanging on to me."

He went on to say, "I have not yet ascended to my Father." I believe Jesus was trying to help Mary understand that now that He was risen from the dead, nobody would be able to take Him away from her again. It was not necessary for her now to cling to Him. So His command was, "Stop hanging on to me."

His commission to her was, "Go to my brethren, and say unto them, I ascend unto my Father and your Father, and to my God and your God." Go tell my brethren. The first message of the resurrected Christ was to go and tell. It came to Mary, Mary Magdalene. His commission to her was, "Go tell my brethren."

And she quickly went. She came and told the disciples that she had seen the Lord and that He had said these things unto her. She told the disciples everything. His memory was in her mind and she said everything that He had said to her. The third revelation verified His true presence.

By these three revelations, Mary's crushing sorrow was turned to joy: by the vision, by the voice, and by the verification. We cannot do what she did, but by believing, we too, can have our sorrow relieved. Do you believe in Jesus Christ as the risen Son of God?

Chapter Ninety-Three

Comforting Joy

As I think back over the Bible account of God creating man, I am certain that God wants us to be joyful. If we go to the first book in the Bible, we find that when God created Adam, He placed him in a beautiful garden. Adam was provided with all that he needed. It makes me sure that God desires us to be joyful.

Sometimes, though, because of unfulfilled hopes, our joys may be dampened, and we're not as joyful as God really wants us to be. Then when those hopes are revived, joy is restored.

We are not much different from the disciples in Jesus' day. The disciples on the resurrection day had real reason to be full of joy because their hopes were revived. So we, too, may rejoice in the fact that Jesus is alive today! He conquered death and instilled joy in all believers because of this great fact.

COMFORTING JOY came to the disciples as reported in John 20:19-23.

> *19 Then the same day at evening, being the first day of the week, when the doors were shut where the disciples were assembled for fear of the Jews, came Jesus and stood in the midst, and saith unto them, Peace be unto you.*
>
> *20 And when he had so said, he shewed unto them his hands and his side. Then were the disciples glad, when*

they saw the Lord.

21 Then said Jesus to them again, Peace be unto you: as my Father hath sent me, even so send I you.

22 And when he had said this, he breathed on them, and saith unto them, Receive ye the Holy Ghost:

23 Whose soever sins ye remit, they are remitted unto them; and whose soever sins ye retain, they are retained.

Comforting joy was experienced in the hearts of the disciples of Jesus by several **ACTS** which Jesus did when He appeared to them after His resurrection.

The first Act was: **His Entrance.**

I want you to note carefully, in the Bible, it is stated that the disciples were gathered in a room and the doors were shut. There was no ready entrance. They were there because they were afraid. They feared what might happen to them because the people knew they were followers of Jesus.

So far as they knew, and so far as the people knew, Jesus was still dead. Excepting, of course, that Mary Magdalene had told them, "He is alive!" They felt threatened by their opponents. Then Jesus came into the room where doors were closed. The first thing He said to them was a quieting, comforting word, "Peace be unto you."

Here was the act of Jesus in coming into the room and speaking peace to the disciples. Yes, my friend, the presence of Jesus always brings joy to the believer. Sometimes He comes in unexpected ways into our lives. I can bear testimony to that.

The second Act was: **His Evidence.**

He didn't wait. He immediately showed them His hands and His side. He knew the disciples would need clear proof that He was, indeed, the same person who had been crucified. So He showed them the marks in His hands and in His side the scars that had been made by the nails and by the spear.

Look what happened when He showed them the evidence: "Then the disciples were glad when they saw the Lord." Comforting joy possessed their hearts when they saw Jesus and were sure that He was the same One whom they had last seen on the cross.

Now listen further to His words, "As my Father has sent me, even so I send you." I want you to catch this because the mission that Jesus began, which the Father had sent Him to begin, now He was transferring to His disciples by that statement, "Even so, I send you."

Comforting joy comes to us when we acknowledge the evidence that the same person who was crucified has risen from the dead and has also spoken to us by this word to the disciples.

The third Act was: **His Endowment.**

We read, "He breathed on them and said to them, Receive ye the Holy Spirit." We know from the record that the Holy Spirit did not come until ten days after our Lord's ascension to Glory. Therefore, I conclude that Jesus performed this act in anticipation of Pentecost. He prepared them for receiving the Holy Spirit at the proper time.

Then He went on to say, "Whose soever sins ye remit, they are remitted unto them; and whose soever sins ye retain, they are retained." This should never be understood to be an arbitrary act of the disciples, because it is very clear in the Bible that the only way for forgiveness of sins is by the shed blood of Jesus Christ. It is only by that way that sins are forgiven. I am sure that Jesus did not overlook that when He made this statement to the disciples.

Comforting joy came to the disciples because they believed on Him. They were glad when they saw the Lord and He gave them this endowment of the Holy Spirit. All who believe on Jesus Christ receive the Holy Spirit.

Comforting joy can be yours, too, if you acknowledge His presence; accept His nail prints, the evidence of His resurrection; and receive His endowment of the Holy Spirit. Will you do so now?

Chapter Ninety-Four

Rewarding Faith

Faith is a part of our human existence. We have been made to believe. The Bible tells us that God has given to everyone a measure of faith. Everyone believes in something. Even those who say there is no God believe in something. For to be honest, they should say, I believe there is no God. They must express some faith.

Now, I would much rather say, I believe there is God. The Bible informs us that even demons believe and tremble. There is put within our being the ability to believe. But not all faith is **REWARDING FAITH**. When I speak of faith, I am talking about believing. To be rewarding faith, there must be a proper object to faith.

The story in John 20:24-31 demonstrates what rewarding faith is. The disciples were staying together, awaiting direction for the future after the resurrection of Jesus.

24 But Thomas, one of the twelve, called Didymus, was not with them when Jesus came.

25 The other disciples therefore said unto him, We have seen the Lord. But he said unto them, Except I shall see in his hands the print of the nails, and put my finger into the print of the nails, and thrust my hand into his side, I will not believe.

26 And after eight days again his disciples were within,

> and Thomas with them: then came Jesus, the doors being shut, and stood in the midst, and said, Peace be unto you.
>
> 27 Then saith he to Thomas, Reach hither thy finger, and behold my hands; and reach hither thy hand, and thrust it into my side: and be not faithless, but believing.
>
> 28 And Thomas answered and said unto him, My Lord and my God.
>
> 29 Jesus saith unto him, Thomas, because thou hast seen me, thou hast believed: blessed are they that have not seen, and yet have believed.
>
> 30 And many other signs truly did Jesus in the presence of his disciples, which are not written in this book:
>
> 31 But these are written, that ye might believe that Jesus is the Christ, the Son of God; and that believing ye might have life through his name.

As there were several **EVENTS** in the experience of Thomas which led him to rewarding faith, so it may be with us.

The first Event toward rewarding faith: **His Refusal.**

When Jesus came first to the disciples after His resurrection, Thomas was absent. We do not know why he was absent. Perhaps fear had so gripped his heart that he refused to be identified with the disciples. Or he may have had other interests or some duty that kept him from meeting with them on that first day of the week.

So he was told what had happened; they had seen the Lord. But he was cautious, "I must see before I believe."

We can sympathize with Thomas. We believe it is proper to require evidence so as not to be led into error. It is important that we are cautious about the claims that people make. His refusal to believe without evidence was quite the proper thing to do.

A second Event toward rewarding faith: **His Rebuke.**

Eight days later, he was with the other disciples. Perhaps he had learned his lesson and gathered with the disciples, the others, in anticipation of what might be a repeat of what happened before.

And it was. Jesus came into their midst, the doors being shut, just like before. There was no ready entrance, but Jesus came and stood in the midst and greeted them just like He had before. It was a word of peace, "Peace be unto you."

Then Thomas was invited to examine the evidence. Jesus said, "Reach here, your finger, and behold my hands. Reach here your hand and thrust it into my side. And do not be faithless but believe." This was a rebuke for Thomas from Jesus.

Jesus must have known about Thomas' refusal to believe until he had seen. So, after the evidence was there, the nail prints and the spear scar, faith was commanded of Thomas, "Do not be faithless, but believe."

And the third Event toward rewarding faith: **His Response.**

His confession was immediate and complete. It did not take Thomas long at all. He cried out, "My Lord and my God." He is to be commended for making a clear and immediate and complete confession right there. He did not falter or hesitate, but his response and confession came at once.

Now notice the commendation that Jesus gave him. He said, "Because you have seen me, you have believed. All who do not see and yet believe are blessed."

My friend, we are among those who have not seen and yet have believed. Thomas saw Him, and the Apostle John recorded it for us. Jesus pronounced a blessing on you and me because we have not seen His nail prints or His spear scar. But when we believe, Jesus said, we would be blessed.

We ought not criticize Thomas until we have believed on Jesus ourselves without any doubt or question. Nor can we hide behind Thomas, for when he was presented with the evidence, he believed and confessed that Jesus was his Lord and his God.

Do you believe that Jesus is the Christ? Listen, "These are written that you might believe that Jesus is the Christ, the Son of God and that believing you might have life through his name." I invite you, I urge you to believe in Jesus Christ as the Son of God, and you can have peace too.

Studies from
John 21

Chapter Ninety-Five

How Jesus Showed Himself

The museums of the world contain monuments to the great men of earth. I have seen some of these in the British museum in London, in the museum in Cairo, and in the museums of other countries of the Bible's history. But the greatest man that ever lived has an empty tomb as His monument. That empty tomb bears witness to Him. No one else has that kind of monument.

When the Romans crucified Jesus, and His friends buried Him, everyone then thought there would be nothing more. But there was more. There is more because He arose from the dead. The last two chapters of John's Gospel give us the record how He arose from the dead and **HOW JESUS SHOWED HIMSELF** to His disciples. This meditation is based on John 21:1-14.

> *1 After these things Jesus shewed himself again to the disciples at the sea of Tiberias; and on this wise shewed he himself.*
>
> *2 There were together Simon Peter, and Thomas called Didymus, and Nathaniel of Cana in Galilee, and the sons of Zebedee, and two other of his disciples.*
>
> *3 Simon Peter saith unto them, I go a fishing. They say unto him, We also go with thee. They went forth, and entered into a ship immediately; and that night they*

caught nothing.

4 But when the morning was now come, Jesus stood on the shore: but the disciples knew not that it was Jesus.

5 Then Jesus saith unto them, Children, have ye any meat? They answered him, No.

6 And he said unto them, Cast the net on the right side of the ship, and ye shall find. They cast therefore, and now they were not able to draw it for the multitude of fishes.

7 Therefore that disciple whom Jesus loved saith unto Peter, It is the Lord. Now when Simon Peter heard that it was the Lord, he girt his fisher's coat unto him, (for he was naked,) and did cast himself into the sea.

8 And the other disciples came in a little ship; (for they were not far from land, but as it were two hundred cubits,) dragging the net with fishes.

9 As soon then as they were come to land, they saw a fire of coals there, and fish laid thereon, and bread.

10 Jesus saith unto them, Bring of the fish which ye have now caught.

11 Simon Peter went up, and drew the net to land full of great fishes, an hundred and fifty and three: and for all there were so many, yet was not the net broken.

12 Jesus saith unto them, Come and dine. And none of the disciples durst ask him, Who art thou? knowing that it was the Lord.

13 Jesus then cometh, and taketh bread, and giveth them, and fish likewise.

14 This is now the third time that Jesus shewed himself to his disciples, after that he was risen from the dead.

As we meditate upon these verses, we notice the **WAYS** Jesus showed Himself to His disciples.

The first Way: **By His Unexpected Coming.**

Did you notice that Peter was the one who said, "I am going

fishing?" This is really not surprising because Peter was a fisherman before Jesus ever called him to follow Him. He and Andrew, James, and John were fishermen. On this fishing project, Peter's companions were Thomas, Nathaniel, James, John, and two others of Jesus' disciples. It's not surprising, I say, that they would go fishing.

They spent the night, however, without catching anything. Maybe that is not really surprising either. If the fish are not running, like they say, then there is not much chance of catching fish. But the surprising part is that Jesus unexpectedly was standing there on the shore as the morning began to dawn. They saw Jesus on the shore and did not even know it was Jesus. They were not expecting Him. No, they were not expecting Him.

That's how He showed Himself to them, by His unexpected coming. I would like to draw a lesson from that for you and me. Is it not true that sometimes Jesus comes to us at unexpected times in unexpected ways? Well, I am so glad to tell you that Jesus will be right there by your side, even though you don't expect Him.

The second Way: **By His Unqualified Command.**

He first asked them this question, "Have you any food?" They answered by saying, "No." They had been fishing all night and hadn't caught anything, so, of course, they wouldn't have any fish. Probably by the way He asked the question and the way they answered it, they didn't have any bread either; they had no food.

Then Jesus gave them an unqualified command, "Cast the net on the right side of the boat, and you shall find." That is remarkable. Here was a man standing on shore commanding the fishermen who were 200 cubits from shore, probably a hundred meters or so. For somebody to stand on the shore and be able to instruct the fishermen where the fish are is surprising, but He did. He told them which side to cast their net. They did, and they caught a great multitude of fish, so that they struggled getting the net into the boat.

Then the reality of who it was came to the disciple whom Jesus loved, we believe it was John. He said to Peter, "It is the Lord." John said that because he knew nobody else would have been able to tell them from a hundred meters away where the fish were.

Let me tell you the lesson that I get from this way Jesus showed Himself: the disciples did exactly what Jesus commanded them to do. Let us think about it, especially, that here was a stranger, for they did not know Him, commanding the fishermen, experienced as they were, to cast their net on the opposite side of the boat, on the right side. Let us ponder that they did exactly what Jesus told them to do. I get a lesson from that for you and me: we also ought to do exactly what Jesus tells us to do. He tells us what to do in God's Word.

The third Way: **By His Unselfish Care.**

When Peter dragged the net to shore, they found they had 153 fish in the net. But Jesus was prepared for them and had already made a fire, and He had laid some fish and bread on the coals already prepared for them.

After they had pulled in the net of fishes, Jesus said to them, "Bring of the fish that ye have now caught." That must have been a wonderful breakfast. Yes, a wonderful meal on the shore of the Sea of Galilee.

Then He said to them, "Come and eat." Everything was ready. Jesus had prepared a tasty, early morning meal for the disciples. When they gathered around, the seven of them with Jesus, He took bread and gave some to them and gave them some fish also. But nobody dared to ask Him who He was because they all knew that it was Jesus. Unselfishly He met their need. He had everything prepared for them, all that they needed.

Now, my friend, I want to draw a third lesson for you and me from this. Jesus unselfishly cares for us too. He provides our needs as well.

What enriching lessons we learn from how Jesus showed Himself to the disciples. Often in our lives, Jesus is there at unexpected times. Sometimes we may not know it at first. Often He commands us, and blessings come when we do what He says. Often His care is shown by how He provides for us.

Do you know Him? Do you know Jesus? Let Him show Himself to you, that He can really meet your need.

Chapter Ninety-Six

The Final Test

Life is somewhat like a school. When we are in school, we face tests. Teachers need to know what the pupils have learned, so they administer tests.

Quite frequently, we get a letter from some listener asking that we pray because that listener will be taking an examination, a test, and wants to make sure that he is going to pass it.

We often face tests. Sometimes they are hard tests. There comes the final test, and the final question, what do you think of Jesus?

If you have been with me throughout the studies of the Gospel of John, you have noticed that we have seen Jesus in many different situations. We've seen Him with the crowds. We've seen Him feed five thousand with five loaves and two fish. We have seen Him before the Roman Governor, before the religious court, and finally crucified. Then John shows us Jesus as He showed Himself to His disciples on the shores of the Sea of Galilee (also known as Tiberias) after He arose.

Our studies in John's Gospel have brought us face to face with the evidence again and again that He is the Son of God, our Saviour. But there is that final test: what do you think of Him? We will find the answer to this test in John 21:15-25, the last part of John's Gospel.

15 So when they had dined, Jesus saith to Simon Peter,

Simon, son of Jonas, lovest thou me more than these? He saith unto him, Yea, Lord; thou knowest that I love thee. He saith unto him, Feed my lambs.

16 He saith to him again the second time, Simon, son of Jonas, lovest thou me? He saith unto him, Yea, Lord; thou knowest that I love thee. He saith unto him, Feed my sheep.

17 He saith unto him the third time, Simon, son of Jonas, lovest thou me? Peter was grieved because he said unto him the third time, Lovest thou me? And he said unto him, Lord, thou knowest all things; thou knowest that I love thee. Jesus saith unto him, Feed my sheep.

18 Verily, verily, I say unto thee, When thou wast young, thou girdedst thyself, and walkedst whither thou wouldest: but when thou shalt be old, thou shalt stretch forth thy hands, and another shall gird thee, and carry thee whither thou wouldest not.

19 This spake he, signifying by what death he should glorify God. And when he had spoken this, he saith unto him, Follow me.

20 Then Peter, turning about, seeth the disciple whom Jesus loved following; which also leaned on his breast at supper, and said, Lord, which is he that betrayeth thee?

21 Peter seeing him saith to Jesus, Lord, and what shall this man do?

22 Jesus saith unto him, If I will that he tarry till I come, what is that to thee? Follow thou me.

23 Then went this saying abroad among the brethren, that that disciple should not die: yet Jesus said not unto him, He shall not die; but, If I will that he tarry till I come, what is that to thee?

24 This is the disciple which testifieth of these things, and wrote these things: and we know that his testimony is true.

25 And there are also many other things which Jesus did, the which, if they should be written every one, I suppose that even the world itself could not contain the books that should be written. Amen.

Amen! There is a final test. Peter's experience demonstrates for us the **AREAS** where we also face **THE FINAL TEST**.

First is: **In The Area Of Loving.**

Peter had vowed before Jesus was crucified that He would go even to death with Jesus. Then when the test came, he denied Jesus. He said, "I do not know him."

Now Jesus was testing His love again. Jesus used the word for love which is of the highest order. In Greek, it is the word *agape*. When Peter responded to Jesus, he used the lesser word, *phileo*. He said, "I love you," with a different kind of love. He was more careful. Peter had learned his lesson, probably, that it's best not to boast when you are putting on the armor. It's better to boast when you are taking it off!

Then Jesus said to him, "Feed my lambs, feed my sheep." If you love me, then serve me. Do My work. Peter was grieved because Jesus, for the third time, used the same word that he did, meaning, "Are you sure that you really love me with the kind of love that you are expressing?"

Ah, my friend, that is a final test, the area of loving. Do you really love Jesus with that high divine love? Or do you only have a regard for Him?

I remember speaking with a man once who told me, "Yes, I believe in Jesus." I said, "If you really believe in Jesus, then you will do what He says." That's the way with us. Yes, we're facing that final test, the test of loving.

Second is: **In The Area Of Living.**

Peter often spoke out when it would have been better if he had listened. He was a strong man, though, to do what he thought was right. Remember him in the garden of Gethsemane when the soldiers came to take Jesus. Peter drew his sword to defend the Lord right there. He did, in fact, cut off the high priest's servant's ear. So

Peter was a strong man. He was impulsive, though, and he needed to be subdued. He was subdued when he realized that all his loud words didn't really add up when the test came.

So Jesus said to him, and I put it in my words, "When you were young, you did what you wanted to do, and you went where you wanted to go. But when you will be old, somebody else is going to take you where you don't want to go. You will be led away against your will; you will be subdued. And when you are, the most important thing for you to remember is to follow me. No matter what happens to you, Peter, follow me." That's what I call the test of living.

We are facing that final test, too. Yes, we are, my friend. The area of living, not doing simply what we want to do, but doing what Jesus wants us to do. That is the important thing. That is why those two words Jesus gave to Peter are so important for you and me, "Follow me." That's what I call the test of living, to follow Jesus.

Third is: **In The Area Of Listening.**

John's Gospel closes with the important test in which Jesus met Peter: Jesus said, "don't bother yourself so much about John. Do what I tell you, have your ear tuned to me. Do what I tell you to do." That was important for Peter. He needed to learn that.

Oh, but my friend, you and I need to learn that, too. There are many people who are very concerned about somebody else when they ought to be concerned about doing what Jesus has said to them. What Jesus has said to you and me is very important. Don't bother yourself so much about John, don't bother yourself about Peter, bother yourself about yourself, yes?

Can you pass the final test? In reality, Jesus must be first in these three vital areas of life: in the area of loving, do you really love Jesus? In the area of living, are you living for Jesus? And in the area of listening, are you listening to Jesus? That is the final test.

HERALDS OF HOPE

For the past 50+ years, Heralds of Hope, Inc. has been presenting the Gospel of Jesus Christ using electronic and print media with a special emphasis on the systematic teaching of God's Word. A primary goal is to encourage deeper commitment to the Bible as the inspired Word of God and a renewed dedication to holy living in light of Christ's imminent return.

Heralds of Hope, an international Gospel radio and literature ministry, was founded by the late Dr. J. Otis Yoder and his wife, Isabelle. HOH aired their first radio broadcast in 1968. The focus of the half-hour broadcast, "The Voice of Hope," is expository Bible teaching with a strong emphasis on spiritual growth and discipleship.

From its offices and studio located near Breezewood, PA, Gospel messages are sent to radio stations in North America and around the world. The Bible teaching on our international program is a mix of teaching by Dr. Yoder and expositions by Radio Pastor, J. Mark Horst. "The Voice of Hope" currently airs on 30+ stations in North America.

Letter responses to our international English broadcasts have come from more than 180 countries around the world! In addition, our partnership with Trans World Radio (since 1974) and other ministries enables broadcasts in many languages.

The current Staff and Board are continuing the founding vision of bringing HOPE to the hopeless and growth to the Body of Christ through the timeless, universal message of the Gospel. Join us online at _www.heraldsofhope.org/listen_.

Interact with us on social media!